Angie Baby

Terry Kerr

*This is for Samantha Roberts,
who stops me looking like a bloody fool.*

The following is a work of fiction. No reference to any persons living or dead is intended or should be inferred. Though real locations are used, I have taken many geographical liberties.

This work is copyright, and may not be reproduced in any way without the permission of the author.

Chapter One

One

You can't plan, thought Hayley Davis from her hospital bed, even through the tears, even as she was rocked and cradled by her husband Graham, even as she took and tried to give comfort. *No one can plan. Or rather, you can…you just shouldn't. What's the point? Plan away, plan all you like, knock yourselves out, and life will batter you anyway. Life watches, and mocks your plans. Life laughs at you. Life batters you.*

So she thought on that bleak January afternoon as she and her husband wept and, in another part of the hospital, the tiny remains of her miscarried child were disposed of.

Two

They hadn't planned on having a baby. They hadn't planned on *not* having a baby. They were young, working, happy, in love, having plenty of bedtime exercise (whilst taking the usual precautions); they were just living the life of a recently married couple.

Then, one morning, just over a year since she'd stood in a church and said 'I do,' Hayley was readying her face in the morning – touch of foundation, hint of blusher, light coat of mascara, not enough to be tarty, just enough to be glamorous, to give the customers of Crouch End's Hair and Beauty something to aspire to – when it suddenly occurred to her.

She was late.

She looked deep into her reflection, stared into her back-to-front cornflower blue eyes and counted back in her head. *Was* she late? She thought she was, she was almost certain she was, but if you weren't actively trying for a baby, who really kept track? She didn't. She'd been having her monthly visit from the Cardinal (as her mother put it), or 'periods' (as everybody else did) for twelve years. Twelve years of cramps, shooting pains, occasional mastitis (and hadn't *that* scared the crap out of her the first time?) stroppy moods…and, well, after twelve years she'd just kind've…well, stopped noticing. It was normal. It was expected. Every twenty-six to twenty-eight days she dug out her Always Ultra and said *Hi guys, how you doing?*

But when had she last?

Hayley replaced her mascara on the dressing table, tucked a strand of blonde hair behind her right ear, and kept staring at her reflection.

November fifth, she thought. Her back-to-front self nodded. Yes, November fifth, at the firework display in the park, whilst watching the Catherine wheels, the fireworks she'd always liked the best, the ones that as a child she thought might hypnotise her, that's when she'd felt that first low, lumbering cramp. And before they'd climbed into bed that night she'd lined her panties with good old deodorising winged cloth that kept her blood in one place and not on the sheets, and she'd drifted off to sleep beside her man, not caring she wasn't pregnant.

After all, they weren't planning.

But now it was – she checked her Samsung – December tenth. Cramps? No. Spotting? No. Thirty-five days. Unheard of.

Of course, all sorts of things could upset a woman's cycle – who didn't know that? Stress, dietary change…but *what* stress? *What* dietary change? Life was good, life was fine and dandy, and she just ate the way she normally did. Which left…well, which left…

Hayley Davis, by nature a trifle fanciful, made a practical decision.

Three

She bought a test on her way home from work, took it to the toilet, watched as her urine turned it blue, and thought about the best way to tell her husband.

Chapter Two

One

If Hayley was by nature a trifle fanciful, then her husband Graham was by nature just the opposite. It wasn't absolute – real life, as opposed to books and stories, was frequently scruffy when it came to character divisions – but, broadly, Hayley was intuitive and Graham was pragmatic. In part, this was reflected in their jobs; Hayley a beautician, Graham a draughtsman with an eye to becoming an architect, a lowly crowd artist in a firm that just may be starting to grow. She made people feel better about themselves as she applied makeup, he drew plans and elevations and worked out stresses.

Graham was like Hayley in that he also didn't plan, but he did have ambition. Why shouldn't he? He had a wife, after all, and a family would surely one day follow, and a man who had no ambition would be a poor provider. Graham hadn't planned on being the best at Technical Drawing in his secondary school; he just had been. And somewhere in his brain, as he held his exam results in his hand and saw that A*, he'd thought *maybe I can do something with this. I'm not sure what, but something.*

What he'd ended up doing was taking an A level in his A* subject at Crouch End College – but at night school, twice weekly, Monday and Wednesday, seven till nine. During the day he worked at every odd job he could. His family wasn't rolling in money, and from an early age his sometimes dour but always practical Scottish dad had been fond of saying, 'We've got to work for our living, annoying though that may be. It's work that buys the food, it's work that keeps the lights on, it's work that keeps the roof from leaking. It may not be fair, it may not even be right – what with half the world living in palaces and the other half queuing for food parcels from Oxfam – but it's the system we're stuck with. Graft, son. That's all we have. Graft.'

So Graham became a grafter – became, a lot of people said (his wife included) like his father. Practical, hardworking, occasionally dour, but not without a sense of humour, and sometimes – just sometimes - incredibly imaginative.

When he came home on that December evening and found Hayley sitting at the dining table nervously folding and unfolding a napkin and he asked her what was wrong and she told him, he stood silent for a moment, then ran to her, picked her up, and spun her round and round, kissing the tears from her cheeks, and screaming inarticulate shouts of joy as if he'd just scored the winner in the FA Cup Final. In extra time. Against Tottenham.

'I was worried,' Hayley said, muffled against his chest, 'about how you'd take it.'

Graham held her at arm's length, searching her face, perplexed. 'Why? Why would you worry?'

'Because we hadn't planned, because we might not be able to afford...'

'Ah, we'd have got round to it one day, wouldn't we?' he asked, interrupting her for one of the very few times in their life together. Graham, as a rule, was very well mannered. 'So it's now rather than later,' he went on, shrugging. 'That's OK. I can get overtime. I can get an evening job if I have to, work in a pub, I don't care. I need you to understand that, love. I don't care. It's no problem. It's never a problem.'

'I love you,' said Hayley, bursting into tears again.

'So you should,' said Graham. 'Face it, you won't do any better.' They laughed and kissed and laughed some more.

That was a good day.

Two

Then they started to plan.

They had to, with a baby on the way. They agreed to keep it to themselves until after the twelve week scan, but all the same, plans had to be made. Graham managed to secure some overtime and Hayley did a few (slightly off tax) private makeovers. A separate bank account was opened, which they called the Baby Buster account, into which every available penny was paid. The spare bedroom (and this was a little tricky to keep secret, but they managed it) was denuded of the crap that had accumulated there and slowly transformed into a nursery. A charity shop provided a cot; mobiles, teddy bears, dolls, changing tables were bought – everything a baby could want and love. Wallpaper upon which Peppa Pig and her friends cavorted lay in rolls under the windowsill.

Plans. Plans for the future. Sometimes, as she lay on the edge of sleep, Hayley could almost *see* the future, could almost see and hear her baby (a little girl, Angie, all brunette curls, turned up nose and freckles) could almost *see* their child explore the world, happy, safe and healthy.

As she almost saw these things, she would smile and stroke the tiny but growing bump of her stomach and would drift into oblivion, happy with their plans.

Three

Which turned to dust after ten weeks.

She was in the bathroom on a Sunday afternoon, changing her pad – spotting was nothing to be afraid of, the Internet said pregnant women often spotted – but when she looked at the used Always Ultra, she knew that wasn't spotting.

She held it in her hand, staring in disbelief. It was soaked in red. *No,* she told herself. *No, that's not right, I'm not seeing that, that's not right, I felt nothing, I feel fine, that's not right, I'm imagining it...*

Then she felt dampness on her thighs, looked down, saw the drips and drops hit the laminate, and once more thought, *but I feel fine...I feel fine...I feel fine...*

Hayley started to whimper. She tried to call Graham's name, but all that came out was a whisper. Then she felt more wetness on her legs and screamed for her husband.

She barely heard him thunder up the stairs two at a time, she barely registered him standing in the bathroom doorway, ashen-faced and horrified. All she could think was, *I felt nothing...I feel fine...*

Four

'No pain at all, no cramps in your lower abdomen?' the Doctor asked an hour later.

Graham had driven to the A&E at St Jude's Hospital faster than a Formula One driver, but he still knew it wasn't quick enough. It was over. He knew it in his heart, and so, from the sobs from the passenger seat, did Hayley. After an endless wait (which was, in fact, less than ten minutes), they had been led into a room equipped with an Ultrasound.

He saw his beloved shake her head, and a horrible, glittery smile appeared on her face – horrible because it was hopeless, and she knew it. 'Nothing, nothing at all, I feel fine. I mean,' tears were coursing down her face, 'that must mean everything's OK, mustn't it?'

Graham said nothing, just held her hand harder. The Doctor evaded that one also. 'I'm just going to give you an Ultrasound, just to check on the situation. We'll know more in a minute.' He smeared jelly on her stomach and passed a machine that looked like a barcode reader over it. He frowned over a monitor as he did so. He reached forward, twiddled with some knobs, then went again with the jelly and barcode.

'Mrs Davis, Mr Davis,' he said at length, and yes, here it came, Graham saw. He looked down at Hayley. She gave a heart wrenching cry. 'I'm so sorry. I can find no trace of heartbeat or life of any kind. The hard truth is I'm very much afraid you are undergoing a miscarriage. I'm so very, very sorry.'

Hayley howled, a sound of such utter desolation that Graham would have sold his soul for her to feel better. He held her, rocked her, then somehow found the strength to say, 'So what happens now?'

'Well,' said the Doctor, 'there are some options. One is to allow the tissue to pass naturally, this may take seven to fourteen days. Alternatively, we can give you medication to speed up the process, though we'd like you to remain in hospital for forty-eight hours if that were your choice. Such medication may be administered vaginally or orally, whichever is your preference.'

Preference? Preference? What is this, a fucking McDonalds?

'Whichever option you decide is fine with us; we're here to make the next few weeks as comfortable as possible for you. I understand this is an extremely distressing situation, and we have excellent counseling facilities we can offer you. Now,' he said, and the professional tone dropped ever so slightly, 'Do you wish some time to discuss what you want to do?'

Graham looked at Hayley. She was weeping, unable to process, so he said through cold lips, 'Yes thank you.'

The Doctor nodded, and made for the door. Through her tears, Hayley called him back. 'Whu-was it...did I...whu-was it my fuh-fuh...'

The Doctor moved to her, took her free hand, and said, ever so gently, 'No Mrs Davis. The horrible, hard fact about miscarriages is that sometimes, for no reason, they just happen. No fault, no blame, they just happen. We have no idea why. But, and I'm aware, believe me, of how little comfort this may be, in ninety-nine cases out of a hundred, the mother is perfectly fine afterwards, and can conceive again. This is not the end of you being a mother.' He disentangled his hand, smiled as reassuringly as he could, then left.

There was silence for a while, then Hayley said, 'Oh, Gray...my Angie...my Angie...' and then they were both crying.

Five

They opted for the medication. Well, in truth, Graham opted for it. Hayley was out of it, and who could blame her? But he looked at her, at her distress – what an awful, inadequate word! – and thought, *No, she has this done sooner rather than later. I will not let her suffer for longer than I have to. This comes out now. Sorry, baby, I am, I really am, but you never were, and my wife still is.*

The Doctor gave her a pill to swallow, then she was led onto a ward on the first floor. 'You'll be handed another pill in twelve hours, then the tissue should pass naturally. You'll experience a feeling like a heavy period...cramps, a heavy flow...' then, to Graham, 'Does your wife have any sanitary products with her?'

'Uh...I don't...I'm not sure...'

'No matter, we have plenty here.' Back to Hayley, who was barely tracking him. 'When you get home you'll need to take another pregnancy test after three weeks, to confirm the miscarriage has taken place. Now,' he said, all brisk and businesslike, 'I'll get the nurse to bring over your medication.'

He left them alone, a desolate man and a broken woman, and they sat there, listening to the beats of their own hearts.

Six

Fourteen hours later, Hayley felt her stomach cramp; a savage, awful pain, and she sat up in her bed, crying through closed eyes. Graham held her, and she squeezed tight on his hand, and after a minute she felt something pass, something taken from her...and she felt an almost irresistible urge to scream, *GIVE ME THAT BACK, THAT'S MY BABY! GIVE IT TO ME, THAT'S ANGIE...*

But then a nurse was there, and she led Hayley to the toilets and Hayley sat in a cubicle and removed the sanitary pad, and dumped it in the yellow metal bin, and then the nurse gave her another, and she was led back to her weeping husband, and he cradled her, and she thought about plans and how pointless they were.

Seven

Some hours later a nurse gave her another pill, and she slept. Graham sat by her, worn out, empty, hollow, a cheap Easter egg. A nurse came by and checked on his wife. 'You should go home and get some sleep yourself,' she told Graham.

'How?' he asked her, and she smiled sympathetically, squeezed his shoulder and left. *Her Mum. Her sister. I should ring them. Hell, I should have rung them before. Mum and Dad, should ring them too. They need to know.* They did, of course they did…but, as he'd said to the nurse, *how?* How could he tell them? Yes, they'd have to know…but *how?*

Tired and ancient, Graham had no idea. He looked back at his wife, at the face he loved beyond all human reason, saw she was breathing regularly, and stood up. He needed a coffee. No, he needed whisky, but coffee would do. There was a machine in the corridor, he had change, even if Hayley woke he'd be there soon enough, there'd be no more than a minute he wasn't beside her…

He almost collapsed against the machine, so exhausted was he, but it was as he put his pound in the slot that he felt it. His heart constricted…no, *contracted*, he could virtually *see* it, his heart squeezed to the size of a grape by an unseen fist. Goosebumps broke out on his arms, his breath rasped in his throat, it whistled in a tiny stream to his lungs. His hair stood up on end, his eyes flew wide, glazed and sightless.

Shock, he told himself, *it's just shock, it'll pass, give it a minute, don't panic, it'll pass.*

And after a while – maybe a minute, though it seemed like eternity - pass it did. He stood at the machine for a little longer, holding himself upright, but eventually Graham was able to breathe normally, to make his drink selection and make his way back down to Hayley, who didn't appear to have stirred.

Yes, it passed, and in roughly a minute. But it hadn't felt like shock. It had actually felt like acute, savage terror, a terror of the unknown, a terror of the future, a harbinger of bad times to come.

Graham, mostly practical, could sometimes be very intuitive indeed.

Chapter Three

One

Hayley came home the next afternoon. There was some pain, not much, but enough for her to be given some tablets and be given the advice 'keep an eye on it.' In a way, she welcomed the pain, even as Graham led her to the Impreza. She welcomed it because it was a reminder, a reminder of Angie, of the child she'd never brought to term. *Soon, even that'll be gone*, she thought as they drove home in silence, *and then there'll be nothing. Nothing to mark her, nothing to remember her by, the little lump of a child who never took a breath.*

She gave a sob, and Graham looked over as she wiped some fat tears away. To his great credit he didn't tell her they'd get through it, or that everything would be OK, he just reached over and touched her hand and told her he loved her. She told him she loved him back. She did, too. If anything was going to get them through this, it would be love.

There were bills on the mat to welcome them; bills and pizza menus and bank statements. The ordinary stuff of being alive, a sure-fire sign that planet Earth was still spinning on its axis. *Pay up, buy a Hawaiian, you have £750 in your current account as of the fifteenth of this month.* Graham absently picked them up as he led Hayley to the living room and helped her to the sofa. She looked at him, loving him, and then said, 'We have to tell them, don't we? Our families.'

'Yes,' he agreed, unhappily. 'I was going to, when you were sedated, but...I didn't want to leave you. I'll do it now.' *There he is, there's my man, he's got something to do, some action to take.* But all the same, she could see he didn't want to. Who could blame him? An appalling thing to have to do, and with her mother the way she was...

'It's OK love, I will.'

'No,' he said, and in the most heroic action she'd ever seen, he tried a smile. 'This is man's work. Listen,' he said, putting it off for a second, 'do you want anything? Drink? Food?'

'Everything I want is here,' she said, and smiled, even as her eye gave birth to another tear, a tear that lived and cascaded down her cheek.

He squatted down before her, took her hands, kissed them, and once more told her he loved her. She told him she loved him back. Then, because it could be put off no longer, he went to the landline and started dialing.

Hayley lay back on the sofa, grimacing a little against a brief stab across her pelvis, closed her eyes and tried to drift, tried to conserve her strength. Twenty-four, too young to feel old, but old she felt nonetheless, and as an old woman she heard her husband talk to her mum. She knew it was her mum because she could hear Graham say, 'Yes…I know…but…yes, but…Anna, she's fine, she will be fine…yes, I know…I know, but…'

More drama for you, mummy. I love you dearly, I really do, but one day – please God soon – I would like you to break this fixation, this addiction. Dad died ten years back, and we miss him, we all miss him, and I know you miss him the most, but you just got hooked on the attention, didn't you? Got hooked on being the martyr. And now your eldest daughter has given you something else to feel sorry for yourself over. I'm sorry. Sorry all these things happened, sorry they affect you the way they do, sorry for thinking this about you, your daughter loves you and she's sorry.

Two

Her mum bulldozed in half an hour later. Hayley's baby sister, Elaine, about twenty minutes after that. True to form, Anna did all but wail and gnash her teeth. 'My poor baby,' she kept saying, holding Hayley and rocking her, 'my poor, poor child, oh you shouldn't have to go through this, oh, I wish it were me, oh, it should be a mother's job to grieve, not a daughter's – like when your poor father was taken from us…'

Over her mum's shoulder, Hayley could see Elaine take a step forward at this, an angry cloud on her face. Elaine was two years Hayley's junior and had little patience for their mother's ways. But Hayley gave the younger girl a brief shake of the head, a bit of a *back off* look, and attempted to *communicate this is what she needs to do, Christ knows why, but it is. And if she's denied her fix she'll just sulk, and her sulks can last years.* Elaine did indeed back off, though she turned to Graham and gave an exasperated, angry gesture which Graham responded to with a shrug, and a muttered 'Come on, let's get the kettle on.'

As they vanished into the kitchen, Anna rolled her litany onwards, familiar tropes from back in the day, *God tests us, and we must be strong, you've got your mum, and your mum will never let you down, and the ever popular, I know how much it hurts, and I know you will recover, I promise you that, I do.*

Hayley, who loved her exasperating mother, let her unwind; let her get this out of her system. She was used to it, after all.

What she wasn't used to was the reaction of Graham's dad. His mum, Linda, she'd loved from the off – Linda was a slightly overweight 'earth mother' type, full of love and positivity, no self-pity and no talk of solutions, just love and hugs, and about as far away from her husband as possible. She was, in truth, a little frightened of Jim, Graham's dad. Oh, he wasn't loud, or violent (as far as she knew, anyway) but that Aberdeen burr (never really softened after forty-odd years of living in London) and his often expressionless face left her…well, yes, why deny it? Scared. She quite prided herself on being a good 'reader' of people, she liked to think she could read the emotional weather on anyone's face, but Jim was just a bit of a blank to her. She could never tell if he was happy or sad, angry or content.

But that day, that long, long day when she seemed to recount the tale of her miscarriage again and again, he utterly astonished her and that astonishment was the first thing, the first small inkling that she may, actually, come out the other side of this. He'd watched as his wife had held Hayley's hand and said all the right things, then made his way to her, sat down beside her and –wonder of wonders – kissed her on the forehead. 'I have no idea what you're going through or how you feel,' he said, very faintly, 'and I'll not pretend I do. But you're my daughter-in-law, and Graham loves you so I love you too. If there's ever a time when you feel you need me, when I'm the one you want to turn to, I will be here so fast you won't have had time to put the phone down. Y'hear me, now?'

Yes, she heard him – though she doubted anyone else would, so softly had he spoken. She heard him and burst into tears – real, awful, racking sobs that tore her insides open. Off in the background she heard her mother asking *what did you do, what did you say* and Elaine shushing her, and if Hayley could have spoken as her father-in-law rocked her, she'd have said, *the right thing. That's what he said.*

Three

Eventually everyone left them and Graham – who'd been feeling very much like a human pinball, bounced from place to place – gratefully led his wife to bed at about ten o'clock, where she finally cried herself to sleep. He, however, lay beside her for hours; exhausted but not tired. Too much had happened, too much to sort out, to get in place. The awful horror show that Anna had put on, for instance. Keeping his mouth closed during that had been almost impossible. *Shut up,* he'd wanted to rage. *Just shut up, you selfish bitch. This isn't about you, it's about us; it's about her, your daughter, why can't you see that, why is that impossible for you, why do you have to be the star of every bloody movie ever made? Why can't you just SHUT THE FUCK UP?*

But, of course, he kept silent. Enough of it must have communicated itself to Elaine, who – even though she was desperate to intercede herself, he could tell that – kept dragging him away, into the kitchen where the kettle was almost permanently on the boil. 'I know, I know,' Elaine had said. 'Trust me, I know. *You* want to punch her. *I* want to punch her. But that won't do any good, will it?' Reluctantly, Graham had agreed. 'Besides, Hales will push her away at the right minute. She's good at judging her. Me? I never grew out of my teen hormones, Mum reckons. I end up screaming at her. But again, that would do no good here, so a whole load of shut up is called for, yeah?'

'Yeah,' said Graham, and sighed. There, all of a sudden, he felt old, faint, weak. He sagged and leaned against the kitchen worktop.

'Right you,' said Elaine, 'when did you last eat?' Good question. He'd no idea. Food hadn't been high on his agenda recently. 'Jesus,' said Elaine, rolling her eyes the way only a twenty-two year old could. 'When did I get to be the practical one? I hate being the practical one. One second.' She brushed past him and opened the fridge door, tutted, then started looking through the cupboards.

'Listen,' he said, 'I'm fine, don't…'

Elaine slammed a cupboard door shut and rounded on him, tears in her eyes. 'You are *not* fine, Gray. You aren't fine *at all.* You're in shock, you're grieving *too,* yeah? So here's the thing, I get that you got some *macho I gotta be strong thing* going down, I do, believe me. But you gotta include *Hales*, yeah? You gotta let her know you're upset, otherwise she'll think you're just a bastard, right? You wanna cry? Give in, cry. You feel weak? Sit the fuck *down* then! I mean, look at this,' she said, her dark blue eyes flashing with hurt, 'I love my sister, she's what I want to be in the world. And can I go and tell her that? No, 'cause our almost certainly clinically insane mother is monopolising her. So I'm here, in the kitchen, trying to find something for my brother to eat, when I should be out there, helping! So don't tell me you're not hungry, even though you probably aren't, 'cause *you* gotta eat and I gotta do *something*, and if you two are going to get through this, you gotta get through it *together*, yeah?'

She wound down then, took a breath, and said, 'Cheese on toast then?'

'Go on,' said Graham, and no, he wasn't hungry, but yes, he needed to eat. 'And thanks.'

'In general, or for anything specific?'

'For calling me your brother, and not your brother-in-law. I've never been a brother to anyone. '

She smiled at him. 'Well, you are now. Cheese on toast it is, and I'm making some for Hales. Make sure she has at least a bite of it, yeah?'

He nodded, said he would, but then his parents turned up and the cheese on toast just sort of got forgotten. But not what Elaine had said. As he lay there, hours later, in the dark, it all came back to him and it all made sense. *Wise beyond your years, kiddo.*

Graham closed his eyes, and eventually fell into a sort of sleep, and there went the first night.

Four

'Coffee,' he heard Hayley say at half eight the next morning. He opened his eyes, sat upright, and there she was, all bed hair and pyjamas and puffy eyes and gorgeous.

'Thanks babe,' he said, and sipped. He was not a religious man, but if there was one thing that could have made him a believer in the Almighty it was hot, strong, black coffee with no sugar. Beer was great, whisky was better, but black coffee with no sugar was divine. 'How long you been up?'

'Since 'bout six,' she managed a pale smile. 'Your snoring was too much,' then, with hardly a beat, the smile dropped. 'We start moving on today.'

Graham was still too far in the Land of Nod to process this. 'We what?'

Hayley swallowed hard, and to Graham she looked like a small child taking nasty medicine, best done quickly. 'The baby. Angie. We have to start moving on, today. Otherwise...' she hesitated, swallowed, then went on. 'I'm not my mum, Gray. I won't be my mum. I love her, I do, hard though that is sometimes. But I won't *be* her. OK?'

He nodded. Of course it was.

'I'm not going to forget it...her...whatever,' Hayley went on. 'It's not going to be like taking a dump, one quick wipe, a flush and it's all over,' again she stopped, and Graham saw she knew full well that was, in fact, what had happened to their child. 'But today, I want us to start again. Put stuff away. The toys, the cot, all the baby stuff. Not throw it out, because we may...well, we may need it again someday. But just...I don't want us tripping over it.' Another beat, then, 'You OK with that, hon?'

He thought it over, but not for long, then decided he was. It wasn't as if they were forgetting, after all. They'd *never* forget. But...yeah, all that stuff lying around...it was too raw. When you cut the skin, you bandaged the wound.

'I'm fine with it babe.'

Five

They started after a fairly desultory breakfast – appetites seemed to be slow in returning – and as they stood in the doorway of the room that was no longer a nursery, Hayley said, 'Ten weeks. We went right over the top, didn't we?'

Graham was startled into a laugh. Yes, they had. The windowsill and the chest of drawers were lined deep with stuffed bears, dogs and dolls, so that not so much as a centimetre of surface was showing; even the mobile above the cot had four Forever Friends bears lazily swinging about.

'I'll get bin bags,' said Graham. 'Get the bears stored in the loft.'

'You will not,' Hayley said, and thumped him on the arm, causing him to exclaim in surprise and turn to her. She was smiling. There were tears in her eyes, but she was smiling. 'You will *not* suffocate those bears and dolls by putting them in bin bags. We'll let them roam free up there. Or as free as they can roam with the cot up there as well…if there's room.'

'Oh, there's room. I'll take the legs off the cot, maybe take the sides off too, it'll be fine. And if you insist, then we shall turn the loft into a toy Safari Park, where the animals shall wander around free.' He hugged her close, because she was his love, and the bravest woman ever. 'But you go up every day and clean the place out, deal?'

'Deal,' she said, but her voice was growing thick. 'C'mon, soonest begun, soonest done.'

Six

In truth, Graham did most of the work. No, in truth, Graham did *all* of the work. That was OK, he didn't mind – a practical problem was his best friend at a time like this. Though Hayley said nothing, he knew she was still in a little pain – the faint frown line on her forehead was enough to clue him into that – but mostly he knew she just wasn't too comfortable in the room. She'd be there for a minute or two, pick something up, put it back down again, then would wander out, returning twenty minutes later with more coffee for him. He didn't press her. Instead he unscrewed the cot, took it up into the loft – actually being grateful for how heavy and awkward it was, being grateful for the sweat he had to wipe from his brow.

When that was squared away, he went back for the wallpaper, six rolls, and he carried them all up at once, again happy at their awkwardness. No, not at that...but he *was* happy. No, not *happy*...he was...

He sat on the bottom rung of the loft ladder and tried to figure out what he was. Not happy, a country mile from happy, so...what?

'Got too much for you, did it?' asked Hayley walking up the stairs with yet another coffee for him.

'Please, hon. I love you with all my heart and soul, and I love coffee too, but no more, I beg you. My dad always said enough was as good as a feast.'

'Your dad's a good man,' she said, and sipped. Then grimaced. 'Jesus Christ, how can you drink this?'

'Through my mouth. And yeah, he is. And your sister's a good girl.'

A second's silence, and Hayley said, 'We're going to be all right, aren't we hon? We're going to get through this?'

'We are. I promise.'

She looked hard at him, as if trying to catch him out in a lie, and gave that smile again. Pale, almost forced...but a smile. Given time, he was sure, it would broaden, deepen, become real again. 'Good,' she said, and went downstairs with the mug, saying, 'I'm putting milk in this and drinking it, last warning.'

'Knock yourself out,' he called after her, and then it hit him, then he realised how he was feeling. Not happy...but *hopeful*. Hopeful the corner could be turned, and turned soon. Yeah, *hopeful*, and that was good enough.

So feeling, he stood up from the ladder and started carting teddies and stuffed dogs two by two up into the loft, then amused himself as best he could by sitting them against the walls, as though they were waiting for something, like a play to start. Eventually there was only one toy left, a doll with a china face and plastic body, maybe a foot tall, a girl in a long lace gown.

As he took that from the windowsill, it happened again. The same thing he'd experienced in the hospital when he'd gone for that drink – bone crushing, breath catching, inexplicable terror. He stared into the doll's dead glass eyes, her plain porcelain face (dark curls, upturned nose, freckles), and felt as if he was dying. The room started to grow dark, to be suddenly in full night, but he could still see this doll, this thing, this inanimate object that was somehow looking at him, looking at him with lifeless eyes full of…full of…

Full of what?

Full of pure fucking evil.

He was drowning, he suddenly realised, that's how he felt, drowning not in water but in dread, unable to breathe, heart thundering, the room dark and cold and alien, the blue of the doll's eyes growing, growing, capturing him, paralysing him, and something was coming out of the black, a remorseless *thud, thud, thud* of…

The phone rang downstairs, loud, dreadful – but the room was daytime again and the breath was back in his throat. He heard Hayley pick it up. 'Hello? Oh, hi mum. Yeah, I'm OK. We're OK. Yes, I promise…'

He dialled the rest of it to nothing, and stared at the thing in his hands. Just a doll, a doll with a china face and a plastic body, bought somewhere he couldn't remember, nothing to be scared of, it was just a doll, what could dolls do? Well, there was Chucky, but Chucky was just in films. In the real world, dolls were dolls and not demons, and they couldn't look at you *at all*, never mind with…well, pure fucking evil.

All the same, it was with some relief that he closed the loft hatch behind it – and this time he didn't arrange it in a semi-comical manner, he just flung the bloody thing through the hole and slammed the hatch shut, then went downstairs to his wife who was telling her mother that no, it was OK thanks, they didn't need her to come round that night, they were doing just fine, thank you. He said nothing about what had happened, because nothing had happened at all.

Seven

They lay on the couch that night, not watching television, not listening to music, just laying together, and at around about nine Hayley said, 'If I feel well enough, I'm going into work tomorrow.'

'Are you sure?' asked Graham. He'd managed to put the afternoon behind him. *Some form of delayed shock, unsurprising, don't fret over it.*

'Yeah,' she said, and snuggled closer to him. 'Don't get me wrong, I'm going nowhere if I feel rough.' After a second, 'Well, it might be just a few hours. What about you?'

'If you go, I go. If you don't, I don't. I got leave, and we're not that busy right now.' This was, in fact, a massive lie, they were swamped with jobs. But what Hayley didn't know, *yadda yadda yadda.* 'I'll leave this call to you.'

'Cheers,' she said, thumping him on the arm, and loving him.

Eight

Graham's bladder made him wake up at four in the morning. He sighed, rolled over, stroked his wife's hair. She moaned, and turned to him, and by the streetlight outside he saw it wasn't his wife, it was the doll, the doll in the loft, and she was smiling at him.

Nine

'Bad dream, hon?' Hayley asked in the dark. He'd sat bolt upright, cold, gasping. His wife sat up too, held him. 'It's OK, it's all right, go back to sleep, I'm here, don't worry.'

But it was a long time before he slept.

Chapter Four

One

Hayley lasted all of three hours in her first day back at work. It wasn't the pain – that at least seemed to be easing – or even the customers. It was the lying. She didn't like lying, hadn't intended to, but when Jodie, her boss and mostly friend, had asked her if she was feeling better now, and what was it, some sort of bug, Hayley couldn't bring herself to say, *no, not a bug. I had a dead baby inside me and I passed it out in a mass of blood and it fitted on a sanitary pad and then it was rammed into a yellow bin. Sorry for the inconvenience.*

Instead she'd smiled, said yes, *a bug, oooh, a nasty thing,* and Jodie had clucked sympathetically, brought her a mug of hot chocolate with marshmallows bobbing along in it, told her to ease herself in, then moved clients around in the book so Hayley wouldn't be swamped.

During that morning, as people sat before her and she painted nails and coloured hair, advised on cosmetics, and the customers talked about the weather and wasn't it cold, even for January, Hayley felt her mind wander. It wandered to the baby, to Angie, to the poor little thing that had never been alive, never been aware, that would never laugh or want a dog, and every time she looked out of the window there was another mother pushing a pram, or walking a child hand-in-hand, maybe dragging it along as it tried to look in a toyshop window. Suddenly it seemed the world was full of mothers and children, the pavements blocked solid with them, a seething, teeming mass of a life that was denied her.

I can have more, we can have more, the kindly Doctor said so, we can fill the world with children if we wish...so why does this feel like an ending?

She put her hand over her mouth to stifle a sob, and Mrs Leonard – who wanted to know if she was an Autumn or a Winter – looked up at her, and said, 'Are you all right, love?'

'Yes, of course.' She even gave a smile to prove it.

Mrs Leonard – twenty-three, two kids – gazed at her. 'Are you sure? You look a bit pale, if you don't mind me saying.'

Yes, I do mind, I mind very much, thank you. I lost a baby three days ago and it hurts, it hurts, it hurts my heart and my head, but I came here to advise you on your colours and to gel your fingernails, I'm working through my heartbreak and you know nothing about it, you've got kids, you can go home and cuddle them all you fucking *well like, so I do mind, I mind so much I'd happily see you dead, so –*

But that last was so harsh, so stark, that Hayley, shocked and scared at herself, stood up on legs that felt like Plasticine, and said, 'Um…well, I've not been so good, and maybe I came back too soon.' Before Mrs Leonard could ask what was up, Hayley turned to Jodie, made her excuses, picked up her coat and left.

Two

Her Samsung whistled as she put the key in the lock. Jodie; *take all the time you need, ok?* and Hayley, as good natured a woman who ever walked this earth, felt the strength run out of her. Should she tell Jodie the truth? Could she take that, the sympathy, the arm around the shoulders? Hadn't there been enough of that? This had been her decision, her attempt to prove she was not and never would be her mother, her attempt at *moving on, getting through* and all the other things people did during a hard time. But how did you know it was the right time? Who told you? How long was too long, how long was not enough? Where was the manual?

She closed the door behind her, stood in the hall, and sent back *I'm really soz. Should be fine for tomorrow.* And maybe that was true. Maybe the first day was always the hardest. Maybe after that it got easier.

She startled herself into a laugh, thinking *sure, like sex. That was crap at first, but after a while I got into it.* But that laugh turned sour as she realised why people had sex; for fun, sure. For babies also.

I'll get through this, she thought. *We'll get through it, Graham and me. I love him too much, far too much to let this get between us. Sorry Angie, sorrier than you'll ever know, but you will not be the thing that sleeps between us at night.*

She took her coat off, hung it on the hook, went into the kitchen, filled the kettle and dropped a PG bag into her mug, then decided to void her bladder before doing anything else.

She climbed the stairs, crossed the landing, walked into the bathroom…then stopped, turned, walked back and stood outside the spare room.

The door was open.

Why was the door open? Hadn't Graham shut it after he'd put the stuff in the loft? Of course he had, Graham was a compulsive door-closer and turner-off of lights. And she was sure it'd been closed that morning as she'd made her way downstairs. Sure of it.

Oh yeah, really? Like all those times you're sure you've turned the gas off, then gone back to the kitchen to check? Or sure you've put your keys in your bag, only to find them in your pocket? Face it, you stop looking after a while. You just assumed the door was closed because Graham's the door closer in this house. And anyway, you left before he did this morning – just for a change - or did you forget that, the way you often forget where your keys are? You kissed him, told him you loved him, and left him eating toast and drinking that treacle he calls coffee. Maybe he came back up here before he left, just to stand in the room, checking if he'd missed anything, or just standing here and feeling sad. Who knows? Then he turned, walked downstairs and went off to work.

Without closing the door?

Well, evidently. Who knows, he could be sat at his desk now, thinking did I close that spare room door? *tormenting himself with it. But here are some facts, you weren't the last out of the house, the spare room door is open, therefore Graham must've opened it.*

Deciding she was tired and her mind was making too much of what was, after all, just an open bloody door, she leaned forward, took hold of the knob, and started to pull. Then stopped.

On the periphery of her vision, her far right hand side, she'd seen something in the room.

She opened the door again, and there, square on the floor, surrounded by nothing else, was a solitary stuffed dog.

Hayley stared at it. A brown and white stuffed dog, slightly hunched on its back legs, pink felt tongue hanging out of its mouth, as though it was about to chase a stick or was thinking about begging for a treat. It had a silly, eager, ready-to-please face.

A sudden chill ran through her, as though the window had opened. Why such a sight, such a harmless-looking, silly old doggy should chill her, she couldn't fathom. But it did. Just a toy dog, on its own, in the middle of the room, missed by her husband, obviously, while his mind was a million miles away and while she was downstairs, fluttering about, unable to settle, not quite doing things; not the sort of thing to chill anybody, was it? It wasn't Jason or Freddy or anything from a scary movie. It was just a dog. Not even a real dog, a real dog that might be mean and bite at the slightest provocation; this was a toy, inanimate, kapok, felt and stuffing. There was nothing to hurt her, nothing to stop her entering the room, picking the damned thing up, maybe taking it to the loft.

But that chill…

Hayley closed the door, went back to the bathroom, urinated, then went downstairs, made her tea and drank it. She turned the television on and watched some daytime rubbish and waited for Graham to come home, and tried not to think about that toy dog, and why it had bothered her so.

Three

'Whassamarra with your gob?' asked Danny, the foul-mouthed Scouser who had the next cubicle to Graham as he wandered past on the way back from the coffee machine. 'Y've had two days off, think y'd be a bit more cheerful. I mean,' he continued, picking up the photo of Hayley that Graham kept on his desk, 'two days with her and I'd be smilin' fit to burst.'

'She's not been too well,' said Graham, not looking up from his monitor. He didn't mind Danny, but he did have a tendency to talk too much, and perhaps unsurprisingly Graham wasn't in the mood for chat. He had, in fact, spent the whole day resisting the temptation to call his wife, and if not call then text, and if not text then nip out to see her during his lunch. *Too soon,* he kept thinking. *It's too soon. I know it's what she wants, but this is too soon.*

'Aw, sorry,' said Danny, still holding the photo. Then, leeringly, 'she 'ad a cold, like? Been feelin' chesty? You 'ad to rub somethin' on it, then?'

'No,' said Graham, still fixated on the angles for the roof of the new shopping mall, 'she had a miscarriage.'

Without looking up, Graham knew Danny's face had crumpled, and cursed himself. Both for saying it and for upsetting someone he basically quite liked. 'Fuckin' 'ell, I'm sorry mate. How's she? Come to that, how're *you*?'

Graham moved his mouse to one side – but not before clicking SAVE, some things were automatic – and said, 'Don't apologise, you weren't to know. And we're...well, no, we're not fine, but...life goes on, y'know?'

'Yeah, I've heard,' said Danny. 'Y'sure you're all right to be back, though? I mean...fuck it, I dunno what I mean, I've no idea about this stuff. But if you need anythin', right, let me know. You was good to me when I got 'ere, I don't forget shit like that, got me?'

Graham managed a smile. 'Yeah. Got you. Cheers, mate.'

Danny gave a sort of clumsy rough nod, then made his way to his cubicle. Graham watched him go – nineteen years old, skinny as a rake, not a care in the world beyond how many pints of Stella he'd neck at the weekend – and felt a bitter gas stab of jealousy. *For two months or so I was dancing for joy inside, dancing for joy and nobody knew. Now I'm miserable and I blurt it out to the first colleague who passes the time of day. What's wrong with this picture?* He checked his watch. Just coming up to one. Nearly lunch. Should he just pop to the salon anyway, *hi hon, just passing, thought I'd pop in, like I've never done before?* Yeah, that's right, nice and normal. No, he should give her a ring –

As he thought that, his desk phone rang. He knew it was Hayley before he picked it up, but just to be professional he said, 'Hello, Maitland's Design, Graham speaking, how can I help you?'

'Hi love,' said his wife. 'You OK to talk?'

'Yeah, course I am,' though he dropped his voice. There were six people in the open plan, and he wanted things kept as private as possible. 'How are you?'

A pause, then, 'I had to come home. Did three hours, then...well, got a bit much. Jodie was fine about it, though. Should be better tomorrow, though. Something we got to go through, I suppose. Time, and all that.'

'You want me to come home?' He was virtually standing. There was a backlog on his machine, things were piling up, but if she wanted him, he'd be there.

'No,' she said, and she sounded calm enough. 'No, I've got *Loose Women* on and I know how much that makes you swear.' A tiny laugh, but it was at least a laugh. 'I'm going to curl up on the sofa, maybe have a sleep. I'm OK, and I love you. Even if you're crap at putting things away.'

'Um, I think you're forgetting I'm the tidy one in this relationship.' What was this, now? Bantering, like they'd done when they'd first got together? Like in the...*what, like in the old days, is that what you were going to say? Come on, man, get a grip, will you?*

'Maybe, but I'm not the one who left a toy in the nur...spare room. Stuffed dog. I'd have put it in the loft, but...' small hesitation, 'I'm still in a bit of pain. Nothing much,' she hurried on, 'but enough so I don't fancy the ladder.'

Now it was Graham's turn to hesitate, to frown. Had he left something behind? He thought back. No, he was sure. The last thing he'd taken out had been that – he almost shuddered – doll, that girl thing he'd had the nightmare about. After that, he'd checked. Empty room. No toys, no wallpaper, no mobile, no cot…just four walls and a floor and a ceiling. So what could she be talking about? And was it worth arguing about? 'I'm sorry babe,' he said, deciding it wasn't. 'Must've been a bit preoccupied. I'll sort it when I get back. Love you loads, take it easy, promise?'

'I will, and I love you more. See you later.'

They hung up then, and Graham went for his lunch at the café round the corner, and ate a ham sandwich and drank black coffee and went over it all again and again. No, he'd taken everything out of that room. He knew he had. He was certain he had. What on earth did it mean?

Four

Hayley's eyes closed during some girly chat about spousal indifference and sexual incompatibility ("Oooh, my first husband, now…what he didn't want me to do!") and had a dream.

She dreamed she could hear something upstairs, like a scratching on a wooden door, something that wanted to be let out, as if for a walk. She dreamed she got up from the sofa and mounted the stairs, ending up before the closed spare room door. She dreamed she opened it, but there was no animal there. There was a little girl, *her* little girl, Angie, in her long white lace dress, facing away from her, looking out of the window.

'Doggy,' said Angie, for in the dream she appeared about three years old.

'You want a doggy?' Hayley asked in the doorway in her dream. 'Well, let's see. We'll talk to Daddy when he gets home. What sort of doggy would you want?'

'This sort,' said Angie in the dream, and turned, but her face wasn't like Hayley had imagined. Angie's face was distorted, spiteful, angry, porcine, slobbery, a massive snarl, jagged cruel teeth protruding from a ravenous, eternally hungry mouth. She raised stick thin, emaciated arms ending in thick, hoof-life hands, and cradled there was the stuffed dog Hayley had seen on the floor, but it's head had been ripped off and blood was pouring down its neck, and Angie was laughing, laughing, laughing and the noise was like a drill chipping through concrete and Angie ran towards her, laughing, holding the toy which was spurting blood out, and she was screaming – no, *squealing* - 'WANT THIS DOGGY, WANT THIS DOGGY, WANT THIS…'

Five

She awoke with such a start she nearly fell from the sofa, but then she felt arms hold her, and in a mad not-quite awake panic she thought it was Angie and she pulled away in terror.

'Easy babe,' she heard a man say, 'easy. You're just having a dream.'

She forced her eyes open, properly open, and there was her man, there was Graham, holding her, loving her. But still…what the hell was he doing home? 'Gray,' she muttered, utterly confused. 'What time is it?'

'Just after six,' he said, sitting next to her and stroking her hair. 'I thought the lights being on would be a giveaway.' He smiled at her, but she couldn't smile back. *God...that dream...*

'Been out for hours,' she mumbled. 'Must've been more tired than I thought. Had a...had a nightmare.'

'I know, you were moaning,' he kissed her forehead. 'It's OK now, all gone. Nothing to hurt you now.'

She was going to say something – though what she wasn't sure – when the doorbell rang. 'Fuck,' said Graham. 'Who's this?' He stood up and crossed to the window, peeking out. 'It's your mum.' Then, turning back to her, 'Shall we pretend to be out?'

This made her smile. It wouldn't have been the first time. 'No, it's fine. She probably needs this. I'll get it.'

Six

Graham followed his wife into the hall, greeted Anna, who bustled into the house carrying enough food to feed Central Africa for ten years whilst saying, 'I'm going to make you two something to eat, no arguments, what you don't have today you can freeze, you're too thin the pair of you, you need building up,' then made his way upstairs to change. As he crossed the landing to the bedroom, he opened the spare bedroom door, to see what he'd left there. But there was nothing, just as he'd remembered. Just an empty room. No stuffed dog.

Seven

Graham didn't get round to bringing it up, not on that evening anyway. There was just too much going on. *How long will it be like this*, he found himself thinking as he stood in the kitchen, boiling yet another kettle. Then, for the first time, an unsettling, almost cruel thought; *was she worth it? Was it even, actually, a she yet? Was it an anything? Ten weeks old, never took a breath, yes God, that's a funny joke, well done, take a bow and end your set with "My name's the Almighty, I'm here all week, don't forget to tip your waitress," and we'll all applaud like seals. But was the baby actually worth all this fuss?*

Down the narrow hall, in the living room, he could hear Anna launch her self-pity rocket into the stratosphere. 'When your poor old dad died, I thought I'd never go on, thought I'd never recover and put it behind me...'

But you didn't, and what's worse, you didn't want to. You grew to love all the fuss and attention it brought you and decided to cast yourself as a star in your own personal soap opera: Anna Buchanan, Widow Woman. It's running and running and nobody will cancel the bloody thing.

He slumped, tired, and then took a deep breath, knowing Hayley would be looking to the doorway, waiting for him, expecting him to take some of this weight from her shoulders. Which he would, and gladly, for she was his love and there was nothing he wouldn't do for her. *Thank Christ she's not her mother,* he thought, for maybe the millionth time in his marriage. *Thank Christ she knows that we've got to* move on. *Thank Christ for that.*

Eight

The phones just kept ringing; the landline, his mobile, her mobile. Calls from Elaine, calls from his mother, even a call from Graham's dad, and every time one phone or the other interrupted her, Anna would give an irritated sigh at being baulked mid-flow, then carry on broadcasting to whichever or them didn't have an ear to a receiver. *Maybe we should get away*, thought Graham as he heard yet again about how hard life could be for someone who was widowed in her early forties, *couple of days, a weekend maybe. Somewhere where the signals are spotty and the Wi-Fi unreliable. Break off. Time for two and two for time. York, that's supposed to be nice. Devon, maybe. Cornwall. Sod it, Margate. I'll suggest it when…*

'Sorry Mum,' said Hayley, putting down the phone, 'Elaine, just seeing how things were. You were saying?'

Anna's wrinkled nose said *Hmph, she can find time to phone* you, *but* me, *her own mother..?* 'About how you must never be left alone, sweetheart. Loneliness is a terrible curse. I know. Ever since your poor old dad died…'

I must ask what did the poor bastard in, Graham thought, as his own mobile rang. *Boredom?* 'Sorry,' he said to the room (and yes, Hayley saw the look of relief he hadn't been quick enough to hide), 'it's my dad.' He took the phone to the hallway, sat on the stairs, and told his dad it was as OK as it was going to be, thanks very much for asking, it was appreciated, it really was, and thought again, *how long does this go on for? How long until I can start talking about Arsenal's title challenge again, or how much I hate Celebrity Big Brother? When do those days come back?*

Nine

Anna finally went home at half nine and an hour later Hayley and Graham were cuddled up in bed, the world shut out. 'I'll try for a full day tomorrow,' she said.

'Good,' he replied. 'How's your pain?'

'She texted saying she'd got home fine, and that we're to eat the leftovers tomorrow,' said Hayley, and without warning they were screaming with laughter, holding on to each other, rolling across the bed. He could see such laughter hurt her a little, but it seemed impossible to stop. It wasn't good laughter – it was too hysterical for that, the kind of laughter that could become a crying jag at the drop of a hat, but it was better than none at all.

It was loud laughter, hard bullets of laughter, and it obscured any noises that might have come from above them, from the loft. Noises like shuffling feet, for example.

Chapter Five

One

The next morning, having kissed goodbye to Graham and made herself up for work, Hayley looked into the spare room and if she hesitated a little too long on the landing, perhaps half reminded of a dream, she didn't notice. There was no stuffed dog in the middle of the floor. *Gray put it away while I was busy with mum. Good lad, I'll thank him for that when he gets home.* But the day went well, she managed a full eight hours, the pain was virtually unnoticeable, and the customers...well, they weren't a problem. As she and Jodie locked up at six, Hayley found herself thinking, *well, there we are. I know one swallow doesn't make a summer, and I know there may be still some hard roads ahead, I accept that even if I don't like it, but there. That's one day down. One not bad day.* So thinking, the memory of a stuffed dog vanished from her mind. For his part, Graham forgot about the whole thing completely. For a while, anyway.

As the week went on, it looked as if Graham might have been granted his wish. Things did, indeed, start to calm down, to return to some kind of normality. Hayley stopped noticing the mothers and children around her – gradually, but it stopped, like a spinning top winding down. Graham started thinking more and more about the tasks on his computer at work. Life, it seemed was going on, just as Hayley's pain was going away. She was glad. She'd never forget what had happened, part of her would always mourn the poor wretched bundle of cells that could have been her first child, but a part of her – a much greater part she would never admit to anyone, not even Graham – was relieved, relieved at the thought they could go back to being normal, and start to face the future together.

Two

Exactly a week after she'd been lying in a hospital bed and felt that heavy pain – something that already was starting to feel it had happened to someone else, something she'd been told about – Hayley walked into the living room to find Graham scrolling through something on his iPad. He gave a little start as he saw her, almost guilty. She snuggled up next to him. 'You looking up porn? I've told you, no way am I buying a schoolgirl outfit, the whole thing's just too Jimmy Savile for me.'

'Shame,' muttered Graham, 'you'd just look so cute in those knee socks. No, actually, I was thinking…'

He handed her the tablet and she saw pictures of hotels, little villages, coastal views, all of which promised OUTSTANDING VALUE. A holiday, time away? God, it sounded appealing. Time to unwind, to ease the creaking bones, maybe to jump each other's bones again and again, time to breathe fresh air that smelled of nothing but cowshit, and go to bed exhausted. Yeah, maybe…

But not now.

'Babe,' Graham asked. 'You OK?'

'Yeah hon, just having a think, give me a second, you know it takes time.'

He smiled at that, and she smiled back, but there was a little unease behind her eyes she wasn't sure he'd picked up on. Why *didn't* she want to go away? They could afford it, and God knew they hadn't been properly away since their honeymoon in Venice. They'd been too busy, working and working, keeping their heads above water, making sure the mortgage didn't go into default. Yeah, times were easier, the worst of the recession flushed away (like a miscarriage) but the recovery seemed fragile, built on spiders' legs, and could they really afford to just blow a few hundred?

But even *that* wasn't it, was it? There was something else, something…deeper? Yes, deeper, nagging at her, like an itch, something that said, *stay here, stay here, stay here.*

'Not just yet,' she said eventually, and seeing the look on Graham's face, hurried on. 'I don't know why, I just don't feel like it's right yet. Y'know *what* I think,' she said, sitting up, breaking the contact, 'I don't know if this makes sense, but…look, we're, well, we're going on, aren't we? Pretty much back to living how we lived before the miscarriage?'

Graham nodded. 'Yeah, I think we are.'

'And that's a good thing, it's what we need. I mean, we've all seen what can happen if you don't. And that's the thing, I think. I want to prove to mum you *can* just move on, not forget, but continue. And do it without even looking like you're making an effort, just by *living*, just by behaving like you always did. This is sounding like I'm trying to beat her at a game, I get that, and maybe I am, but I want to prove that getting on isn't something you need to take a...I dunno, a pill for. Get me?' She studied him, stared deep into the brown eyes she'd often thought she'd like to swim in.

'So, if we went away, then came back all smiley and happy...' he said, slowly, testing it.

'Yeah, it'd give her some superiority, I think. "Oh yeah, they got over it because they could afford to go away, I couldn't afford that, I was a widow, I just had to get on with it." Seriously, hon, am I making sense?' She had to keep asking that, because part of her didn't think she was making sense *at all*. Part of her was, in fact, worried sick at this line of reasoning. It seemed alien.

But it seemed like she was making sense after all, as Graham smiled at her, kissed her nose. 'Course you are,' he said. 'When have you never, except when you said you thought Jim Davidson was funny. And here's the thing, even if you weren't, I'd agree with you.'

'Because you love me.'

'Because I love you,' he agreed, smiling wider.

'Good,' she said. 'And because you love me, you can go for a takeaway. I seriously cannot be arsed cooking tonight.'

'What do you want?' he asked, kissing her nose again (and oh, that was making her hot, hot for the first time in a while, more proof that things were back the way they once had been), 'Indian, Chinese or Italian?'

'Surprise me,' she said, and as he stood up to go, she took hold of his hand and said, 'now and tonight, if you want. You can surprise me tonight.'

Something that might have been a tear popped up in his left eye. 'If you're a good girl for teacher.'

'Go on,' she said, swatting him away, 'before I change my mind, you dirty perv.'

'All pervs are dirty,' he called over his shoulder as we walked into the hall, retrieving his coat from the hook, 'that's why they're pervs.' The door opened. 'See you later, babe.'

'See you hon.' As the door closed behind him, she found herself thinking, *well, he stood for it.* But she couldn't understand *why* she thought that.

Three

She heard it as she was in the kitchen, putting plates on the warmers and pulling cutlery from drawers. Directly above her, from the spare room.

Sobbing. Soft, subdued sobbing, as if from a child who'd cried themselves out and was about to sleep, or from a child who expected no comfort, who was used to crying alone in the dark.

She froze at the open drawer, knives in hand. She ran a million thoughts in her head. Mid terrace...maybe the Patterson's next door (who didn't have a baby) on the left (who didn't have a baby) were looking after a baby (one they must've found outside Waitrose)...or maybe their television was on (even though she was in the kitchen, which backed onto *their* kitchen) or maybe the radio she'd never heard before that they played in their kitchen was tuned to Radio 4 and there was a drama about a baby that sobbed or maybe...

Maybe there was a sobbing child in her spare room.

Except there wasn't, there couldn't be, because there was no child here, unless maybe one had run in, unseen, while Graham had opened the door. Some kind of stealth child. Stranger things had happened. Cats did it sometimes, ran into strange houses to get out of the rain...It'd happened to her, once, when she was younger, and...

Except there's no rain, except children are not cats, and there is no child sobbing in this house. Got that?

Got that.

But there was. She could hear it; hear it clearly, even down the stairs, even though it (she) wasn't drawing attention to itself (herself). There was *something* up there anyway, *something* making a noise. And hadn't she once heard that cats' mewling could sound like a baby's cry?

'OK Moggy, here I come,' she said aloud, with a bravado she did not feel. She placed the knives on the kitchen table, crossed into the hall and climbed the stairs, slowly, breathing through her nose, treading lightly...

There was a noise, behind the door that was revealing itself to her, step by step, that closed door, and it wasn't a cat, no cat could sound so desperate, so lonely, so wretched...it was a baby.

No, a child, no longer a baby, no longer a toddler, a child...no, it was a baby, it was...

'IT'S NOTHING,' Hayley screamed to her empty home. And suddenly she was furious, beside herself with an anger she could barely contain. She stormed up the final few steps, ran across the landing, and flung the door open...

The room was, of course, empty, and the noise stopped suddenly, as if cut off. She stood there for a second, panting, her eyes scanning every inch of that space and there was nothing untoward, nothing amiss, nothing there that shouldn't be, just a room, nothing more, nothing less. She took a second more, got her breathing under control then closed the door and went back down to the kitchen. If she'd looked up, she'd have seen the hatch to the loft close itself, very slowly and virtually silently, as if something was hiding there. But Hayley didn't. Instead she got the cutlery and plates ready and Graham brought home Crispy Duck and she ate it and said nothing about what had happened while he'd been out.

Four

The sex was over and – contrary to the good old cliché – Hayley had drifted off and Graham was still awake. Dozing, and with a silly grin on his face, but awake nonetheless.

They'd taken it slow, and it'd been mighty fine. Slow out of consideration for her residual pain, and slow because...well, slow seemed to be the way they needed it, face to face, eyes locked together, slow, gentle strokes until the end, and as he came he held her, hands behind her head, cradling her, looking straight at her, deep into those stunning blue eyes. She'd told him she loved him, but the words had been unnecessary. He could see it all over her face, read it in every line of her naked body. *Yeah*, he thought as he held her – as soon as he *could* think – *we'll do OK now, we'll do fine. This is the start of it, the start of us being good again.*

They'd said little else, just held each other. There was some distant, sad expression on her face as he slid out of her, but she didn't expound upon it and he didn't press her. If she'd wanted him to know, she'd have told him.

So eventually she'd slipped away to wherever she went in her dreams, and he lay there, dozing but not asleep, silly grin on his face, feeling Hayley's occasional twitch and hearing the sporadic mumble in the back of her throat. *I'll join her soon,* he thought.

Except he didn't. He didn't mind it, not for half an hour or so. He felt at his most protective of her – maybe something men weren't supposed to feel in the early 21st century but hey, who was there to arrest him, in their own bedroom as the day broke on a late January morning? His woman had been through something brutal and if he wanted to feel as if he was protecting her, he would. He was a slightly old-fashioned man in that way, influenced by his slightly old- fashioned father and if people – not that there were any people in that room, beyond his beloved – didn't like it, well then, they could fuck off.

Still he didn't fall asleep. He raised his head, caught the bedside clock. 12:15. Up in seven hours for work. But hey, never mind, even if he lay there for another three quarters of an hour before catching the Zs, that would still be six hours, and six hours was enough for anybody.

His bladder was filling. Graham turned onto his side and pretended it wasn't. *There's something I bet you never get in books, not even ones by that Stephen Vaughn bloke. Sex makes you want to piss. There's a secret that's never been past the bedroom door. Anyway, I'm fine. I don't need to get up. I'm comfortable, I'm warm, I don't want to wake Hayley, everything's OK, everything's fine in Graham's bladder, let's count us some sheep – or think about how unbelievable Hayley looked as she rocked underneath me, slow, slow, fused like glue, let's pretend there's no need for me to get up at all.*

Of course, the more he pretended his bladder was fine, the more he felt it fill, the more he felt the pressure build. *Go away,* he thought, now becoming irritated. *Go away, let me sleep.* But it didn't. Another look at the clock. 12:45. 12:45, still awake, bladder now painful, and *oh, fuck it.*

Moving with all the stealth of a safecracker (or so he thought), he gently lifted the duvet and tiptoed out of the room, along the landing, and into the bathroom. Without switching on the light he voided in a wonderful gush, resisting the temptation to sigh with relief. He dropped the lid down to deaden the flush, washed his hands and…

Heard something on the landing. No, not on the landing, but outside the bathroom. A sort of *clump* noise. *Must've woken her after all, some safecracker you are,* he thought with some amusement as he dried his hands. *Any minute now she'll walk through that door, more asleep than awake and probably bump straight into you.*

But she didn't. Nobody joined him at the towel rail, and there were no more noises. Must've been next door, he reasoned, with all the clarity of a man who'd just emptied his bladder at nearly one in the morning. He exited the bathroom, turned left, and saw the hatch leading up to the loft dangling open.

Oh, that's what it was. Damn thing. If either of us had been standing underneath that would have given us a good whack. Mustn't have set the catch properly, easily done. He reached for the pole that was tucked nicely away behind the bathroom doorframe, inserted the nick into the notch, and pushed the hatch closed. Just as he was about to make the three quarter clockwise turn that would have secured it, he heard a little girl laugh. A quiet laugh, a *let's not wake the parents* laugh, but still, a laugh.

He ran cold, standing there naked in the early morning, and a half remembered sensation flooded through him. *Dread, terror, the harbinger of bad times to come,* he thought randomly. A little girl's laugh in the dead of night in a house where no little girl had ever trod, and then, just after the laugh, a low, lilting child's voice, from above him, from *directly above him* in the loft, said 'Daddy? Come and play with doggy. Come and play with *me.*'

If Graham hadn't have just been to the toilet, he would have pissed all over the floor. *No,* he thought. *No, that's not happening, just isn't, I heard nothing, nothing to hear, nothing happened...*

Just in front of him, to his left, the spare bedroom door was open, the door he was sure had been closed less than five minutes ago.

There are no voices, no little girls, nothing is happening here. I am going to take one step, then another, then a third and soon enough I shall be lying by my beautiful and sexy, sleeping wife and I will put all this behind me. All what *behind me? All* nothing *behind me, that's what.*

He managed it. He took one step forward, and without looking inside he reached out, grabbed the knob of the spare room door and pulled it shut. He took another step, and another, each one taking him closer and closer to his beloved and as he got to the bedroom door, he heard, from above him, 'See you soon, Daddy.'

I heard nothing, he told himself over his hugely beating heart. *I heard nothing. Nothing to hear, so I heard nothing.*

Slowly, quietly, he climbed into bed beside Hayley (who appeared not to have moved at all), and spooned her, seeking her warmth, seeking comfort.

He didn't sleep a wink. For some reason he kept thinking of that doll, that china doll with the brown curls, the blue eyes, the upturned nose and freckles. *Come and play with doggy. Come and play with* me…*see you soon, Daddy.*

Five

'Jesus hon, you look like shit,' Hayley said to Graham as he entered the kitchen the next morning. He said nothing, barely looked at her, and sat at the table. She crossed to him, concerned. He was pale, heavy circles under his eyes, and looked like he'd had a rough night on the whisky. 'You coming down with something?'

'Had a bad night, hardly slept.' Not only was he not looking at her, nor was he making a move for the kettle, and the latter especially wasn't a good sign. Graham couldn't function without a good two spoonful's of Nescafé at almost hourly intervals, and first thing in the morning the kettle was virtually the only thing he could see.

'Well, I did my best to tire you out,' she said, and this at least was greeted with the ghost of a smile. He took her hand, kissed it, rubbed it against his cheek. 'You should stay here, you're going to be no use at work.'

She thought she saw him tense at that – no, almost shudder – but that had to be an illusion. She herself had slept like a log and had still not quite entered the land of the living. 'It's OK babe, I'll be fine,' he said. His smile widened a little. 'I promise.'

'If you're sure,' she said. 'Stay there, I'll get you a coffee. Extra strong?'

'Please.'

So she busied herself with mugs and coffee and kettles, and looked after her man, and after he'd finished his drink he kissed her, told her he loved her, and left the house for work. *I hope he's OK*, she thought. *I hope he doesn't drive off the road or into a bus or anything. Please God, if You're there, look after him. Thanks. It's Hayley, by the way. Hayley Davis.* She checked her watch. 8:35. Time to brush her teeth and make final preparations to her face.

It was only as she climbed the stairs that it came back to her, and she stopped just before the landing. The sobbing she'd heard (*thought* she'd heard), that child crying. She found herself hardly breathing for a minute, her ears straining…but she heard nothing.

Of course I heard nothing. Nothing to hear.

So thinking, she went into the bathroom and started making herself ready for another day.

Six

'Fuck me, mate,' said Danny, 'how much did you neck last night? I 'ope you weren't drivin'.'

'I didn't have a drop,' said Graham, dragging the mouse across a support strut on his screen and deleting it. Damn thing wasn't even straight. *Can't even freehand a decent line,* he cursed, and resigned himself to lining up the entry points and leaving the computer to sort the lines out. It was cheating, a kind've Painting by Numbers approach, but screw it. He was tired, tired and…

'Well, you must've been doin' sumptin'' Danny persisted, and today that bloody Scouse accent was like a road drill. If it wasn't a sure life sentence, Graham would have killed the younger man just to shut him up. 'I mean, like, is everythin' all right? With the missus an' that?'

OK, keep a lid on it. He's being considerate, it isn't his fault you're tired. Tired, and shitting yourself, to be frank. Because no matter what you keep telling yourself, that happened last night. *The hatch* dropped, *the voice…*he shuddered, *the voice, the girl's* voice, *you heard it. It actually* happened. *Maybe just in your head, but it* happened.

Except it hadn't, it couldn't have, it was impossible, so therefore it hadn't happened. Algebra, one of the design fundamentals. Say a structure needs to take x weight; well then, the structure needs to be y size, therefore it needs z materials. Simple, straightforward. So, apply that to the previous night – well, the early hours of this morning. There was no child in the house, so therefore there had been no child's voice. Both side of the equation balanced, everyone was happy. 'No, she's good, mate,' said Graham. 'And getting better.'

'Nice one, glad to 'ear it. I know she don't know me, but give 'er me best, woncha?'

'I will, sure.'

Danny wandered over to his own desk, and started tapping his keys, and Graham found comfort in his reasoning. *Yeah, algebra. No child could have spoken because there was no child to speak, therefore you didn't hear what you thought you heard. Therefore you did only* think *you heard it. And why did you think you heard that? Well, stress, the stress you've been under. Come on, people do all sorts of weird shit when they're under stress. Talk to themselves, sing to themselves, chew their own earwax, dress up as Spider-Man and hang off a bridge. But the stress is diminishing now, things are getting back to normal, and soon all of this will be nothing but a memory you can't quite recall.*

In the meantime, though, he was shattered. *Early night tonight, TGIF and all that cobblers, early night and a lazy weekend. Yeah, do me fine.*

Seven

'Can you fit me in?' asked Elaine. Hayley jumped a little, turned, and saw her younger sister, half in the salon, half outside in the drizzle. 'I know, I should have rung ahead, but I only found out half an hour ago.'

'Come in and I'll see,' said Hayley, and crossed to the appointments book. Jodie had often spoken about getting a computer in to log the appointments, but had done nothing about it. 'What do you want doing?'

'Just nails, really. Shellac, with a sparkle.'

'Hot date?' Unsurprisingly, there was space in the book. January wasn't a boom month in their business. Who went to a party in January? Thank God for Christmas. Christmas could carry a beauty salon until March. 'Yeah, sit down, I'm free until half past.'

'Ta, appreciate it.' Elaine took the seat behind the table and Hayley sat before her, arranging her equipment. 'And no, not a date. Me and a couple of the girls are going to the Town Hall tonight. To see a psychic. One of them had to drop out.' And together, she and Hayley said, 'Unforeseen circumstances,' and laughed. She was a good kid, Elaine, a good sister. Together they had weathered their mother's storms, and it had bonded them, like survivors from a small shipwreck. 'I've never been to one before,' she went on, 'and I know they're all crap and cold reading, yeah, but Emma from our place has seen this one before and said she was brilliant. Anyway, it'll be a laugh.'

'Which one are you going to?' called Jodie from the other side of the salon, where she was putting heated rollers into a teenage girl's hair. The girl herself didn't look up, just continued reading her Facebook updates on her iPhone.

'Oh, erm...hang on, I'll get it...' said Elaine and Hayley coughed a smile into the back of her hand. Yeah, a good kid, a good sister, but the mistress of artifice. This slightly empty-headed *hang on, um, be there in a sec* façade that she used to disarm people could get a little wearing if you were around her for a while. Elaine had a ton of ambition, Elaine had purpose, Elaine wanted to be MD of that bank she worked in someday, but Elaine didn't want anyone to know that, she wanted to fly under the radar. *Foil the enemy and fox your friends,* she'd once said after too much fizz. 'Lillian Manning, I think that's it.'

'I've seen her,' said Jodie. 'Yeah, she *is* good. She was in the back of the Red Lion a couple of years ago. Told my cousin all sorts of things she couldn't possibly have known. Put the wind up me a bit, it proper did.'

'Well, she's gone up in the world, got to give her that. Back of the Red Lion to the Town Hall, business must be good,' said Hayley. Then, specifically to Elaine, pointing to the nail bottles, 'Which one?'

Elaine hesitated, pointed, shook her head, then chose another. Hayley was often reminded of that old detective show they'd play on cable on Sunday afternoons. All Elaine needed was a crumpled mac and a glass eye. 'Ah, it's nothing but a night out, and it's January, and I'm fed up, and it's cheap, so hey,' said Elaine. 'If she's good, so much the better. If she's crap, I can get some cheap laughs out of it. I mean, what else am I to do? Sit in the flat and look at the phone which has forgotten how to ring, yeah?'

'You could call mum,' said Hayley, avoiding eye contact, applying the first layer to her sister's right hand. 'She was saying only the other night, you don't call, you don't pop round...'

'Balls, I was there yesterday evening. Apparently it's *you* who doesn't keep in touch.'

'Hey, I've got an excuse. Even got a note from the hospital,' she said, without thinking, then almost clamped a hand over her mouth. If she hadn't been holding a nail bottle, she would've. Was she actually *joking* about her miscarriage?

'God, right, sorry,' her sister said, her brow knitting in concern. 'I mean, I've not forgotten, but...how are you?'

Had my mind play a trick or two on me, but aside from that... 'OK, I think. Yeah, OK and getting better. I'm determined I'm not going to be mum on this one.'

'Yeah, good deal. I mean, you've already got her hips, that's enough of a cross to bear.'

'You want this on your nails or across your mouth,' asked Hayley, holding up the nail polish.

'Can't blame me for nature,' Elaine smiled. Then, more seriously, 'You know I'm there. Yeah?'

'I know. And thanks.'

They left it there, that was enough between them, and the conversation turned to Elaine's big night, and who knew, this Lillian Manning might just tell her if she was going to meet a dark, handsome stranger. Someone like Richard Hammond, but taller.

Eight

'Who here has a sister…works somewhere with…oh, chemicals I think. There's a smell.'

Yes, thought Elaine at nine o'clock that evening, *it's the pure rank odour of bullshit. Prime 100% bullshit, fully British, accept no substitute.* That it should come to this, twenty-two years old, sat in Crouch End Town Hall on a Friday night, watching a pudgy, middle-aged woman in a bell-tent dress virtually resort to *I'm getting the name...John* was...well, sad. This Lillian woman wasn't even funny. In fact, the longer the night went on, the angrier Elaine had become. She was some kind of vampire, a parasite, convincing this packed audience - and at twenty quid a ticket no wonder she was pudgy - of mostly elderly men and women that all was good, all was well, and in the spirit world you basically got to sit around and read *The People's Friend* all day with no sodding arthritis to drag you down. People had been reduced to tears as their parents (or children who had been taken too soon) popped up to say not to worry, being dead's a great laugh.

'Not a bad smell though,' Lillian went on, eyes scanning, doubtless looking for the tics and twitches on an audience member's face that signalled someone here had a sister who smelled nice. Elaine looked to her left and saw Charlotte, whose idea this had been. She was sat forward, mouth open, taking it all it, taken in by it all. *That's the last time I come to you for advice*, she thought. *Anyone who thinks this is real has no business telling me how to deal with an irate account holder whose Direct Debit has bounced.* Elaine looked to her right, and her other colleague, Vicky, was stifling a yawn. They exchanged *Jesus Christ* glances, then Elaine flicked her eyes to Charlotte. Vicky leaned forward, saw Charlotte, almost laughed, then suppressed it. Elaine looked away quickly, turned her glance to the stage. She couldn't bray laughter like a donkey, no matter how much this old fraud deserved it. *Three hundred years ago you'd have been burned at the stake, you witch. God, I could be home now with my Rampant Rabbit and my copy of* Fifty Shades…

'Her name's…Hayley,' the woman on the stage suddenly shouted. 'And you,' she pointed straight at Elaine. 'You're her sister. Your name is Elaine. Am I right? Stand up if I'm right.'

Elaine looked at her companions – Charlotte's face was a round O of astonishment, Vicky's a *why not* – and stood, still not taken in. This was a trick. 'Yes. I'm Elaine.'

'And your sister is Hayley, she's a beautician, she did your nails today, you didn't have an appointment you just turned up. You weren't supposed to come here, someone dropped out,' Lillian laughed, 'unforeseen circumstances. Shellac, with a sparkle.' No questions now, just rapid-fire speech, but still…well, who *didn't* get stuff done before a night out? And Elaine's crew were a good twenty years younger than the average age of the audience. OK, the names, they were good, but it would take more than *this* to convince her.

'Your dad passed, ten years ago. Suddenly, a heart attack, he had a condition, no-one knew, not even him, came out at the autopsy.' Lillian went on, and her head was slightly tilted towards the lights. 'He's fine though, he's happy, he says he loves you, and you must forgive your mother's funny ways. Your sister, Hayley…he says he's sorry about what happened to her. Her baby. She had a miscarriage, recently, a week or so ago, it would have been a girl. He says if he could, he'd hold her. There's a Scot…your brother-in-law? No, related to him though. He'll…I'm not sure I understand this…he'll come through in the end. Do you know what that means?'

'No. I don't.'

Lillian faced her directly. 'You don't believe any of this, do you?'

Elaine felt everyone turn and look at her. Some of the audience were curious, but the majority of them were looking at her with frank hostility. *Well done, Lillian. Put me on the spot, try and frighten me into compliance. Sorry, you picked on the wrong girl here. I've faced worse than you down. My mum and her 'funny ways' for example.* 'No,' she said once more. 'I don't.'

Lillian smiled, and it was such a genuine, warm smile that – just for a second – Elaine was completely disarmed. 'It's all right, don't worry. But what I'm telling you is true. And your sister, Hayley, is experiencing something to do with the other side. Her husband also. They've not told each other, but they are. It's something they'll need help with. That's why you were brought to me tonight, why your friend dropped out and you took her place. Soon, you'll need to turn to me. Then you'll believe. Now,' she went on, addressing the rest of the crowd, 'who here had a son? Jason? Taken before his time?'

The audience turned away from her, and Elaine sat down, Charlotte glaring at her, arms folded, Vicky patting her consolingly on the leg. *I'll turn to you when hell freezes over,* thought Elaine, *and not before.*

Nine

Hayley sat in her front room, TV on low, Graham asleep on her lap while she stroked his hair. *Poor baby,* she thought. *He's shattered.* He'd barely been able to eat his meal, his head dropping onto his chest as he tried to insert the scrambled eggs into his constantly yawning mouth. As soon as she set the Sky box to show the latest episode of *Game of Thrones* he'd laid across her, closed his eyes and departed for Dreamland. She didn't care. She felt...at peace. Yes, rested, complete somehow. *You don't ask for much, not like that sister of yours.* Her mother's voice, a constant litany of admonition, of playing people off against each other, drifted to her across the years.

No, she didn't ask for much. If you didn't ask for much you were happy with what you received, that was Hayley's philosophy. Elaine had drive and Graham had ambition, but Hayley...well, she took what she was given. She had a certain artistic flair, she could make people pretty and that cheered them up, so she'd become a beautician, and that wasn't a bad thing, was it? It didn't start wars, did it? She had a home, she had her man, and the future might or might not hold children or riches and whatever turned up, turned up. Recent history had taught her a lot about planning.

No, she thought, stroking her man's head, *this is fine, this'll do.* She remembered when she'd first met him, that night at whatsername's party, the redhead she'd been at college with, doing their BTEC in Hair and Beauty, oh God, what *was* her name? Something exotic, Chantelle or Chandelle or Chandelier, something like that. Champagne? Did it matter? All that had mattered was Graham, a friend of a friend of a gatecrasher, standing in the kitchen talking to another man, someone taller, and she'd had to squeeze past them both to refill her Chardonnay (*Chardonnay? Had her name been Chardonnay? No, not quite*), and he'd said, 'Here, allow me,' had taken her glass, filled it, handed it back and their fingers had touched and that had been it, thank you very much, Hayley, at twenty-one, had met her man.

He'd asked for her number that night, she'd given it gladly, and he'd called the next day, arranged a date in *The Moon on the Water* in town, and she'd lost herself to him. She was twenty-one, not a kid, and not a virgin, but she had genuinely never felt the way she had when she sat in his company. Warm, respected, sexy, protected, hot...he wasn't perfect, God no - he sulked too much if Arsenal lost for instance, and sometimes he could be a little *too* courteous (she knew how to open doors, and occasionally she wanted to walk on the outside on the pavement, just to see what it was like), but then he put up with *her* Dido CDs and *Made in Chelsea* on the telly. *It's the grit in the pearl that makes the oyster,* her dad had said once, and had he been talking about mum, even obliquely? Maybe. It had all been a long time ago.

She'd been fourteen, Elaine twelve, when their dad had died, very suddenly of a heart attack. In a way that was typical of her memories of him; no great fuss, no great drama, he'd gone to bed one night alive and hadn't been the next day; the first they'd known about it had been their mother's screams, and Anna, not too tightly bolted onto the face of the world in the first place had sailed right off into orbit.

He'd never met Graham, he'd been in the ground seven years when she'd met her future husband, and sometimes – mainly late at night – she'd wonder what they'd have made of each other. She liked to think their quiet natures would have complemented each other, but who knew? Nobody, that's who. And she'd never find out anyway. Sometimes she missed her dad a lot, like on her wedding day, when she'd almost ruined the makeup that Jodie had worked so hard on by bursting into tears at the mirror when it finally, *really* sunk home that Uncle Edward was to walk her down the aisle and not her own dad, he wouldn't see her looking so lovely in her dress, he wouldn't give the speech, telling everyone how proud he was…

It'd been Elaine, not her mum, who knew what was up, who'd run to her, held her and whispered very softly 'He loved you, if he was here he'd burst with joy,' into her ear. It had helped. A little, but sometimes a little was enough.

Hayley sat on the sofa on that Friday night, her sleeping husband across her lap, lost in her memories, while the barely watched TV played on, and she was nostalgically happy, mellow, at peace. Some sad things had happened in her life, but things balanced out. Her dad had died, but she'd met Graham. She'd miscarried, but something good would turn up sooner or later to even that up. Her phone whistled its text alert, and Graham muttered and stretched. Somehow she managed to retrieve it from the sofa's arm without waking him. From Elaine; *fucking bollocks! I'm off to get pissed and maybe pull. Seeya soon.*

Hayley smiled, sent back a smiley face and put the phone down. *If you do pull,* she thought, *be careful. And if you can't be careful, be good.*

On her lap, her husband twitched again.

Ten

He was wandering the corridors of the hospital, looking for his wife, who had been induced, her dead baby taken away and probably burned. Something about that wasn't right, it hadn't happened that way...but he wasn't sure exactly what was wrong with it. It was dark, there were no lights anywhere, and he'd just stepped out for a coffee but when he'd turned back he'd forgotten where her ward was and everyone had gone, not a doctor or nurse or even a visitor in sight, so he was wandering the dark corridors and listening to his footfalls echo and calling for her, calling his beloved's name, but he couldn't even get that right, because although he knew her name was Hayley, he kept calling 'Angie! Angie!'

This hospital was enormous, the size of the world, and the walls were a million feet high, stretching away farther than the eye could see, and the circular holes in the ward doors were too high for him to look in, so all he could do was call that wrong name and hope the right woman would reply. He was anxious, frantic. She'd miss him, she needed him, he needed her, he wouldn't let her down, he never had, he never would, he had to get to her.

He reached a crossroads, four corridors branching off to infinity; dark, shadow-filled mysteries. In front of him, out of the shadows, stepped his sister-in-law Elaine. Her head was canted at ninety degrees to her neck, a bone jutting horribly through the tight skin. 'Have you seen Angie?' he asked.

'Have you tried that way?' Elaine asked, and pointed to her left. He looked, and a child was floating in the air, horizontal, spinning around and around, laughing like an idiot. He turned back, meaning to tell Elaine he couldn't go that way, but she had gone. His dad was there instead.

'Dad, I'm looking for Angie, have you seen her?'

'She's not here son, this is the land of the dead. She'll be round though, if y'd care to wait. Then again, who won't be?'

Before he could ask his dad what he meant by that, another man walked up and put his arm round his dad's shoulders. Graham knew him but had never met him. The man who would have been his father-in-law. 'He's not wrong,' the newcomer said. 'That's why I'm here. Now Jim,' he said, leading his own dad away, 'let me tell you why George Graham was a better manager than Wenger. One, a sound defence...' Then they were gone down the corridor into oblivion.

'Please,' Graham said to no one, 'where is she? *Where's my wife?*'

But no one answered him, so he fell to the floor and cried.

Eleven

Hayley let him sleep till eleven – he looked so peaceful – but by the time she'd watched everything she wanted, she shook him, waited till his eyes focused, then finally said something she'd always wanted to. 'Wake up, hon. It's time to go to bed.'

Chapter Six

One

Graham might get Saturdays off but at Crouch End Hair and Beauty Saturdays were busy, busy, busy – even at the beginning of February. As Hayley rolled up her sleeves and dug in, as she did nails and applied blusher, she realised that she was…well, grateful. Yes, grateful for the return of the routine, of the normality.

She entered the house at just before seven, stuck her head round the living room door and saw Graham jump as Arsenal put a fourth goal past someone she'd never heard of. 'You'll be wanting it tonight then.'

'Babe,' he said, smiling, 'there's not a moment I can see you that I don't want it.' He took her hand, kissed it, then set his eyes back on the screen.

If this is all we ever have, if there are no more children in the future, if it stays like this, I could be very, very happy indeed, Hayley thought, then wandered off, back into the kitchen, picked up one of Graham's Stephen Vaughn paperbacks, turned on the radio and started to read. It wasn't bad. Bit too much swearing, but not bad at all.

At half seven, her mum rang, *all how are you*, and then *yes, but how are you* really, in response to Hayley's 'We're doing fine, mum. We're going to be OK.' From the other room she heard the post-match analysis die down and Graham entered. He opened a cupboard door, took out a bottle of gin and a bottle of whisky, and Hayley repeated her mother's line very clearly for him to hear. 'Dinner, at yours, tomorrow? Um, well...' She looked at Graham. He shrugged and nodded. 'Yes, lovely, thank you. Six? No problem. Yes, love you too. And I'm fine, I promise. Yes. Bye.' She hung up and took the gin he'd poured. 'Thank you,' she said, for more than the drink.

'No probs,' he said, sitting close. 'I mean, she needs to cluck around you, it'll do no harm, it'll save you cooking and am I just the best husband in the world or what?'

'You are, by a country mile. But no, still no schoolgirl outfit.'

He sighed, puffed out his cheeks, and said, 'Thank God for my lively imagination then,' and she punched him on the arm and then kissed him and without warning there were clothes hitting the floor, and this time they didn't take it slow, not at all.

Two

She was brushing her teeth at eleven the next morning when Graham entered the bathroom and wrapped his arms around her waist. 'Dad just rang, he's got some concrete flags he wants shifting.'

She spat Maclean's into the bowl. 'But (a) he didn't tell you that, and (b) he didn't ask for help, right?'

'Two for two. Y'know my dad, wouldn't ask for help if he was trapped under an elephant and an elephant hauler drove past really slowly with the driver hanging out the window saying, *hey, who wants a hand lifting an elephant?*'

This made Hayley giggle harder. Graham wasn't funny often, but when he was it was normally something as surreal as that. And of course, it was Jim to a tee. And like father, like son. *I must ask to see some photos of Jim when he was younger. Did they look alike as well?*

'What *actually* happened was I asked him how he was; he said they're having the drive re-flagged – which wasn't what I asked, but never mind – and the flags were delivered yesterday. I ask where they are, he says stacked by the gate…'

'And you didn't say, "I'll come round to help," 'cause you know he'd have told you not to.'

'Three for three. He doesn't even know I'm coming, or he'd probably drag Mum out to a garden centre to avoid me. I'm planning just to be passing, *thought I'd pop in and, oh while I'm here*...that OK with you?'

She kissed him. She'd never tire of kissing him. 'Of course it is. And thank him for what he said when I came home from...well, the hospital.' She saw Graham frown a little at the word *hospital*. 'It helped. A lot.'

'I will,' he said, but that sprightly mood of his was clouded a little. He kissed her back – but this kiss was a little cold – and went downstairs, she heard the door close after him, and a minute later the car drove off. *It's not a quick fix,* she thought, and went to dress, *that's obvious, just mentioning the hospital brought it back. But we're getting better. That's what we have to hang onto. We're getting better all the time.*

Three

She'd broken his bloody dream, and it disturbed him. When she'd woken him on that Friday night he'd known he'd dreamed *something* – there were vague images and patterns floating around somewhere in his subconscious – but the details had been nicely submerged until she'd said *hospital*.

Bad dream…horrible dream, but just an anxiety nightmare, he told himself, turning towards Shepherd's Bush. *Stuff's still working its way out, and often it's after all the rush and panic and when the world goes back to normal that you relax and it all comes spiralling out, or so I think I read somewhere.*

And there was a lot of stuff to come out, wasn't there? Those awful, heart-wrenching feelings of terror, once in the hospital, once in the house. Couple of disturbing dreams. That strange thing that had happened on the landing, that little girl's voice that he could have sworn had drifted down from the loft. *Yeah, a lot of stuff to work out. It'll be OK though. It'll fade.*

Four

'Something on your mind son?' his dad said, about an hour and a half later, when half the flags had been retrieved from the gatepost and neatly stacked against the wall.

Yes, there was. But what was uppermost in his mind wasn't Hayley or the tricks anxiety was playing on his cognition. Right now, it was his dad, red-faced, breathing hard, and starting to look old. *But he's not old, he's only what? Fifty-three, fifty-four? That's not old these days. I mean, fifty's the new forty, or so it said in one of Hayley's magazines.* No, fifties weren't old, but that Sunday, Jim *looked* old. Crows' feet, more grey, bald patch nicely spreading. In days gone by, he'd have shifted these by himself and hardly broken a sweat. But now those muscles looked flabby, and was that a gut forming over his jeans? A small one, but a gut nonetheless?

When Graham had been a boy, he'd idolised his dad almost to the point of religious awe. Imposing, powerful, even more so for the fact he rarely spoke, and almost never found it necessary to shout. When asked what he wanted to be when he grew up, he always answered immediately, 'My dad.'

But Graham was no longer a boy, he was a man, a man the age his father had once been, and he suddenly felt the speed of time pushing him along. *The speed of time,* yes, that was it, wasn't it? People spoke about the speed of light, or the speed of sound, but the only one that mattered was *the speed of time,* that onrushing wind caused by the flying passage of hours and days and months and years...

'C'mon,' his dad went on, 'you've been in a blue funk since you got here. Is it Hayley? You said she was feeling better, son.'

Son. Very rarely my name, nearly always 'son.'
'No, it's not her. She's getting on.'

'Aye, she's a good lass,' Jim agreed, putting his hands behind his back and straightening his spine (and Graham saw that wince, no matter how cleverly his dad tried to hide it.) 'She's strong. And strong enough to be weak sometimes. There's not much I've got time for in the world today, son – most of it passes an old man like me by – but I am glad that every so often us men are allowed to be weak as well, sometimes. Takes a fair bit of pressure off.'

'You're not old, Dad,' said Graham, but nervously, as if he'd had his thoughts read.

'I am, though. Your granddad wasn't much older than me when he died, and I thought he'd go on forever. Been forty-two years next month since he brought me and your grandma and your uncle Peter down here, when he got that job on the ships. Forty-two years, son, and I remember every mile in that bloody old Morris Minor. Took us the whole day. Set off at six in the morning, got to Rotherhithe ten o'clock at night. Stopped off once in Birmingham, and that was just to use a pub toilet. Forty-two years, and I've never forgotten it. Can't remember who Arsenal played last week, but I remember that all right. Twelve years old, scared and excited, not knowing what it was going to bring, hearing these people talk in their funny voices, I couldn't understand them, they couldn't understand me, a little bit o'bullying at school, nothing I couldn't handle, not if you're from Aberdeen. Lived in London ever since, but y'know? Aberdeen's still home. Don't tell your mother that, though I expect she knows. Sometimes it's the secrets we keep that glue us together. We moved here, to this house – what, '88? '89? - me and her, not long after we were married, and that seems like yesterday too. But it wasn't, it was a whole heap o'years back. You come along soon after, and that's five minutes back in my head, but you're twenty-five now, a husband yourself, and, oh my, the years do pass.'

Graham stared at him, fascinated. This was the longest he'd ever heard his dad speak for, and yes, he was looking older, but for the first time Graham saw his dad not just as a dad, but as a man, a man who'd lived an actual life.

'Seen a lot o'things come and go, and some of the stuff that's come I don't care for, and some of the stuff that's gone I wish were still around, but I'll tell you what I have learned, son - things *are* what they *are*. Y'can shake your fist and swear at them as much as you like, but it'll change nothing. You may as well be that King, sitting on his throne, commanding the tide not to come in.'

Graham smiled, and was suddenly reminded of a game his dad had taken him to years back. He'd have been nine, maybe ten, one of the first Arsenal games since they'd left Highbury, and Fulham had beaten them – Fulham! – one nil. What was worse was that Arsenal had battered them, absolutely trounced them, sixteen shots on goal to Fulham's one, eighty-eight percent possession, but Fulham had scored and Arsenal hadn't, and they'd lost and on the way back home on the Tube, surrounded by people in their red-and-white scarves, Graham had burst into tears. His dad had put an arm around him – something that happened rarely – and said, 'Crying won't change it, son. Go ahead, if you must, but it'll still be the same tomorrow. Think about all those times we've come away the winners, think o'those other poor sods we've known, crying all the way back to Newcastle or Liverpool. Cry if you like, but remember that you'll be laughing soon, probably on Wednesday when we beat Inter.'

Had they won that European game? Maybe, he couldn't remember it, though he could look it up when he got home if he wanted. He'd even forgotten the conversation until just now. But yeah, it was a good attitude to have. If you could remember to stick to it.

'You and Hayley,' Jim went on, 'you'll do OK. I like her, have done since I met her. I know it was a bad do, what happened, but…'

'But if you're crying on Saturday you might be smiling on Wednesday,' Graham said, smiling, and watched as Jim's face wrinkled, puzzled. *It's OK that you've forgotten, I'll remember for both of us.*

'But there is something on your mind, son. I can tell. Y've no need to share it if you don't want to – or if it's not right – but I'll listen if and when you do.'

Graham hesitated, opened his mouth, then said, 'Nothing important, Dad, I promise. Just stuff to be worked through. But we'll get there.'

At that moment, the front door opened and his mum stood there, arms folded, that look of half-exasperation, half love that only women can manage on her face. 'Will you two get inside? It's freezing out here. Kettle's on.'

She turned, went in, and father and son smiled at each other and followed her.

Five

Flumph.

Hayley stopped reading, looked up at the ceiling and that cold blanket of fear dropped over her again, the one she'd felt when she'd heard the crying, the crying from upstairs, from the room that would have been the nursery, the room where she now heard...

Flumph.

Something soft hitting the carpet, again and again.

Bright February afternoon light shone through the kitchen window, it was a Sunday afternoon in 2015, in a mid-terraced Crouch End home. It wasn't midnight in Dracula's castle, it was somewhere ordinary, somewhere normal, a place with a washing machine and a kettle and a sink and an electric cooker and a fridge. It was the world of the mundane, of Sunday afternoon football and Pot Noodles in the cupboard, a world where you could have crunchy peanut butter sandwiches for lunch if you wanted, but Hayley was terrified.

Flumph.

That wasn't normal, and it was happening, just like...the crying...

But that was next door, or my imagination, or a cat on heat, so shut up and...

Flumph. Flumph-flumph. Flumph.

Could it be a leak? Hayley's mind seized on that thought like a dog with a rag. OK, bit of a pisser, getting a plumber out on a Sunday and all that, but better than...well...

Flumph. Flumph-flumph-flumph. Flumph.

She could just sit there, ignore it, pretend it wasn't happening, wait until Graham got back, until he said, 'What's that noise,' and she could pretend she hadn't heard it, and Graham could go upstairs and find the leak, after all she was reading this book and enjoying it, thank you very much, so why *shouldn't* she just ignore it, why shouldn't she just read her book, well *Graham's* book, why shouldn't she, what was it to anyone, I mean, who wanted to climb those stairs again like she had the other night, scared, footstep after fearful footstep?

Flumph. FLUMPH-flumph. Flumph-FLUMPH.

But if it was a leak, it sounded like it was getting heavier, and the tank was up there, in the loft, and what if the whole thing just came crashing down? What would she say then? *Oh sorry, didn't hear it, I was reading – good book though, yeah?*

No...she had to see. Then turn the water off at the stopcock, find a plumber...

She was in the hall and mounting the first stair when she thought, *the stopcock's in the kitchen. Where you just were. So...if you think it's a leak, why didn't you just turn it to OFF and sit tight? Is it because if you'd done that and the noise had continued, you'd have to face...*

'I have to face nothing,' she said aloud, and climbed the stairs, her right hand gripping the banister knuckle-whiteningly hard, and oh God, the stairs...how many were there? They seemed to be going on and on forever and she was nowhere near the landing...

FLUMPH-flumphflumph-Flumph, FLUMPH.

She could see no sign of water dripping from the ceiling. In fact, that noise was coming from her left. From ahead of her, to her left. From the spare room.

The door of which was open.

Through which she could see, clearer and clearer with every passing step, every step that brought her inexorably but with agonising slowness closer to that doorway, a shadow. A shadow bouncing up and down. And every time it came down it was making a *flumph* noise.

It seemed as if Hayley stopped moving and the spare room advanced towards her, such was the swooning sense of horror that clamped down upon her. A shadow, a definite thing in a room where no thing should be, bouncing up and down, like Tigger, Tigger who had so delighted her as a girl.

As she reached the top step and somehow found the strength to put her right foot on the landing, the shadow stopped. So did Hayley, hardly breathing, frozen, utterly perplexed. For a minute she stood there, silent, breathing shallowly through her mouth…then she made herself take a step forward. Then another. And a third. There she stood, before the open doorway. She looked inside.

That stuffed dog was back, in the middle of the room (*you want a doggy*, she found herself thinking) looking at her with its stupidly happy eyes and lolling felt tongue. If you picked that up and bounced it off the floor, on that thick carpet, it would probably make a *flumph* noise. If you were pretending it was running about, like a naughty, silly doggy, it would make a *flumph-flumphFLUMPH* noise.

Trouble was, there was no one to do that. No one at all.

Hayley Davis had no idea what to do next.

Chapter Seven

One

Graham declined his mother's offer of food - after all Anna was bound to cook up a meal for the five thousand that night, she always did. Instead, he hugged her, shook his dad's hand, and drove home, thinking. *Cry on Saturday, laugh on Wednesday. Not a bad philosophy, or motto, to live by. You could do worse.*

He opened his front door and was nearly knocked off his feet as his wife ran to him, held him - no, clung to him - babbling almost incoherently. Something about the spare room, something about a dog...

Want to play with doggy, Daddy?

'Easy babe, come on, take a deep breath,' he crooned, easing her into the hallway and closing the door behind them. No easy task, as Hayley just didn't want to let him go. She was a barnacle. A hysterical barnacle. He managed to disentangle her and hold her at arm's length, looking deep into her eyes, trying to hold them with his own, trying to stop her from glancing constantly up the stairs. 'C'mon babe, please, look at me, that's it, look at me, now breathe. Breathe in with me, yeah? Deep, in through the nose,' *thank God for that first aid course work made me take,* 'and out through the mouth. Together, yeah? You and me?'

He breathed in deeply, saw that she managed to do the same, then exhaled while she copied. *OK, so far so good. But what was this? What had happened?* He'd been gone less than four hours. *Four hours is long enough for everything to turn to shit, Gray old son. You know that now. Four hours is* more *than enough time.* 'From the start, babe. Just tell me, do you need an ambulance? Do you need…?'

'Nuh-no,' she stuttered, hitching, but trying to control herself. 'It, it's not me, it's…' she looked away from him, looked above him, then came back. 'In there,' she said.

'From the start, babe. From the start. Look at me,' he added urgently as she looked as if she was going to lose control again. 'From the start.'

Haltingly, stutteringly, she managed to tell him everything. He listened and grew cold but at no point did he think she was lying. Not her. Not Hayley. 'OK,' he said, and then for the want of anything else to say, 'OK,' again. He took a step to the stairs.

'Where are you going?' she almost shrieked, grabbing at him.

'I have to see,' he said.

'I've *told* you what's there, I've *told* you, what do you have to *see* for?'

Why indeed? He shrugged and almost laughed – a scared laugh, nervous and high pitched. 'I have to,' he said, and started up.

Two

It won't be there, Hayley thought as she climbed after him, close. *It's* never *there. In all those horror films you see, it's always gone when the girl takes the man to look. It's like a law.*

Graham crested the stairs, walked the landing, put his head into the spare room and she heard him say, in a tiny, trembling voice, 'Oh. Fucking hell.'

Staying on the landing, she looked past his elbow, and it wasn't gone at all, there it was, a silly stuffed doggy with a lolling red felt tongue, square in the middle of the carpet, ready for a play. There was silence for a second, and she saw Graham tremble slightly. 'Is that the one,' he said eventually, 'the same dog you saw in here the other day?'

'Yes.' It was as much as she could say.

He turned his back to the room and looked her full in the face. 'When I came to put it away, the room was empty. No dog, no nothing. I thought…I'm sorry, I thought you were upset, confused. But…'

Hayley stared at him, and for a split second was angry, very angry. *How could he think that? Hadn't she told him? What, did he think she was going round the bend? Did he?*

Hey, don't, rein it in, it's Gray. 'But?'

He looked as if he was going to tell her something, then said, 'Downstairs, in the kitchen. I need a drink.'

Three

His mistake, as he was to discover later, was in not telling her everything there and then. Instead, like a lot of people would have done, he took a look at his wife's face, saw what he thought she could cope with, and held stuff back. *It's still the truth*, he told himself. *Just not all of it.* He meant well, but as his mother could have told him, Hell was full of souls who meant well.

He told her about finding the trap open to the loft, how he'd nearly hit his head on it, but not about the little girl's voice asking if he wanted to play, telling him she'd see him soon, about her calling him 'Daddy.' He told her that twice, once in the hospital and once in the spare room, he'd felt suddenly terrified, scared beyond belief, but he didn't mention the doll, the one he'd held that second time and the one he'd dreamed of; the dreams, in total, he kept to himself. *Hey, they're just dreams. Where do you stop when you head down that road?* '*Oh, and there was another with Amy Childs sucking me off?*

So he kept some things dark and told himself it was for the best. After all, what had his dad said earlier? *Sometimes the secrets we keep are the glue that holds us together.* Maybe that was the second fine bit of philosophy he'd received from his father.

Four

Hayley, on the other hand, told him everything – which in her case only amounted to the crying she'd heard on Friday night. She was surprised, and a little disappointed he'd held stuff from her, but not shocked; after all, *he* was only hearing about the crying now, wasn't he, forty-eight hours after the event? And all this...well, wasn't it too *unbelievable* to be told? I mean, what were you supposed to do when faced with stuff like this?

Trust one another, she found herself thinking. It was odd, a little sour thought in a head that didn't support such thoughts easily, but she chewed it around for a while and decided that, yes, on some level that was right. Weren't marriages built on trust? Wasn't love built on trust?

Yes, but, she argued back, *we're talking late night Horror Channel double bills here. Yeah, there* are *ghosts, thousands of people see them every day, but there are thousands of people who see llamas every day and you don't expect one in your spare room, do you?*

No, but if you did come home to find a llama in there, what would you do? Ignore it, hope it would go away? Or call someone? Get on the phone to Animal Rescue or the RSPCA or the nearest farm and say, 'Sorry to bother you, but it appears we've a llama here. Is it one of yours? If not, what do we feed it? I've some pizza in the fridge.'

Incredibly, she laughed. Graham stared at her, then joined in. 'What's so funny?'

'Llamas,' she said, then laughed again.

'Of course,' he answered. 'That makes sense.' He reached across the kitchen table and took her hand, squeezed it. She squeezed back, smiled, because she did love him, but...

He should have trusted me, should have told me the truth from the start. 'What do we do?' she asked, trying to shut that nagging voice up.

'Babe,' he said, 'I don't have a fucking clue. All I know is, we're supposed to be at your mum's for tea in an hour.'

For a terrible second, she was so angry she could have launched herself across the table and clawed his eyes out. 'I know that,' she said, removing her hand, digging her nails into her palm to distract herself. 'I can tell the time, Gray. I want to know what we're going to do about what's going *on* here!'

Graham flinched and a part of her was sorry immediately, wanted to take it back – after all this time they'd maybe only rowed half a dozen times, and then about stupid things. Even those rows hadn't lasted the night, those had been the product of tiredness mainly; but here, in their kitchen, she could feel a real row brewing, a proper one, a screaming match, and most of her was scared of it, because once something was said it could never be taken back...but a black, cold part of her – a part of her she hadn't been really aware of until that afternoon – wanted it. Wanted it badly.

'Babe,' he said, and he seemed nervous, as if finding his way in a dark room, carefully taking it from word to word, 'I don't know what's going on here, let alone what we do about it. I don't...I mean,' he went on, never taking his eyes off her, keeping his voice calm, 'yeah, something weird's happening, I got you. But...hey, if you want me to calculate the stresses on a bridge and how much concrete you'd need for it, I'm your man. I can even design you a really nice one. But I'm out of my depth with this. Sorry.'

Hayley took a deep breath, reached out to him, took his hands again. 'Yes, of course. So am I.' Who wouldn't be? But it made sense. Had she *really* expected him to say, *'It's not a problem, I'm a ghost expert, I forgot to tell you, I'll nick upstairs and sort it out, maybe unstick that awkward drawer in the dressing table while I'm at it.'* Which left them...where, exactly? Well, just where they had been half an hour ago. But, if nothing else, the problem was in the open now, it was acknowledged, they were being honest with each other, and that was enough.

In the meantime, in the real world, her mum would be expecting them, and what was she to do about that? Ignore the whole thing, stay here, in this place where...well, stuff sometimes happened...or get out, do real things, even if such real things involved a meal with her self-pitying mother? *If I decide we're going nowhere, that we're staying in tonight, just on the off-chance that something happens...and say it doesn't...then what about tomorrow? Do I stay home from work, make Graham do the same? Do we never leave the place again, become prisoners, just in case there's a noise we can't explain, just because there's a toy that sometimes turns up where it shouldn't? We stay here, waiting, lose our jobs, lose the house, lose each other...do we stop existing, or do we carry on?*

'Tea,' she said, 'Mum's. In an hour. Yeah, that's what we'll do. I'll go up, get washed and changed.' She leaned over to him, sniffed, then said, 'and you'd better shower, you smelly bastard.' They laughed together again, and that was good. Then she stopped and said something she'd not said since she was five years old. 'But I need you to stay in the bathroom with me. I can't be alone up there.'

'That, my love, will be no problem.'

Five

'I'm getting the word...*sprouts*,' said Elaine an hour and a half later, her hands to her temples, brow furrowed in concentration, and Hayley put both hands across her mouth to stop from laughing.

They were sitting in her mum's dining room in Seven Sisters, just the three of them while Anna was busy in the kitchen, and yes, there was that familiar odour wafting through the house. Elaine was taking them through Friday night's adventure, and by God was Hayley glad she'd come out. She needed this. She needed her kid sister on a roll like this.

'Sprouts,' she said again, questioningly, then more firmly, 'sprouts! Who here knows someone who's eaten sprouts? Might have liked them, might not have, oooh the spirits are very strong tonight!'

'Oh come on,' said Hayley, and sat here, in that place, the smell of food around and good electric lighting around the place, her waterproof mascara about to be seriously tested if Elaine kept this up, 'it can't have been all like that.'

'And worse,' her sister said. 'I saw it on Derren Brown; she just stood there, yeah? Talked bollocks like that...'

'Elaine,' admonished Anna from the kitchen.

'Talked *rubbish* like that,' Elaine corrected herself, blushing a little, 'making the most appalling generalisations and these poor, stupid basta...people kept going for it. And she was so fuh...really *smug,* that's what hacked me off the most. "Did you know someone who died?" Look, most of them were in their sixties, of bloody *course* they did!'

'Elaine,' from the kitchen again.

'Bloody's not swearing, mum,' Elaine called over her shoulder. Then, under her breath. 'Cunt, cocksucker and twat are swearing,' and that set Hayley off again. 'Jesus said bloody all the time,' Elaine called back.

'He did not,' said Anna over the rattle of pots and pans.

'He bloody did,' said Elaine, but quietly. To Hayley and Graham, 'Anyway, she asks if they knew anyone who died, everyone sticks their hands up. "It's a man." Half the hands go down. "With brown hair and brown eyes." She's down to two thirds. "Initials J or G or something like that." Now the herd's really thinning, so she's scanning around, looking for the eye movements and little twitches that give the really gullible away. "J? Joseph? No...not Joseph? James, yes you love, you knew a James who died, didn't you?" And then it's all "Don't you worry, he's got a penthouse flat and a yacht and when you get up there and join him he's going to fudge your brains out."'

'I am *sick* of telling you,' said the kitchen voice.

'No one swore, mum,' Elaine called back. 'Fudge is a sweet.'

'Although,' said Hayley, again keeping her voice low, 'a finger of Fudge is just enough.'

'Ain't no man fingering *my* Fudge,' Elaine whispered, 'though what you two get up two in the privacy of your own bedroom is your own business.'

They were off again, hands over mouths, trying to keep their laughter down, and Hayley thought, *I am so glad we did this. God, did we need this.* She sneaked a look over at Graham, who was also laughing, if a little less enthusiastically than them. *Well, I suppose that's how it is. Families and that, always closer than outsiders.*

But wasn't Graham part of her family now? In fact, wasn't he her *new* family? That was a very strange thought, so she ignored it, brushed it aside, and concentrated instead on sitting at that table, the familiar smells of overcooked food wafting from the kitchen, and laughing at her sister, her funny little sister.

'It was horrible,' Elaine went on after that giggling fit had calmed down. 'I was really, really angry at her, yeah? Fudging *ghoul*.'

'Elaine,' said Anna, bringing a gravy boat and a bowl of evil looking Brussels sprouts to the table. 'I know the word you're pretending to say. Honestly, it's like you're six years old.'

'Do you need any help, Mrs Buchanan?' Graham asked, half rising. Even after all this time, Mrs Buchanan, not Anna. Never Anna, never an invitation to call her by her first name. *What does that mean?* wondered Hayley, not for the first time. But for the first time, she wondered, *does she think he's not permanent?*

'Bless you dear, but you stay sat there. I never allowed their dear old dad into the kitchen except to wash up, and I'll certainly not allow my son-in-law. You stay there and try and keep these two in line.' She squeezed his shoulder and made her way back.

'Creep,' said Elaine, and flicked the Vs at him.

Graham shrugged, 'Just trying to earn some Brownie points.'

'Was it *all* cobblers?' Hayley asked, trying to distract herself, to put these awkward thoughts away, to get back to how it was.

'Well, law of averages means she must have got a hit or two. If you throw enough sh...mud at a wall, some'll stick eventually. She did one clever thing, I'll give her this. She picked me out as outright hostile – not hard, considering how I was scowling at her, made me stand up and gave a load of stuff out to me, and every time I nodded, she'd turn to the audience with a *see, I've convinced the sceptic, aren't I great, throw me a bone.*'

Anna marched in from the kitchen with a bowl of roast potatoes in one hand and a bowl of mashed in the other. 'Can we change the subject, please? I want no more about these things in my house. And Elaine,' she went on, almost slamming them on the table, 'I haven't told you yet how angry I am at you for going. You know you shouldn't be meddling in such things.'

'Mum, I'm not meddling in anything,' said Elaine, and Hayley could hear it all again, every snapped remark, every icy response. *For ever and ever, amen.* 'It was just a very silly woman putting on a bad act that sad people fall for.'

'It's *meddling*,' Anna said, mouth in a thin line, eyebrows drawn together. It was the voice of *come in now*, the face of *don't sit there, you don't know who's sat there before you or what they've got*. It was the face of *no argument*. 'You know what the Bible says about such people. Or would, if you went to Church more often. Or at all.'

Elaine opened her mouth, and Hayley could see a full broadside response about to pour out, but then she closed it again, smiled over-sweetly, and said, 'I know mum, you're right, I'm very sorry.'

Anna, who knew many things but was ignorant of when she was being mocked, smiled back at her, then turned to Graham. 'Leg or breast?'

Graham, managing to ignore Elaine who coughed into her palm, asked for a leg.

'Go on,' whispered Hayley, after Anna had gone back to the kitchen, 'what did she say to make you give her credibility?'

'Some really good guesswork,' whispered Elaine in reply. 'She even got your name right. Said I had a sister Hayley who worked as a beautician, said I'd been there that day and you'd done my nails.'

Hayley sat back in her chair and frowned. That was *way* too good to be guesswork. She looked over to Graham, who dismissed it with an eyebrow raise and a shrug. 'C'mon,' she said. 'Admit it, that's spooky.'

'It's clever, that's as far as I'm going. Look, most people make themselves look pretty when they're going out, yeah? It's a fair assumption I'd had something done, and all she had to do was look at my nails. I mean, she got me standing up, easy peasy lemon-squeezy. OK, I've no explanation for how she knew your name, but I also have no explanation for how that guy walked through the Great Wall of China that time. All I know is, it was a trick. A clever trick, but a trick.'

'Yes, but...'

'But nothing Hayles, a trick, and one she has to spoil by going too far.'

'Oh?'

'Yeah, starts going on about how you two are experiencing – oh, how did she put it? "Something to do with the other side," something like that anyway, about how you've not told each other. Y'know, real Hammer House of Horror bol...cobblers.'

'Are we *still* talking about this,' said Anna, bringing two plates brimmed with hacked about chicken to the table, 'I thought I'd made myself quite clear. There you are dears,' she went on, placing the food before Graham and Hayley, 'tuck in, enjoy. And you, young lady,' to Elaine, 'not *one more word* about it, understood?'

Elaine nodded, then made a zipped shut motion across her mouth, and for once she was true to her word, the rest of the night passed without another mention of Lillian Manning, it passed with Anna telling them how lonely she was, about how few friends she had, and Hayley tried to nod and look sympathetic, but all she could think was…experiencing something to do with "the other side"…a sister called Hayley who's a beautician…they'd not told each other…

How did she know? How did she know? How did she know?

Six

Elaine spent the rest of the meal thinking, *why did I keep stuff back? Why didn't I tell them everything? Why didn't I mention the fact she knew about the miscarriage? The Scots relative? Dad's heart attack? Why?*

Because I saw Hayley's face, that's why, she realised as the last of the coffee – no booze at her mother's table, not even Lambrini – had been drunk and coats were being struggled into and kisses and hugs exchanged at the door. *I saw how she looked, the widening of the eyes, the biting of the bottom lip. Part of her believes that crap. Part of her has* always *believed that crap. And I will not feed that. I love my sister, so I will not feed that. Sometimes, loving someone means doing what's best for them, even if they don't like it.*

In that respect, if in no other, Elaine was very much her mother's daughter.

Seven

Hayley kept her counsel until after lights out, when she was huddled to her man (and yes, she'd tensed as they'd arrived back, she was frightened at what they might find, but the house had been quiet, the spare room empty, everything normal, and after an hour or so she'd relaxed) but still…

'OK hon, how do *you* think she knew?'

She heard Graham sigh, an *I was expecting this kind've noise*, and once more she was irritated at him. She hated this, but couldn't stop it. 'I don't know. But Elaine's right, some kind of trick.'

'A trick? You think?' She wanted to roll away from him, he was being so stupid, but she made herself remain where she was.

'What else could it be?'

She kept silent for a second, debated whether to keep silent for all time, then thought, *no I will have my say here.* 'Gray, something's going on. We know that now, we've talked it through. I don't know what, neither do you, but we know *something's* not right here. You going to agree with me on this?'

'Well, yeah but…'

'No. No *buts*. We've both seen and heard stuff that we shouldn't have. And it's been since…the miscarriage, and it's all in that room, the nursery that would have been. Right?'

Graham rolled away from her, propped himself on an elbow, looked at her, and by the streetlight she could see the disbelief in his eyes. 'You're saying…what?'

'I'm stating facts,' she said. 'Mad facts, maybe, but facts. You want me to go over them again?' He thought, then shook his head. 'Right, stuff's going on and it's all around that room, and it's all since I lost the baby. Then Elaine goes to this woman and she knows something, she says what she says…'

'If Elaine remembered it right. I mean, it was a couple of days ago, and she'll have had a drink or two since then, and maybe before she went in. You know your sister. That's what people like this so-called medium depend on. I saw a programme about this stuff...'

Don't shout, don't scream, no matter how much you want to. 'OK, granted. But it's still enough for Elaine to remember it, to bring it up tonight, you'll give me *that* much, won't you?'

'Well...yeah.' A brief silence, then, 'but so what?'

'So we call her, this woman, we get her round here and she tells us what's going on.'

She saw her husband almost recoil at this idea, and realised that no matter how hard she'd tried, a row was on its way. He'd slammed the shutters down. 'Babe, that's...' He managed to choke the end of the sentence off, but she finished it for him.

'What, *stupid?*' She sat up, pulled her knees to her chin. 'Is it *stupid* to want to know what's going on here? Because *something* is, isn't it?' He said nothing, seemed to be searching for words. She kept on, and her voice was rising. 'Or do you want to ignore it, hope it'll go away? Or just pack up and move? Yeah, 'cause we can afford that, can't we? Or do you want to live with your mum and dad? Or with my mum? Elaine's got a spare room, she could put us up.'

'Babe,' he tried to say, but it was too late. She was too tired, too stressed, too much had happened, and she was venting now, she *had* to vent.

'No, no *babe*, no *nothing*. I don't *care* what you think, not on this. *I don't want weird shit going on in my home*, you understand that? When the boiler breaks, you get a plumber, when stuff like this happens, you get...'

'Stuff like what?' he interrupted, and oh yes, he was angry too, here it came, here it is, arriving at Platform 9, the 22:45 Argument, calling all stations to Screaming. 'What exactly do you think's going on here?'

'WE'VE GOT A FUCKING GHOST,' she bellowed, not caring who heard, and once the sentence was out it could never go back.

The one thing she didn't want him to do was laugh in her face, that was the one unforgivable act. So of course, he laughed in her face, a half-angry, half-dismissive laugh. 'Oh, you don't...'

'It's a fucking *ghost,* you arsehole,' and she was up, out of bed. She had to. Had she been closer, she would have hit him. 'How *else* do you explain what's going on?'

'I don't,' he said, and she saw him clench his fists, tightening himself up, trying to keep control. *Oh God,* part of her moaned, *how did we get to* this? 'I can't, not yet, I don't know enough,' she started to talk, but he raised his voice and overrode her. 'But there *aren't* any ghosts, Hayley. They're up there with Hobbits and Unicorns, just made up stuff, things for gullible people to believe in…'

She could interrupt too. Oh, what a lovely night. 'Like *me,* you mean? Like stupid *me?*'

'That's not what I'm saying. Listen to me, please!'

'I will when you say something worth listening to!'

'When it's what you want to hear, you mean?'

'Yes!' And that was it, wasn't it? That was at the bottom of this awful scene, this terrible shouting match. She just wanted him to say *yes, dear* and go along with what she wanted, and what, just once, was wrong with that?

He took a breath, held it, and let it out slowly, shudderingly, and appeared to understand. He climbed out of bed, slowly, and moved to her, put his arms to her. 'OK then,' he said. 'OK, if that's what you want, we'll get this woman down. I'm sorry, I love you, and if that's what it takes, that's fine, we'll do what you want.'

I want you to say you believe me; I want you to say I'm right and you're wrong. But she was suddenly very tired, almost sick, and she hated rowing, she wanted to be held, she wanted her husband. 'Thank you,' she said, and allowed herself to be led back under the duvet. He held her, stroked her hair, kissed her forehead, and after a while she fell asleep.

Eight

Graham lay awake until sometime after two. It wasn't the argument so much that kept him awake, it was a terrible, disturbing thought that had occurred to him just before he'd conceded.

She may be having a breakdown.

It was in the set of her back, the stare in her eyes, the way her fingers splayed out, her insistence that they had…*I mean, can anyone believe this…a ghost? OK, yes, some funny stuff had been going on, but come on now, a ghost, that's…*

What, exactly, has been going on?

That was an interesting thought, so Graham pondered it. *Well, there's the stuff, you know, the dog in the room, the noises, and what you heard on the landing, the dreams…*

But who cares about dreams? Dreams don't count. And what actually *happened on the landing that night?*

Well, the hatch to the loft was open, and I heard a voice, a little girl...

Come now, did you? I think you were half asleep weren't you? Maybe dreaming a little, and I think we've already decided dreams can be discounted from all this. So...what? The loft hatch came open? Well, you didn't shut it properly, did you? Hardly supernatural, is it?

Those times I felt...in the hospital, and holding that doll...

Understandable reactions to stress, I thought you'd sorted that one out. Right, what's next?

Well, the things Hayley's seen and heard. The crying, the toy dog...

Says *she's seen and heard, get your facts right.*

Graham twitched violently, and Hayley mumbled in her sleep, turned over and settled back. *Yes...says she's seen and heard, that's right, isn't it?*

Sure is.

I saw the stuffed dog in the room though...I saw how scared she was...

Yes, there was a toy dog in the room. This time. And the time before? Nothing. And what did you actually see, *Graham old son? A toy dog on the carpet. Oooh, scary toy dog. What might you have missed? What might have happened while you were out?*

I don't know...I don't get what you're trying to say...

Oh come on, it's obvious! OK, dog in room when you get back. Dog not in room when you leave. Now, how do inanimate objects get from place to place? Do they walk, hop, skip or jump? No. They can't *can they? So they're...*

He kept himself from twitching this time, but he was cold all over. *No.*

Oh, how else could it have happened? I'm not saying she did it deliberately, *I'm not saying she knew what she was doing, but get with it, Graham. Get with her lineage, look at her mother, it's in the genes, grief is an addiction, attention is an addiction...*

She's doing this for attention? No, that's mad!

Madder than the idea of a ghost? She's been through a lot, been through a bad do, bound to affect her one way or the other, wouldn't blame her for being a bit mad, she needs a rest, time away, a beach somewhere, oops, sorry you tried that, she didn't want to know, and isn't that suspicious in itself, Gray? Here's what we do, we go along with Mrs McGillicudy or whatever this madwoman's name is, we let Hayley have that, then you say 'Hey, you had yours, here's my turn, we need to get away, oh and maybe you should see a doctor when you get back?

All of that made sense, but still...*I'm not sure, you know. Not sure I was sort-of dreaming when I heard that girl talk to me.*

Of course you were, you had to be, because there are no such things as ghosts. Algebra, the equations now balance. Now off to sleep with you.

Troubled, Graham slept.

Chapter Eight

One

Hayley was sitting on the bus, phone in hand, text written when she thought, *no, I've a better idea.*

The text read *Hey Elaine, what did you say that psychic's name was?* and her thumb was actually on the SEND button when she stopped, wondering what her sister would make of her. What she would say. Elaine's opinion of that woman was quite clear, what would her opinion of Hayley be when she read that message? *Oh, c'mon, you don't* believe *that bullshit, do you?*

Did it matter? Yes, obviously it did, otherwise SEND would have been pressed without a second thought. But second thought there was, so she deleted it, closed the phone, and sat back. Then she had a better idea, one that would involve less ridicule.

Two

'Elaine had a great time on Friday,' said Hayley as she entered the salon, took her coat off and pulled the pinafore over her head.

'Oh,' said Jodie, slightly blank. 'That's nice for her.'

'She went to see that psychic, remember,' Hayley went on, turning away, fanning out the bottles of product on the nail table, hoping Jodie wouldn't notice the flush on her cheeks. Lying wasn't something that came naturally to her. 'The one you said was good.'

'Oh God, right, yeah sorry. She enjoyed it, yeah?'

'Yeah, said she was spot on.' Fiddling with more stuff, keeping her head down. 'Um, what was her name again? You said you'd been to her.'

'Um...hang on, Manning, that's it. Lillian Manning.'

Yeah, that's it. Lillian Manning. She'll have a website, a CONTACT ME button. Bound to have.

Hayley changed the subject to the weekend's TV, the weather, parents eh? and Jodie joined in, and at five past nine the first customer arrived and the day started, but there was a terrible excitement in her heart, a sense of danger, a feeling that things were about to be made clear and sorted out.

Three

She went to Garfunkel's for lunch, and over a BLT and cappuccino scrolled along her Samsung. *Thank God for smartphones, smartphones are the greatest invention since heated rollers.* Google gave her LILLIAN MANNING, PSYCHIC EXTRAORDINAIRE, and a link to her site. That gave up promises of TAROT, PALM & DISTANCE READINGS. Apparently she could tell you things just by looking at a jpeg photo. There was a list of personal appearances, and there, near the bottom, was what she was looking for. CONTACT ME.

Without a second's hesitation, Hayley opened the tab and typed in a message. At the bottom she included her phone number. Once it was sent, she ate her sandwich ravenously. She felt as if she'd taken the first step, and the first step was always the hardest.

Four

Lillian Manning hadn't asked to be psychic, any more than she'd asked to be left handed or for hazel eyes. It just happened, and after a while she'd learned to be grateful. After learning to be grateful, she'd learned to make money out of it.

When she'd been six years old, lying in her old bedroom in her parents' house in Muswell Hill, the door had opened and an old woman had walked in. She was wearing a headscarf and a heavy woollen coat – which was odd, as August 1976 had been a scorcher.

She hadn't been scared, she remembered that. A little puzzled, but at the age of six most kids live in a world of wonder with every day a bizarre passage of astounding sights and sounds. What, after all, was one more?

'Hello,' Lillian had said.

'Oh, hello dear,' the old woman had said, looking about her. She appeared as confused as Lillian herself. 'Do you know where I am, I seem a little lost.'

She's like Mr Wood from down the road, Lillian thought. Mr Wood was 'a little bit soft,' according to Lillian's mother. Mr Wood sometimes stood on the pavement and stared around him as if he could see things other people couldn't. She'd once been in the shop buying her *Look-In* when Mr Wood had entered and asked the shopkeeper what time the next bus to town was. The shopkeeper had told him, as far as he knew, and Mr Wood sat on the floor. When the shopkeeper asked him what he was doing, Mr Wood had said he was sitting at the stop, waiting for the bus.

Some people were mean to Mr Wood, and some of the kids she was at school with knocked on his door and ran away or threw stones at his window. Michael Murphy had spat at Mr Wood in the street and called him a spaz. All of this made Lillian sad. Mr Wood wasn't nasty or cruel, he just seemed, in her mother's words, 'a bit soft.' But there was no meanness in him, he just seemed a bit...lost.

Like this lady, she'd thought. A bit lost, in the wrong house. 'You're in my bedroom,' said Lillian, and when that didn't seem to get through, she repeated her address, just as she'd been taught. 'Number 6, Carswell Street, Muswell Hill, London.'

'Oh dear,' said the old lady, 'I don't think that's right,' and promptly vanished.

At this, Lillian screamed. No matter how nice the old lady had seemed, how harmless, just vanishing like that was scary. She heard footsteps pounding up the stairs and her father ran in, asking her what was up, and she told him, through her distress, and he told her to hush now, it was just a dream, just a dream, hush now.

But it hadn't been just a dream. Even at the age of six she'd known that. It just took her a while to find out exactly what it *had* been.

Five

From that point on, she could see people who weren't there. Not always, not even all that often, but it happened. But it wasn't until she was ten that she really began to understand what was going on. She'd been at school, it was playtime, and she'd been playing netball with the other girls (she was tall for her age, and a fairly proficient Goal Attack) when she'd heard her father call from through the wire fence.

She ran from the game, ignoring the cries from her team mates, and went to see her dad, whom she adored. He was standing there, very smart in the suit he wore to THE OFFICE (Lillian had no idea what he did there, just that he dressed up and looked all posh and all sorts of things happened at THE OFFICE that she didn't really understand) but today he had a sad face on. 'Hi Dad, what you doing here?'

He looked at the floor, then back at her and said, 'I have to go away for a while. I'm sorry. It wasn't my idea.'

'On biz-ness?' Lillian knew that sometimes THE OFFICE sent Dad away on biz-ness. Her mum joked about it, but sometimes the jokes were like Michael Murphy's, hard and sharp. There was edge when mum asked if Mrs Dury would be going along as well.

'No my love,' he said. 'Just away. I won't see you for a while.'

This dismayed her, for sometimes Lillian's mum would drink white lemonade that smelled like aniseed when her dad was away and her voice would go all funny and she would sleep a lot. 'What will you bring me back?'

'What would you like?'

'A Cabbage Patch Doll!' She really wanted one of these. Emma Costello had received one for Christmas and Lillian loved it.

'OK,' her dad said, smiling, but it seemed a tired smile, a bit sad. 'That I can do.'

'Lillian,' she heard from behind her. She turned, and there was Mrs Hunter, one of her teachers, walking towards her. Mrs Hunter had a funny expression on her face, like she'd been sucking a lemon. She turned back to her dad, to tell him that, but her dad had gone. *He didn't kiss me goodbye*, she thought. *He always kisses me goodbye.*

Mrs Hunter had asked Lillian to go with her, and had taken her to the office and Mr Simmington the Headmaster was there and he told Lillian he was going to take her home. When Lillian asked why, he looked at Mrs Hunter and just said, 'Your mum will tell you. Hurry now, and get your things.'

Her mum had told her when she'd been deposited at home. Her dad was dead. He'd had a heart attack on his way to work, and they all had to be very brave. Lillian burst into tears, and so did her mum, but as she cried she'd thought *but he promised to bring me something.*

She slept with her mum that night, her mum having drank quite a bit of the aniseed lemonade, but woke up early, wanting a wee. As she passed her room on the way to the toilet, she saw something through the open door, propped on her bed. She stepped in.

It was a Cabbage Patch Doll in its box.

That's when she knew. She could talk to the dead. And sometimes, get a present off them.

Six

Lillian was in some ways mature beyond her years, so she told no one about what she could do, or about how sometimes out of nowhere a spirit would contact her, mostly just to pass the time. At times, it could be highly embarrassing, such as the time a young boy materialised in front of her while she was masturbating. That put her right off her stroke, and no mistake. Mostly though it was just something she became accustomed to, the way her friend Mary could roll her tongue.

When she was twenty and working as a Receptionist in a hotel in Pentonville, Lillian saw a programme about mediums on TV. There was a big woman with bouffant hair on it and film of her in a big theatre giving her 'readings', but the man who was hosting the programme was calling the woman a liar. Not outright, just hinting at it. And then he said she could make a thousand pounds a night doing one of these 'gigs,' as he called it.

A thousand pounds. A night.

From that point on, she knew exactly what to do with this strange gift of hers. After all, actors were paid, writers were paid, typists were paid...why *shouldn't* she make money out of her talent? It was hardly unfair, was it? She had some flyers printed, put them up in pubs, booked back rooms wherever she could find a space, and slowly, far too slowly, began to make some cash. And if she exaggerated a bit sometimes, so what? She was genuine, after all, she *could* see the dead, and more often than not they *did* come through with the odd titbit of mostly monotonous information (one thing she'd learned about the dead, their conversation was most often as dull as ditchwater.) If sometimes they didn't, well...she *might* make things up, just to send the customers away happy, to make sure they paid up. She had bills after all, like everyone else, and the books on cold reading she'd bought – just to make sure the evening went well, most of the time she didn't need them *at all* – weren't cheap.

So OK, she wasn't in the grand a night league yet – and after fifteen years she was beginning to think she never would be – but as the years had gone on, she'd managed to turn her talent from something that brought a few quid in on the side to something that provided her primary source of income. She was a full-time psychic. Not a grand a night, no – but six hundred quid a night wasn't too shabby, was it? Eight or nine gigs a month did her well enough. And with the private readings on top of that...Yeah, she posted a healthy enough tax return, she could afford her mortgage and her car, she could take two holidays a year, and she was helping people come to terms with grief and loss and loneliness, and what, exactly, was wrong with that? Yes, a little lie here and there as an aid, a little scan of the tics and twitches that gave people away sometimes, but they were just oil to the gears. The engine itself was sound. It was only like telling someone their arse didn't look big in jeans, or that you loved them just so you could get your hole filled.

Most of that previous Friday had been a dud, and that was the truth. Nothing much happening in the spirit world, nobody wanting to play – there might have been a concert on, John Lennon and George Harrison playing along with Elvis and Jimi Hendrix, some big distraction like that. But brilliantly – and thankfully - someone had come through while that pouty-faced sceptic was standing, had told her what was going on in pouty's sister's life, and that had convinced everyone else, and they'd all gone away happy, spreading the word, and today her inbox was full of requests for private readings, including...

```
Hello Mrs Manning, my name is Hayley
Davis. My sister came to see you on
Friday and you said you knew that my
husband and me were experiencing
something to do with 'the other side.'
I was wondering if you'd care to come
and take a look and tell us what is
happening. If you could call on 07459
252521 I'd be most grateful. Thank you.
```

Bingo, thought Lillian, and picked up her phone.

Seven

Graham had mostly put away his thoughts about Hayley's mental state as he'd worked through the day – not forgotten them, as deep down he suspected there was quite a bit of truth in them, but put them away. Sometime after three that afternoon he'd decided the best thing he could do was keep an eye on her, monitor the situation, as his boss Mr Maitland liked to put it, and see if she deteriorated. If she did, there'd be a conversation. She wouldn't like it, but they'd have to have it. He loved her too much to let her become ill. If she resisted him, he would drag her to a doctor, sit on her if he had to. She was too precious to be allowed to wither.

So when he came home and she ran at him, all excited, and said 'Mrs Manning's coming round tonight to sweep the house,' he was totally nonplussed.

'Mrs Manning?' *Who the hell was that, some kind of housekeeper? After all, she was going to 'sweep the house.'*

'The woman, the psychic Elaine saw, the one who knew what was going on with us. I found her website, contacted her and she rang back saying she could tell it was a matter of some urgency so she's coming round tonight!'

Inside Graham screamed, he grabbed Hayley by the shoulders and told her what an idiot she was, that it'd be a cold day in hell when some phoney set foot in his house why wouldn't she just *grow up*. Out loud he said. 'What did you tell her?'

'Nothing, I swear,' she looked young, eyes wide...but slightly mad. 'Not a *thing* about what's been going on, I just repeated what she'd said to Elaine, that we were having something to do with the other side, and she said it's not a problem, she'll be here about eight.'

'What's she charging?' As it came out of his mouth, Graham could see it was the wrong thing to say. Those wide eyes narrowed, her brows grew close.

'She's not taking a penny,' she almost growled. 'She's doing it for us, for the spirit. All she wants is a cup of tea.'

Give a little, get a little, thought Graham. *Give her this one, indulge this bit of madness, then you can at least prove you've gone some way down that road and stomp on the rest of it.* 'OK then,' he said, and forced a smile he hoped looked more genuine than it felt. 'I'll get changed and throw a sandwich down me.'

Hayley became a child, a happy, glowing...but slightly mad...child again. She hugged him, hard. 'Thank you! Thank you!'

As he made his way upstairs, with a heavy heart, Graham profoundly hoped this would be the last of it, that this stupid woman would wander round, tell Hayley what she wanted to hear, and then everything would go back to normal.

Eight

The doorbell rang at eight precisely, and Graham opened it to find a pleasant enough looking woman in her mid-to-late forties standing there, a sort of matronly type, slightly overweight. 'Mrs Manning?'

'Lillian, please,' she said as he ushered her in and took her coat. 'Through here?'

He followed her into the living room and watched as Hayley stared at her in almost religious awe. *Bite your lip, swallow it down, give a little, get a little.* 'You must be Hayley,' Lillian said. *Must she? Don't you know for sure?* Hayley nodded. 'Well then,' Lillian went on, 'let me tell you a little about how I work. I don't want you to tell me anything about what's been happening here, or if it's been centred in any particular place. I'll simply walk about a bit, if that's all right with you, and give you my impressions.'

Sure, thought Graham. *Can you give us one of Tommy Cooper? My dad does that one and it cracks me up.*

'Of course, yes, that's fine with us, isn't it Graham?'

Go on, tell her my name. 'Yes, not a problem.'

Lillian stared at him. 'You're a sceptic.' Graham started to speak, but she held up her hand and laughed. 'Good, I'm glad. Important to have a sceptic present, keeps us grounded, stops us getting carried away. Now,' she went on. 'It's not here, is it? No, upstairs I think.' She walked past him to the hall, Hayley followed, and Graham brought up the rear.

Lillian stopped at the top landing, looked around her, then homed in on the spare room. 'In here. Don't say yes or no, I know. In here.' She opened the door and stepped inside, and the look of triumph – almost *angry* triumph - Hayley gave Graham startled him.

They followed. Lillian was standing in the middle of the room, casting about like a dog who'd lost a Bonio. Then she turned, looked at Hayley, and her eyes filled with tears. 'Oh you poor love,' she said. 'A baby, you lost a baby. Recently. Don't say yes or no. But you did, unborn I think. A miscarriage...and there's something...' she broke off, puzzled, then said 'Angie! The name Angie! That's what you were going to call her, I know. Yes. And...there's a girl in here, in this room. Older. Not ten, but older than yours...Angie. That's *her* name! *Was* her name. She passed...oh, long time ago, twenty years, thirty maybe...she was looking forward to a sister. *Yes*, that's what she's saying. She's lonely. Wanted...wants someone to *play* with. You bought toys for your child...dolls...teddy bears...a dog, a funny dog, with a tongue. She loves that dog, loves the toys...she wants to play. She's...' she broke off again, confused, shook her head. 'There's no harm, no threat, she's just lonely, wants the toys back, wants to be played with, that's all.'

To give her credit, Lillian had been convincing at all that. Yes, it was bollocks, but she presented it well. But when Graham looked over to Hayley and saw the tears rolling down his wife's face, his mood changed. *You're a fucking vampire,* he thought, unknowingly echoing Elaine's thoughts. *Get off on this, do you?*

'That's it, I'm afraid,' said Lillian, making her way to Hayley and holding her hands. 'All I can get. There's a lonely little girl here who was so looking forward to having a sister to play with, and she loves the toys. All she wants is the toys back, to be spoken to once in a while. She's a good spirit to have in the house, I promise you.'

'Shouldn't she have moved on by now?' Hayley asked, and Graham managed not to laugh. Laughing would be bad.

'Spirits have no sense of time, not as we understand it. And she's so young, I don't think she even knows that she's passed.' But again, just for a second, that puzzled look. Then it went. 'She'll find out, in time. When she does, she'll move on, I promise you. Now then, did we say something about tea?'

Nine

They said their farewells about an hour and a half later, after Lillian had consumed not one but three cups of tea, and had sat around their table blathering about 'confused souls on the other side,' how 'death is only a corridor to the other realm' and 'some souls get lost in that corridor, or are unwilling to move on.' Apparently quite a few of them 'felt they had unfinished business, messages to impart,' and that's why they contacted people like her.

Like that kid in The Sixth Sense, Graham thought. He took little part in the conversation, confining himself to nods, shakes of the head and the occasional, 'Oh, really?' *She sees dead people. If she turns around and tells one of us we're ghosts, then I'm picking her up and throwing her out of the window.* But he kept his counsel, reminding himself over and over again he was doing this for Hayley, for his love, conceding a little ground so she could never accuse him of being intractable.

At half nine, Lillian finally rose, said, 'Thank you so much for your hospitality, but I must leave you young people to your evening.' Hayley fluttered around her like a bird, and Graham could see quite clearly how Lillian puffed herself up at this, how it fed her ego. *I can see it, why can't* she?

At the door, Lillian turned to them, and said – mostly to Hayley – 'You should count yourself very lucky. Not many people are blessed to have such a lovely spirit in their house. All she wants is to play and be happy. She'll make the odd noise now and then, but nothing alarming. Just give her that opportunity, won't you?'

'Yes,' said Hayley. 'Yes we will. Won't we, Graham?'

'If that's what it takes,' said Graham, taking each word carefully, 'then that's what we'll do.'

Hayley might not have noticed how perfectly phrased that sentence was, but Lillian Manning did. She gave him a look that just screamed *oh, young man, what you don't know would fill an encyclopaedia*. But she said nothing, just hugged Hayley, nodded at Graham, and left. Walked towards the Audi Quattro parked in the street, the one that Graham knew cost almost twice his year's salary.

Hayley shut the door and turned to him, those gorgeous blue eyes ablaze in triumph. 'You see? You *see!* The things she *knew*, the miscarriage, the fact we were going to call her Angie, how could she know all that if she wasn't genuine? If she didn't have the gift?'

He could have argued. He could have repeated Elaine's theory; *just because I don't know how a trick was done doesn't stop it being a trick.* But he didn't. Yes, it was a trick, and a cruel trick, a trick that duped the sad and the desperate, a trick that had been perpetrated on the woman he loved, but he didn't argue. He was tired. He wanted his wife and his life back. So he didn't argue. Instead he told the absolute truth. 'I don't know, babe. I really don't.' The smile she gave him – almost angrily triumphant – showed him he'd said the right thing. 'So what are you going to do?'

'What she told us to, make Angie happy. Put the toys in the room, maybe buy her new ones. I...' here she faltered, and once more he saw tears in the corner of her eyes. He'd seen that too often recently. 'I can't bear the thought of her being sad. Being lonely. Nobody should have to put up with that, should they?'

About this he didn't need to lie. 'No babe. They shouldn't.'

He stepped forward and held her, rocking her slightly. God, he loved her. Loved her so much it hurt sometimes. 'I know I've been a bitch,' she said, but Graham wasn't fooled. This was her *generous in victory* voice. 'And I'm sorry. But it'll be better now.'

'I know,' said Graham, and then, to test the waters, 'I know you were a bitch.' Thankfully, she giggled a bit, gave him a light swat on the arm. 'But it's OK. Love you, babe.'

'Love you, hon.'

They stayed that way for a while, and it was good.

Ten

Lillian sat in her living room an hour later, cocoa in hand, thinking about the evening just gone and feeling good about herself. She'd helped. She'd helped a nice family (well, the woman was all right, the man was a Grade A Dick in her opinion) she'd also helped that poor little girl, trapped between worlds, lost and alone. She'd helped, and without a single trick. That poor lost soul, standing at the window, turning to her, and saying 'Where's doggy? I want doggy to play with. I love doggy.' Ah God, if she hadn't seen stuff like that a million times she'd have just broken down and cried. Death could be cruel sometimes. Oh, mostly it was a release, people who were in pain set free for the life everlasting, that was a good thing, proof that God was just, but oh, those poor ones who were lost, the children especially, sometimes it just tugged at your heart. But she'd be OK now, if those two followed instructions. She'd find peace and happiness and the attention she so desperately craved, and then, after a while, she'd pass on.

Yes. Good work. Good work deserved a cup of cocoa. And the tot of rum she'd laced it with. Good work, honest work, not a single trick.

Not from you, anyway.

She almost spilt her drink. A sudden shiver had run through her. Whose voice was that? Her dad's? It sounded like him – or at least her memory of him, she'd had no contact since the day he'd died (and none at all with her mother, who'd passed five years back.) 'What do you mean?' she asked the room.

Think. Think.

Even if it wasn't her dad, it was someone, a genuine spirit voice. But what did they mean, *think?* Think about *what?*

Tricks.

'But I didn't do any tricks,' she protested out loud. 'I did it for real. I saw her, the little girl, and...' She stopped there, shivering so violently now that she had to put her mug on the table. 'No...not from me, that's what you said, isn't it. Not from me. So from...what, the husband? That Graham? Is that what you mean?' Nothing. The spirit voice was gone. *Had* he played a trick on her? If so, it was a good one. But she didn't think he had, he was just a sceptic, a man of the material world, who didn't believe it existed if you couldn't pour it in a pint glass and drink it. She'd seen enough of those, even resorted to the odd bit of cold reading just to shut the bastards up. *Think,* the voice had said. *Think.*

So she did. She thought about the presence she'd felt as soon as she'd entered the house; a light, skittish one, a slightly mischievous one, a presence that had grown stronger as she'd mounted the stairs. And as she'd opened the door, she'd seen her, Angie, by the window, and she'd turned, all smiles, then asked about the doggy, a little girl with curls, freckled, a turned up button nose…

Think. Think.

Lillian replayed it all, every detail. The little girl, turning. Her long white lace dress. The smile. Asking about doggy…

The smile.

Was that it, the smile? It had just been a little girl's smile, bright, wide, shark like…

Lillian sat bolt forward, almost knocking the coffee table over. Yes, just for a second, a shark's grin on that little face, far too wide, full of teeth, teeth like razors. And a couple of times, when she'd been groping for the impressions, hadn't there been the *slightest* sensation that she was being *led*, shown what she *wanted* to see?

She stood, suddenly panicked, and nearly picked up the phone to call them, to tell them to *get the hell out of there right now,* when her own sense of self-confidence came back. *Easy, easy, you're spooking yourself. Worse, you're second guessing yourself. Remember, the spirits are all impressions, feelings, empathy. What did you feel* most? *What was the strongest?*

Love. Loneliness. Desire to play. Joy. Harmlessness.

Then that's all there was, that's all there is to say. Anything else is 20/20 hindsight. You've been doing this long enough to know. You're an expert. You know your stuff. So sit down, stop listening, finish your drink and go to bed. You did good, you know you did. You know you did.

So Lillian Manning, a mostly genuine but occasionally fake medium, supreme in her arrogance, sat down and calmed herself by adding another tot of rum to her cocoa. She'd been right. She *knew* that. Just a little girl, of no harm to anybody.

Eleven

In Crouch End, Hayley and Graham slept, their room still and quiet bar the occasional snore and sleep mumble. The wind blew outside, and at a little after one some rain lashed the windows, but they didn't hear it. They slept on.

But above them, in the loft, observed by no living soul, something did not sleep, something with dead glass eyes and a frozen china smile. It sat like that fabled rough beast, its hour come round at last, and its dark heart danced with glee at the thought of the pain to come.

Chapter Nine

One

After she'd kissed Graham goodbye and sat in their bedroom making her face up, Hayley thought to herself, *we've a ghost in our house.*

She paused, and really thought about it. An actual, authenticated by-God *ghost,* really in their house, not in a story, not in a film, but a genuine from-another-world *spirit.* Shouldn't she be scared? Ghosts were *always* scary in stories and films, rattling chains and running their bony fingers along your spine. Yes, by rights, she *should* be scared. Along the landing, not ten feet from where she was sitting, was a ghost, the disembodied soul of a little girl, dead but still roaming the earth – roaming their spare room, to be exact.

So she *should* be scared, but she wasn't. Yes, a ghost...but a little girl, lost and lonely, just wanting something or someone to play with. Who could be scared of *that?* Not *her.* Not Hayley Davis.

She finished her makeup and walked along the landing, opened the door and stepped into the spare room. 'Angie,' she heard herself whisper. Then, stronger, 'Angie? Are you there? It's me. Hayley.' She probably should have felt stupid, talking to an empty room, but she didn't. She didn't because she now knew the room wasn't empty. Somewhere here, somewhere she couldn't see, was a little girl, hanging on her every word. 'It's OK love, I know you're there. I've got to go to work, got to earn the pennies. If you want to bring the doggy down to play with, you go ahead, it's all right. I might – if you're a good girl – even bring you a new toy later. But only if you're good.' The more she spoke, the more...well, *complete* Hayley felt. The more she felt *right,* like this was what she was *meant* to do, maybe even *made* to do. 'If there's anything you want, you just say, and if we can, we'll do it for you. You be a good girl, now, and I'll see you later.' And then, just before she closed the door, she said the words she'd longed to say to her own child. 'Love you, Angie.'

Two

'Someone's in a good mood,' said Jodie a couple of hours later.

'Am I?' asked Hayley. She was doing a stock take, pulling things from the supply cupboard and making a list for the next Cash & Carry run. 'We're low on pink, yellow and red gel. And jewels.'

'Gotcha,' said Jodie. 'And yes, you are. You do realise you joined in with not *only* ABBA but *also* the Spice Girls *and* One Direction while you were sorting Mrs Carney's facial? OK, ABBA, and Spice Girls at a push, but *One Direction? Seriously*, girl?'

'I don't know any One Direction songs.'

'I know, I could tell, what you were singing bore no relation to what was coming out of the radio. Which doesn't change the fact you were making the attempt. Minus three points on the Cool Wall.'

'I didn't realise being cheerful was a crime, lock me up officer, it's a fair cop.'

'It isn't,' Jodie said, smiling, but sympathetically. 'But just recently you've been...since you weren't well, had that bug, you've not been yourself. And today you have been. It's nice to have you back, that's all.'

'You know something? It's nice *to* be back.' She looked back in the cupboard. 'And we're down to the last case of Insette.' *Back to myself,* she thought, making a note on her list. *Back to myself. Funny. But then, it's a funny old world, one you can't plan for. It takes a ghost to make me myself again. As Harry Hill used to say, 'What are the chances of that happening?'*

Three

On her way home, she stopped off at Toymaster's and picked up a teddy bear, a daft-looking brown and white thing that had a growl in its stomach. It was perfectly adorable, the sort of thing she'd have loved as a little girl, the sort of thing she'd have loved and hugged till the fur was worn smooth and the growl all worn out. She was halfway to the checkout, purse in her hand, when she stopped. *Why am I bothering? We've plenty of stuff in the loft, tons for her to play with.* Then, with a wry chuckle as she placed the bear back on the shelf, *anyway, she knows how to get the stuff down herself, doesn't she?* Still, all the same, she'd have a word with Graham, ask him if he'd mind bringing all the toys back down. The more Angie had to play with, the less bored she'd be, and the less bored she was, the happier she'd be. Stood to reason.

Four

It seemed liked Angie hadn't wanted to play with any toys at all that day, the spare room was still empty when Hayley looked in. 'Hey sweetheart,' she called. 'You OK? You had a good day?' Nothing, no noise at all, just the traffic outside. 'Well, I'm back anyway. And Da...Graham will be home in a bit. You want anything? Anything at all?' Still nothing. 'Well, if you do, let me know.' Another chuckle. 'I'm sure you'll find a way. Shall I leave the door open?' No answer. 'I will, just a crack. Love you, Angie.'

She changed her clothes and pottered downstairs, made herself a cup of tea and went into the living room, switched on the TV and watched something mindless, waiting for her husband.

Five

'Quittin' time, nobhead,' said Danny as he retrieved his coat and baseball cap from the coat rack. Graham looked at the clock. Six on the dot. Yes, quitting time. Time to drive home and cuddle up with his wife and watch some telly and eat a meal and maybe have some loving later on, the way normal folk did.

But they weren't normal folk anymore were they? I mean, normal folk didn't have the ghost of a little girl in their spare room.

'Y'arright?' Danny asked. 'Y'looked like a dog 'oo'd swallered 'is own dick.'

That was too much for Graham, *way* too funny an image on top of everything else. He rolled back his chair and bellowed laughter. Danny stood there, looking on indulgently until the storm passed. 'Seriously, mate. Y'OK?'

'Yeah, yeah I'm fine. Thanks. For the concern as well as the laugh.'

'No probs, no charge, just remember to tip your waitress. Burra mean it, like. Y've looked like boiled shite again today. Is it y'missus? She still…y'know?'

'She's getting there,' said Graham, but thought *getting where? Where exactly are we?*

'Well, tell 'er I was askin', won't y'. Y'know, shite wharrappened to yis.'

Yep, and getting shite-er all the time. 'I will, cheers.'

'An…if y'wanna talk, y'know, get t'gether over a bev or somthin', lerrus know. Still don't got many mates down 'ere, an' even though y'an Arsenal fan, you're norra bad nobhead.'

'Thanks, mate,' he said, genuinely touched. Of course, he wouldn't take him up on that – not without risking a trip to the nice hospital where they gave you the canvas jackets as a consequence – but for a kid like this, not even twenty-one, and a bloody *Everton* fan at that to take such an interest, to be concerned...well, that said something about something, but right at that moment he was too tired to make out what. 'You should come to the Emirates one Saturday. See what a proper ground looks like.'

'Go frig yerself and your dog,' Danny smiled, and departed with a cheery 'Up the Blues!' As he left the office, Graham felt his good mood vanish along with him, and for the first time in his life he realised he genuinely didn't want to go home. He wanted to stay here, at his desk, dealing with angles and deadlines and calculations, things he could understand and quantify.

But Hayley needed him. Somewhere inside he knew that, he felt that, but did *she* know that? Did she know that at some stage this madness would crash down around her, and then she'd need picking up? And what of *him*, what of *his* needs, what of...?

Oh, stop whining, you selfish bastard. Who's your love? Who did you promise to stand by, in sickness or in health? Your day will come, if that's all you're after. One day it'll be all about you, and hallelujah let's have a party, break out the streamers and the funny hats, but you *are her husband, and that carries with it certain responsibilities – and don't pull that face, you know what you signed up for when you put your name on that register. OK, she's a little bit off the deep end right now, but that'll sort itself, in time, so shut up and put up. Got me?*

Graham did, albeit reluctantly. He saved his work, switched off the Mac and made his way home.

Six

'Can you do me a favour?' she asked as he entered the hall. No *hello hon, how was your day*, no welcome home kiss or cuddle, just *can you do me favour*. 'Later on, I mean, when you're settled?'

'Yeah, sure.' He felt heavy. He didn't like that bright – almost over bright – glitter in her eyes. It was almost a permanent fixture these days. He shrugged off his coat. 'What is it?'

'Could you get the toys out of the loft, put them back in the nursery? For Angie? I nearly bought her something new today and then I realised we still had that stuff. Seemed pointless, really. Didn't it?'

Several things about that speech horrified him, but he kept quiet. Barely, but he managed it. The first was, *she's calling it 'the nursery.'* The second was, *she's calling it 'Angie.'* But it was the third that disquieted him the most, the almost puppyish begging for affirmation, that she was doing the right thing. 'Yes,' he said. 'I suppose it was. I'll do it now,' he said, and made for the stairs.

'Oh, no rush.' But Hayley seemed elated, almost dancing around him. 'I mean, get changed first. It's dusty up there.'

'Fair point.' He stopped halfway up, looked back at her. He hardly recognised her. The figure in the hallway looked like someone trying on a halfway convincing Hayley disguise kit. *How far do I let this go? What happens if she never snaps out of it? What do I do then?*

For the first time, Graham Davis was faced with the very real possibility that he could fall out of love with his wife.

'What?' asked Hayley, and there was the oddest look on her face. She was smiling...but she was also wary, as if she was checking out a dog with a waggy tail but might bite at any moment. 'What are you looking at?'

I don't think I know. 'Just my love,' he said, and the wariness left her face. Her smile became her real smile, genuine, warm and as sexy as hell.

'Oh, you know what to say, don't you? Just for that you might get something special tonight.'

We better keep it quiet, don't want to wake the dead. I mean, I want to be the only one who puts the willies up you. He coughed a laugh back. 'Well, if I'm on a promise I'd better get started. And make us a big tea. I'll need to keep my strength up.'

'Stuff that, I'll phone for take-out. You'll burn it off,' she said, and headed to the living room. Graham waited until she was out of sight, and dropped his smile. He thought again, *how long do I allow this?* Having no answer, he mounted the rest of the stairs, changed, and set about his job.

Seven

He brought them down as he took them up, two by two, and arranged them on the shelves, on the windowsill, on the floor. He looked at them, bears, dogs, pigs, a giraffe, a silent menagerie on parade and went to leave, to put the loft hatch back in place and make his way downstairs, maybe even to invite Hayley up for the seal of approval.

At the doorway, he turned and looked back. Something was wrong, but he wasn't sure what. It was like those damned Activity Books his parents used to buy him to keep him quiet on long car journeys. THESE TWO PICTURES LOOK THE SAME BUT THERE ARE FIVE DIFFERENCES, CAN YOU SPOT THEM (answer on page 16.) He'd hated them as a kid, could never do them, always had to turn to page 16 and cheat, and he hated this one even more because...well, this wasn't a book. He knew *something* was wrong, the way he'd known those pictures were different, but he just couldn't *quite* make it out. It was maddening, like trying to recollect a song lyric when you were singing in the shower.

He closed his eyes and tried his level best to conjure up the image of the room as it had been – what, only two weeks ago? Three at most? God, could it *really* have been only twenty-one days? *You can pack a lot in if you try. Next time we have one of those time management seminars at work I'll really have something to say about how productive you can make your day.* There were toys hither and yon, a cot, rolls of wallpaper ready to be hung, a china...

He opened his eyes. Yes, that china doll, or at least the doll with the china face. The body was plastic, but the face was definitely china. The one he'd taken up last, the one that had given him that case of the creeps.

The one he'd taken up last, that was the important thing. The one he'd virtually thrown into the loft because...well, he just didn't like touching it, there's no one else around, may as well tell the truth. And if he'd thrown it in last...

'Then it should have been right at the front,' he muttered. But it hadn't been. It wasn't that big a loft, about six feet by ten, not even the full length of the roof, and it wasn't full, not even when all the baby stuff had been up there. Now...well, bar the cot, wallpaper rolls, hot water tank and a couple of boxes of old football programmes, it was empty.

So where was that bloody doll? he wondered. Then he decided it didn't matter. Then he decided once more to tell the truth to himself. He didn't *want* it to matter, he didn't like the thing, he just *didn't*, and if it had decided to dematerialise then *whoop-de-doo, thank you God, that'll do nicely. While You're at it, can You sort out Hayley's madness? I'd be grateful, Lord. And three points on Saturday, while You're at it.*

But still...he'd promised Hayley to get the toys out of the loft. *And I have,* he protested. *Behold these things here, these creatures of nylon and stuffing; what are they if not toys? Tottenham's back four? Toys, toys everywhere, so let's all have a drink.*

But what if she noticed? *Noticed what, one horrible, creepy-faced, nobody-likes-it-doll? How's she going to notice one doll in all that crowd?*

Of course, yes, you could *take that chance...but have you seen the way she looks at you nowadays? That faint, wary, will-he-won't-he-bite look? You want to see that some more, maybe forever?*

'Fuck you,' Graham muttered, and made his way to the loft ladder. *I'd better get a truly amazing shag out of this – actually, this* deserves *the schoolgirl uniform, I don't care how* Operation Yewtree *she finds it.*

He mounted the steps and stuck his head through the hatch, looked about, saw nothing doll shaped and so started to descend. *Hey, I tried. Not my fault.*

Yeah, tried really hard, didn't you?

With a heartfelt heavy sigh, he heaved himself back into the loft. He scooted forward, bent at the shoulders, careful to keep his feet on the beams – there were boards down, but he didn't trust them – and searched by the light of that sixty watt bulb. He moved the pieces of the cot, one by one, from the wall. No doll. He looked behind the boxes of programmes. A dead spider in a decades old web, but no doll. He even lifted the top off the water tank (half hoping he'd see the thing bobbing about face down, like the bitch had drowned.) Nothing but water and a ballcock that looked like it had six weeks left on it before it rusted through.

Cot, boxes, tank. That's what the loft held. Just those things and nothing more. Well, and the corpse of Incey Wincey spider, and good riddance to the eight legged freak. *Well, if she asks I can swear on a stack of Bibles that I did my best. I can swear also that I put it up here in the first place, I'll go on the* Jeremy Kyle Show *and take the lie detector, I'm covered, officer.*

He clicked off the bulb, descended the steps, pushed the ladder back into place and shut the hatch, making triply certain the lock was engaged.

On his way to the stairs he looked into the spare room, hand on the knob, ready to pull the door shut.

The doll was looking at him, sat square in the middle of the floor, eyes fixed, that horrible smile seeming to mock him.

He stood, rooted, for what seemed like a million years. It was hard to pull a breath in. He could feel his eyes bulging. *How the blinding blue fuck…?*

The doll, being a doll, didn't answer. It sat on the carpet, smiling. *Wouldn't you like to know,* that smile seemed to say.

No. I wouldn't. I would like very much not to know. Because…because…

'Because I just wouldn't,' he said, very quietly. With shaking hands, he pulled the door shut. *What the eye doesn't see the heart doesn't grieve over,* that was one of his dad's sayings, and right then Graham had never heard a truer word spoken.

A ring of the doorbell, loud and shocking, made him jump. 'Curry's here,' Hayley called from downstairs.

'Right,' Graham tried to say, but his voice went through three octaves. He cleared his throat and tried again. 'Right.' *Better. Almost normal, in fact.* 'I'll just wash my hands, down in a sec.'

'Cool,' she called, making her way to the front door, 'I'll plate up.'

On rubber legs he staggered to the bathroom and ran the tap. Looking in the mirror he saw an old man looking back. *How am I supposed to go downstairs and eat dinner after* that? *How?*

Because the alternative is telling her.

So? Would that make a difference? She already thinks there's a spook in the house.

The difference is, she'll think you agree, that there is, when of course there isn't, because there are no ghosts, and SHUT UP about the doll, there's an explanation we just haven't found yet, but I know this; you talk about this and you're not so much adding fuel to the fire as pouring an entire Texaco station on it and lighting a match – comprende, amigo? The less 'evidence' she has, the quicker this whole thing will pack up and go away. So keep your mouth shut, eat your dinner, and give your missus a right seeing to later and everything will work out fine.

'OK then. OK.' He ran his hands under the water, wiped his face, and made his way downstairs, hoping to God it wouldn't show, that he wouldn't betray himself.

Eight

After the meal, Hayley went to the bathroom, urinated, then looked in the spare room. *Oh, thank you hon,* she thought. It was perfect, just what Angie would want, all the toys to play with, the doggy with the red felt tongue dead square in the middle of the floor. She stepped inside. 'Is it all right?' she whispered. She didn't know why she whispered, just that it felt right. Just that she didn't want Graham to overhear. She wasn't a stupid woman, she knew he was largely indulging her, but that didn't matter. Even if for the wrong(ish) reasons, he was doing the right thing, and he was doing it because he loved her, and Hayley truly believed that if two people loved each other enough then everything would turn out right.

'Angie,' she whispered. 'Do you like it? Do you like *them?* The doggy's there, I know you like *him.* Does he have a name?' Silence, just the faint soundtrack of the TV from the living room. 'You let me know if there's anything you want, and I'll make sure you have it.' Although...how was she going to do that? How was Angie going to communicate with her? That needed some thought. In the meantime though, she contented herself with looking at the room, all the toys, all the things a little girl could ever need, her favourite doggy on the rug, the doll with the china face propped up on the windowsill...

As she looked, she felt two small arms encircle her right leg, and squeeze. Just once, very quickly. Then, faintly, a pattering of tiny steps, away, away to the window. As if someone tiny had impulsively run up to her, hugged her as best they could, then ran away, shy. 'Oh hon,' she said, and a tear dropped down her cheek. 'Oh Angie. Oh my baby.'

She waited for five minutes, but nothing more happened. She wiped the tear from her face and made her way to her husband, closing the door behind her, and in the light from the window, the china faced doll's eyes gleamed.

Nine

In the middle of the night, Hayley awoke with a perfect idea. She knew how Angie could talk to them. It was easy, *simple-pimple* as they'd said in school, and Graham didn't have to know. She didn't have to buy a thing. Everything was downstairs. Happy, she went back to sleep, and dreamed no dreams.

Ten

Before she left for work, she stood in the nursery with a notebook and pen. 'Angie,' she said, clearly now, since Graham was already out. 'I'm going to leave these for you. If you need anything, please, write it down.' Then, as an afterthought, '*can* you write? Have you learned? If you have…then, please. Take these things and let me know. If you haven't…well, I'll think of something. I'm off to work now, you've all the toys to play with. Keep busy and it won't seem like any time at all before I'm back. Be good, my baby.'

As she let herself out the front door, she contemplated on how Angie must've been playing already, since the doll was no longer on the window, it'd been by the door, as if waiting for her, as if saying hello.

Chapter Ten

One

While Hayley had been having her great idea, over in Highgate her sister Elaine had woken screaming from the worst nightmare of her life. Her phone had rung, and she'd looked at the screen to see HAYLEY MOBILE CALLING, and as she'd thumbed the button she'd heard someone - a woman, maybe a girl, sobbing helplessly. She'd called Hayley's name, over and over, but only the crying came in reply. Then (such was the logic of dreams) she was outside her sister's front door, knocking in panic but the door swung open, it was unlocked and who the hell left a door unlocked in London in 2015?

She'd made her way into the hall, calling their names, louder and louder, and as she'd reached the bottom of the stairs she'd heard that sobbing, coming from above so she'd run up them, two at a time, but this was a dream and the landing kept running away from her, the stairs turned into an escalator, she was carried forward, powerless, and on the landing she saw it, the thing that was crying, a terrible stunted *thing* that almost *looked* human, but no, it was a *pig*, a thing with a pig's face, a pig on two legs and wearing a dress, and that should have been funny, pigs in clothes were *always* funny, but this pig had a human body and human arms and legs, and it was crying, sobbing, tears running down its snout...but this pig was *laughing,* because this pig had tricked her, this pig had tricked everyone, this pig was...

'Piggy's got us all fooled,' said a faint Scots voice from her right, and she turned, and there was Graham's dad, and she almost smiled despite the pig that was growing closer, closer, because (and wild horses wouldn't have dragged this out of her, but this was a dream, and you can't lie in a dream, not even to yourself) she had a bit of a crush on Jim, he was her older man fantasy, and that might have been a bit weird but hey, it was no one's concern but hers.

She tried to ask him what he meant, but he turned from her and walked away down what looked like a hospital corridor, and when she looked forwards again, the pig was almost on top of her, and it was snuffling, its snout dripping, its mouth watering; the pig was going to eat her. It reached out with its terrible (girl) human hands and grabbed her by the neck and said 'Yum yum my bum,' and its hot breath was in her mouth.

Two

Which is when she awoke, screaming in terror, waving her hands in front of her face, trying still to bat that horrible thing away. It took her almost ten minutes to calm down, to realise she was OK, she was in her own bed, that it was just a dream, and twenty minutes to be ruefully grateful that she was between boyfriends.

But still, *never again a dream like that, please God*. Sleep was impossible so she stomped to her living room – still spooked enough to expect that thing, that awful pig-human to be lurking round every corner – and opened her laptop, powered up Facebook, and played three games of Candy Crush Saga. That calmed her down somewhat, but running around the back of her mind, like a hamster in a cage, was the thought, *Hayley's in trouble, Hayley's in trouble.*

It wouldn't go away.

Three

If anything, it grew louder and louder during the day, interfering with her work. She misplaced two files, deleted an email that really should have been read (and humiliated herself by phoning the other party up and asking for it to be re-sent, *gosh, dopey me, eh?*) and totally forgot she was due to take the minutes at the weekly review meeting.

'Pull yourself together, Elaine,' her boss said at half two that afternoon. 'This is sloppy. C'mon, pull your socks up.' At this, some of the others in the office tittered, and Elaine could have shot them all. Twice. Yes, it was true she affected a slight air of inefficiency in order to disguise her intent, but the keyword was 'affected.' She was going to go far in this company – she just didn't want anyone else to notice. They may try and block her progress. Business was ruthless in the 21st century. She could put up with people *thinking* she was just a tiny bit ditzy – but she hated actually *being* a tiny bit ditzy. She hated being told to 'pull her socks up' by the boss who didn't notice just how efficiently she was chipping away at his authority, how much of his work she was squirreling away and doing herself, one day to present all of this to the board of Directors and be presented with that balding dinosaur's job as he was hauled onto the street like a wino from a White Hart Lane pub. Oh, she hated that.

All because of that bloody dream, the sleep it had cost her and that nagging, persistently nagging voice that said, *Hayley's in trouble, Hayley's in trouble*. So Elaine, being Elaine, decided to do something about it.

Four

'Hey you,' said Hayley in her ear. 'How you doing?'

'Bored,' said Elaine, even though she was anything of the sort. 'Bored and fancy destroying any plans you and Gray have for tonight. Can I come round? I'll bring wine.'

'Course you can, be great to see you. Don't bring much though, some of us have to work Saturdays.'

'Yeah, poor you. OK, see you about eight. Everything good there?'

'Oh yeah,' said Hayley, and there was a tone there, something furtive, that Elaine really didn't care for. 'Everything's brilliant. See you later, customer coming.'

'Yeah, see you later.' Elaine hung up, not quite as reassured as she'd hoped. That tone…what did that mean?

Five

She knocked on the door at ten past eight and was almost shocked when Hayley opened it. She covered it well, she didn't think it played on her face at all, but her thought was, *My God, what's* wrong *with her?*

Hayley was glittery, brittle, almost over-bright, hyper-excited. She danced around Elaine as she ushered her in, took her coat, retrieved the bottle of wine and skipped into the kitchen to open it. She looked to Graham, who in contrast had never looked older or more tired in all the time she'd known him. 'Uh, hi Gray,' she said, still discomforted by her sister's behaviour. I've not seen her like this since...well, was it when she met Gray? All excited, not telling anyone, all…

All *I've got a secret*.

Yes, that was it. Hayley was a terrible liar, couldn't utter an untruth without blushing or examining the carpet. She was even worse when she had a secret. She always wanted people to *know* she had a secret, which to Elaine kind of defeated the purpose of a secret in the first place. She was all, 'No, honestly I've not got a secret and even if I had, which I haven't, I wouldn't tell you what it is, because I haven't got one, honestly, oh all right since you're pestering me, his name's Graham and I met him at a party, now stop *bugging* me.'

'Hi,' said Graham, standing slowly, almost painfully. *Is he going grey? Tell me the truth, have you started going grey, Gray? Or were they out of Just For Men this week?* He hugged her one armed, the way he always had. She gave him a look of concern, and he almost seemed to understand it. He gave a half-shrug and shook his head slightly.

'What you doing still standing?' said Hayley, trotting – yes, *trotting* – into the living room, three glasses cupped in her hand. 'Go on, sit down, get comfy.' Elaine took her glass and made her way to the sofa, Hayley close behind her. 'Been ages since we had a chat, just the two of us.'

'I'll go to the pub, shall I?' asked Graham, taking his glass and sitting on the armchair.

'You might have to,' cautioned Hayley, 'you know how we girls witter on.'

'Yeah,' said Elaine, joining in, but not wanting to join in. 'We'll be talking about boys and whether Oxy-10 can *really* clear up your spots before the Prom.' They both laughed at that, but…no, this was weird, wrong, distorted. They were like poorly rehearsed actors playing at being Hayley and Graham. Elaine, who'd never had a relationship that had lasted more than six months, had often looked to these two as proof positive that it *could* work, that there *was* actually someone out there that you would want to spend your time with. But these two…

Look, they've probably just had a colossal row, it happens, and they're putting on a show for you. So go along with it. I mean, Jesus, what is it with you today? And yet, beating away at the back of her mind, *Hayley's in trouble, Hayley's in trouble...*

'I might take my drink into the kitchen then,' said Graham, standing. The standing meant *might* was *will*. 'Play on the iPad, get a couple of games of Bejewelled Blitz under my belt.'

'Go on then,' said Hayley, and once more Elaine felt discombobulated. She was virtually shooing him out of the door. 'But no looking at those dirty schoolgirls. Or if you do, delete your search history, there's a good boy.'

Graham stopped, gave her an almost hurt glance, then looked at Elaine and forced a big smile. 'She's joking.'

'Hey, whatever floats your boat, mate,' said Elaine, wishing to God she could be somewhere else. Like Krakatoa in 1888. 'You want to hear some of the stuff men have asked me to do.'

'Trust me,' he said, 'I really don't.' Without a look at Hayley, he left.

Elaine turned to her sister and said, 'Look, I'm sorry. I'll go.'

Hayley looked puzzled. 'Go? You've just got here. What do you want to go for?'

'Well...' Elaine fidgeted, and looked at the doorway. From the kitchen she could hear the Windows startup chime. Hayley frowned at her, clearly not getting the mime. 'You and Gray,' Elaine whispered. 'Is everything OK?'

'Everything's fine. And why are you whispering?'

'I just thought,' still whispering, 'you'd had a row or something.'

'God no! We had one on...' she thought back, tilting her head to the ceiling. 'Friday. Or Sunday, something like that, but it's way over now, like dinosaur over.'

'You promise me? I just thought...well, you sure you're OK?'

'Oh Elaine,' Hayley said. 'I have never been better.'

God, of course! How could I have been so stupid! It might be a bit soon, but if she's looked after from the start... 'Are you,' she said, still whispering, 'pregnant again?'

'No,' said Hayley instantly, but still...she looked at her glass, her face the colour of wine.

'You are, aren't you? It's OK, I won't tell anyone, I swear.'

This time Hayley looked her square in the eyes. 'No. I'm not.' Then that shifty, pleased, shiny look again. 'But...well, there *is* a baby. No, not a baby. A little girl.'

'So...what? You're adopting? I thought you could still...'

'Oh yes, we can. And no, we're not adopting. We've been adopted.'

Elaine shook her head. 'Don't get you.'

Hayley sipped her wine, thought, then said, 'You remember years ago, when we were kids, and there was a big storm, and when we went to put the bins out, a cat ran in? Remember that?'

Despite the weirdness and the sensation – low, but persistent - that she wasn't talking to her sister *at all,* Elaine laughed. Yeah, she remembered that cat. Their mother, who had a passionate hatred of all animals but cats in particular, had screamed the place down, frightening the poor little bugger even more than it was already. It was a scraggy, soaked ginger Tom, all sorry for itself, and all it wanted was a place to dry off. Maybe a saucer of milk. And a tickle behind the ears wouldn't have gone amiss either. 'I hated mum that night, making us throw the poor bastard out again. God knows what happened to it.' Indeed for years afterwards, whenever Elaine had left the house she'd looked around for that little ginger cat, hoping it was around and doing fine.

'But think, if Mum hadn't, we'd have kept the thing, he'd have been *our* cat. We didn't look for it, it found us. And *this* is like *that*.'

'What is?'

After a second, Hayley told her.

Six

When she'd finished, Elaine looked at her, drank half a glass of wine in a single gulp, and said, 'You want to go over that one more time, please?' To her horror, Hayley started to, delighted, just as she had been years back when she'd told her secrets. Elaine held her hand up, stopping her, and drank some more. *She's slipped her wheels completely. It's all been far too much for her, Jesus, the poor cow. How did I not see this? Wait, maybe I did, maybe that's what the whole bad vibe thing I've been going through is about. Maybe* this *is the trouble she's in.*

'I know it's a bit much to take in,' said Hayley, smiling.

'Yes, I'll say.'

'But it's happening. I swear to you,' and Elaine looked at her, hard. *Yes, she believes all this. Does that make it better or worse? Oh, and if I find that Lillian Manning I will pull her trachea into some interesting new shapes for doing this. And then I will nail her feet to the floor. And laugh.* 'C'mon,' Hayley said suddenly, and stood. 'Come and take a look.'

Elaine did not want to stand and take a look. Elaine wanted to do *anything* but stand and take a look. At that moment Elaine would have watched an entire night of *Strictly Come Dancing* than stand and take a look. But this was her sister, her older sister, and Hayley had never let her down before, never resented playing with her (well, much), had always looked after her. This was Hayley, the woman she respected above everyone else, the woman she'd almost made into a mother substitute. Hayley wouldn't hurt her. Hayley wouldn't allow her to be hurt.

She took a deep breath, necked more wine, and said, 'Go on then.'

Seven

As her sister led her up the stairs, the nightmare from the night before came rushing back with brutal force. *If there's a pig up there, then I'm sorry sis, but I'm leaving an Elaine shaped hole in your front door. And I'm not paying to replace it, either.*

No pig, but a sensation of...what? Oppression? A thickness of the air, something cloying, almost as if a hand was pressing down on her chest, making it hard for her to breathe. *Something nasty, anyway,* she thought.

Hayley opened the door, stood back, and said, 'Just look at it.'

Elaine did, and looking at it was as far as she wanted to go, thank you very much. Certainly she didn't want to step in. No, the landing was good enough. Even though...*well, what was there to be scared of? Some stuffed toys, that's all. Who the hell was scared of a teddy bear? Or six? Or nine? Or fifteen hundred and fifty-three, by the looks of it.*

'This is what Lillian said we should do,' said Hayley, and Elaine recognised that tone. Their mother's indulgent voice. That scared her on a whole new level. 'Fill the place with toys so that she can play.' Then, to the room, 'Angie? Are you there? Can you hear us? This is Elaine, my sister. She's come to see you. You want to say hello?' The room, of course, remained quiet. Hayley turned to her, smiling ruefully. 'I think she's shy with new people.'

'Why wouldn't she be?' said Elaine. Her lips felt cold. 'I was.'

'She'll get used to you, the more she sees you.' Hayley stepped into the room, and Elaine somehow managed to resist the urge to shout out a warning. 'I put this notebook here for her and a pen, to see if she had anything to say. Maybe she could write it down.'

'And has she?'

'No,' said Hayley, sadly. 'Maybe she can't write. Ah well. I'll find a way. But she's happy, I know that.'

'Do you? Good.'

'Yes, by the way she hugged me. Ran up to me, hugged me, and ran away again.' The smile was now wistful, almost tearful. 'Must be so strange for her. I mean, this was her home, so Lillian says. And then new people come, and she can't find her own mum and dad. Oh, the poor love.' She dropped the notebook and pen on the floor.

'Yes,' said Elaine. 'Poor love.' But it was not any ghost child she was thinking of. 'Well then. More wine?'

'Why not,' said Hayley, and stepped onto the landing, closing the spare room door. But not before saying a faint, 'Goodnight my baby.'

More wine. Like a gallon, thank you.

Eight

Somehow, and she never knew quite how, Elaine kept up the conversation until after eleven. They spoke about other stuff, work, TV, the lack of available men in her life, was their mum getting worse or were they just less tolerant as they grew older, just stuff, the sort of stuff they had always talked about…but Elaine saw the way that her sister's eyes kept flicking to the ceiling, the way she was always just a beat off, slightly disconnected.

At five past eleven, Elaine stood and said, 'Well, I'd better let you good people get to your beds. Thanks for tonight.'

'Not a problem. And thank you. For listening, I mean.'

Standing there, looking at her elder sibling, Elaine felt two massively conflicting emotions. On the one hand, she wanted to take her by the shoulders and shake some sense into the stupid bitch. On the other, she wanted to take her by the shoulders and hold her, hold her so hard she might break her in two. In the end, the latter won out. 'Love you, Hayles,' she said.

'Love you too, kid.' Then, louder, 'Gray? Elaine's going home now.'

He appeared in the doorway and, oh yes, he looked older, he did, she'd been right about that. And who could blame him? 'Gray,' she said, 'you mind walking me to the Tube? I heard someone got mugged round here not long ago, and I'm only a little'un.'

'Elaine,' said Graham, 'you're five foot six and could batter a Mexican wrestler. When did you turn wimp?'

'Oh hush you,' said Hayley, and pushed them both to the front door. 'You men are supposed to protect us. Walk her to the Tube, it's only down the road.'

'I thought you lot were liberated now,' said Graham, pulling his coat on.

'We only tell you that to fudge – sorry, fuck, I can say what I like here - with your heads,' said Elaine, putting her own coat on. 'C'mon, hero.'

'Back in a minute, babe,' said Graham, and kissed Hayley on the cheek, the way you'd kiss an aunt.

Nine

They hadn't got as far as the end of the road before Elaine said, 'She's in trouble, isn't she?'

Graham stopped, and sagged against someone's wall. 'How much did she tell you?'

'Everything I think, unless you know better.' She gave him a brief recap. 'That the lot?'

Graham looked like he was about to say something, but didn't. Then, 'Yeah, that's the full SP.'

They stood looking at each other, shivering in the chill early March air. 'Do you think it's the right thing, to indulge her like that?'

For a second she thought he might cry, but he kept it together. 'I don't know, Elaine. I'm past being out of my depth, I'm in the fucking ocean. Y'know what I was doing on that computer tonight?'

'Looking on the St Trinian's Upskirt pages?'

'D'you know what I was doing the *rest* of the time,' he said, smiling, and she was glad. She'd hated that old man look. 'Trying to find some advice on treating psychosis. Because that's what it is you know, a psychosis.'

'Jesus.' That was a horrible word, a bleak, final, awful word.

'Yeah,' he nodded. 'All the symptoms fit. Fit so neatly she might have been copying them. "Fixations on specific incidents." That's the best definition I've found. And that's my Hayles right now. Fixfuckingated.'

'Was it any help?'

'Well, Sandra from the sixth form who just wouldn't do her homework cheered me up a bit,' and now it was her turn to smile, 'but aside from that...half the sites say get her to a shrink right away. A third say get her to a shrink if she doesn't get better. The rest say play along and it might pack up in its own good time, particularly if it's definitely related to a specific stress-related event.'

'You reckon this one is?'

He shrugged. 'Probably. If not it's an incredible coincidence, wouldn't you say?'

'So...what? Leave it and it might go away of its own accord?'

'That's one plan. If it doesn't I'll have to take her to a head doctor.'

'Good luck with that,' Elaine muttered. 'Oh Jesus, Gray. This is so *fucked up*. The way she was when she took me up there...'

Graham blew steam out. 'I know. She thinks I can't hear her. She goes up, talks to the fucking room, and I...' he stopped, unable to find the words, and Elaine hugged him.

'If you need me, call,' she said. 'Any time. She's my sister and I love her and I want her to get well. But you're the closest thing I've got to a brother, and you need my help as well – don't say you don't, of course you do. Whatever help I can give, anyway. Got me?'

'Yeah,' he said, and grinned. A genuine grin, the first one she'd seen that night.

'Great, then walk me to the Tube, and quick before I piss myself.'

'Why didn't you go in ours?'

'You kidding? There's a ghost next to your toilet.'

Ten

As soon as they'd gone, Hayley tiptoed up the stairs to the nursery. She pushed open the door, walked in, looked around...and on the floor, on the notebook, was written:

<pre>
      NIGHT NIGHT MUMMY
           LUV YOO
           ANGEE
</pre>

'Oh baby,' she whispered, hugged the notebook to her heart, 'oh my Angie, I love you too. I love you too. I love you too.'

Chapter Eleven

One

As was their Saturday routine – established early in their relationship and too late to change now – Graham awoke first, even though he had no work to go to. He plodded downstairs and filled the kettle, then placed two rounds of bread in the toaster. While getting the butter and marmalade from the fridge, he pondered his life. Four months ago, just four months back, everything was…well, as good as it could get. And now? *Now I've a heavy heart, a heavy head, heavy tread.*

His reading the previous night hadn't encouraged him. Not that he'd expected to find a link with YOUR MISSUS THINKS THERE'S A DEAD CHILD IN THE SPARE ROOM? CLICK HERE TO FIND YOUR MAGICAL SOLUTION! But still, it would have been nice…

Ah, he thought, as the toast popped up and without looking he rammed it back down again, *that way you end up like Hayley. One wave of a magic wand and everything is fantastic again. Even if the wand is waved by a lunatic and the solution is bollocks.*

He hated thinking of her that way, he really did. If there was a way of reaching inside him and cutting those thoughts out, he would. As the toast re-emerged and he got about the job of buttering, he wondered if it might not be an idea just to give in and join her. It was attractive, in its way, like those geeks who hung around in chatrooms and banged on about old football matches and rated ex-players out of ten and debated such important matters as whether the Arsenal team of 2006 could have beaten the Brazilian national side. *They're happy. Hayley's happy. I'm the miserable one. I'm the one in the minority, and at what point is it wrong to be in the minority?*

When the majority is mad, that's when. If the majority says there's a giant teapot in the sky when there plainly isn't, do you join in?

More heaviness, yet another sigh as he poured boiling water over the PG Tips. God, he hated this. Had he done the wrong thing in supporting her delusion? *Give a little, get a little,* that had been his line of reasoning. But the converse of that was *give 'em an inch and they'll take a yard.* Wasn't that what had happened here? Hadn't Hayley taken her yard? If not yet, then when? How far was too far? When did it cross the line? Where was the line? And did the whole of the ball have to cross it? Was there technology available to help?

Just four months ago I had none of these worries. In fact, I didn't have many worries at all bar is my job safe? Can I provide if it isn't? And now, oh God help us. God. Help us both.

But God offered no help then, so Graham took the tea and toast up to his wife, whom he still loved with all his heart and soul, but who was beginning to scare him.

Two

An hour later and she was gone, off to make people prettier. She'd left with a spring in her step – a skip, almost – and a long, lingering kiss that he could still feel on his lips, the sort of kiss that makes you forget about everything else that may be going on and drag the kisser to bed. But he couldn't do that, because she had to work, and he didn't.

Frustrated, he decided to clean the house, then shower, then vegetate in front of Sky Sports News and see who won what.

He polished the living room, hoovered, polished the kitchen table, wiped the worktops, hoovered, polished the banister, hoovered the stair carpet and landing, cleaned the bedroom, hoovered...but didn't touch the spare room. He paused before the closed door and...well, listened. *Madness,* he thought. *There's nothing to listen* for. A distant memory of a child calling goodnight, asking if he would play with doggy, a little girl calling him 'Daddy' came back to him, but he bit down hard, and it went away. Of course, he heard nothing, because there was nothing to hear. Laughing at himself, but still not opening the door to clean, he unplugged the Hoover and walked into the bedroom to pick out clean towels. Whilst there he 'made the bed'; or rather pulled the duvet into some kind of shape.

Which is when he saw it, poking out from under her pillow. A square of paper, folded.

Odd, he thought, then reached out his hand...and pulled it back. *It's the secrets we keep that glue us together*, his dad had said, less than a week ago. Here now was such a secret, hidden under his wife's sleeping head for...how long? No way of knowing. A secret thing, something she didn't want him to know about, something for her eyes only. *If she wanted me to know, she'd have shown it to me, not keep it under her pillow like...*

Like a kid. Yeah, that's what kids did, wasn't it? Keep their important things under pillows, so no one could steal them? Did adults do that? Did they?

Well, obviously. She's an adult and she's done it.

Ah, but she was an adult who was...not too well right now, wasn't she? Maybe *he* was the adult right now? After all, she needed taking care of, and he was the one to do that, that was something adults did. Something else adults did was sometimes act in their children's best interests, whether they liked it or not.

He reached out a hand, picked up the note, and read it. He read it six times in total and each time he did, he grew colder and colder. 'My God,' he said when he could speak. 'My God, what's this now? What's this now?'

But God was still keeping quiet.

Three

He made a coffee with three spoons of Nescafé and boiling water and sat in the kitchen, wishing fervently for an alcohol dependency problem so he could throw some whisky in it. *We are in very serious trouble,* he thought as he drank. *Worse trouble that I thought. This...oh God...*

He'd put the note back, hoping it was in the same place. But now he was wondering whether it was a good idea or not. Maybe he should retrieve it, confront her with it when she came home, some form of shock treatment. It was a depressing thought – but what wasn't a depressing thought these days? It was all too easy a scene to imagine, like one of those daytime true life dramas Hayley loved to watch on a Sunday afternoon. *But I have to do* something. *I can't ignore this. This is…huge.*

He looked at the clock. Nearly twelve. How time flew when you were living a life of lunacy. Almost six and a half hours before she came home and he had to deal. Time enough to formulate a plan. *Nearly twelve and still not dressed – my, what would the neighbours say?* Yeah, step one: get dressed. And stuff having a shower, Graham decided he was going to take a bath. A really long, hot bath. Maybe something would occur to him while he was soaking.

He downed the last of the mug in one, shuddered as the caffeine hit his nerves, and went upstairs.

Four

It was like a Turkish bath, or one of those old Sherlock Holmes films you saw late at night. He lay in the tub, saw nothing but steam, and thought *Watson! The game's afoot!*

Then he decided he was chasing his tail right now. This latest lunacy, piled upon all the others, had knocked him sideways. *No thinking, just a soak, just a relax, just a bath, just something to ease my bloody tense muscles, that's all.*

Thinking that, he closed his eyes and dozed. He remembered meeting Hayley at that party, the one he strictly speaking hadn't been invited to, back in the day when he and his mates would circle north London and listen out for the noise of revelry, knock on the door and say politely 'We met John at the pub, he said we could come, is that all right?' Oh, nine times out of ten they'd be told to fuck off and end up in the park drinking Special Brew (though never to excess, they were a cheeky crew but no more than that, never in trouble, none of them had even been spoken to by the coppers, they kept to themselves) but there was always that tenth time, that time the door would be opened and someone would say, 'OK then,' and invite them in.

Sure, there were risks, some people needed to be looked out for – like that exclusively male party they'd crashed back in…when? '01? The one where the men had eyed them like cattle, and they were no bigots, not him and his crew, but for all that they quite liked their arseholes the size they were, thank you very much, and they'd split at the speed of light. Or the time when the party had got out of hand and a fight was started and Graham's mate Tim had seen that guy pull the knife out and my God had they run…

Dozing in the tub, Graham smiled for the first time in a while. Why not? Good times, good mates…ah, he needed to contact them all. Properly, not just some rude, random message on a Facebook Timeline. Get them together, go down a boozer, sink a few, tell stories about the old days…

Like the time he'd met Hayley. Stunning of face and figure, and smiling in a friendly, open way as she chatted. Not a vapid *I'll smile at grass, me* way, or a calculated *look at me and how beautiful I am* kind of way, either. Just…smiling, smiling because she was happy, she was comfortable in that space, and oh boy did she make his heart beat. In the one crafty move of his life he'd positioned himself by the drinks, and waited. Sooner or later she'd come over, and then he'd introduce himself, and after a while, she had…

Dozing harder, he smiled wider.

Until the noise of the bathroom door closing disturbed him.

He sat up, wide awake now. Damn it, why had he run the bloody water so hot? He could hardly see anything, just steam, steam and more steam...but yes, he'd heard it. The *snick'd - clunk* of the bathroom door being pulled shut, the way it sounded the handle was just pulled, not turned.

Pulled. Or pushed.

Despite the heat in the room, Graham suddenly went cold. Pushed? Yes, because he'd left the door open, hadn't he? He always left the door open, they *always* left the door open, unless they were taking a dump. So that noise...which he had heard, had to be somebody pushing the door closed after they'd...after they'd...

Christ, I can't frigging see!

After they'd let themselves in.

Absurdly, he found himself thinking of that doll, the doll that had somehow made its way from the loft without him seeing it. Somewhere in his bathroom, that doll, moving in the mist, the steam, the fog he'd created, that old London pea-souper. In a second the steam would darken, and there it would be, that doll, that terrible, inhuman, blank-faced, evilly grinning *doll,* reaching out with its fake human hands, reaching, grabbing, strangling...

Strangling, or worse. He *was* naked after all.

He stood up and shot out of the water like a Polaris missile, grabbing for the towel rail, trying to look everywhere at once, panic-stricken, dragging breath in and out like an exhausted dog. *It's here, it's here, I can feel it, looking at me, hating me, wanting me dead, I can feel it...*

He pulled the towel from the rail and wrapped it around him, covering him. 'C'mon then,' he heard himself mutter. 'C'mon. C'mon!'

Nothing came at him for a full five minutes. Five minutes after *that*, still nothing came at him. Wary though, still wary, he reached behind him and opened the window, shivering as the brisk early March air hit his wet shoulders. Slowly, far *too* slowly, the steam dissipated.

Nothing came at him as, bar himself, the bathroom was empty. But the door was closed. Not just swung to, but closed. And if the noise he'd heard – that he was *sure* he'd heard - was right, it had been pushed shut. Pushed shut by something that could just about reach the handle, maybe, but not quite turn it.

Something about the height of...well, that doll.

In here. It was in here, looking at me while I was dozing, while I had my eyes shut, looking at me, grinning, plotting, waiting...

He actually punched himself, a right uppercut to the jaw. He had to stop that gibbering somehow. A galaxy exploded in front of him, he staggered, almost fell back into the bath, managed to steady himself in time.

No doll, he told himself. No doll. Because dolls don't walk. So there was no doll in here and SHUT UP I WILL NOT LISTEN!!! It didn't happen. Nothing happened. Nothing.

But just before that scared voice was shouted down – for now, at least – he heard it say, *who's maddest? Those who see the teapot in the sky or those who see it and deny it's there?*

Five

For all his bullet-headed rationality, Graham virtually ran from the bathroom to the bedroom and would not look away from the doorway as he dressed. Also, as he made his way downstairs, he decided he did not see the faintly damp footprints that made their way along the landing. The faintly damp small footprints. That led from the bathroom to the spare room.

He went downstairs and switched on the TV. He cranked the volume and watched as the results came in. And as they did, he felt better, because football was real.

Six

She's real, thought Hayley and she added the tiger stripes to a client's nails, a young girl who was 'out on the lash' with her mates that night and was desperately excited about all the things she was going to be doing and the shots she would down and the boys she would meet. *She's really* real.

Not that there'd been any doubt in her mind, not even before she'd felt that cuddle. She'd known the child was there, ever since Lillian had told her, and probably before, if truth be told. But now there was absolute, incontrovertible and absolute proof. There was a spirit in their house, her name was Angie, and she'd *got through,* she'd made *contact…*

And you hid her note. You bundled it under your pillow and didn't show Graham. Why?

Good question. She'd meant to show him, she'd had it in her hand ready, almost dancing with excitement. She couldn't wait to see his face as she presented him with…with…well, the evidence, the proof. She wanted to see his eyes grow wide, his mouth open; she wanted him to hold her, to embrace the truth…

And to rub his nose in it, be honest. Yes, there was that. She wanted to take the note – that precious piece of paper that an actual spirit had written on and not so much rub his nose in it but ram it down his fucking throat. It was a dismaying thought, but she wouldn't deny it. She had been right all along, and he'd been patronising, and now she had proof. So she stood in the hallway, reading and rereading those words and just before the key turned in the lock she put it away in her back pocket. Why? Well...just because. Just because it seemed like the thing to do, that's all. Just because...well, Angie was hers. Angie was shy with strangers, her behaviour with Elaine had proved that. Angie might not have wanted him to see it...after all, if she had, wouldn't that note have been addressed to him as well? So as he'd let himself in, she crammed the folded note into her back pocket, kissed him, asked if Elaine had got to the station OK, then said she was tired and was going to bed. In that bed she had read and reread the magic paper again and, as she'd heard his tread on the stairs, she'd tucked it under her pillow, close to her sleeping skull, as once she'd hidden love letters from teenage boyfriends.

No. Angie was hers, at least for the moment. When the time came, she would share, of course she would, Hayley Davis was not a selfish woman. When would that moment come? Well, that was for Angie to let her know. She'd ask, yes she'd ask, but if Angie didn't want it, it wouldn't happen. Hayley was building trust here, after all, and trust could be so easily broken.

So she did the nails and listened to the young girl prattle on, and counted the minutes until she could go home, never once considering that once she would have counted the minutes until she saw the living, but that now she was counting the minutes until she could commune with the dead.

Seven

Six o'clock couldn't come soon enough, but eventually it did. She practically ran out to the street, barely remembering to call a goodbye to Jodie over her shoulder. Of course, the bus was late, and of course it was drizzling, and of course she had forgotten her umbrella, so by the time she'd let herself in it was nearly seven and she was damp (though not in a good way) and ravenous and desperate to see if Angie had left her anything else.

'Gray,' she called, closing the front door.

'In here,' he called from the kitchen. Good, he'd made something for her to eat. She really couldn't be arsed cooking tonight. Tomorrow, they'd have a roast – and her roasts battered the *hell* out of her mother's – but right now, she wanted a bit of pampering, then a hot bath. Why not? She worked hard, she deserved it.

But as she entered the kitchen, she saw no evidence of cooking, smelled no smells, just saw her husband sat behind the table, a strained, pallid look on his face, and before him...

The note.

She felt slightly faint as she saw it. Then angry.

'What's this?' Graham asked her. No, not asked. *Accused.*

'Where did you get that?' she said, ignoring the question.

'It was under your pillow. I...'

'How *dare* you,' she snapped, hot blood in her cheeks. She ran forward and grabbed the note, clutched it to her chest. 'How *dare* you go rooting through my stuff!'

'I didn't go looking,' he said, trying to stay calm himself by the looks of it. She didn't care. Why *should* she care? 'I was tidying, making the bed; it was under the pillow...'

'Under *my* pillow! This is mine, Graham. She left it for me!' Then, briefly, she saw a way this could be turned from an argument, and she went for it. 'Don't you see what this means, though? It's proof, evidence, whatever you want to call it. There was nothing on the paper when Elaine was here – ask her, she'll tell you. But there was when she'd *gone!* It's real, don't you see? Real! You have to admit that now!'

Something danced in his eyes as she said that, not for the first time either. Something...what, shifty? Yes, that was the word. Like when she'd ask *did you have the last Twix* and he'd deny it, even though she'd known there was one in the fridge that morning and now there were none. Yes, shifty. Deceitful, even. 'Do I? Do I really?'

The anger was back now, roaring in her ears at his obtuseness. She felt like Galileo, trying to convince the Pope that the Earth revolved round the sun and not the other way round. 'Look at it,' she virtually ordered him. 'Look at it, Gray! You've got eyes, you've got a brain – use them! That is a note written by a little girl, a spirit – don't you understand what that means?'

He said nothing for a very long time, just stared at her, that shiftiness gone. After a minute, tears began to gather and roll down his cheeks. 'Babe,' he said at length. 'I think...aw God...I think you need to see someone. To talk to someone.'

'To who?' she asked, confusion mingling with her anger now. What was this? Why was he crying? 'Lillian, do you mean?'

'No. I don't mean her. I mean...' he gulped, wiped his eyes, and unable to look at her, said, 'a doctor. You need to see a doctor, babe. I thought...if I gave you this, oh I don't know, this delusion, this game, it would help you get over the miscarriage. But it's getting worse, and I can't...I don't know what to do. I mean, that...' he flapped his hand at the note she was holding close to her heart.

Hayley almost stopped breathing. For a second she was back in the hospital, being told her baby hadn't managed to even become a foetus, that she would have to pass it into a sanitary napkin, so sorry. Except this was worse. This was *Graham*, her lawfully wedded spouse, the man for whom she'd forsaken all others - and there'd been a *lot* of others – the man who was supposed to love and support her, for better or worse, in sickness...

Sickness, that was what he was saying. She was sick, mentally ill, a nutter, a total spacker as they'd said as kids. *My God. Damn him. Damn him, the bastard.* 'I'm going upstairs,' she said, icy, containing herself - just. 'I'm going to take a bath. Then I don't know what I'm going to do.'

He stood, moved quickly – almost ran – to her and grabbed her by the elbows. 'Hayles,' he said…no, begged. 'Don't ignore this, please. Sometimes we have to hear things we don't want to. But babe…'

'Take your hands off me,' she said, still contained, but the walls of her temper were flaking.

He didn't. 'Just listen, please. That note, that thing you have there.' He swallowed, heard a dry click. 'I think you wrote it.'

Eight

She didn't accept it. He saw that as soon as he spoke. *Of course she doesn't, she's too far into it. How could I not have seen how far into it she was? Or maybe I did see, and just didn't want to admit it?*

Yes, that's likely. There's been a lot of that recently, hasn't there?

He threw that thought aside; it wouldn't help what was happening right now. His wife was writing notes as if from a ghost, and that wasn't a sign that all her ducks were in a row, but he loved her, he wanted to help her, he wanted her to help herself.

'I said let me go,' Hayley repeated, and her voice was flat, final. He did, and stepped back. 'Like I said, I'm going for a bath. After that, I don't know.' She turned and he heard her make her way upstairs. After a while Graham sat down at the table and wondered what the hell to do next.

Nine

She soaked until she resembled a prune, and though she warmed she did not thaw. *I will not back down,* she thought, drying her hair, pulling on the towelling gown. *Not on this. Not when I know I'm right.*

But what to do about *him?* About what he believed? He thought her insane, how did you get beyond that? How did you reconcile after that? He was being willfully blind, she could offer him all the proof in the world and he'd just pretend not to see it. *Who are the mad?* she pondered, unconsciously echoing Graham's thoughts from earlier that day. *Those who accept what they see, or those who deny it's even there? Don't you see, Graham? You're the mad one, not me. It's you who needs help.*

She stopped outside the nursery, then opened the door, knowing full well he was sitting downstairs, listening, stacking it all up against her. *Fuck him,* she thought, and stepped inside, flicking on the light. She picked up the china-faced doll from by the door and cradled it. 'Hello Angie,' she said, her voice sad. 'Mummy's home. How're you? Did you have a good day? Did you?' She walked to the middle of the room and picked up the notebook. Nothing, blank pages throughout. She put it back on the floor, open, and rested the pen on top. She walked to the window and looked out onto the alley below. 'Did you play with all your toys? Or did you sit on the sill and watch to see if anything happened? Maybe you had a little sleep? Maybe you're still asleep now, and hearing me in a dream.' She laughed a little at that. Then sighed. 'Oh Angie. Oh my love. What am I to do? How am I to...' then she caught a hold of herself. 'I'm sorry, little one. Nothing to talk to you about, nothing to...'

She broke off. The doll in her arms...was it *trembling* slightly? The way a muscle might tremble sometimes?

Behind her, the sound of pages turning. Still the doll trembled. *The book,* she thought. *If I turn, I might see her...*

But she didn't turn. Angie was shy, after all. If she turned to look, she might run and hide. So she stared out of the window, felt that *thrumming* of the doll in her arms, and heard *scritch-scratch* as the pen ran across the page. *Come on, Graham,* she thought, bitterly. *Come on. Come on in* now. *Dismiss* this *as mental illness, will you? Or will you be too busy screaming, your hair standing on end?* That was a funny thought; she'd like him to look like that.

The doll stopped trembling, the noises behind her ceased, the house fell silent again. She carefully placed the doll on the floor and turned back to the notebook. On it was written

DON'T CRY MUMMY
ANGEE LUVS YOU
ANGEE MAKE HIM SEE
XXX

Ten

He looked up in dismay some time later as Hayley entered the living room. She had the spare duvet and a couple of pillows in her arm. He stood, utterly at a loss, trying to find a way to make this right, to make her see sense, and came up dry. 'Babe...' he started.

She held up a hand like a police officer on traffic duty. Halt. 'No. Let me speak.' Her voice was flat, but her eyes were still full of that unnatural energy. The combination was disconcerting. 'I don't want to be around you right now. I don't know why you said what you did.' He opened his mouth to interrupt but she spoke louder and faster, 'And right now I don't *want* to know. Maybe later, maybe when you've calmed down and are thinking better. But right now I'm tired, I don't want another argument, and I don't want to be around you.' She threw the bedding on the sofa. 'One or other of us is sleeping down here tonight. I don't care which.'

Four months, he thought again. *That's all it took, four months. On top of that, our first night alone, bar the time she was in hospital. And at least there was a reason, at least I physically couldn't be there. But this...here, in the same house...*

He sighed and admitted defeat. He didn't want another row, either. What was he, after all? A doctor? Counsellor? Psychiatrist? No, a draftsman, that's all. Plans, elevations and side views, that's all he understood. 'OK. If that's what you want, fine. I'll sleep down here.'

She nodded, as if that was what she'd been expecting. 'I'll say goodnight then.'

He didn't bother to tell her it was only eight o'clock. He didn't say anything. What would be the point? He just watched as Hayley left the room and climbed the stairs. Then he gathered his bedding together, sat down, and watched the TV without taking it in. Three hours later, halfway through *Match of the Day* he decided enough was enough, switched the set off, and made the best bed he could. Switching off the light, he settled down and pondered the future.

Eleven

Hayley wasn't hungry, though she should have been. She wasn't tired, though she should have been. She wasn't even angry anymore, though God knew she had reason enough for that. No, in truth she was elated.

She'd worked very, very hard at keeping that from Graham, now that she knew not only that he would *not* see, but that he didn't *want* to see. Part of her was saddened by that, but by far the greater part was thinking *ah, what the hell?* It was almost like when she was a teenager and had crushes on boys who wouldn't look at her twice. For a long time she'd virtually thrown herself at them, dancing before them, saying *look at this, look at me, I'm here, I'm here* until her friend Gill had taken her to one side and said something like, 'Leave it out, don't be desperate. If they want you, they'll find you. If they do, happy days. If they don't, what the hell? Whoever lost something they never had?'

Sound advice that was, but then Gill had been a sound sort of girl. And what had happened to her after sixth form? No idea. No real idea what had happened to any of them. Once, not long ago, that thought would have brought a slow, rolling wave of nostalgia, almost of panic as the realisation set in that it was true, she was ageing, that soon she'd wave bye-bye to her twenties the way she'd waved bye-bye to her teens, next stop middle age, mind the doors and the gap between the train and the platform.

But not now, not that Saturday night, because despite being apart from her husband, despite the fact he thought she was a raving nutter, she was elated.

She had Angie, after all. Angie, her baby. Who needed friends, who needed husbands, when you had a child? Hayley lay on her bed, hands locked behind her head, staring up at the ceiling, and smiled. It was a very beautiful, peaceful smile. Maybe Graham would come round and see the truth. Maybe he wouldn't. She found she didn't really care. A part of her, a small but growing part, didn't mind if he *never* saw the truth. That way, Angie would be hers and hers alone, for ever and ever and ever.

Twelve

Graham came awake in the dark, utterly confused and disoriented. Why was the bed so narrow? Why did his neck hurt? Where was…?

Of course. Hayley was upstairs. And he was on the sofa, alone, because she just wouldn't see the truth. He settled back and made himself as comfortable as he could, which wasn't very. It was disconcerting sleeping in a room where the traffic sometimes rattled the windows and it was downright criminal to be sleeping on a sofa when there was a big bloody double bed about twelve feet from his head.

He banged his head on the pillow, rolled onto his left, snorted, then rolled onto his right, snorted again, then rolled onto his back. God alone knew what time it was and he didn't want to pick his watch off the coffee table to find out. It was bad enough being awake when he should have been able to reach out and cop a feel of his sleeping wife's backside without knowing exactly *when* he couldn't reach out and cop a feel of his sleeping wife's backside.

Is this my life then? Is this our *life now?*

He banged that thought on the head and sat on it. The middle of the night was no time to think such things. The middle of the night was the worst time to think anything serious. The middle of the night was for sex dreams or dreams where you scored the winner in the World Cup Final despite having only just returned from a career threatening broken leg or dreams where you cut the ribbon at that hotel complex you'd designed in Shanghai, the one the world's press had declared the Eighth Wonder of the World. The *worst* thing you could do in the middle of the night was count your problems as you listened to the two of you breathing. Yeah, because night worries never hit both people at the same time. Whoever you were with would be laying there, giving it the old sleep-breath, all heavy and slightly snotty, a bit grunty, like a pig – oh, and that occasional pause just long enough for you to think they'd died until they exhaled for a million years – yeah, that was the way of it, one awake, one sleeping, breathing...

Except he was alone. So who the fuck was *breathing in his left ear?*

He turned sharply, and oh dear Lord, he was eye level with the doll. Its glass eyes glittered in the dark (like Hayley's, he thought in panic), and that wretched grin seemed wider, broader...and did it have teeth, fucking *teeth?*

Didn't matter, because it was reaching for him, actually had its arms out, and was coming closer, walking, the damned thing was *walking*...and those tiny plastic hands were flexing, flexing, like the mouths of Venus flytraps.

'Daddy,' it said, in a little girl's voice, a dead voice, and he hitched in his breath to scream, but the doll wasn't walking anymore, that fucking thing was *running*, running at *him*.

He flung the duvet back, almost got his feet caught, and half stumbled onto the floor. He rolled, stood, and ran to the door...but he didn't open it. He flicked on the light, turned back to the room, keeping flat against the wall, and saw it.

It lay flat on the floor.

But it came at you. Arms out. It came at you, to strangle you. To kill you.

He waited for some other voice to shout it down, to call it preposterous...but none did, because his hammering heart and the taste of coppery fear in his mouth weren't to be denied. Sometimes, no matter how insane it was, you had to see the teapot circling the sun.

No dream, no pretending you didn't see the damp footprints, no editing hearing that voice from the loft...*yeah, OK Hayley, guess what? You were right. Here come da ghost. But you're wrong, 'cause this ain't no ghost of a little kid.*

This fucker's out for blood.

He did not sleep again that night. He stood there till the sun came up, never taking his eyes off the doll.

Chapter Twelve

One

'Why lie?' Hayley asked him, hours later, exasperatingly calm. 'Why would you do that?'

Graham gaped at her. They were sat in the kitchen, neither of them dressed, one with coffee and one with tea, the doll on the table. He'd managed to reach across and pick it up as he'd heard Hayley make her way downstairs. Just touching its awful, warm plastic arm had revolted him, but he'd managed it. He'd followed her into the kitchen, saw her eyes widen in surprise at what he was carrying and had made her listen to him. He may not have made the best job of telling her what had happened – he was no raconteur – and he wasn't sure he'd quite made it clear just how terrifying the whole thing had been, how insane...but for her to accuse him of simply making it up...

'Don't you want me to be happy?' She went on. 'Why wouldn't you want that? Why do you want to take it off me? First you say I'm mad, that I'm making it all up, and you say...' she looked at the doll, laughed, then back at him. With contempt. 'That this tried to kill you.'

'Hayles,' he stuttered. 'Listen...'

'No, *you* listen,' she interrupted, still smiling that awful, contemptuous smile, 'listen to how insane you sound.' She picked up the doll. She waggled it around. 'This is a thing. It doesn't move. It can't move.'

'Then how was it in the living room?' he said, playing his trump card. 'I didn't bring it down. Did you?'

She stopped, that smile dropping from her face – then, 'Maybe it was Angie. Yes. She said...' Then she stopped again, almost biting her bottom lip.

'Go on.'

'She said she'd make you see,' she continued, but slowly. 'She wrote me another note. I was in the room this time, I heard it. It said "Don't worry Mu...don't worry, I'll make him see".'

What was that word she stopped herself saying? Mum? Mummy? What is this?

'So maybe she took the doll down to show you,' Hayley continued. 'To prove to you that she was real.'

'And then...what? Decides to kill me for a giggle?'

Hayley laughed openly at him, a hard, brittle laugh, and for an awful moment Graham wanted to slap her, to bring her round. 'She's a little girl, Graham. A lost and lonely little girl who's just found a family. She wouldn't harm a fly.'

'But she's *not* a little girl, is she?' said Graham, his temper snapping. 'She's a *ghost*, isn't she? OK right, so she wanted to make me see, wanted to make me believe, well, guess what? *It worked!* You were right, I was wrong, *there's a ghost here!*' Even as he almost shouted this, he was aware of the lunacy of it. But it could no longer be denied. The time for taking the blinkers off had arrived. 'But Hayley...she's...it's...' he ran out of words then, couldn't bring himself to say what he wanted to say.

But she made him. 'She's what?'

'Evil,' he said, and looked away from her.

Once more, that harsh laugh. Once more, he wanted to smack her. 'Evil?' She asked, when she'd calmed down. 'Of course, yes. Why didn't I see it? Why am I so stupid?' Horrifyingly, she turned the doll to her, and spoke to it. 'You're evil, I can see it in every freckle on your face! What's that, Angie? You want me to kill everyone?' She dropped the doll on the table. 'Ooooooooh, I'm possessed, I'm that little girl from *The Exorcist*. "Your mother sucks cocks in hell, let Jesus..."'

'*SHUT THE FUCK UP,*' he screamed at her, standing. He just about managed to stay where was. If he'd moved it would have been dangerous. It didn't matter anyway. She looked at him as if he had slapped her. 'OK, I'm sorry,' he continued, although...*was* he? Was he *really?* 'Don't you see? I agree with you here. There *is* something in this house. Maybe it's even a ghost. I don't know. I don't know what it is. But I do know it's...wrong. There's a bad vibe about it. We...we have to find a way of getting rid of it.'

That was exactly the wrong thing to say. Or maybe in a situation like this there was no right thing to say. Hayley stood, faced him down. 'Over my dead body,' she said. Then, even more chillingly, 'I've lost one child this year. I will not lose another.'

Oh thanks, God, I needed something else to mess with my head. 'Hayley...this isn't your child,' he said, and the astonishment that had replaced his anger made him talk to her as if she was a child herself. 'This isn't *anyone's* child.'

'She's mine if I want her to be,' she said, with the finality of a door closing. 'And I do. I want her to be mine until she can move on, to the other life. That's what any mother would want.'

He made one final try. 'You're not her mother.'

She smiled. 'I am. If I want to be, I am.'

Two

Graham felt the slide of reality in his head. 'I need you to listen to me,' he said, controlled. 'Please. We have to go. We have to leave this house.'

'No.'

'Hayley, I'm begging you. If we stay…something bad will happen.'

'If we *leave*, something bad will happen. Angie will be all alone. Would you abandon a child? You're many things, Graham, but I didn't think you were cruel. Until recently. I think I can make a counter proposal.'

'Which is?'

'You leave. At least for a while. You're not happy here, so why stay? I'm going nowhere. I'm staying with Angie, with my daughter. You go. Pack up and leave, come back when you've accepted the situation, don't come back if you don't. What do you say?'

The strength ran out of him, the world swam into ugly grey dots. He grabbed the table and lowered himself into the chair. *It's me or her…and she's picked* her. *No. No, I will not accept this!* 'You can't…I won't…'

'Stay then, and put up with us.' That brittle laugh again. '*Put up* with us! *That's* the foundation for a strong, happy marriage, isn't it?' She leaned in, close. 'You get it? You have to change, or you leave.'

He looked up at her, her bobbed hair, cornflower blue eyes...the woman he loved...and didn't recognise her. He didn't see her anywhere. *What do I do? How can I walk out and leave her with...that? How can I stay? But at least, if I'm here, I can keep an eye out, protect her.*

Oh yeah? Against that? And what about Hayley, or the madwoman who's replaced her? What do you do there? Don't you see, you've got two choices here, and they're both awful. He looked from Hayley to the doll, sprawled across the table, and wanted to beat its disgusting face to a pulp. Impossible. Impossible that it had somehow come to life and attacked him. Utterly ridiculous. Didn't happen.

But it had. And if it had happened once, it would happen again. Until it succeeded... succeeded in...*killing* him?

Fuck this and fuck that, this isn't Chucky XX: Chucky Does Tranny. It's a Christing doll, and even if it comes at you in the night you can kick that bastard across the room and stomp it to pieces and Jesus Christ WHAT AM I THINKING?

He put his hands to his head and moaned. Maybe he'd just gone mad. That was a nice, comforting thought, and the *fact* it was so comforting scared him a little. How bad did things have to be before madness seemed the good choice?

But he was married, a married man. No matter what, he was married. Whoever stood before him looking like his wife, he'd made vows, vows before God. He wouldn't walk out. He wouldn't leave her to this...whatever...on her own.

'OK,' he said eventually. 'I'll stay. Whatever you want, I'll stay.'

A terrible smile of triumph split her face. 'Good! Now that we're sorted, you want some breakfast? I don't know about you, but I'm Hank Marvin.'

Once, back in the day, after an argument was resolved they'd have kissed, cuddled, maybe even got right down to the horizontal bop there and then. But this time they didn't even touch. 'No, not for me,' he said. 'There is one thing I'd like to ask though. If you would.'

'Oh yeah? What?' The words were pleasantly enough delivered, but her eyes...narrowed, watchful.

He jerked his thumb at the doll. 'That thing. Could we...y'know, get rid of it? We could get her...get *Angie* another, if you...if she'd like. But that one...' He couldn't go on.

'Oh, sure,' she said, turning to the fridge, from where she pulled rashers of bacon and slammed them on the worktop. 'I'm not sure she even likes that anyway. She never plays with it.'

Three

The smell of the cooking bacon hit him five minutes later, and he bolted from the kitchen and pounded up the stairs two at a time. No time for the toilet, he offloaded a thick stream of bile into the basin instead. He broke down into shivers and groaned helplessly. *What do I do? What do I do? What do I do?*

Four

Hayley listened to him, and smiled indulgently. *There, there,* she thought. *He'll be better for bringing it all up.* 'Boys are silly,' she said – well, whispered – to the kitchen. Well, you never knew. Angie might be there. Even if she wasn't, she might be able to hear her. 'Be glad you're not a boy. They've got wired wrong at the factory.' There! Was that a giggle? Faint, stifled – but audible? *Angie's* giggle? 'They get up and down all mixed up in their tiny little heads. Sometimes,' she went on, flipping the bacon over, no longer whispering, now speaking almost normally, 'sometimes we have to be a little sharp with them. Don't get me wrong, they have their uses...but oh, they can be so stupid.' She pulled some bread out of the cupboard and retrieved some butter from the fridge. 'But it's OK now; we've made him see sense. Everything will be OK now.'

Something rustled behind her, and she turned sharply, hoping to see Angie. But there was nothing, only the doll on the table, and that certainly hadn't moved. That was gibberish. It hadn't moved a bit. Not one centimetre.

Five

It had, of course.

Six

Somehow, they passed the rest of the day together. God alone knew how, but they did. The distance between them never lessened, the silences between sentences didn't shorten, their conversation flowed like treacle, but they somehow passed the day. At around four in the afternoon, Hayley picked up the doll from the kitchen table and theatrically dropped it into a bin bag. 'There,' she said to Graham. 'All gone.' She made a huge point of striding to the wheelie bin and made damn sure he saw her throw the thing inside. She returned to the living room, wiping her hands. 'Another job done.'

Of course, she spent a hell of a lot of the day in the spare room talking to...whatever...but it kept her happy, and Graham said nothing. For his own part he hardly left the sofa, staring at a TV screen that meant absolutely nothing to him whatsoever, trying to keep his mind from falling apart.

We've a ghost, he thought. *Upstairs. And it's not Casper, unless Casper's had a radial personality change. This isn't fun, it's not good, it's not nice and it's somehow...well,* changed *her? Altered Hayley's personality, warped it, so she can't see just how dangerous it is. Or is it like Bruno?*

Bruno had been a German Shepherd owned by a previous girlfriend, Amy. Bruno had loved Amy. Bruno followed Amy everywhere and wagged its tail whenever she spoke. According to Amy, Bruno was just the *cutest* little doggie, yes he was, yes he *was*. Yet, cute or not, Bruno fucking *hated* anyone who came near Amy. Graham had only to put his arm near her and that bastard would prop up onto his hind legs and growl, huge, nasty brown eyes fixed on his, tongue lolling, foam dripping. 'Oh, he's just protective of his Mummy,' Amy would say, giving the sodding thing a cuddle, as Bruno looked him in the eye and sent *touch her and I'll rip your throat out and lap the blood and wag my tail while I'm doing it. Got me?*

It wasn't a relationship that lasted long, suffice to say. But...suppose, once you accepted the fact there was a ghost in the spare room, then why was it *one* thing to her and another to *him*? Could it actually *be* like Bruno, hyper protective and territorial? He mulled that one over as, unseen, Antiques Roadshow gave way to Songs of Praise. Suppose that this...girl...had misread Graham's scepticism as outright hostility, even aggression? Would it not be logical for it to react in some protective way towards Hayley?

Logical? Logical? *You're (a) sat watching* Songs of Praise *without turning over and (b) thinking over a problem that appears to involve a ghost and you're using the word* logical? *Listen to yourself! Regardless of how the bloody doll made its way down the stairs and attacked you, regardless of its bloody motivations*, it still happened! *You* can't *attack a problem like this with logic! What you do is get the hell out of there, pack up and go. Knock her out and carry her if you have to. But your sodding house is haunted, you arse! And even if you want to go down the 'protective dog' route – which you shouldn't – what do you do with a dog when it attacks someone? You get it bloody well put down!*

He shifted in his chair, briefly took in a choir of extremely well dressed middle-class people singing about how brilliant God was, then slunk back into his thoughts. *So...I got me two choices, am I right? Bodily drag my wife from the house or attack the damn spook with bell, book and candle?*

Pretty much.

On TV, the well dressed people told him God had made their pretty colours, not to mention their tiny wings. *No, I've got a third choice. I can wait, see what happens now I've accepted what's going on. Maybe it'll all settle down. Maybe Hayley will return to normal. Maybe we'll learn to live with it, the way you learn to live with a boiler that doesn't heat your water properly but goes 'boink' in the middle of the night?*

Yeah, that seemed a plan. Well, no, it wasn't a plan, but it was the closest he could come up with. Wait and see. Like Jim Henson's plan. Which hadn't worked so well for him, had it?

Chapter Thirteen

One

Wednesday of the following week saw Graham called into the boss's office. 'You wanted to see me, Mr Maitland?'

Maitland, who could have done with including the phrase *no thank you, I'm full* into his vocabulary, sat back in his lovely, comfy swivel chair and actually tented his fingers. Graham didn't think he'd seen anyone do that before outside of *The Simpsons*. He nodded to the chair opposite and Graham sat, understanding this was not going to be the news that he'd won a fortnight's all expenses trip to Los Angeles and a night in bed with Scarlett Johansson. 'I've been looking over the quality of your work for the past month,' Maitland said, with a fine absence of preamble. 'It's deteriorated badly. In fact the plans you drew up for the Costco development in East Ham I've had to hand over to that young Scouse lad to finish.'

'Danny,' said Graham. Maitland stared at him, uncomprehending. 'Daniel Highsmith,' Graham explained. 'That's the Scouse lad's name.'

Maitland didn't even bother to acknowledge what he'd said. 'You've been with us...four years?'

'More or less.'

'And you've shown promise. Or you did, anyway. We thought reasonably highly of your work. Everything to time and to the clients' specs. But over the last month, it's all gone to shit. I understand you're married?'

'Yes.' He supposed he was expected to be fazed by this change of direction. He wasn't.

'Any kids?'

None who ain't see-through. 'No.'

'But a wife. And a house, a mortgage?'

'Two for two.'

Maitland sat forward, a spark of anger in his deep set round eyes. 'Are you taking this seriously?'

'Yes.' He almost added sir, but didn't. Partly because it might sound insolent, mostly because he didn't want to.

'Good. See that you are. Because the harsh truth is this, Davis – I could spit from this window and hit five draftsmen who are every bit as good as you and two more that are better. Got me? You are not irreplaceable. I can pick up someone with your talents at the local Art School and set him to work at *half* what I'm paying you. And if I do, how do you go on paying your mortgage? How do you explain it to your Building Society? Or your wife? What do you say to her when you're living in a cardboard box under the railway arches?'

To be honest, I think we could get by on her wages and opening up the house to the public. Fifty quid a pop to see the ghost. Then I'd come back here, buy this place, and swap our desks and see how you sodding like it, fatty. But he kept quiet.

Maitland grunted and pulled a letter from his in-tray. He flopped it across the desk at Graham, who made no attempt to pick it up. 'In accordance with our disciplinary procedure I must inform you I'm issuing you with a written formal warning about the quality of your work. Please sign to say you've received it and return it to me within twenty-four hours. I've also written in there that I expect your work to improve immediately and to that end I shall be reviewing your work at the end of every day for a month. Is all that clear?'

'Quite clear,' said Graham, and stood, taking the paper with him.

Once in the corridor, the door closed behind him, he saw a very upset Danny prowling around by the Klix machine. 'Eh mate,' he said. 'I'm sorry. I wanned to give y' the heads-up, like, but he said if I did he'd fuckin' suspend me. Y'arright?'

'Trust me,' said Graham, 'that didn't scare me.'

'Look,' the younger lad went on, 'if y' need 'elp with anythin'…'

Graham pulled in a deep breath. 'You'll be the first I call, trust me. And thanks mate. Don't worry about it.'

Danny hesitated, smiled, then pottered back to his desk. Graham stayed a second longer. *That didn't scare me,* he'd said, and for a second – well, the whole time he'd been in the room – that'd been true. But out here, leaning against Maitland's door, well that was a whole different story. Lose his job and the house would go, no two ways. Hayley didn't do badly, but her wage alone wouldn't cut it. If he got another job with another company – which wouldn't be easy without references – there'd be no guarantee he'd be on anywhere *near* the salary he was on now.

Four months ago, he thought yet again. *Just four months ago. If I'd gone back home with this news just four months ago, I reckon Hayley would have been upset, sure, but would have simply said, 'Oh well, if it comes to it my mum will take us in. Or your parents. Or maybe even Elaine. Something'll work out.'* But now? Oh now, that house, that room, that child were her obsessions. She'd been prepared to separate before giving that up. If he went back tonight and handed over this letter she'd probably accuse him of doing it deliberately so they'd have to lose the place, so she'd have to give up...Angie.

OK, it was quieter now, there was that. No madness with dolls. No nightmares or scary noises. But she still went into that room three or four times a night and *spoke* to the bastard thing! Yes, it had settled...but it was still mad. Sometimes he wondered if she ever left the house at all, if she ever actually went to work, and yesterday he'd had to stop himself from taking the Tube a stop or two just to walk past the shop and make sure...but stop himself he had.

After all, she was happy. Yeah, talked to an empty room, but she was happy. And it *had* gone quiet. And to keep all these ducks in a row he had to straighten up and fly right and get his mind back on the job.

Only four months.

Two

Hayley, unlike her husband, wasn't screwing up at work, but she *was* having a hard time keeping her concentration. Hardly surprising, really, considering. In fact, she was enormously proud of the fact her work wasn't suffering, proud of the fact that the only comments were positive ones, proud of the way Jodie had told her that she was a joy to work with these days, that her positive attitude and brilliant smile were brightening the place even on the darkest days. In fact, if she didn't know better, Hayley might have begun to suspect her boss might have started boarding the other bus.

Oh, but the world was wonderful these days. Better than she could ever have expected. Even Graham seemed to have come round. OK, so he didn't join in, and he was a little quiet, but at least he appeared to accept and understand Angie. He'd at least dropped his objections. And as for that crap about the doll! What an idiot, really! As if Angie would hurt him, as if she'd hurt *anyone*. Angie was the loveliest little thing, perfect and special. Most likely she'd taken the doll to show him – she had said in that note that she would make him see after all – and he'd been having a nightmare and got the two mixed up. Easy.

Oh, the notes...more and more, sometimes two a day. Little things, but oh how they touched her heart. 'What did you do today?' she'd ask the room, facing the window, making sure she didn't look at the paper, and that *scritch-scratch* sound would come, and there would be written something like PLAYED WITH DOGGY or HAD A SLEEP or WAITED FOR YOU COZ LUV YOU MUMMY. To see such things, to read such things, to *hold* such things, things that came to her from beyond this world...oh, they made her feel...made her feel...

Blessed. That's how they made her feel. *Blessed.* Out of all the people in the world, all those millions, all those *billions,* she and *she alone* had been picked out, pointed at, chosen to receive such a magical gift. She was like that young girl in Fatima, the one who'd seen the Virgin Mary. *I am special, I am blessed, I have been chosen,* she would feel as she picked these notes up and read them with tears of joy in her eyes. *Thank You, God,* she'd think. *Thank You for making my sorrow turn into joy.*

She'd started to think about going back to Church - then again, if God was everywhere, she reasoned, why bother? God knew what was in her heart and her soul, and God had probably sent Angie to her, so God almost certainly knew how she felt, so why bother with the trip? Why not just, before falling asleep, think a little thank you to the Big Guy in the Clouds? Surely He'd get the message. He was God, after all.

So she didn't go to Church, and she did go into work, and when she came home she spent time with her daughter and her husband, and to Hayley life had never been better.

Three

She let herself in at six and made straight for the nursery without taking her coat off. 'Hello darling,' she said, opening the door. 'Mummy's home. How're you?' She walked to the window and looked out. 'Did you have a good day? Get up to anything exciting? I hope you were good – oh, what am I saying, of course you were good, you're *always* good, what a silly Mummy I am!'

Scritch-scratch went the pen across the page behind her. Oh, the temptation to turn, to see Angie bent over, the pen probably clenched in her fist as she dragged the pen across the page. Frowning slightly, concentrating, making sure she did her best writing, trying to impress. But Hayley stayed looking down at the alley. Maybe one day – hopefully soon – Angie would be able to write while she was looking – maybe one day she wouldn't have to write at all, maybe one day, she'd speak, and oh – what a day *that* would be!

The sound stopped. She gave it a couple of seconds and turned...and was there something, by the door? A faint shape? A sort of shadow that wasn't actually a shadow, a kind've shadow in negative if such a thing was possible? An almost-mist, maybe two foot tall, sort of a smudgy rectangle shape? If there was – and she wasn't sure – it was gone in a second. Maybe it was only wishful thinking, but her heart sped up all the same. *She's on her way*, she found herself thinking.

But still, there was a note to be read before anything else. Hayley crossed to the book and picked it up. HE WILL BE LATE, it said. 'Who will?' she asked. 'Graham?' No answer from the room, but at that second her Samsung bleeped. She flipped the cover and read GRAHAM MOBILE CALLING, hit the green button and said, 'Hi.'

'Hi,' he said. 'Sorry, but I'm going to be stuck here for a while. There's...well, bit of a work crisis.'

'OK,' she said, looking at the paper in her left hand. *There's my clever girl.* 'What time do you reckon?'

'With luck, half eight. With no luck, half nine. There's a fair bit fucked up,' he said, and gave a harsh, almost bitter laugh she didn't care for *at all,* 'and God alone knows how long it'll take to unfuck it.'

'No problem, what will you do for dinner?'

'Might pick up something on the way back. Probably will. A sandwich or something.'

'OK then, see you later.' She hit the cut-off button and put the phone back in her pocket. 'You're right, he will be! Still, more time for us, eh? Let me take my coat off and get something to eat, then I'll come back up and see you. Love you Angie.'

At no time did she think it was odd that during the conversation with her husband they'd exchanged no terms of endearment, that she wasn't disappointed he'd be late, or that neither of them had said 'I love you.' Nor did she think it odd that she had said 'love you' to a ghost.

Instead, all she wondered as she made her way downstairs was *I wonder if she'd like a game or something? Snakes and ladders, that's easy. I could teach her that.*

Four

For the fifteenth time that day, Elaine picked up her phone, scrolled to Hayley's number...then put it down again, totally unsure of what to say. Yes, she could have just rung and chatted about nothing, the way she would every so often, but the things that had happened on the previous Friday seemed too heavy for her to ignore, and too heavy for her to acknowledge.

So she did nothing, just worried. She thought of calling Graham, finding out from him, but somehow that seemed like a betrayal, as if she was going behind Hayley's back. *I mean, if things went really tits up, he'd call me, wouldn't he? Surely he would. So...shall I just assume that no news is good news? I mean, yeah, – sooner or later I'll call, or just knock round. But...*

But she was scared; yes that was the top and bottom of it. Scared of the look on Hayley's face, that awful glitter in her eyes. Scared of what might be happening. So if Elaine didn't look, she wouldn't see. Cowardly, maybe. But that's how life was, get used to it.

Five

It was a bad night for the dead to clam up, but clam up they had, and Lillian was beginning to sweat a little.

There she was, playing a big gig in Ealing – four hundred paying customers crammed into that Little Theatre – all hanging on her every word, all desperate, eyes bright and mouths open, and there was nothing from the other side at all. It was a tricks night, a night of narrowing the field, taking random shots into the dark and seeing what hit, and it only took one wrong turn, one bad call and her reputation could be finished. Or worse, finding someone who was only *pretending* to play along only to denounce her. 'Yeah, saw that Lillian Manning. Shit. I pretended she was getting it all right, like they did to that fella off *Most Haunted,* then I shouted "Ha bitch! I never had no Uncle Peter who had a funny walk! Lying cow!"'

But still…they'd paid for a show, so she had to give them a show. But Jesus this was scary.

She faced them all, all those white faces in the black, and said 'Who here...oh, this is very strong...who here recently lost a woman, an elderly woman...she's all bundled up against the cold, oh, she says she *hates* the cold. What's that, dear? Oh, and the heat. Yes,' back to the audience, and there were waving hands everywhere, *pick me, pick me.* 'Yes, too cold in winter, too hot in summer – oh, she could be a trial! White hair, bouffant? Does that sound like anyone?'

Some hands went down, not many. There was an old man in the front room who looked a bit wet-eyed. He would do. 'Was it your wife, dear?' He nodded. Lillian put her head to one side, as if listening. 'What's that, dear? No, you can see for yourself he hasn't. Oh, please speak up...yes,' back to the old man, 'she says you should have worn your scarf on a night like this. Quite strident, she is.' The old man smiled and nodded, wiped his eyes with the heel of his right hand. 'I don't like to say this,' said Lillian, dropping her voice (but making sure she could be heard. She'd taken Drama classes back in the nineties, she knew projection), 'but she could be a little bit of a nag, couldn't she?' A fresh fall of tears from the old man, but he nodded, smiling. Did she feel guilty? A little. But there were those bills to pay, after all. And she quite fancied Antigua this year. Maybe for a fortnight. Meet some young bartender with tight bum cheeks and a package like a Cumberland sausage. Or if not a man, a woman. Lillian was happy either way. Could happen. 'Well she says...her name's, oh speak up dear? Begins with...oh, come on, you're not backward about coming forward, tell me your name,' she kept her eyes on the old man, and without knowing it he said the name *Enid* to himself. An easy one to pick up. The plosive names could be the worst. She'd had a horrible time in Hatfield once, trying to read *Philomena*. 'Begins with an E...Edna – no, oh speak up love, no need to be shy. *Enid!* Thank you, Enid. Yes,' she went on, the poor old man weeping openly, 'I'll tell him, yes. You, sir, need to wrap up warm in this weather. Remember, she's watching over you, wants you to be well. And – yes? Oh, she says find something better to do with your day! What does that mean, sir?' *Please God they don't notice I haven't got a clue what this man's name is.*

'I like bowls,' the old man said.

'You like bowls,' she repeated, louder. 'Oooh, she's shaking her head! Says what a waste that is! But what's that, dear? Yes. She says, despite it all, she loves you, she misses you, and she'll be waiting for you. Aw, bless her heart.'

The old man put his head in his hands and wept, and the people he was with comforted him, and the audience collectively *ahhh'd.* A quick glance at the clock at the back of the auditorium told her it was nearly nine, almost interval time. They'd down a couple of pints or a sherry or two and come back slightly less focused for the second half. Alcohol always made the second half run smoother. 'Now then, what's this I see,' she started to say, looking about her, making judgements, seeing who looked the likeliest, when – finally - the other side came through in style.

In the aisle was a child that wasn't a child. It was maybe two foot tall and wearing what looked like a long white nightgown. But it had the head of a pig. Its wet snout flexed and contracted. Droplets of moisture ran from the nostrils and fell on the steps with a wet slap. It snuffled and grunted at her, tiny evil eyes fixed on hers. It pointed an arm that ended in a dirty trotter at her and it grunted louder, a one-two-three snuffling, awful sound that seemed to mock her.

Lillian Manning felt terror in her soul. She stopped speaking, her eyes bugging. The audience leaned forward expectantly, but she couldn't see them. All she could see was this thing, this homunculus, pointing that dreadful 'hand' at her, pointing and jeering, pointing and laughing, pointing because it had...it had...

Fooled her, somehow.

Her heart stopped, and she clutched a hand to her breast, pounding, trying to beat life back into it. But that sensation, burning from it...*you're not the only one with tricks,* it said. *My master taught me tricks you know* nothing *about, you stupid cunt!*

Snuffling, louder snuffling, almost a guffaw of snuffling damp sounds, and then it threw back its head and *squealed,* the loudest, most appalling pig squeal ever, a sound of triumph, and it was gone, didn't fade away, was just gone, and a second later so was Lillian, gone into the dark.

Six

She came around briefly in the dressing room, surrounded by paramedics. There was a plastic mask on her face and the hissing of an oxygen cylinder. Two men were above her, clad in green. 'Lillian,' one was saying. 'Can you hear me? Make a sign if you can hear me love.' She managed a small nod. 'OK Lillian, we're going to get you to hospital. Little ride in an ambulance. Y'ever been in an ambulance, Lillian?' She shook her head slightly. 'Well, today's the day. We're just gonna roll you onto the stretcher, won't hurt a bit I promise.'

Behind them, the pig thing walked into the room, and laughed its horrible, animal laugh. Lillian blacked out again.

Seven

At ten past nine Graham let himself in, almost exhausted, his eyes stinging from the amount of time he'd been staring at that bloody Mac. Maitland had been right, as much as it hurt him to admit it. With Danny's help (up until seven, anyway) Graham had gone through his last month's output and saw that it did, indeed, suck the hairy root. They'd mostly repaired the damage, and then Graham had quadruple checked the work he'd done that day and made damn sure they're wasn't a line out of true, that all the angles added up, that the stress calculations were one hundred percent accurate. The thought of continuing like that for a while was depressing, but less depressing than the thought of living on the street, even less depressing than…

Well, the thought of coming home at all.

Yeah, that was true enough. Unpalatable, but true. This place, these four walls, once his haven and his refuge, once the place where peace reigned and love found in the warm thighs of his woman, wasn't a place he really wanted to be in just right now. No fun at work, no fun at home, no fun anywhere. *So this is what the Yanks mean by a rock and a hard place. Often wondered.*

'That you, Graham?' Hayley called from upstairs. From the spare room.

'Yeah,' he said, hanging his coat up. 'Sorry, should have rung ahead, give you time to get Johnny Depp out the back.'

Once that would have got a laugh. Or at the very least an acknowledgement. Now Hayley just skipped down the stairs sparing him nary a glance. Certainly no hug or kiss. 'Did you eat?'

'No.' He dragged his feet into the living room. 'I've gone past it, I reckon.'

'Oh, don't be silly. I'll make you something.' More skipping into the kitchen. 'Sandwich do you? Got that bacon to use up. Or,' bit of a pause, the sound of things being moved around in the fridge, 'or nothing, really. Just the bacon. That OK?'

'Yeah, that'd be great. Thank you.' He wasn't the remotest bit hungry, but he didn't feel like a discussion on anything right now. Right now he wanted to sink into the sofa for an hour or two, then go to bed. Besides, right now his tactic was agreeing with everything she said.

He settled back, closed his eyes, listened as the faint sound of the grill pan banging up and down faded and there was nothing but the world outside, the occasional car, the blue strobing light of an emergency vehicle, the *tak-tak-scrape-tak* of a young woman (or man, this *was* Crouch End after all), dragging their high heels along the pavement, Hayley's snuffling, snorting, slobbering hot breath on his face...

But Hayley's in the kitchen.

His eyes sprang open, and there, perched on the arm of the sofa was that fucking *doll*, nose to nose with him, grinning, grunting, *breathing*.

'*JESUS,*' he screamed, and lashed out. He hit the thing square in the chest and it flew across the room, hitting the wall. Graham tried to stand, but his knees betrayed him as he saw the doll scamper to its feet, like a spider, and glare at him.

Then, horribly, it winked.

In that hideously co-ordinated way the bastard thing scuttled to the open door, and he heard its footsteps pound up the stairs. He dragged a ragged, whistling breath in, and was suddenly beset with the shakes.

'What the hell,' said Hayley, running in from the kitchen. 'Graham? What's happened?'

He couldn't speak, he just curled up, shaking, his eyes screwed shut, the way he once had when he was a kid and heard the wardrobe monster in the dark.

Eight

'It was the doll,' he managed to say, two hours later. He was still packed into the corner of the room and wouldn't come out, but at least he was talking, which was – sort of – an improvement.

'What do you mean?' she asked – in truth, she was exasperated by all this behaviour. The bacon had been ruined.

'The *duh...doll*,' he exclaimed, eyes cutting beyond her to the doorway. She looked over her shoulder, saw nothing, then looked back. Her knees were beginning to ache. It was undignified, squatting like this, trying to coax words out of him. He was a grown man, after all. Why wouldn't he *act* like one for a change?

'Graham, there's no doll. There's nothing here but us.' *And Angie,* she nearly added, but Angie was in her room, almost certainly asleep for the night. It was well past her bedtime.

He grabbed at her arm, shaking like he had palsy. 'It was *there,*' he managed. 'On the sofa. I heard it bruth-breathing, and I opened my eyes, and it was *there,* the bastard thing was *there.*'

'What thing?' she asked. Honestly, it was like getting blood out of a stone.

He looked at her as if she was the one who was mad. 'That doll. The wuh-one that...the one from *before.*'

'Oh, Graham,' she admonished. 'I threw that out, didn't I? You saw me do it. They came for it yesterday. It's gone. Probably crushed to a pulp by now.'

He stared at her for what seemed like a long time. 'It came back,' he said at length.

Hayley took a deep breath, controlled her temper. This was just getting too much. And she thought he'd stopped all this foolishness. 'It was just a *doll*,' she said, crisp, the way her mum would sometimes talk. 'Plastic and china. It's not a little person dressed up. It's not going to get up and walk around. That doesn't happen, except in films. We're not a film, we're real life, so stop being silly.' He stared up at her, and oh how she wanted to smash that look of disbelief from his mouth. Instead she went on, still using that snapped-off syllable by syllable tone of her mother's. 'You say you saw it when you opened your eyes, yes?' He nodded. 'Well then. You came in, tired – not surprising, you've worked late – and you had a doze. Who can blame you? You had a bad dream. Then...'

'It was *not* a dream,' he growled. Little flecks of spit hit her in the face. 'Its breathing woke me up; it was there, right at me.'

'Dolls don't breathe.'

He lunged forward, still sitting, grabbed her elbows. 'I threw it across the room,' he said, 'it hit the wall. It got up and ran out of the room. It went upstairs. I heard it run up the stairs.'

'Did you? Then why didn't I? I was only in the kitchen, not Timbuktu. Why didn't I hear it?'

He floundered, looking away, totally at a loss. Hardly surprising, her logic really was impeccable. 'I don't know,' he muttered. Then, seizing on an idea, he said, 'because it didn't *want* you to hear it! Yes, because it's *only meant for me*. Don't you see?'

She left it a second, then said, 'OK then. You say it went upstairs. That you *heard* it go upstairs, yes?' He nodded again. 'Right then. Let's go and look for it. If we find it, then you were right and I'll apologise. If we don't, I was right and *you'll* apologise. Fair deal?'

She didn't think he'd answer. She thought he'd sit there until Judgement Trump without answering. But eventually he said, 'OK then.'

Nine

Graham Davis had never really considered himself a brave man. Conversely, he'd never really considered himself a coward either. In truth, he'd never really had much of an occasion – until recently – to test himself in these ways. On that Wednesday night, though, he found out exactly what he was made of.

Somehow, he found the courage to walk up the stairs. Somehow, he found the strength to put one foot in front of the other and to climb higher and higher. As he did, he was almost overwhelmed with terrible nostalgia – he was a child again, forcing his way to bed after staying up late watching old Hammer horror movies, never knowing when his ankle would be grabbed by something that had flopped out of a grave, waiting to see if the Frankenstein monster would be hiding in the bathroom.

Except this *wasn't* like that, not really, because scary as that had been, it'd also been sort of fun, hadn't it? There *were* no monsters, no vampires, no ghouls (whatever they were). They were, as Hayley had just pointed out, only in films. Christopher Lee was just an actor, and when the Director called 'Cut!' everyone took off their makeup and went home. That was the charm of those movies (although 'charm' wasn't a part of his vocabulary back then). They were made-up fears, just a lark, a bit of a game, like jumping out from a corner and shouting 'Boo!' They couldn't hurt you, because they weren't real.

But this, here, now, in his ordinary, slightly boring Crouch End mid-terraced house, *was* real. It was *actually happening.* For true and all, he was mounting the steps, Hayley slightly behind him, fully expecting a doll, a fucking *doll,* to come running at him, hands outstretched, breathing that horrid wet slobbering breath, evil in its glass eyes, to push him down to the ground, tumbling, maybe breaking his neck…

But somehow, he kept going.

'Where do you want to look first?' Hayley asked. 'I'll be with you.'

'Bathroom,' he said. She didn't believe a word of it, and wasn't even bothering to hide it.

'OK.'

He stepped inside, scooting to the wall, pressing his back against it. He heard Hayley hiss disapprovingly as she flicked on the light. She stepped beyond him, looked into the tub. 'Nothing,' she said. 'You want to come see?'

Two steps took him to her side. He managed to look in. Nothing, except a few stray pubes. He jerked around, unwilling to keep his back turned to an open door. There was nowhere else to hide in here, they didn't even have a mirrored cabinet to keep their shampoos and stuff in. 'Where next?' she asked.

'Spare room,' he managed. That's where it would be. Hidden with the other shit.

'Come on then.'

She led the way across the landing, and opened the door. Incredibly, before stepping in she said, 'Angie? Sorry to interrupt you, my love. Just need a look around. Won't be a sec.' She entered.

And she thinks I'm *mad,* he found himself thinking, and followed.

Ten

It wasn't there. The hundred watt bulb in the ceiling lit the room like a floodlight, and it wasn't there. He made his way on robot legs and pulled every toy off the shelf, off the windowsill, and it wasn't there. He even managed to open the wardrobe, which was totally empty.

'No doll,' she said.

He couldn't speak to her. He just left the room and stood on the landing, listening as she said, 'Sorry babe, go back to sleep,' and turned off the light. She faced him as she closed the door. 'Bedroom?' He nodded. 'And if it's not there, which it won't be, what are you going to do?'

'Apologise,' he managed to say.

'Good! Come on then.'

No doll in the wardrobes there, either. No doll in the laundry basket. No doll behind the curtains. 'Do you want to check the drawers,' she asked, and he hated that smile on her face – no, he hated *her*. For one awful second, he hated her *entirely*. He shook his head.

There was, of course, one place he hadn't looked, and it was this that brought that almost-swooning nostalgia back in force. How he found the courage he didn't know, but somehow he lay flat on the floor and looked under the bed, the place where monsters always dwelt, the place they popped up from in the middle of the night, grasping, clutching, tearing...

No doll. Couple of Stephen Vaughn paperbacks sprouting dust, but no doll. He stood, and as he did he felt the world rush from him, the grey clouds cross his eyes. He staggered, grabbed the bedpost, remained vertical and after a while things straightened themselves out.

Once, she would have come to him, or maybe laughed gently, affectionately, but now she just stood, leaning against the door, arms folded, that hideous half smile unmoving. 'Better now?' Without waiting, she said, 'and what do you have to say?'

'I'm sorry,' he said. *Sorry I ever met you.*

'It was a dream, wasn't it?'

'Yes. Must've been.' *No.*

'Glad that's sorted,' she said, and clapped her hands together. 'I don't know about you, but it's late and I'm going to bed. You need to use the bathroom?' He shook his head. 'I'll brush my teeth then.'

As she left him alone, Graham sat on the bed and realised the truth of his earlier thought. It was terrible, appalling, but undeniable. He really *was* sorry he'd ever met her. That was worse than a ghost in the spare room or a killer doll on the loose. That was the worst thing of all.

If he'd been less wrung out, he'd have cried. But he *was* too wrung out...certainly too wrung out to even consider there was one place in the house the doll could've been hiding...but even if he had considered it, it was doubtful that even his courage would have got him up those loft steps.

Eleven

Early Thursday morning, Lillian awoke in her hospital bed – a hospital bed only a few feet away from where, quite recently, Hayley Davis had received some devastating news – and tried to look around her. It wasn't easy, her neck felt as if it was carved from oak and there was a plastic mask around her nose and mouth, but she managed it. It was as dark as it ever was in a hospital (which meant, not very) and around her the comforting drone of monitors hummed away. A nurse passed down the ward, looking left and right, unhurried, calm, professional.

What happened to me, she wondered. *What was that...thing...I saw?*

There was never a second's doubt that she *had* seen it; when you spent your life in contact with the other realm you saw all sorts of things, not all of them pleasant by any means, but she'd seen nothing like *that* before, that terrible hybrid, snuffling and gobbling with pure malevolent glee...

But it was gone now, whatever it was. It was gone and she lay in a hospital, and despite the stiff neck and the hissing of the oxygen mask every time she took a breath, she felt quite fine, thank you very much. Oh, it had been a scare, no argument, but everyone had a fright from time to time, and she was sure she'd rise above it.

Then nurse came back down the ward. She was a little short to be a nurse, Lillian felt, almost a dwarf, but these were the days of Political Correctness after all, of diversity in employment, and she supposed that even a dwarf could have the right qualifications to be a nurse. Even if she did need a stepladder to get the meds off the top shelf.

That almost made her chuckle as the Dwarf Nurse stopped at the bed opposite, her back to Lillian, and reached out to pick up a chart from the end of the sleeping patient's bed. Reached out with very stunted hands. It almost dropped the chart, but managed to hold on, raised it to eye level...

It. I thought of her as 'it.'

Something seemed very badly wrong all of a sudden. A dark cloud rolled over Lillian's eyes as the Dwarf Nurse replaced the chart (with difficulty) and pointed at the man in the bed opposite.

As it pointed, the poor bastard's monitors went flat. He spasmed in his bed, arms flailing wildly, kicking his legs like he was doing the Hokey-Cokey. His left leg was in, then it was out, then he was shaking it all about.

Oh my dear sweet God, that's not a nurse, that's...

But it had turned to face her before she could finish the thought. It was that *thing* again, right here, right in the hospital, and it had followed her, and it was...

Dancing with joy. Its stubby pig's trotters were clapping, its horrid feet tapping out a rhythm, its wet, awful nose pulsing, twitching, drooling. Genuine nurses, real people came rushing to the old man's bed, fussing, hitting buttons, calling for doctors, pulling defibrillator carts, and none of them saw the pig-thing. But Lillian did. She saw it caper and gibber, and just before she fell back into the black, she saw it wink at her, as if they were in on this joke together.

Chapter Fourteen

One

Graham sat in the car later that morning, looked at his watch, saw it was getting on for twenty past eight, went to turn the ignition over, then stopped. He tried again, stopped. He had to move sometime, at any moment Hayley would be leaving the house and making her way to the bus stop and it just wouldn't do for her to find him there, sitting behind the wheel, not going anywhere.

But where would he go? To work? What, after no sleep whatsoever? After nine hours of listening to Hayley's contented snoring while he examined the Artex on the ceiling he'd never quite got round to chipping off? Hearing her snores and coughs and muddled talk as he listened out for *something else?* Something in the dark, something stealthy, something that would hide and hide well, until that moment when it would leap out of whatever space it had vanished into, grabbing, snuffling, grunting…

I was wrong, he thought. *I was wrong and she was right. I was on the side of logic and reason and rationality, and she was on the side of madness and lunacy…and she was right and I was wrong. What the fuck does it all* mean? *How can I sit in the office, behind my desk, dragging a mouse about the mat when…when…*

And the *worst* of it? The fact that having a murderous...ghost...*wasn't* the worst of it. The worst of it was the fact that all night he'd been listening to his own thoughts, the *really* dangerous ones, the ones that kept repeating *I wish I'd never met her*. Did he *really* mean that? Or was it just his overtired, overstressed mind looking for an easy solution to all this madness, this madness that had overcome his life? He'd no idea. Three o'clock in the morning was a bad time to try and figure anything out. Three o'clock in the morning was the time of No Fucking Ideas, the time of Oh The Light Will Never Come.

Go to work after all that? Were you joking? He pulled his mobile from his pocket and rang Danny's desk phone. Unsurprisingly, Danny was there already. *The early berd gets werms*, he'd said often enough. Of course, Graham stayed later. 'Maitland's Design, Daniel Highsmith speaking, how can I help?'

'You can take that fake posh voice off for a start,' said Graham, surprised at how normal he sounded. 'You sound like a pouf.'

'Calls are monitored and recorded for training purposes,' said Danny, and Graham could tell he was grinning, 'which means you're fucked. What's up, mate?'

'Listen, hate to ask, especially after all you've done so far, but can you cover for me? Hayley's...not too well.' He bit off a bray of laughter at that.

'Oh sure, don't worry. Fatty Maitland's at a site all day anyway, be a piece of piss. How bad is she?'

'Stomach flu,' he said, unsure if such a thing actually existed or not, but it sounded good.

'Ah, gross. Don't envy you that, mate. Take care of her, she's a right fit sort.'

'I will. And thanks mate. I owe you.'

'Yeah, y'do. Biiiig time! An' don't think I won't cash in. No go, hold the puke bucket.'

'Will do. Cheers, man.' He hung up, one problem down, another to go. As in, what was he going to do with his day, now he was playing truant? Hang around till Hayley went to work, then go back home, watch some TV, avoid the killer doll, make the dinner and tell her he'd knocked off early, isn't this a nice surprise? Unlikely. Spend the day in the park, feeding ducks, and freeze to death? Less likely. A look at the dashboard clock. Eight twenty three. Any second now she'd be on her way. Any second now he had to be gone.

He sat a second or two longer though, looking at the street he'd called home for three years, a monstrously boring suburban row of terraced houses. Trees lined the pavement. Cars droned along, kids being taken to school most likely. It was unutterably normal. And he, Graham Davis, no longer belonged here, because his world was no longer normal. It was a terrible thought in a life that was suddenly full of terrible thoughts.

Eight twenty-four. He turned the ignition on, selected first, released the handbrake and drove, not having a clue where he was going.

Two

Except maybe he did, as forty minutes later he found himself turning towards Shepherd's Bush. *No, I can't,* he found himself thinking as he realised the direction he'd travelled in, seemingly at random. *I can't bother him.*

He found himself an empty parking slot just by the Green and pulled in. No, he couldn't, that was right. Tell his dad all this? Never. He wouldn't burden him. Hadn't he been thinking only a couple of weeks ago that his dad wasn't looking too fresh these days? A little old? Ever since taking early retirement from the contractors he'd kept busy – building sets for one Amateur Dramatics company or other, mending neighbours' doors and fences, that sort of palaver – but it didn't seem to be *enough* for him, somehow. Jim was a man who made things, built things, constructed things. He had a hunger for it, it drove him; a day he wasn't actively using his hands was a wasted day. How could he help with *this*, with what was going on in Graham's life?

No, Graham thought. So thinking, he drove off to his parents' house.

Three

There was no answer to the doorbell, so Graham let himself in, feeling as he always did these days in that house, as if he was a visitor to the set of a TV programme he used to watch. *That was where I used to watch telly. That was the shelf I knocked the glass swan off. This is the kitchen we used to eat our tea in – Dad called it tea. Mum called it dinner. Dad called lunch dinner. It was all very odd north of the border, apparently.*

This was the place of Christmas mornings and birthday cakes, the place of discipline when he'd been sent home from school for fighting or had rolled home drunk at nineteen, it was the place of Sundays in the park and homework to be done, of Hallowe'en chocolates and staying up to watch *Match of the Day*. It was the place that had once been his world, and now it was smaller, less powerful, less immediate, but still warm, still safe, still a place he felt he belonged.

He looked out of the kitchen window and could hear the faint sounds of sawing from the shed nestled down the garden. For the first time that day – for the first time in what seemed forever – he smiled. How many years had he heard the sound? All of them that he could remember. Things being made. Things taking form from blocks and poles and rods; tables, mantelpieces, shelves, bookcases. It was magic. One day, nothing but a loose conglomeration of wood; the next, a dining table. *Hey presto, at no time do my hands leave my wrists. And for my next trick, a bookcase! Or a guitar for your cousin Stewart! Or a toy plane for your fourth birthday! You imagine it, I can make it!*

He let himself out into the garden and walked down, standing for a second at the open shed door, watching his father run the blade through the wood, slice it in two, unscrew the vice, screw another piece in, and start sawing again. He saw himself, in his memory, a small child watching the sawdust make stars of itself in the light from the window, stars that floated on the breeze and tickled his nose, his father working, but always listening. *No, I don't think Batman could beat Superman in a fight, son. Superman's got all that strength and the x-ray eyes, hasn't he? And he can fly. But why would they fight, anyway? They're goodies, as I understand it. They'd surely be fighting the baddies, not each other. You're right, son, English is hard, I never quite got it myself, all those adjectives and stuff. But nothing good came easy in this world, and English is the single most important thing you'll ever learn, otherwise you'll never make yourself understood. No, I won't let you use the saw, but come here and you can use the plane. That's it, one hand there, the other here. Press down hard and evenly, then push. See? You did it! Now pass me the small jar of screws, get me a little Phillips. Cheers.*

Graham coughed lightly, stung by those memories. It was hard to think it was all so long ago. His dad gave a little start as he turned and saw him, then smiled. 'Hello son. What brings you here?'

'The car.'

They laughed together. Jim put the saw down carefully on the workbench. 'You having a day off?'

Graham's smile dropped. 'Yeah. Couldn't…' Couldn't finish, that's what he couldn't do. Suddenly it was all too much. How could he say it? How could he tell *anyone?*

Jim let him stand in silence for a second, the way he had when Graham had been a kid and had to fess up to something wrong he'd done. When Graham still didn't speak, he said, 'Well something's up, I can see it all over you. Always said you'd never make a poker player, son.'

'Where's Mum?' Graham asked.

'She's out at her knitting circle. I think it's socks for our troops or something. So if you want to tell me something it'll just be between us. If you don't, you can make yourself useful and at least make a brew.'

Again, Graham choked. This was too much, too much to lay on anyone, least of all his dad, his dad who wasn't as young as he once was. 'It's OK, I'll just…'

'Hayley, is it? Problems there?'

It was Graham's turn to jump. 'How did you know?'

'When a man looks like you do right now, like he's had no sleep and he's carrying the world on his shoulders, it's one of three things – money, job, wife. And I know Hayley's not been well, don't I? Seemed a fair choice. So, what's the matter?' Still Graham hesitated. 'Like I said, if you'd rather it's between us, I'll not tell. If you'd rather tell your mother, that's fine, me and you can pick over the weekend's results, either way.'

In the end, Graham told him. Told him everything.

Four

It took longer than expected – he kept forgetting things, or losing the order and backtracking – but eventually he was done, ending with the events of the night before and the way he was now thinking about his wife. Through it all, Jim's expression never wavered. His eyes widened a little here and there, but he kept silent, just nodding every so often to prove he was listening, and he understood. 'And that's when I came to see you,' Graham finished. 'Except I didn't know I was coming to see you. I just ended up here. So.' And how scared was he now? Oh, very. 'When are you going to have me committed?'

Jim kept quiet for a second, then said, 'That shelf behind you, son. Pick around, behind the jar of nails – the three inch ones – and toss me what you find, will you?'

Still scared, Graham did as he was asked, and his hand clasped around… 'Dad!' Shocked now, not scared. 'You gave these up! *Years* ago!'

'Aye, so you were told. Toss them over anyway, will you.'

Reluctantly Graham passed his dad the pack of Silk Cut. He watched as Jim opened the pack, poked around, found one, popped it into his mouth and lit it with a lighter he retrieved from his jeans watch pocket. He didn't cough over it.

'No, I didn't quit. Sorry I lied, but I didn't. Cut right down though, two or three a day and only when I'm working. Never in the house. Your mother knows. She wants to say something about it, but never does, the way I say nothing about the Cadbury's Fingers she buys and eats without telling anyone. It's what I told you about the secrets a marriage keeps. It's what we choose *not* to see that makes up happy. But this,' he went on, exhaling smoke, 'this is something you can't *afford* not to see.'

Something like relief crashed over him. 'You believe me, then?'

Jim looked at him in mild surprise. 'God, aye. You're no liar, son, never have been. Could never pull the wool over anybody's eyes, whatever that means. I mean, I'll give you this, it sounds mad, but just because something *sounds* mad doesn't mean it isn't happening. It sounds mad to me that Jews and Arabs blow each other up over who owns what, or that spraying deodorant under your arms means we get more skin cancer, but that happens too. And I think, deep down, we all know there's weird stuff going on. Listen,' he said, taking another drag, and blowing it out, 'your grandfather once told me about a time he was in Germany – or West Germany as it still was, doing his National Service. Couldn't tell you whereabouts, I've long forgotten, but for the sake of argument let's say it was in the Black Forest somewhere. Anyroad, they're guarding the camp, him and three or four others. Once an hour one of them has to do a sweep of the perimeter, make sure no one's been cutting the wires or whatever. So, comes to your grandfather's turn. Gets halfway round, nodding and saluting to his mates, whatever they do, when he hears footsteps coming towards him. He turns, rifle at the ready – even though there were no bloody bullets in it – and issues a challenge. German soldier steps out. Seems a nice guy, they get chatting, he's barracked a little further down, on a furlough, going back to meet his girl, that sort of thing.

Your grandfather thinks it's a little odd he's in uniform, that he's making his way on foot in the middle of the night, but as he said to me, he didn't know what the Krauts got up to. Anyway, they walk together, checking the perimeter, nodding and saluting, chatting away. The Kraut gets his fags out, your grandfather takes one. Said it tasted horrible, but he smoked it to be polite. Eventually, the Kraut says *it was nice talking to you, Jock* – everyone called him Jock – *but I have to go now*. Walks off into the wood. Your grandfather gets back to his post. An hour later the next squaddie on perimeter duty comes round, looks at him and says "You going off your nut, Jock?" Now he had a temper, did your grandfather, a mighty quick temper, and he's ready to get mad at this. "What you saying?" The squaddie then tells him that when he – your grandfather – had done his perimeter check everyone had seen him talking to himself, having a very animated conversation with thin bloody air. No Kraut soldier by his side. Oh, of course he thought they were having him on, and he didn't speak to them for quite a while – *there* was a man who could hold a grudge – he thought they were ganging up on him 'cause he was a Scot, but then he got to thinking about the man's uniform, the fact he was going on his furlough late at night, and on foot, and how none of that made sense. He said to me that he came to believe he'd met, walked with, talked and shared fags with, a ghost.

'He was in poor health when he told me this, son, on his way out, and maybe some things had been added to the story and some others taken off - it happens when you tell a story – but he had no reason to lie. He had no reason to tell it to me at all, he just felt he had to one night. I think it had troubled him for nigh on forty years and he needed to get it off his chest. So I tell you this, I believe you the way I believed him, because there's nothing to gain from either of you lying.'

Graham stared at him, fascinated. Jim stubbed out his smoke, put the butt in the packet, considered taking another, then with clear regret didn't. 'The point I'm making, I think, is that everyone either has had or knows someone who's had a spooky thing or two happen to them. I don't pretend to know what they are really, or what they mean, but I'm not one of those people who have to see something to know it exists. I've never seen Australia, but I know it's there. The question we have, if I read this right, is what you're going to do next.'

'That's the trouble, Dad. I haven't got a clue.'

'So let's run through your options. This thing, this doll, is nasty, right?'

'Yes. I think…I think it's out to get me.' He should have laughed at that, because it was a stupid thing to say. A doll! Out to get him! But he didn't laugh, because it wasn't stupid.

'And she doesn't see it?' Graham nodded. 'She only has eyes for this little girl that's in the spare room?' He nodded again. 'It's simple then. You have to get out. Take her with you, if you can. Without her if you can't.'

Five

'What?' Graham asked, a full five seconds later. This was as unexpected as his dad buying him a season ticket at White Hart Lane for Christmas, and about as welcome. *Or was it,* he thought, deep in his brain. *C'mon, isn't this what you* wanted *him to say? Isn't this what you* knew *he would say? Isn't that why you came here?*

'Graham,' his dad said, levelly, solemnly – not 'son,' but 'Graham.' 'There's something in your house that isn't natural, that appears to be actually hostile towards you. If it was a burglar or a squatter, I'd tell you to punch the bastard out. If it were someone moving in on your wife, I'd say do the same. Your mother would tell you to sit down and talk it out, but believe me, a punch to the jaw is the only language some people understand. But *this is not a man,* is it? This is something else, and it's dangerous, and what good will punching it do? Now I love Hayley, I really do, she's the closest I'll ever get to having a daughter, but you are my only son, and I'll put your safety before anyone's, barring your mother's. You hear that? Yes, fight for her, make Hayley see she has to leave, because she has to, but if she won't listen you get the hell out, son. You get the hell out and come here. That's an order.'

Run away, Graham thought. *Abandon ship.*

'I know what you're thinking,' Jim went on, picking up the smokes and giving an *oh, fuck it* shrug. 'You're thinking it's cowardly, that you're giving up, that you'd rather go down fighting than run away. Aye, that's something I've given you, something I got from *my* dad. But let me tell you something I've learned in my life; *pick your battles*. Only fight if you've a chance of winning. If you've a better that *even* chance of winning.' He pulled a cigarette out and lit it. 'And against this, have you? Have you a better than even chance of winning?'

Graham left a long pause, almost disgusted with himself, and said, 'No, Dad. I don't think I do.'

'Well then,' said Jim. 'You know what to do, don't you?'

'It still feels like quitting,' Graham said, looking at the sawdust covered floor. As a kid, he'd sometimes draw in that, or write his name. 'Y'know, the vows and stuff…'

'Aye, but it isn't. From what you say, Hayley's so far gone she probably wouldn't notice you've left. Any maybe this'll be the shock that brings her back to the real world.'

'Yeah. Maybe.' He thought it over, long and hard, and everywhere there was a bad decision lying in wait. *What do you do when every choice looks bad, when every choice is a bad choice?*

He stood in his dad's shed and wondered.

Six

As Graham had been parking up outside his parents' house, Lillian awoke once again, and found a vision of loveliness beside her bed. She was a tall, Spanish looking doctor, all olive skin, raven black hair and eyes so brown you could swear they were black. Lillian twitched a little. *Hey, I can't be too sick*, she thought. *Never heard of anyone at death's door getting horny.*

'Hello Lillian, I'm Doctor Thompson,' the vision said, smiling. 'I hear you put on a show last night.'

That stopped any good feelings right there and then. Remembering what had happened, first at the theatre, then in the dressing room, and finally in the ward the previous night. Lillian craned her head upright – less pain than the night before, but still as stiff as a sailor's cock – and, sure enough, the bed opposite was empty. She pulled her oxygen mask aside.

'Easy now,' said the doctor. 'Don't overtax yourself just yet.'

'How...I mean, what's wrong with me?'

Doctor Thompson flicked through the notes she held. 'Nothing, so far as we can see. All the standard tests are negative. We may want to book you in for a CAT, maybe an MRI, but we may think about those as outpatients' appointments. Frankly, there are sicker people out there who need the bed. The plan is twenty-four hour obs then you can go home.'

'Obs,' repeated Lillian, unhappy. It had a terrible, ominous ring to it.

'Observations.' Then, smiling wider and showing perfectly even white teeth, 'But all your functions seem healthy, you're the right side of the grass, breathing unaided with a perfectly healthy heart and you're tracking everything I say. We'll give you the cognition tests later – draw a clock, put the numbers inside, that sort of thing – though for what it's worth, I think you'll pass those. We've tested your reflexes while you were under, and they're all in fine shape; none of your bones are broken, all we can find is a bruise on the back of your neck, probably when you fell. So, all I need to know is; what happened to make you fall?'

Lillian was a far better liar than Graham – after all, on any given night up to half her 'act' was a lie. 'I think it all got a bit much,' she said. 'The lights, the show…hadn't eaten properly…you know how it is.'

'I don't, as it happens. But that seems to fit. If you have another blackout we'll run a load more tests, but based on the evidence we have so far I'd say this was pretty much a one off. So if I was you, I'd lay back for a day, watch some TV, enjoy our famed hospital food and if you need anything, press the call button.'

She went to go, but Lillian called her back. 'The gentleman in the bed opposite,' she said. Doctor Thompson's eyes – those miraculous brown eyes – dropped a little. 'I woke up in the night and saw...' a dancing pig... 'well, a commotion. Is he...?'

'I'm afraid Mr Webber passed in the night,' the doctor whispered. 'I wasn't on call, so I don't have the details. I'm sorry if it upset you. Anyway,' she went on, louder, professional, 'must get on.' This time she breezed away, taking her eyes and her figure out of Lillian's eyeline. She lay back on the pillow and examined the peeling paint. *I'm sorry if it upset you*, she'd said. *And it did, just not the way you think. Because Mr Webber wasn't in any danger, was he? Oh sure, monitored up the wazoo, but isn't everybody here? No, middle bed in the ward, no special precautions, not in Intensive Care...yes, it's a hospital, and death visits here often, death is an old acquaintance, not welcome but expected, like snow in January. But not for him, not for Mr Webber. Not until that thing came and pointed at him*, marked him...

Killed him.

She didn't move, but she felt that apparently fit heart of hers flutter. *Yes, killed him. It was prowling, wasn't it, stalking up and down the ward, looking for someone who looked likely, someone to kill. If so, what was it, that thing? How did it relate to the thing that was in the theatre last night? Is it one and the same? Is there a family? A whole host of those bastards floating about? And why did it come to me? And why did I only faint, when poor old Mr Webber crossed over?*

That one seemed obvious. As a warning.

Yes, of course. A demonstration of its – or *their* – power. 'Next time it's you, bitch.' *They know me, they've seen me, they've marked me. I just don't know what they're warning me against.*

Of course, that was the worst. How could you avoid something bad if you weren't told what the bad thing was? Back in the 1920's pregnant women were advised to smoke; it was apparently not only good for you, it was good for your baby, she'd seen that on some programme or other. *What don't I do? What don't I do? What don't I do?*

Wrestling with a terrible dilemma, Lillian lay in bed and trembled.

Seven

Hayley, in stark contrast, was in heaven. Like Graham, she hadn't gone to work. Unlike him, she'd stayed at home. She'd used her mobile to call Jodie and tell her a sob story about the backdoor trots, yeah she was off to bed with an Imodium, please cancel her appointments and apologise profusely, yes, almost certainly tomorrow. Then she'd hung up and ran back upstairs.

Standing in the nursery, Hayley caught her breath again and said, 'Oh. Angie.'

She was standing there, her little girl, fully three dimensional, and smiling. Her smile was like sunshine in Eden.

Eight

She hadn't believed it at first. When she'd popped her head in on the way to the bathroom – just to say good morning – she'd expected to see nothing but the toys and the book on the floor. Maybe, if she was lucky, get a hug. Or *very* lucky, see that misty outline again. But no. Miracle of miracles, there she was, solid, real, as real as everything else in the world – a little girl, maybe two foot tall, in a long white lace dress, curly hair, bright eyes, a freckled nose.

Oh my Lord, thank You, Hayley had thought, standing there, jaw open. *She's perfect. She's what I always dreamed of, oh thank You Lord.*

She couldn't speak. It was too much. Far, far too much. She was overwhelmed with rapture, a word she'd only associated with an old pop song before then, but upon setting eyes on Angie she knew *exactly* what it meant. Rapture, bliss, a sense of…completion. *Yes, completion. I am now complete. A complete woman. I am a mother, and that is why men and women exist, to make children. I was unsure before, but now I know. Looking at her I see it now, I understand the plan. Everything else we do is a side-salad,* this *is the main course.*

'*Ohhhhhhhhhhhh,*' she'd said, not so much a word as an expression of joy, the sort of noise she made when Graham had brought her to orgasm.

'Hello Mummy,' Angie had said, speaking in a broken not-quite-language-cemented way. 'Can we play games today?'

'Oh Angie my love,' she whispered. 'Oh of course we can.'

Nine

They played at tea party with the toys – that doggy with the lolling tongue was very naughty and kept trying to steal Jolly Tall the Giraffe's scones while Jolly Tall was looking at the ceiling – and they played peek-a-boo and they played Hide and Seek (difficult in one small room, but they made the best of it.) They sang 'The Wheels on the Bus' and Hayley taught her 'Row, Row, Row Your Boat' and then 'Round and Round the Garden,' which Angie just loved. In fact, when it came to the bit at the end, where the Teddy Bear took one step, two steps then *tickled her under there,* Angie just lay on her back and giggled, kicking her feet in the air, the feet which seemed not to fit properly into her black buckle shoes.

'Oh Mummy, you funny!'

'I'm glad you think so. Now, tomorrow I'll get us some games – board games. You ever played Snakes and Ladders?' Angie sat up and shook her head, but slowly, almost apprehensively. 'Oh, it's all right my love, there's no *real* snakes. Just drawings. I'll show you tomorrow. And there's...oh, all sorts! Things I had as a girl. Connect 4, Hungry Hippos – that one will make you laugh – Pop Up Pirates...'

'Was you once a girl like me?' Angie asked, curious now.

'Yes, my love. Once. A long time ago now.'

'Will I grow up big like you, Mummy?'

Oh, didn't *that* break her heart? No, she wouldn't, would she? Her growing was over, her life was over, she was the definition of static – but how did you tell her that? How did you say, 'No honey. You're going to stay exactly as you are for ever and ever, because you're a ghost, and ghosts never change, ghosts never grow.'

At that thought, something began to grow in her head, something odd and unsettling. She squashed it. She was playing with her daughter and didn't want anything to disturb her.

'If you get plenty of sleep, do as you're told and are a good girl you will,' said Hayley.

Angie giggled, but then that solemn face came back. 'You love me, Mummy?'

'Oh, ever so much.'

A puzzled frown on the little girl's face. 'Why doesn't the man love me?'

'What man, sweetheart?'

'The man what lives here with you. The nasty man what shouts.'

Another odd thing...when Angie had first mentioned 'the man,' Hayley had genuinely no idea who she was talking about. *What man, sweetheart* had been a genuine enquiry. It was only when she followed up with 'The nasty man what shouts' that she'd remembered him...Graham...her husband...and was it *right* that 'nasty man what shouts' should be the association? *Well, yeah. Ever since she's known him, he's been...well, let's say 'cranky.' Not himself. All that wild crap about 'killer dolls' for instance! No wonder that's how she thinks of him, she's never known any different.* 'Oh honey, he *does* love you.'

'Does he love you, Mummy?'

She blinked a little, for a second unsure. 'Yes, of course he does.'

'Then why will he go? Why is he going to go then?'

Hayley sat back, looked hard at the little girl before her, the little girl who only a few minutes before had been kicking her feet and squealing with laughter like a little piglet, practically grunting with delight, and was now sat with dismay all over her face. 'What makes you think that, Angie?'

''cause he is,' Angie said. 'He's going to go and leave us. Why? Why do that if he loves us?'

Hayley thought that over, and eventually said, 'You know what, honey? I've no idea. But you want to know something else?' She leaned in close, and Angie leaned in too, they were nose to nose. '*I don't care*. If he wants to go, we'll let him. Then we can play as much as we want.'

This made Angie laugh delightedly again, and Hayley couldn't help herself. She leaned in and kissed the girl on the nose, and Angie laughed some more, so Hayley kissed her on the nose again and again. Her cold, wet nose.

Ten

She made Angie go to bed at six, went down to the kitchen and at half past she heard Graham's key in the lock. He called to her from the hallway, and the tone of his voice said it all. 'In here,' she called.

Graham entered, and stopped by the door, eyes wide in his hollow face. 'Jesus,' he said. 'Are you OK? You look…'

'You want to look in the mirror before you throw stones,' said Hayley, arms folded.

He stopped talking, made his way to the table and sat. He couldn't look her in the eyes. She let the silence spin out. Eventually, he said, 'We have to talk.'

'Do we?'

'Yes. This thing...what's going on...it's not right, is it?'

She still said nothing. This was his play, let him make it. She already knew her answer before the question was asked. That made her powerful. 'I mean,' he went on, 'what I saw last night...and before...it happened. Hayley, I know you don't believe me, but it did. I need you to see that. There is something in this house, I know that now, I agree with you now, but it's *wrong*. Please. Please *believe* that.' She still kept quiet, though inside there was a rising anger. How could he *say* that? How could he say that about *her daughter?* 'If we stay,' he said, 'things will go bad here. I can't have that. I know things haven't been great between us the last few days, but we can get over that, I know we can. But we have to leave here.' He reached out and grabbed her hands. She didn't pull them away. She wouldn't give him that satisfaction. 'I love you,' he said. 'I love you and want to keep you safe, and the only way I can do that is by taking you with me. I'll carry you if I have to. I'll drag you out by the hair if I have to. But we have to leave. And now.'

'No,' she said.

'Listen...' he said.

She cut him off. 'I'm going nowhere. If you so much as touch me I will phone the police and have you arrested for assault. I'll take a court order out against you. You hear me?' Her voice was uninflected. 'This is my home every bit as much as yours. Upstairs, asleep, is a little girl who loves me and needs me and I will *not* abandon her.'

'*She's dead,*' Graham screamed, standing. He ran his hands through his head as if trying to rip the hair out by the roots. 'Can't you *see* that, she's *dead!* You're obsessed with the dead! Have you any idea how mad this all is?'

'Hush. You'll wake her.'

He stopped as if slapped. He took a deep breath and tried again, his control paper thin. 'You're not well, Hayley. This place...it's making you sick. Please. Please *see* that. For me, for us. Wake up to what is *actually happening* and see that it's not right.'

'I'm not going anywhere. I live here. You may stay, you may go, you're an adult and I can't stop you doing anything. But I stay,' she went on, her voice rising for the first time in the conversation. 'I stay and look after Angie. Am I making myself clear?'

'You'd let me go?' he said, shoulders drooped, looking a lot like his father. 'You'd choose her over me?'

'*You're* making me choose. I don't see why, but you are.'

A long silence fell. He kept looking at her, looking away, looking back. Several times he started to speak, then closed his mouth. He sat down for a while, then stood up again. Eventually he said, 'Hayley. I can't stay here.'

'Goodbye then,' she said.

Eleven

Is this it, then? Graham thought as he looked at her dirty, unwashed face, her clumped hair, her pyjama-clad body. *Is this how we end?*

How could he walk out on her? How could he stay? What could he do?

Look at her, though. She's jumped the tracks completely. His heart broke, he felt it go. There was hardly the ghost – *ha fucking ha* – of the woman he loved in the person who sat opposite him, entrenched.

She doesn't think I'll do it. She thinks I'll give in, for her sake. For a quiet life. But it wouldn't *be* a quiet life, would it? For somewhere in this house – maybe watching him right that second for all he knew – there was something that actually hated him, which wanted to harm him, maybe even kill him. She couldn't see that, because she was crazy.

Yes, crazy. It was time to tell the truth. No fannying about now. He had to face the *truth*. She wasn't listening to reason, to sense, and he *was* making sense. So...what? Club her, drag her out, like he'd threatened, only to have her call the police like *she'd* threatened? What then? *Maybe that's for the best, maybe the whole story would come out and they'd section her and she'd get help at last...*

Yet another cheery thought in a life that was just full of shit right now, thanks a bunch God. His beloved wife – and he did still love her, despite everything, he'd love her for ever – even if she was dragged down the corridors of some awful asylum, foaming at the mouth, arms in one of those canvas jackets (and something about the notion of hospital corridors brought back a vague memory of a dream, but it danced away before he could grab it) he'd still love her, but...*is that what you want for her?*

No. Of course it wasn't. What he wanted was to go back in time and put it right somehow. Or go back in time and not meet her at all, save himself all this. Weak, yes. But he still wanted that.

If I stay, I face a life of sleepless nights, waiting for that face to pop up out of nowhere and rip my throat out and drink my blood, or maybe something less messy like squeezing my nose shut and putting a hoof across my mouth until I suffocate.

(Hoof?)

He shook that away and continued his internal argument. *If I go, I leave her to the mercy of...whatever's here. How can I do that?* Terribly, the answer came. *Because she's happy here.*

Oh yes, that was the worst of it. She was happy in this place, with her ghost. She loved it more than she loved him, that was quite obvious. This was where she wanted to be, needed to be, *had* to be, and this was where he *couldn't* be. All of which led to only one answer, didn't it?

'I'll get packed then,' he said, and the silence that followed was the silence of the grave, for she raised no objection. She just nodded.

Twelve

He was gone an hour later, into his car and away. She didn't see him to the door. She sat in the kitchen until she heard the door shut behind him, then she ran to the nursery. As she'd suspected, Angie was awake, standing in the room, biting her bottom lip anxiously. 'I hearded shouts,' she said.

Hayley rushed to her, picked her up and held her close. 'I know, honey, I'm sorry, so sorry, but it's over now, no more shouts, I promise.'

'Has the man gone?' Angie asked.

'Yes,' she answered, putting Angie down again, and stroking her hair. 'The man's gone, now it's just us, and we can play all the games we want and no one can stop us ever again.'

In the light from the street outside, Angie smiled.

Chapter Fifteen

One

At eight o'clock on the night Graham moved out, Elaine sat up from browsing on Facebook and thought, *what's happened?*

She'd been unable to shake that feeling for a while now, the feeling that there was a thunderstorm coming, something edgy and restless in the air, something electric that made you prowl and snap or just flick yourself off, *anything* for some relief. But at eight o'clock on that Thursday night, she felt something *snap*, somewhere in her head. *What's happened?* she thought again.

Her hand reached out for the phone, she needed to call Hayley and see. For she knew it had something to do with her, her and Graham, she could tell...but she pulled her hand back and rubbed her mouth instead.

She was scared to find out. Yes, no question, she was scared. She didn't want to know. It would be bad news. She didn't want bad news, no one wanted bad news – and anyway, why go looking? Bad news would find her soon enough. *Don't buy trouble before it's on sale,* that was one of her mother's less stupid sayings, one of the few Elaine could get on board with. Yeah, if there was trouble, she'd find out soon enough. She didn't need to know yet, it'd turn up.

Sooner or later.

So she went back to Facebook and scrolled through the status updates and shared photos and did her best to put it all aside. She managed well enough.

Two

Lillian was discharged on the Friday morning with a clean bill of health and a hearty 'Don't overdo it,' from Doctor Thompson. *Oh honey,* Lillian thought, *if I was ten years younger I'd invite you back and you could overdo me anytime.*

But still, as she climbed into the cab and gave her address, she found herself looking back at the hospital, scouring the windows, looking to see if something was waving her off, something stunted, something with a wet undulating snout, something inhuman. But the sun was reflecting off them so she saw nothing.

It's still there though. It or them. Still there. She shivered.

'Y'all right, love?' the cabbie asked.

'Fine thanks. Just a little shiver.'

'Goose walked over your grave,' he said.

Not a goose, a pig. A terrible pig-human. But otherwise, yes. I think that's about right. And while it walked over it, I think the bastard laughed.

Three

A little while earlier, while Lillian was being formally discharged, Graham awoke in a narrow single bed and thought, *Where the hell* am *I?*

The answer came back, but slowly, reluctantly. He was back in his old childhood bed, the bed he'd left years before when he'd rented his first bedsit in Islington. Back home, back in his parents' place, back where it all started, back in the room he'd read his comics in, back in the room where he'd lined up his cars and his Action Men, back in the room where he'd stashed his first porn mags, back in the loveless single bed.

He groaned a little, but quietly. He wasn't sure of his parents' routine these days, wasn't sure if they were up, didn't want to disturb them if they were. But the sour defeat of his situation pressed hard upon him. Turning up at their door late the night before, bags in each hand, listening to his mother flutter about him, telling him not to worry, all marriages have their bad patches, you'll make it up, realising then that his father had kept quiet about the troubles, sitting in the front room where he'd once watched *Pokémon* and *Star Fleet*, trying to put a brave face on the fact he'd...run away. Given up. Deserted his post. Left his wife.

Danny Highsmith had a poster above his desk – some photo from *The Walking Dead* showing a zombie with its face rotting off and the caption underneath WELCOME TO THE FIRST DAY OF THE REST OF YOUR LIFE. Was this the rest of *his* life, living back at his parents', separated then divorced from his wife who was sitting happily with her ghost daughter? Was it? And if it was, how would he cope?

One day at a time, he told himself as he looked at his watch. Seven on the dot. If he was quick he could fit in a shower before heading off to work – he was in Shepherd's Bush now, another forty to fifty minutes on his journey. *One day at a time*, he thought again as he untangled himself from the duvet, *just like the alcoholics do.*

Four

Hayley rang in sick again that morning. Jodie was slightly less sympathetic, but Hayley managed to charm her – if that was the right word – with a story of how those backdoors just wouldn't keep closed; this may be more than just something she ate, this could be a virus. Could be a bad one. Oh, she knew it was inconvenient, and she was really, really sorry, but (a) she wouldn't be at her station for more than five minutes, not the way her bowels were today, and (b) she didn't want to pass it on if it was a virus, which seemed likely – if Jodie caught it as well, they really would be in (excuse me) shit street, wouldn't they? And what about the customers? No, best if she just stayed at home, and of course she'd make it up later, when she felt better, and oh dear Jodie, better go, I can feel it coming out again, yes, sorry...

Once she'd hung up, she called to Angie, told her not to worry, she was just stepping out for a while, and without washing, changing her clothes or cleaning her teeth Hayley went to the shops in the High Street, picked up some board games and went home again, oblivious to the way people stared.

During that day she taught Angie how to play Ludo and Hungry Hippos. Angie took to them surprisingly well, especially the latter. She laughed and laughed as the clattering plastic Hippo ate the marbles, and Hayley laughed at her daughter's pleasure.

She didn't think of Graham once. Nor did she think about how Angie was able to touch things now. She was a happy Mummy with a happy daughter. What *else* was there to think about? What else *mattered?*

Five

'Thanks for yesterday, mate,' said Graham as he plopped down behind his desk. 'What do I owe you?'

'Dunno, I'll think o'somethin'. An' no sweat. I mean, not quite *anytime, dude,* but y'get the drift.'

'Yeah. I do.' He opened the files Danny had completed yesterday and scanned them. For a brief second he stopped thinking about Hayley. 'Jesus Christ, these are *good.*'

'I'm an unappreciated talent in me own lifetime, like that Dutch fella with one ear. And you thought, wha'? That I'd piss them off in me dinner hour and make y'look shite?'

'No. I truly didn't.' Horrified, Graham discovered there were tears threatening to fall. He needed to get a grip. A look over at Danny's poster helped somehow. WELCOME TO THE FIRST DAY OF THE REST OF YOUR LIFE. 'If you need to cut and run at any time, don't hesitate. Got me?'

'You know it, bud. Tell you what y'can do mate, get the coffees in.'

He did, with no complaints, and at lunchtime he took the lad out and bought him something to eat. Danny didn't object. At three that afternoon, Maitland emailed him a job that would take forever to complete. At any other time, this would have set off a rant of some description, something nice and eloquent about how the fat bastard should be run over in the street in front of his kids, it's a Friday afternoon for God's sake, but on that particular Friday, Graham welcomed it and declined Danny's offer to share the load. This was good. He could work late that night, come in over the weekend as well, keep himself occupied, stop himself from thinking.

He picked up the desk phone and had punched in four numbers before ramming down the cutoff button. He didn't live at that number anymore, did he? *Should I call anyway, see how she is? I mean, I still love her; I still want her to be well.*

His fingers held over the buttons for a second, hovering, then punched in his parents' number. *No, not today.* He'd contact her over the weekend maybe. He told his Mum he'd be late back, not to worry he'd pick something up to eat, yes it was all good, don't worry, and went back to his job, to the REST OF HIS LIFE.

Six

It was like an itch she couldn't reach, maddening, causing her to squirm and dance, robbing her concentration. *Something's happened*, she kept thinking, like the time she'd kept thinking *Hayley's in trouble.*

It buzzed through her all the Friday at work, and all the Friday at home, and when the phone had rung Elaine had jumped at it, almost ripping the headset from the cradle, but it was only her mum.

'How are you, dear? I got worried because you've not been in touch, and you living all alone like you do.' You had to admire Anna, two guilt trips in one sentence, that took talent. *You never call and you've not found someone yet* (unspoken subtext: your time is running out to give me grandchildren). Elaine apologised as if she meant it, said she was fine, then asked if she'd heard from Hayley. 'No, but that's not surprising. Too busy to talk to her old mum. Still, never mind, I've got plenty to occupy me.' And to prove how occupied she was, Anna gave Elaine a complete rundown of what had happened on all the soaps, the talent shows, and the latest scandal to hit about a former Radio One DJ. Elaine kept her side of the bargain by listening and making vocalisations, but all through that interminable conversation she kept thinking, *something's happened.*

Seven

By eleven o'clock on the Saturday morning it was just too much and Elaine rang Hayley's mobile. No answer, straight over to Voicemail as if it was switched off. 'Hayles, it's me. Give us a call when you get this will you?' Then she rang the house phone. It rang out and out until the BT voice clicked in with, 'The person you are calling is unavailable. Please leave a message after the tone…' and on and on, with instructions about what she could do if she wanted to re-record her message. Eventually the tone bleeped, and she said 'Hayles, it's Elaine. Tried your mobile, got nothing. Trying this, got nothing. You OK? Call me the *second* you get this, y'hear?'

She hung up, and drummed her fingers on the shelf. Then took out her mobile, found Graham's number, pressed SEND and let out a faint scream of exasperation as his Voicemail told her to leave a message. 'Gray. Elaine. Tried your home, tried Hayley's mobile, tried this, no one's talking. What's going on? What's wrong? Oh…fuck it.'

She jabbed at the cutoff button, threw her Nokia across the room, then retrieved it, stuffed it back in her pocket and ran for the door.

Eight

Sitting on the Tube forty minutes later (a seat she'd almost committed murder for, but she wasn't standing, not no way, thank you), Elaine almost laughed. *Hey, maybe I'm psychic. Cool beans and hot peas! I got me a show I can take on the road and fill out town halls with. 'I'm getting the words 'Something's happened.' Mean anything to anyone?*

It was a hollow laugh though, a laugh that had never found anything funny. That nagging nervousness was growing louder. Louder. Loudest.

Nine

First stop was the salon; Saturdays, after all, were their busiest days during the year. 'Hey Jodie,' she said as she made her way in, heart sinking as she saw the harassed look on the other woman's face and the empty station where Hayley normally sat.

'Before you ask, no chance of fitting you in, sorry,' Jodie said, stirring some foul-looking gloop in a plastic bowl ready to smear it on some teenage girl's fringe.

'No, it's OK, I can see you're busy. Um, is Hayley about?'

'If Hayley was about,' Jodie said through gritted teeth, 'I'd be able to fit you in. And also see my boyfriend. She's sick, didn't you know?' Elaine shook her head, unhappy. That panicky feeling burst like a soap bubble and filled her with acid. 'Leastways, I *think* she's still ill, not heard from her today. I'd have rung, but...' The shrug she gave suggested that she hadn't rung because she was (a) too busy and (b) would have sworn a lot.

'How long's she been off?'

'Since Wednesday, she rang in Thursday and yesterday, but nothing today. And, look, if you don't mind...'

'Yeah sure, I'm off.'

She ducked back onto the street, looked about her for a bus, realised she had no idea which buses made their way to Hayley's, then set off in a brisk stride.

After ten minutes, though, she was running.

Ten

Forty minutes later, she was hammering on Hayley's front door, more and more frantic as she received no reply. *God, what's happened? What if she's collapsed? What if she's dead? What if...*

And where the fuck *is Graham?*

She looked around for his car, saw no sign, then hammered on the door again. Where was he? Were they at the hospital? Where? Where the hell was everybody?

Eleven

In the nursery, Hayley and Angie sat, giggling silently, with their fingers over their lips. Hayley was painfully reminded of being at school as a little girl, not much older than Angie was now, trying not to laugh in class even though someone had made a funny noise or passed a note that said JOHN METCALF HAS SNOT ON HIS TEETH. Oh, it was painful. Oh, it was delightful. Oh, it was everything she'd ever wanted.

'Shhhhhhhh, Mummy,' whispered Angie, and they both giggled louder. They clasped their hands over their mouths and rolled on the floor, just having the best time ever. *I pity anyone who's not me*, Hayley thought. *I really do.*

Twelve

This was pure agony for Elaine, absolute agony. She thought of kicking the door down, then realised she had no idea how to go about it. It always looked easy on TV, but *those* doors were almost certainly made of balsa wood, and this one wasn't. She thought of calling the police – actually had her phone in her hand to do it – then stopped, having no idea what to tell them. *I got a bad feeling about my sister and no-one's opening the door, send all units, a chopper and the full riot squad please.* Right. That was likely, in a town where you could lie murdered in the gutter for ten years and people chucked coins at you, thinking you were homeless. Coins if you were lucky.

I mean, let's be rational here, she tried to tell herself. *So what, she cops a sickie from work, we've all done it. Her and Gray decide to take a break, right? Long weekend off somewhere, take a trip to Margate, ride the rides, see the sights; a second honeymoon. OK, it's March, not too clement, bit of a chill – but if they're staying in bed the whole time, what does it matter if it's blowing a hurricane? Who's the bloke with that Razor, the one who said 'the simplest explanation is the most likely'? Sure, it'll be something as innocent as that, and boy, won't we have the best laugh when all this is over?*

But that niggling, biting feeling that something was wrong just wouldn't go away. She looked up at the silent house, curtains drawn, and walked away, down the street, hands deep in her dufflecoat pockets, sure she was doing the wrong thing but not knowing why.

At least cover all your bases, she suddenly thought, and stopped. *You've checked Hayley's work, what about Graham's? Have a knock there, see what's what.*

Elaine very suddenly wanted chocolate – a mint Aero, to be precise. She thought better with chocolate; well with food in general, and it was nearly two. Well after lunchtime. *Anyway, Graham didn't work weekends. Much. If he had overtime, then yeah, but...*

Why not try there anyway. Google the number, give them a ring. If someone's working, they'll answer. And look, a greasy spoon! Stuff chocolate, get yourself a fry-up. You deserve one. Besides, it is a little chilly. Get in the warm.

All of which sounded good advice, so she took it.

Thirteen

Graham was sat at his desk, concentrating damned hard – maybe a little too hard – on the job in front of him, when down the office, a phone rang.

The place was deserted, just him on shift. He had the numbers to all the key codes so access wasn't a problem, and he'd found the silence therapeutic. No chatter, just the drag and click of a mouse and the occasional keyboard click. Of course the job was a nightmare – the plans Maitland had agreed to were virtually impossible – but he took his time, doing this one perfectly, angling to spec and to spec only, no embellishments, no improvements. He didn't even correct the poor line on the double curve the plans specified, he just drew them; plan, elevation, side view as directed. He'd almost self-hypnotised, forgetting everything but the job in hand, when that damned phone rang.

Who the hell would phone here on a Saturday, he thought, making no effort to move from his chair. The phone would get to him anyway – the system was geared to ring five times at each receiver in turn, something which deterred most callers. But only if they'd rung the main switchboard number, anyone who wanted to contact them direct could dial their desk numbers.

So the phone rang five times, clicked off, another phone rang five times, clicked off, a third phone...

Persistent buggers, I'll give them that. But still, who'd ring here on a Saturday?

Hayley, maybe.

He stopped dragging the mouse and automatically saved his work. *No, she'd ring me direct, or on my mobile – which, of course, I've switched off.* He dragged his phone from his pocket while that ringing bounced around in the background and switched it on. 1 MISSED CALL FROM ELAINE, it said. He frowned at that, was about to hit the redial button when another message popped onto the screen. 1 NEW VOICEMAIL FROM ELAINE. This time his thumb was on the green icon when it was his desk phone's turn to ring.

Without thinking he snatched it up and said, 'Maitland's Designs, Graham speaking. How can I help?'

'You can tell me what the fuck you're doing there,' said his sister-in-law.

Fourteen

She listened, while chewing on a sausage made of Flubber, as he related the story of his important job in a flat, dead voice. When he'd finished, Elaine said, 'Well boo-hoo for you. So what's up with Hayley? And don't tell me she's fine, Gray, 'cause I know different.'

'What exactly do you mean?' A little worry there. Not much though. Not *enough.*

'I mean she's not been in work for three days now, I mean she's not answering any of her phones and I mean nobody's answering at the house. So, you saw her this morning – what gives?' She slurped her coffee and grimaced. That sort of thing lubricated brakes.

'I didn't,' said Graham, after a pause.

'Didn't what?' Beans now. The beans were OK, she trusted the beans. She'd seen the can they came out of.

'I didn't see her this morning.' He gave a heavy sigh. 'We're...sort of separated.'

Very slowly, Elaine swallowed. She took another slurp of brake fluid. Calmly said, 'Repeat that, please.'

'We had a...discussion, I suppose. About what was going on. There's stuff I haven't told you, but never mind that. It came down to me or the little girl. She chose the girl. I moved out, went to my parents'.'

The nagging worry was louder now, raging...but louder than it was a cold, surging fury. 'You did *what?*' Around her, she saw people jerk their heads towards her and didn't care.

'Look,' Graham said in her ear, 'you weren't there; you don't know...she's lost it, Elaine. She didn't want me there, so I thought it best...'

'You thought it best to *fuck off* and leave my sister – your *wife* – alone? When she's clearly *having a breakdown?* You decided to *pack up and leave?* Oh, how very *brave* of you! Don't you understand how vulnerable she is? Christ, she could have done *anything,* and you just FUCKED OFF?' Now the entire café was staring at her and she found she cared even less, if possible. This was bad. This was very, very bad.

'I was trying to give her space…and it's not just that, Elaine, there's this thing…look, I need to see you.'

'Get bent,' she snapped. 'I'm going back to yours now and smashing a window if I have to, and if she's swinging from the lights I swear to God and all the saints I will kill you.'

'Jesus, no – don't…' he started to say, but she cut him off, stood, stormed to the door. She almost wanted to give the café patrons a snappy comeback, a sort of *take a picture, it'll last longer,* but didn't. Time seemed too short for that. She ran into the street, ignoring her ringing phone.

Fifteen

'Mummy,' said Angie suddenly, 'aren't you hungry?'

In the space of a second, Hayley was. Just before, no. Just after, yes, a stabbing, ravenous hunger. When, exactly, had she eaten last? She tried to think back, but couldn't remember. For a moment it seemed as if she hadn't eaten for days, but that was ridiculous. Nobody went for days without eating. Not in England, anyway. 'Yes love,' she said. 'I am a bit. Why?'

'Oooh, I dunno, but your tummy made a tiger noise!' At this, Angie screwed up her face and went, '*Rooooooooaaaaaaar*,' and that just slayed them both.

'Well, in that case,' said Hayley, after she'd recovered, 'I'll best make me a sandwich or some soup or something.'

'No Mummy,' said Angie, very serious. 'You wants more. Go to the shop and get one of them big sticks of bread with cheese and ham and stuff.'

'A baguette? There's no need, sweetheart, I've got all the stuff here.' But still, now she'd mentioned it...yeah, a crusty French baguette, crammed full of ham, cheese...maybe even a couple of tomatoes...oh yes, that sounded *just fiiiine*.

'No, you have big bread stick. I'm a-sleepy now, wanna take a nap.' She gave a massively exaggerated yawn that was a cute as a button. 'I love our games.'

'Yes, me too. Will we play lots?'

'Yes, Mummy, For ever and ever. But me wanna sleep now, then play games when I get up.'

'OK my love. You know best.'

Angie curled up on the rug and closed her eyes. *I must get that cot down, put it back together*, Hayley thought. *Give her somewhere proper to sleep.*

Hayley stood, closed the nursery door quietly behind her, grabbed her bag from the bedroom and tiptoed down the stairs, closing the front door gently, her mind now set on finding the biggest baguette she could...and maybe a huge pot of tea to wash it down with. She stepped into the light, blinking a little, and set off in search of somewhere she could find them.

Two minutes later, her sister came around the corner and knocked again.

Sixteen

This time, to her amazement, the door swung open at her knock. 'Hayley,' she called. 'Hayley, are you in here? You OK?' Then, feeling ridiculous (but wasn't *everything* about this day ridiculous?) she added, 'It's Elaine.'

Nothing came back, nothing came out into the street, no answer, no cheery *hey, how you doing, come in, I've got the kettle on – yes, I know, it doesn't suit me, ha-ha.* And who would leave their front door open anyway? Their *London* front door? The door that had been so securely locked only half an hour before?

Feeling that this was wrong and growing wronger with every second, Elaine stepped inside. She peeked into the living room, reeling a little at the stale, unaired smell. Nobody, just some dust on the tables to say hello. 'Hayley,' she called again, and that fright dropped from her throat into her stomach like a lead ball, her bowels soft and loose. 'Where are you?'

Silence, still. Elaine put her head round the kitchen door, so certain was she that she'd find her dead sister there that she actually *saw* it, Hayley sitting in one of the chairs, head back, throat cut, blood pooling everywhere, her sightless eyes fixed on the ceiling...

Elaine almost screamed, closed her eyes, opened them again and saw nothing but an unoccupied kitchen. *Get a grip, girl.* So...downstairs, nothing. Which left...

She almost ran out into the street instead of turning right in the hallway onto the stairs. She took the first two, then called her sister's name again. It bounced back at her from the walls, mocking. Two more steps...and then the dream came back to her, the nightmare that had awakened her some days back, awakened her as she screamed. *Oh my dear God, was that...was that some kind of warning? A what do they call it, prophesy?*

Regardless, it didn't matter. She had to keep climbing, she had to see, no matter how scared she was, how utterly sure something terrible was waiting for her, she had to keep climbing, because this was her sister, because she had to know.

She reached the top landing and was about to call again when the *thing* ran out from the spare room, that awful, inhuman *thing*, that child with the capering, laughing pig's head, it ran at her with its hooves (trotters?) outstretched, and it screamed *'AUNTIE ELAINE'* at her in a gurgling, bubbling voice, and Elaine lost her footing, fell backwards, fell backwards down the stairs, and she heard a terrible snap and there was a bright white flare of pain and she thought *oh fuck that smarts* and then all was black and she thought no more.

Seventeen

Her lifeless body lay there, twitching a little, and the thing that was on the landing looked at it, laughing. Then it made its way to the bottom, and laid its head on the woman's corpse. It opened its enormous mouth.

There were some ripping noises as it went to work.

Eighteen

Hayley came home half an hour later, closed the door quietly, and went into the kitchen to eat her baguette. It was scrummy-dummy. She washed it down with a gallon of tea. That was scrummy-dummy too. When that was done she sat quietly, waiting for her daughter to wake up, then they could play some games. *I pity anyone who isn't me,* she thought again. *I really do.*

Chapter Sixteen

One

She was still thinking that about fifty minutes later when she heard someone let themselves in the front door. The first thing she thought was, *who's that?* The thought it might be her husband never entered her head, until she heard him call her name.

'In here,' she said, lips thin. He stood in the kitchen doorway and gaped at her.

'Where is she?' he said at last.

'Upstairs, asleep. Or at least she was. Could you keep your voice down, please?' Such an aggravating, selfish man he was.

He blinked at her. 'Why is she asleep? What are you talking about? That makes no sense.'

She stood, walked towards him, and didn't notice that he flinched back a little. 'All children need a nap in the afternoon, didn't your parents teach you that? Didn't they teach you *anything?* Apart from how to be a little prince, that is?'

He shook his head, but weirdly, as if he was half asleep. 'Not that...whatever. Elaine. Where's Elaine?'

She grabbed him by the arm and dragged him into the kitchen, closing the door behind him, somehow resisting the temptation to trap his fingers in the jamb. 'How would I know? At home, or off with some bloke, landing on the moon – and will you please keep the noise *down.*'

'She's not been here?'

'Of course she hasn't, no-one's been here. I've been here all day with Angie.' As far as she was concerned, she had been. Hayley had forgotten entirely about her trip to the shops.

Graham looked puzzled and sat at the table. *Did I tell you it was OK to sit down? To make yourself at home? Did I?* 'She said she was coming here. She rang me, said she'd been round, she'd been here and at the salon, no sign of you, and she was coming back. She said that, about an hour ago.'

'Did she? Must've been lying, playing a game or something. You know what she's like.' Again, Graham was gaping at her. How unattractive that looked, thank you very much. Had she once really stuck her tongue down that throat? Had she once really gone down on someone who looked like that? Jesus Christ, what had she been *thinking?* 'Don't stare at me like that,' she went on. 'You know what she's like. Proper little drama queen. It's all me, me, me with her. Gilly one-note on the kazoo.' She sat opposite him, revolted by him, but determined to keep her ground. This was her place. This was *their* place, her and Angie's. No way was she going to give ground. Not to him.

'Have you been to work this week?'

'No,' she said, keeping her eyes straight and her voice level. 'I've been ill.'

'I'll say,' he muttered, and nearly – nearly – received a slap for it. 'But Elaine never came here?'

'Going deaf?' She asked, smiling. 'Nobody has been here. We've been in all day. Are you receiving me?'

He said nothing, just gave her a look which was one part annoyance and nine parts condescension. He pulled his mobile out and hit the redial button. He sat, listening, then switched it off. 'Straight to voicemail.'

'So?'

He shrugged, wiped his hands over his eyes, and slumped. 'I dunno. I don't know anything anymore. She called me a coward.'

'Did she?' Hayley was growing bored. Who cared about this? What mattered was Angie would be waking up soon, and Hayley wanted to be there when she did. In case she was cranky. Children sometimes woke up that way, and Hayley wanted to be there, just in case. She'd sing a song. That'd cheer her daughter up. The one about catching the fish alive, maybe.

'She said I shouldn't have left you alone, that I'd...'

'But I'm *not* alone, am I? And you didn't want to stay, you made that plain. And now,' she said, standing, 'I'd like you to go.'

'But...Elaine...I mean, she may be...'

'I don't care about Elaine, I don't care about you, I care about my duties as a mother. So get up, go back to wherever you're sleeping and stay away. Y'hear me? *Stay away.*'

He dragged himself to his feet. Looked at her. Looked like he might speak. Didn't. After a minute standing there like a mime in need of greasepaint, he left. As soon as she heard the door close, Hayley ran upstairs. Sure enough, Angie was sitting on the rug, rubbing her eyes. 'Hello Mummy,' she whispered, and all was good in Hayley's world.

Two

Graham stood on the doorstep, wondering if there was a word to describe how he felt. The best he could come up with was *desolate*. Even that didn't cover it, not entirely. Hayley...*God!* How *thin* she seemed. Could she *possibly* have lost what looked like half a stone since he'd seen her last? She looked like someone checking out of Belsen. Add to that her dirty hair, dirty face, dirty clothes, unwashed teeth...Jesus, she *stank*. He'd tried hard not to flinch away, but some things were automatic.

Elaine. There was another thing. Where the hell was she? He rang her again, listened to the Voicemail welcome, switched off. Had she been winding him up, like Hayley had said? (And add this to the list: Hayley and Elaine loved each other as well as sisters could ever love each other, bonded perhaps by their mutual need to avoid their mother's behaviour. When had Hayley ever spoken of Elaine like *that* before today?)

He shook his head. No, Elaine's anger, her fury, her worry had been real. No wind up. She had been coming here, to check on Hayley. He knew that in his heart. So where the fuck had she got to...? And what should he do about it? Stand here, waiting, just on the off chance?

You've only Hayley's word that she didn't turn up, he found himself thinking, and that was nice, that made his day even better, thank you very much. *Would she lie? If so, why? And Elaine's phone, going to Voicemail. Straight to Voicemail. No ringing out. Straight to Voicemail. As if it were switched off. Or dead.*

No. She wouldn't lie, he told himself, and shivered. Four months ago he'd have been certain of that. Hell, *ten days ago* he'd have been certain of it. But these days she played Mummy to a ghost girl and shared a house with a killer doll. Who knew how that messed with your sense of morality?

He moaned, a low, terrible sound. *What do I do? Please, God – tell me. I'm begging You. WHAT DO I DO?*

If Elaine had come round...and Hayley was lying...what did *that* say about how badly his wife had deteriorated? And why did the Voicemail worry him so?

He started walking, uncaring about where he was going, uncaring about the car parked up outside the driveway. He just had to keep going.

He found a pub, and went in. Inside the pub he found a whisky. Then he found some more.

Three

Lillian was exhausted and by two that afternoon had curled up on the couch for a nap, Debussy oozing from the speakers, and had drifted into a very pleasant, dreamless sleep.

Until a *thump-thump* from upstairs awoke her. She sat up, clutching her chest. *It's here, she thought. That thing. It's here. It followed me from the hospital, and soon it's going to run into my living room, point at me and I'll just drop dead, like that old guy in the bed opposite, and that bastard pig-thing will dance around me, laughing.*

She lay there for a while, but the sound didn't come again. She debated going upstairs to have a look – after all, she thought as sanity restored itself, something may have fallen out of a cupboard – then decided she was fine as she was, thanks all the same. She'd had a trying twenty-four hours. A *very* trying twenty-four hours *indeed*.

But she couldn't reclaim that serenity. Her mind kept turning, turning to that awful, horrible, inhuman, unhuman thing. *What was it? Evil, that's what it was. No doubt about it. Yes, but* what *evil?* She knew evil existed, of course – in her line of business it was a given fact, like ghosts. The netherworld, the space between here and there was full of...things. Mostly just wandering lost spirits, confused, aimless, but harmless, more or less. Oh sure, some could get quite aggressive when you confronted them with the truth, that they were finished on Earth and had to move on – some of them didn't like that message *one little bit* – but the worst they could do was throw some stuff around the room or flush a toilet. Nuisances, mostly, often called 'poltergeists' by people who really didn't know what they were talking about. They were a pain, but you could get through to them. Eventually. If you wanted to put the hours in.

So yes, the space between worlds was mostly filled with poor lost ones. But sometimes, like shadows in the mist, you could see *things* lurking, watching. Shapes you could never quite make out. Shapes you didn't want to make out, shapes you never wanted to come lurching towards you, arms outstretched, a big welcoming smile on their massive grinning lips...No, when you glimpsed these things, you turned away, shut your eyes, you ignored them and hoped they'd ignore you. Because if they noticed you, they might...just...decide to...

Follow you home.

One more, her heart skipped a beat, and her clutching hand moved from her breast to her throat. *My God, is that what happened? I saw that in the hospital...it saw me...it followed me...and now it's in my house?*

But that wasn't what had happened. No, she recalled, struggling to be calm, she'd seen that thing first at the theatre, standing in the aisle. Then in the dressing room. Then in the hospital. *If it's following you, it didn't come from there, the hospital. It came from...from...*

Another thought struck her. Was it punishment? Punishment for her occasional…embellishment? For the abuse of her gifts? Something that didn't take kindly to her tricks? Maybe God - whom she was *certain* existed - had set this thing upon her as a warning? *No more tricks, honey, or Porky here comes and bites you on the tit.*

That didn't sit right, not with her concept of the Loving and Forgiving God who looked on us all with compassion, but there seemed *something* in it, all right. She'd been struck by the word *warning* all the time since she'd seen it. It had pointed at her once and she'd passed out…it'd pointed at the old man and he'd died…*see what we can do,* it'd been saying, hadn't it? *See how clever we are.*

We?

Call me Legion, for we are many.

Fear that she had never known - fear that she could have gone her whole life without experiencing - hit her like a sledgehammer. Compared to this, what she'd felt when she'd set eyes on that thing was a mild fright. 'A man afflicted with demons…' she whispered. 'And Jesus cast them out into…into swine…and the swine drowned themselves in the river. But before…' Her voice gave out, but she knew the rest well enough. Jesus had asked the demon's name, and it had said, 'Call me Legion, for we are many.'

Swine. We are many.

Not the *same* demon – and yes, *of course* it was a demon, an Imp from Hell itself – but one of many. A different one at the theatre? Yes. The hospital…oh, what a place that would be for them. Death was a regular visitor there, didn't keep to the hours stated on the boards, Death turned up when he wanted… so where better for them to…to…

Feed.

Feed. Of course, feed. What else? Feed. Upon what she didn't know, and didn't care. She'd been warned. *Stay out of this*, and even though she didn't know what *this* was, she had every intention of obeying. If she stayed still, stayed very small, hid under a blanket and made no sound at all, maybe they'd forget all about her.

She *wanted* to be forgotten about. She really did. She never wanted to be woken from a nap by a *thump-thump* from upstairs ever again.

Four

'I wanna report a missing person,' slurred Graham to a policeman at ten thirty that night.

'Sir,' said the duty officer with a heavy sigh that said *It's a Saturday night in North London and any minute now World War Three will kick off outside these doors and I have no time to deal with a drunk, so fuck off. Sir.* 'I suggest you go home and sober up, and if you still want to make a report you can come back in the morning.'

'Burrit's important,' he stumbled on, wondering firstly why he suddenly sounded so much like Danny from the office and secondly why this arsehole wouldn't take him seriously He'd been unable to get Elaine on the phone since he'd left his old home – oh, how that hurt – and he'd spent four hours in the pub, downing drink after drink, punching redial after redial and getting nothing but that bastard Voicemail and he was now seriously worried. As well as seriously pissed. 'Hur name's Elaine Buchanan an she lives at...' he gave a huge burp, hiccupped, felt vomit at the back of his throat, swallowed it down, nearly fell, caught the desk and steadied himself, 'sorry. She lives at...'

'Sir,' the copper said, 'you're very drunk, and I cannot understand a word you say. So please, go home, sober up. If whatever your problem is hasn't resolved itself by then, by all means come in and see us. In the meantime, I cannot help you.'

'I wanna see your superior officer,' Graham said, drunkenly offended. And also drunkenly terrified.

'I didn't get a word of that sir. Now please, go home or I shall escort you off the premises. If you refuse to go quietly I may arrest you for drunk and disorderly and violent conduct against a Police Officer. Do I make myself clear?'

Oh, he did. This lack of understanding was strictly one-way, it seemed. OK then, the Boys in Blue would do nothing. So he'd do it himself. He'd go to Elaine's flat. See if she was there. *That'd* show them.

He turned on his heel and staggered out onto the street, wondering where the hell the bloody Tube station was from here.

Five

'One more, Mummy, one more about Tigger and Roo!'

'No honey,' said Hayley. 'It's late, past your bedtime already. You go to sleep, and we'll play more tomorrow.' Children needed boundaries and rules. They were happier that way.

Angie opened her mouth to protest, then sighed. 'OK then. Night Mummy.'

'Goodnight angel.' Hayley leaned over and kissed her daughter on her slightly bristly chin. 'Shall I leave the landing light on and the door open a little?'

'Please. Keeps the bogeyman away,' she said, smiling.

Angie settled down on the floor (*tomorrow, the cot*), and Hayley stepped onto the landing and pulled the door to, leaving just the faintest crack of light playing across Angie's beautiful face...and on that glint...that reflection of light on something silver...something metal...

'Mummy?' Angie had opened one eye and was looking at her. 'Wanna go sleepy now.'

'Yes, of course baby. Night night.' Hayley walked to the bathroom, urinated, and went to bed without washing her hands, or anything at all. She didn't think of that odd, reflected light at all, the way it had glinted back off something on the floor, something rectangular. Maybe four inches by five.

After all, what would a child – little more than a baby – want with a mobile phone?

Six

Graham had heard the phrase 'Beer taxi' before – Danny in the office had used it often enough – but had never really known what it meant until that Saturday night. It was truly like the transporter they'd had on that old *Star Trek* show – one minute he was exiting the police station, gruffly affronted and also terrified, the next he was standing outside Elaine's flat in Highgate. *Fair few miles covered there*, he thought. *I'll feel that in the morning. Also, I walked all that way, pissed, at night in London. Did someone miss the sign on my back with MUG ME written on it?*

He stared at the bells on the front door, decided they were in Chinese, squinted at them, decided one had FLAT 5 written on it, and pressed his finger to it. He couldn't hear it ring, so he just kept on pressing. He put his whole weight behind it, almost totally supporting himself on his right index finger.

Time, of course, has no meaning to the drunk. He could have been standing there for five hours or five seconds before he decided she wasn't coming down. He frowned, mulling it over, wanting another drink. Also, not to be crude, a piss. He took a step back, onto the street, saw nowhere he could get one or do the other, and so looked up at the building. A double fronted terrace, carved into boxes. Two windows downstairs. Two more on the first floor. Two more on the third. Counting twice – well, you had to be sure at that time of night - he decided top right, third floor was Elaine's. No light – but then none of them was lit up. *Need a stone*, he thought. He cast about, looking for one. *Typical. You can never find a stone when you need one.* This made him laugh, a laugh which was joined by a drunken burp that started in his toes. For a second he thought he might vomit, and hung onto the gatepost as that wave of nausea passed. *Stone. Something. Gotta see if she's in, if she's safe. Fucking coppers. Gotta do their job. Bastard filth.* His squinting eyesight found something that looked likely – not so much a stone, looked like half a slate off the roof or something. *This'll get her up.* He threw it as hard and as far as he could.

It hit, of course – one of the immutable laws of the Universe, never to be broken, is that drunks will never hurt themselves when they fall over, will never charm a woman into bed unless she's worse off than he is, and will never miss when hurling half a slate at a flat window in the early hours of a Sunday morning. He stood there for a second, noting no change, then looked around for something else to chuck, then – miracle – the light went on and the window opened. A man in his fifties looked out, and didn't seem happy. 'What fuck you doin'?'

Greek? Turkish? Dunno, could be an Armenian. Still, he's doing OK with the swearing, got that down. 'Get Elaine down here,' he yelled up. Another immutable law of the Universe is that drunks have no volume control. 'Need to see Elaine.'

'No Yell-nane, go away crazy man.' Some babble behind him. He turned and babbled back. Then, to Graham. 'You go or I call police.'

'Don't bother, they're not fucked. Get Elaine down here, I can hear her. Send her!' More lights were snapping on. *Good, come one, come all, roll up and see the show!*

'You crazy. No Yell-nane. Go now!'

The window went down, but Graham could see his shadow behind the net curtain, watching. *No you don't, arsehole.* He looked about him, saw nothing more to throw, then staggered down the street again and found a Bud bottle left by some late night reveller. He took it back and hurled that at the window. It hit the sill and shattered into a million pieces. *'ELAINE! ELAINE! ARE YOU ALL RIGHT?'*

Shadows moved behind lots of windows now, people peeking at him…but one window remained black. With a drunk's reasoning, Graham saw he'd *really* fucked up this time. Elaine's flat was *next to* the Armenian's. Or the Turk's. Or whatever the hell he was. 'Hey mate,' he yelled, 'sorry. Got the wrong fucking flat. Sorry mate. Mate?' His mate didn't seem to want to accept the apology. *Fuck him, then. I was only trying to be polite.* There was nothing left to throw, at least that he could see, so he resorted to shouting her name, over and over, and wasn't it a little scary that her window remained dark when everyone else's was at 100 watt Heaven? He kept shouting, then screaming, but before he could act on his next impulse – to kick the door down and storm the building – he became aware of the blue flashing lights and the hand on his shoulder.

'Keep it down will you, sir? People are trying to sleep.'

Seven

Whilst Hayley slept, something in her house opened the spare room door and went for a little walk. First of all it went to watch the woman sleep. It'd be easy. It'd be easy anyway, but especially now. Lying there, in the dark, unprotected...easy, but no challenge. And when you pretty much lived forever, challenge was what you were after. Otherwise...well, you may as well just give up.

It withdrew, then made its way downstairs. It opened the bin. Threw the phone in it. Closed the lid again then went back to its room...well, the room it mostly stayed in. The room she *thought* it stayed in, anyway, shut the door behind it and fell fast asleep.

It had a full stomach, after all, and that always made it sleepy.

Eight

At nine o'clock the following morning, Graham was led from the cell to the station desk, to be greeted – if that was the word – by his father.

'How much trouble's he in?' Jim asked the desk sergeant, a young woman.

'None, really,' she said, giving Graham a slight smile. 'He was a little drunk – no, a lot drunk – last night, hurled a slate and a bottle at a window, did a bit of shouting, but when the officers showed up he behaved himself.'

'I should bloody hope so. I'm so sorry for this.' Then, to Graham, 'Why the *hell* didn't you call us? Your mother's been worried sick about you.' *And me,* was the unspoken subtext. On top of that, *how old are you? I'll tell you how old, too bloody old to be acting like a fifteen year old after his first bottle of Strongbow!*

Graham would have wilted, *should* have wilted. He'd been up all night in that metal box, gradually coming to his senses as he heard bedlam break out all around him. He had vague, confused memories of everything that had happened – refusing to tell the officers where he lived, desperately trying to tell them what was wrong, and then, eventually, telling them he wasn't going anywhere, he was staying right here, thank you very much, and then being frogmarched to the van, and –hey, beer taxi! – next thing he's sat in a cell minus his shoes and belt, trying not to vomit in the corner. On top of all that, there was his dad, looking sterner than he'd ever seen him – worse, looking *disappointed*. Yeah, he should have wilted. He just didn't. There was too much at stake.

'What's he being charged with?' Jim asked the desk sergeant.

'Nothing, not even D&D. Just a warning, not even an official caution.' She handed Graham an envelope. 'Check this over and sign, please.' When he stared at her blankly, she went on, 'your belongings.'

He nodded, opened the envelope and was sorting through keys, phone, his wallet and diary – *and shoes, hell of an envelope* – when he asked, 'Who do I see about reporting a missing person?'

'What the hell d'you mean, son?' his father asked.

Graham ignored him, signed the form, and looked at the officer on duty. 'Please. It's important.'

The duty officer looked first at him, then his dad, then back at him. 'You want to make an official report?'

Graham turned his phone on. There were no missed calls from Elaine. Three from his parents' number, but none from Elaine. This he found terrifying. How many messages had he left her? *Christ, you'd think she'd have replied, even just a text to say WILL YOU SOD OFF?* 'Yes,' he said, and something in his face must've got through, as she nodded and picked up the desk phone, started muttering down the line.

As he did, Jim caught him on the arm and pulled him to one side. 'OK son, what the bloody hell's this? You're missing the whole day, we get a call from the Rozzers at half past two saying you're being detained overnight, y'smell like y've bathed in bloody whisky,' in his distress, Jim was sounding more Scottish than ever, 'so what the *hell*'s going on?'

'It's Elaine, Dad,' he said, swallowing. There was a horrible dry click as he did so, and he was ravenously thirsty all of a sudden. 'She's missing.' Then he told the truth that was in his heart. 'I think she's dead.'

Nine

'Baa baa black sheep, have you any wool? Yes, sir. Yes, sir – three bags full! One for the master and one for the dame, and one for the little boy who...Angie? You all right, sweetheart?'

She'd started to join in, then had broken off suddenly, as if listening. For some reason, that alarmed Hayley quite a bit. The look on her face...watchful, alert...far too grown up for her little girl. But after a second, that sunny smile was back on her face. 'My Mummy's *so* pretty!' she said, then ran and hugged her.

Oh, this was the best. Was there *ever* a better feeling than being hugged by your child? Was there? Could there be? Hayley wanted this to go on forever, for them never to disentangle. But they did, and part of her died. 'But you might be prettier,' Angie said.

Totally unoffended - this was only the brutal honesty of a child, after all – Hayley asked how. '*Welllll...*' Angie drawled, head on one side, 'my Mummy's hair used to be bright mellow.'

'Yellow, honey,' Hayley corrected gently.

'*Yell*...low,' Angie said, carefully. Then, 'but its blacker now. And you used to have red on your cheeks and your mouth and now you've not got none.'

'Haven't got any,' she replied, then thought about it. True, she'd not thought to put makeup on for...how long? And her hair? God, when was the last time she washed it? Never mind her hair, when was the last time she'd taken a bath? Brushed her teeth, even? Jesus, she must look rank! No wonder Angie had said what she did. 'Your old Mum's got a bit slovenly, I'm sorry.'

'What's slov...slovenly?'

'Dirty. Messy. Like a little messy piggy!' At this she buried her head in Angie's chest and oinked. Angie laughed, very, very hard at this. 'OK babe, point taken,' she continued when she'd straightened up. 'Mummy's going to take a bath, wash her hair, and make herself all pretty. Will you be all right while I do this? You want a toy to play with?'

'Yes! Doggy! Give me doggy!'

'*Please.*'

Mildly admonished, Angie said 'Please.' And held her arms out.

Hayley took doggy from the shelf, handed it to her little girl, kissed her and headed off to the bathroom. In the nursery, Angie grinned.

Ten

They sat in the interview room, Jim refusing to leave his son's side, and Graham went through the preliminaries with the officer ('Detective Lewis, CID – yeah, just like off the telly,' he'd said with a weary grin.) He'd given his name, addresses – postal and the one he was currently residing in – date of birth, and the name of the person he was reporting as missing.

'How old is Miss...um,' Lewis looked at his paper, 'Buchanan?'

'I'm not entirely sure,' Graham said, taking a swig from the cup of water they'd provided. It wasn't enough to quench that raging thirst – he had a feeling nothing would be, not even Lake Superior – but it was marginally better than nothing. 'Twenty-two, twenty-three. She's younger than my wife.'

'I see,' Lewis muttered, leaving a space on that bit of his form. 'She's what relation to you?'

'Sister-in-law. My wife's sister.'

'And you and your wife are separated, if I read these addresses correctly. Yes?'

'Yes.'

'Long time?'

'Just last week.'

That was written down. 'And what makes you think your sister-in-law is a missing person?'

Graham very deliberately took Lewis through the events of the day before. That wasn't a problem, everything before the pub was nice and clear. It was everything *after* that which was a bit hazy.

Lewis listened, jotted notes occasionally, then said, 'What time did she phone you? When she said she was going to see your wife.'

'It'll be logged in my phone. May I?'

'Be my guest.'

He took his Nokia out, scrolled through RECEIVED CALLS. '15:35.'

Duly jotted. 'And you've heard nothing from her since?'

'No. I went round to see Hayley about an hour, hour and a half maybe, later. Hayley said she'd never turned up.'

'Where were you when you took Elaine's call?'

'At work. Maitland's Designs, in Camden.'

Jotted down. 'Your wife said she'd not seen her sister?' Graham shook his head. 'Do you know where Elaine was when she called you?'

'No. But she said she'd been at the house a few minutes ago, and I could hear…well, cutlery and plates in the background. There's a few cafés round our way. She could have been in one of them, but I'm not sure.'

'For the sake of argument, if she *had* been in one of them, how long do you reckon it would have taken her to reach your house?'

'No more than ten minutes.'

'So, from…let's say your call ended at 15:50. Ten minute walk, by four she'd be at the door. But your wife says no one came. Not a big window for Elaine to vanish in, busy road, broad daylight…'

'But not impossible. And she's not answering her phone, hasn't replied to any messages,' a small, embarrassed cough, 'and I'm pretty certain she wasn't home last night. All of which makes me uneasy, Detective.' He felt like a horse's arse calling someone 'Detective,' but then he'd felt a horse's arse since the hand on his shoulder early that morning.

'But still, look at it from our point of view. Your sister-in-law is free and over twenty-one. We can plot her movements up until about a quarter to four yesterday. It's not yet eleven this morning. Not even twenty-four hours, Mr Davis.' He sat back, arms folded. *You see how it is.*

Yeah, Graham saw. Lewis was sat opposite an unshaven, hungover man in his mid-twenties who's been held for, basically, arseing about in public the night before and was spinning a very thin story that wasn't really a story at all. If only he could make this guy see... 'The thing is, Detective Lewis, there's some stuff you need to know.' Beside him, he felt his dad tighten up, and Lewis – no doubt an expert body language reader – sensed it too.

'Oh?'

'Well, I'm not sure my wife is a reliable witness.'

Lewis sat forward. 'Look, there may be some bitterness between you – I've been separated, I know how it goes – but try not to let it cloud you, mate.'

Mate. He's Good Cop. But he's on his own. Does he have to do Bad Cop as well? 'Actually I don't feel bitter towards her at all. I still love her, I want to get back with her. But she's…had some kind of breakdown. She had a miscarriage a few months back.' A grunt of sympathy from the policeman. 'Since then…well, things haven't been so good. And when I went round there yesterday it looked like she'd not washed for days – and,' he went on, turning to his dad, 'you know what she was like about her appearance.' Back to Lewis. 'She's a beautician by trade, has to look the part or the clients lose confidence. But she's not been to work for days either. I was shocked at how she looked. Thin, like she's not been eating. Eyes didn't track well. And that dirt…she hadn't even cleaned her teeth for ages.'

'Mr Davis,' said Lewis, turning to Jim. 'You look shocked by this.'

'I am, sir,' said Jim, gently respectful, but never taking his eyes off Graham. 'Hayley's…beautiful. Takes pride in her appearance. To hear that…no, that doesn't sound like her at all.'

'I'm worried about her, too,' said Graham. 'But I know that's not your business. All I am saying is I'm not sure she'd have noticed if Elvis and Michael Jackson had turned up and sang a duet in our living room.' He saw Lewis try to hide a smile at that, but by Christ he didn't find anything funny. 'She's not a well woman. I don't want to say this – I don't want to *think* this – but even if Elaine had turned up, I'm not sure Hayley would have noticed. But please, I don't know how to say this so you'll take me seriously, but I am *certain* that Elaine's in trouble. Even if you do nothing, can you please note I was here, that I told you this, take her description? *Something. Please.*' Tears were coming, tears of exhaustion, tears of despair, tears of fear. 'I'm begging you.'

Lewis sat back again, thought for a while, then said, 'OK, here's as far as I can go for now. I'll take a drive to your sister-in-law's. See who's in and who's not. Chat to a couple of neighbours, if they're about. Then I'll go and see your wife. And if no-one's seen her, or she doesn't get in touch by five tonight I'll list her as a missing person. But,' he went on, sitting forward, 'I'm doing this because, despite last night, you impress me as an honest lad. I ran your name through the computer, came up nothing. Not even a speeding ticket. Last night seems a little out of character. Frankly, though, Elaine seems a low priority case.' Graham started to speak, but Lewis overrode him. 'Sir, listen. Yes, you know her better than I do. Yes, you'll know what she's likely to do and what she isn't likely to do. But given her age, her social group, for all I know she might have decided to say "I'm off to Monaco for the weekend." You follow?'

Graham reluctantly nodded. He could read between lines. *We're up to our eyes in stoned junkie homeless thieves and murderers. We're drowning in paperwork. There's guns on the street and knives in the throats. One white middle class girl decides to duck her phone calls? Well, so fucking what? BFD, pal. Take a ticket, take a seat, we'll get to you in 2050, if we're not dead by then.* 'Thanks. I appreciate that.'

'No problem. Give me the description then get the hell out of here, get some rest. And if you don't mind me saying,' he wrinkled his nose, 'your wife's not the only one you could do with some Radox.'

Eleven

Hayley luxuriated. She'd lit the candles, washed her hair, her body, scrubbed her teeth till the gums bled, then topped up the water and soaked again. *Oh, bliss.*

But life was *all* bliss these days, wasn't it? All of it. OK, she might have got overexcited a little – forgetting to wash, how silly – but then, she hated leaving Angie, even for a second. But never mind, she'd been reminded now. Now she wouldn't forget again.

Now she'd be fine. In fact…well, she'd be *more* than fine, wouldn't she? In fact, she'd be *excellent*. Excellent, convincing, charming…who *wouldn't* believe a word she said? Not that she was expecting to talk to anyone. But if she did…oh, she felt like she could charm the birds from the trees, make an Arsenal fan buy a season ticket to Spurs (as someone she distantly recalled had once been fond of saying.) She was an empress – beautiful, composed, calm and reassuring…a beneficent ruler, generous and loving.

Eventually, she stepped out of the bath and towelled dry. She pulled on her robe and made her way to her bedroom – wincing a little at the unaired smell. She opened the windows, let the fresh air in, selected a powder blue top and jeans from the wardrobe, then sat down at the mirror to do her face and blow-dry her hair. *It's the little touches that matter*, she thought. For a second she wondered, *matter to whom*, then decided she knew. *Mattered to her. And to Angie. Most importantly to Angie.*

Twelve

'I don't know no Yell-nane,' said the Turkish gentleman. 'I tell crazy man who smash bottles, I no know this name.'

Lewis smiled at him, even though he was giving his usual inward sigh. *I love London,* he thought. He was from Hatfield originally. In Hatfield – even now – if you left your milk bottles out for too long people noticed. London? *Nah, nobody looked past their noses. Wasn't safe, might get them shot off.* 'Elaine Buchanan,' he said. 'Lives across the hall.' He pointed with his thumb at the door he'd got no reply from after he'd rung the front doorbell and the woman from Flat 1 had let him in the building. She didn't know any Elaine either. ''Bout five foot five, dark blonde hair, blue eyes. Have you lived here long?'

'Half year. Lease just came up, we sign. We good people,' he seemed to think Lewis was on his case. 'Make no trouble.'

'I'm sure,' said Lewis. 'It's the young lady I'm looking for. You sure you haven't seen her? Not even once? If you've been here six months…'

'Oh, I see her, sure,' he said, slightly relieved. 'Time to time. She smile, say hello – y'know? Didn't know name. Quiet mostly, no trouble her.' He sniffed. 'Not like Greeks downstairs. Them, huh!'

Lewis gave a *yeah, bastard Greeks eh*, smile and said, 'You say "mostly" quiet? What does that mean, sir?'

'Few night back, she scream in night. We hear in here. Was loud. But I see her next morning, she says hello. I ask, she says bad dream. But that only thing, only problem.' He cast a filthy glance down the stairs.

'And you haven't seen her for the last couple of days.'

He thought. 'No. Maybe Thursday last time I see. Maybe Wednesday.' He shrugged.

Yeah, London, thought Lewis. *For all you know it was a month back. We stopped looking out for each other a while back, didn't we? The human race, God bless it and all who drown in its shit.* 'Thank you very much for your help, sir. Sorry to have disturbed you.'

The Turkish gentleman – he'd given his name but Lewis had forgotten it, far too hard for him to pronounce, and how nice a guy did that make *him?* – went back inside. Lewis stood on the landing for a minute, walked back to Elaine's door and listened. No TV, no radio, no footsteps, no nothing. He thought about knocking again, then didn't. He'd go and see her sister instead, maybe with a mask over his nose if her husband was to be believed.

Thirteen

Except he didn't, as the woman who answered his knock was a heartstopper. So much so that Lewis actually took a step back and was momentarily wrong footed. Not what they'd approve of in Hendon, but what the hell? *This is what he walked out on,* he thought, and on top of that, *arsehole*. Her hair was immaculate, makeup also, and those enormous blue eyes…oh, he'd have sold his soul for a woman who looked like that when he was younger.

'Yes,' she said, after a pause. 'Can I help?'

'I'm sorry,' said Lewis, rolling his tongue back in his mouth and mopping the drool from his tie. He held up his warrant card. 'Detective Lewis. I was wondering if I could come in and have a word, Mrs Davis.'

A worried frown crossed those blue eyes, and Lewis, who considered himself an expert in body language, saw confusion, apprehension, but no fear; the usual reaction of someone totally innocent who finds a copper on their doorstep. He called it the *oh fuck who died* look. 'Oh God. Yes, of course.' Flustered, she stood back, allowed him in, and stood twittering, hands fluttering. She wouldn't have closed the door if Lewis hadn't pointed at it. 'What's happened?' she almost begged. 'What is it? Please.'

'Well, we're not sure anything *has* happened yet, Mrs Davis.' He pointed to the living room. 'Shall we?'

She led him in – the room, like the woman, was spotless, fragrant – and sat on the sofa. She took the armchair. She didn't so much sit as perch on the edge. 'This is just an enquiry. Your husband Graham was at the station this morning…'

'Oh God, what's happened to him? Is he all right?'

Separated, but still concerned. He pulled his notebook from his pocket and flipped it open, but made no attempt to write anything. 'He's fine. Might have a bit of a sore head, but he's OK.' He saw her relax, just a touch. She was twiddling her wedding ring around in a circle, and he kept an eye on that. He knew how to read signs. 'He wanted us to check on the whereabouts of your sister,' he made a show of looking down at the empty page in his notebook, 'Elaine. He'd like us to file an official missing person report on her.'

'Yes,' she said, nodding. 'He was here yesterday, saying something about talking to her, that she'd been on her way.'

'And she didn't turn up?'

'No, I was home all day. I've not been too well, didn't go into work.'

No let-up in the ring twiddling, no suddenly looking *too hard* in the eyes, no involuntary swallowing or dropping of the voice. 'The only person you saw was your husband?' He doodled a squiggly line.

'Yes. I'm not sure what time he came round, early evening I think. Could have been about fiveish. Could've been later.'

No exaggeration, no embellishment, no *well, it was exactly 5:05, I know because I looked at the clock like I always do at that time. I was thinking maybe I'd have some dinner or check the final scores on the Red Button – I don't know, how lucky are United, eh? He knocked four times, and he was wearing a blue coat and a hat with a feather in it.* Just the facts, ma'am, as best as she could remember them. 'When was the last time you saw your sister?' he said; if she was covering something a sudden change of tack never hurt.

'Uh...I think a week last Friday,' she squinted into the distance, still fiddling with her wedding ring, her voice at the same pitch. 'Yes. She came round, we had some drinks and a chat. Nothing fancy. Split a bottle of wine and talked about crap, really.' She smiled at the memory, then that smile faded, she looked right at him. *Oh my word*, he found himself thinking. *All that and a bag of chips.* 'She's not missing, is she? She couldn't be. Please.'

'Well, we're unsure at the moment,' he said carefully. One, because they weren't sure of anything. Two, because his heart was thumping a little too much. Also, he might have to be careful about his sitting position if she kept looking at him like that. 'Have you spoken to her since then?'

'Oh…um,' more thinking. 'No. No I haven't.'

'Is that unusual? Do you normally speak quite often?'

'We don't…well, sometimes. Sometimes a couple of times a week, or a load of texts in one day. Sometimes we go for weeks without speaking. I mean, we won't have had a row or anything, it's just like…sometimes we've got nothing to say. You know?'

Lewis, who had four brothers, knew *exactly*. Sometimes they were on top of each other, sometimes they weren't. The normal pattern of families, that was, in his experience. 'I don't wish to pry, but you and your husband separated recently?'

'Yes, that's right.' A small, sad smile, but she kept on twisting that ring. 'I had a miscarriage a little while back. For some reason that caused us problems. I'd like to think we can make a go of it.' *If you can't,* thought Lewis, *give me a call.* 'Maybe we just need a little space, like they say on the soaps. He's a lovely man, but…' she gave a little shrug. *Who knows the future,* that shrug said.

'Have you spoken to Elaine about that?'

'No,' she said, and now she *did* drop her voice – but it wasn't a lie, he was sure about that. 'I was ashamed. Still am. Nobody's blameless when people split up – even if only for a while. I thought if I said nothing, and we did get back together, then nobody needed to know.'

'I understand.' He did too. It'd had taken him a while to 'fess up to his split. *If you carry on as if it's business as usual, then you get through the day.* 'OK Mrs Davis,' he said snapping the book shut and hoping he could stand without poking her eye out, 'I've taken up enough of your time.' He stood, and well….if she didn't look at his beltline he'd be fine. He made for the front door, and she followed him. 'If she gets in touch, or you manage to contact her, please let me know. I'll do the same. Try not to worry, nine times out of ten these things sort themselves out.'

'Yeah,' she whispered, 'but there's always that tenth time, isn't there? I'd better call Mum, see if she's heard anything.'

'Please do. And let me know one way or the other.' He dug his wallet out, produced his card. 'Any of those numbers, don't worry about the time.' *I'm single,* he almost said. *So, you know...you don't have to worry about disturbing anything. Unless you* want *to disturb something.* He blinked, astonished at himself, then took another look at her and wasn't astonished at all. She wasn't a suspect in anything, after all. He was convinced she'd spoken the literal truth the whole time. Hell, he was single, over twenty-one – by some margin – what was wrong with looking at a nice fit sort?

'Oh yes, I will, don't worry. God. I hope she's all right. I might go round to hers, see if she's OK.'

'You have a key?' said Lewis, almost slapping himself on the forehead. Why hadn't he asked that before?

'No, but...y'know...' She trailed off, gave a weak, hopeless smile.

'I suggest you stay here, call your mum, let me know what she says. In the meantime, I'll keep you informed.' He wanted to say more. No, he wanted to hug her, give her comfort that way, to press against her, take her upstairs, maybe see the sights and ride the rides, but instead he let himself out onto the street, went to his car and thought for a while. *Let's see. He says she's a tramp. I see she's a babe. What's that about? Just being nasty? Trying to discredit her for some reason? Why? Makes no sense. And she's telling the truth, her story jibes with his –* he *was telling the truth too, about that at least, if not his wife's relationship with a flannel. Which leaves me with…well, just a woman who says she's going somewhere and doesn't arrive. Neighbours haven't seen her, so what's new? Her last known locale was…where? She called him, he could hear cutlery in the background, a café. Not far from here. Her husband said there was a couple. Why not have a scan round, see what could be seen. I could walk, but stuff it, it's cold. I'll take a crawl up there, show the card, ask around, get a sandwich. I'm starvin', Marvin.*

He let the clutch out and drove off.

Fourteen

She closed the door behind the copper and went back upstairs. 'Angie?' she asked, pushing the door open. 'Hon?' But Angie was curled up on the rug, thumb in her mouth, other arm around doggy with his lolling tongue, so Hayley closed the door quietly and went downstairs for something to eat.

It was funny, but as she pulled slices of bread from the loaf and rammed them in the toaster, she thought that while that...man...had been in the living room (and her memories of him were already starting to fade), she'd felt...well, full of life, somehow. Vibrant. Sexy, even. But now...well, now...for a second, as she felt dark curtains close in her mind, she was a little scared. *What's happened to me,* she thought...then forgot that she'd thought that. Forgot the man who'd been there. She stood by the toaster, waiting for the bread to pop up. When it did, she'd eat it. After that, she'd see if Angie wanted a play. Yeah, that'd be a good time – that was *always* a good time.

In the dark room above her, something sat up and very quietly giggled wetly to itself.

Fifteen

Lewis hit paydirt first time out. He'd ordered a sausage sandwich and a mug of tea, and as the guy brought them to his table he surreptitiously flashed the card. 'Detective Lewis,' he murmured. 'Just like to know if there was a woman in here on Saturday, about three. Five foot five or so, dark blonde hair, blue eyes. She might have had a row with someone whilst talking on her mobile.'

'Yeah, reckon so,' the guy said, relieved no doubt that Lewis wasn't from the Council and checking for rat droppings. 'Dunno 'bout the eyes, but yeah. There was a girl sat right there, as it happens, screaming into her phone. I was behind the counter an' even *I* could hear it. Givin' some poor bastard a right earful. Then she gets up an' legs it out the door, leaves half her Full English. Hate that. Waste, innit? Some poor bastard African would've been grateful for it.'

Lewis looked at his sausage sandwich and thought, *you reckon? I think they'd prefer to starve.* 'You're sure of the time?'

'Saturday's a busy day, lotta traffic in an' out, but yeah. Threeish is about right.'

'Did you make out anything she actually said?'

'Nah, not 'specially. Like I says, I was behind the counter. She might've used the word "coward" but I wouldn't wanna swear in Court on that.'

'No. OK then, thank you.' Relieved, the waiter (*hah!*) went away, and Lewis reluctantly bit into his sandwich. Waste not, want not and all that. And how much closer was he to anything concrete on Elaine? Not at all, really – but Graham's story about their argument on the phone was more or less substantiated. Which meant Elaine had been here. It was perhaps a ten minute walk from here to the house. So somewhere between here and there, on a well-lit relatively busy road in Crouch End on a Saturday, she'd just...popped out.

I'll check for hit and runs when I get back. Traffic incidents. There's a junction back there. I mean, you never know, do you, and...WHAT THE FUCK'S THAT?

It was, in fact, a pig. Sitting opposite him. In a café. A small pig in a white lace dress. Its snout was twitching, drooling, its tongue drooping. It almost seemed to be smiling at him.

The last thing Detective Lewis – just like on the telly – thought was, *Oh mate, I'm sorry if I'm eating your brother.*

The pig grunted, pointed a trotter at him, and Lewis felt a huge piece of sausage sandwich block his throat. He coughed. The blockage stayed where it was. He tried to cough again. But no sound came. The blockage seemed to grow. He could feel his face become hot, his heart spasming. He tried to stand, couldn't. He tried to drag air in through his nose, but it lodged in his throat and went nowhere near his lungs, lungs he could visualise now as balloons, balloons that were deflating. He gagged. He retched. He tried to push his hands into his chest and perform the Heimlich on himself, but his arms were too heavy. He could feel his eyes bugging. Around him, dimly, he could hear people asking if he was all right and someone asking if anyone knew first aid, but all he could see was the pig, the pig in the dress, the pig opposite him, and as his lights went dark and his air ran out, he saw the pig laugh.

Sixteen

'Mummy, Mummy,' Angie called from the top of the stairs, 'I had the most lovely dream!'

Chapter Seventeen

One

At five o'clock that Sunday, Graham rode the Tube from Shepherd's Bush to Crouch End, walked to his front door, thought about knocking, and didn't. Instead he slouched back to his car, gave it the once over – nothing broken – and drove it back to his parents', to their disapproving and worried glances and stilted conversation. He waited for his phone to ring with some information about Elaine. It didn't. He waited for Elaine to ring. She didn't. He thought about ringing Hayley or Anna, to see if anyone had heard anything. He didn't. He took some consolation – as much as he could – from the fact that Elaine would now be officially a Missing Person and all the resources available to the Metropolitan Police would be hurled at finding her (in his mind he saw coppers beating at grass with sticks, or forming a human chain and scouring pavements, just like he'd seen on TV) but then he'd sigh and remember the expression on that idiot Lewis's face, the one that said *she's over twenty-one, she can go where she likes*.

I can't just sit here and do nothing, he thought, but that's just what he did.

'How worried are you, son?' his Dad had asked earlier that evening.

'Very,' he'd replied. 'So worried I can't think what to do for the best.'

Jim hadn't even attempted to comfort or quieten him. He just let him worry. Sometimes that's the best parents can do for their children, let them worry and don't lie to them about how it will all come out all right in the end. Sometimes it didn't. Everyone knew that.

Two

Maitland sat in his chair, gleaming at him in triumph. Graham hardly took him in, even when he said, 'You're sacked. Clear your desk and get out.'

Graham shrugged, and stood up. Maitland called after him, 'Don't you want to know why?' He stopped, turned and stared at the fat bastard, face a blank. Who cared? 'You walked out of here on Saturday and left the place wide open,' Maitland rejoiced. 'And don't try and deny it, I ran the security tape. Got a call from the police. The *police*,' he said again, as if Graham hadn't heard him. He'd heard, he just didn't care. 'They told me they'd driven by, saw the place wide open on a Saturday, no cars in the car park, had walked in to check – place was empty. "Why," I said, "we're not open on a Saturday, I authorised no overtime." So I came down here to check everything was OK. Nothing stolen, thank God, otherwise I'd be after you in Court – so count yourself lucky, young man – but when I ran the tape and saw you just get up from your desk and run out of the building without locking anything behind you, I thought, "Well, *there's* gross misconduct for you!" Not a tribunal in the land would argue that, Davis! Not one! So clear your desk and get out. Now.'

Graham turned and moved to the door again, and once more Maitland called him back. 'Haven't you got anything to say to me?'

'Yeah,' said Graham. 'You're a fat bastard and nobody likes you.'

He was so depressed he couldn't even enjoy that. He walked on stiff legs to his desk and pulled the photo of Hayley from its frame. As he placed it in his jacket pocket, Danny said, 'What's up, mate?'

'Got sacked. Don't care.' The younger man's face fell in shock. 'You're a good lad, Dan. Don't forget that. We'll go for a pint sometime, yeah?'

With that he left the building, like Elvis, for the last time.

Three

Twenty minutes later he was at the police station. 'Is Detective Lewis on duty today?' he asked the duty copper. 'I'd like a word with him, please. My name is Graham Davis, we spoke yesterday.'

The duty copper had a very sad face. 'I'm afraid Detective Lewis had an accident yesterday evening,' he said. 'He died. We're all very upset about it here. Can I help you at all?'

'No,' said Graham, the wind knocked out of him. His sacking hadn't bothered him, but this...*Accident, died.* The words chased themselves around his head, playing hide and seek. 'No. It's fine, thanks.' He walked out into the overcast day and nearly fainted. He grabbed hold of a litter bin and managed to stay upright. Just.

Accident. Died. Yeah, right. He pulled his phone out and called Elaine. Straight to Voicemail, yet again. He rang Hayley. Ditto. He rang the landline. It rang out and out and out...then the BT woman, asking him to leave a message. *Accident. Died. Accident.* Finally he rang the HAYLEY WORK number. He thought he'd have no luck there also, but eventually a very out of breath Jodie answered. 'Crouch End Hair and Beauty, Jodie here. How may I help you?'

'Hi Jodie. It's Graham Davis, Hayley's husband. Is...um, is Hayley there?'

The woman on the other end – who Graham had only met maybe half a dozen times – dropped her voice. 'No she isn't,' she snapped, 'and hasn't been for a while. What's going *on?*'

'Jodie...I've...I've no idea, I'm sorry.'

'Yeah well, you tell the customers I'm having to turn away how sorry you are. Tell her how sorry you are when I have to sack her. I'm losing money hand over fist here, mate!'

'I know.' God, this was so wrong. *Only four months*, he thought again, and a bubble of sorrow burst in his gut, rank and stale. 'I wish...' But he couldn't go on.

'Have you two split up or something?' she went on, the anger drained but the exasperation remaining. 'I mean, if you're calling here...'

'It's complicated,' he said, then almost laughed. 'I'm so sorry, Jodie. And if she was feeling right, I know Hayley would be too.' Yet more confirmation if (*accident, died*) confirmation were needed about how wrong things were these days. Jodie was almost a second sister to Hayley, and she loved that job. To just abandon them both...

'Well, look...tell her I can just about keep her job open till Friday. After that...' the sentence tailed away, then came back, 'and I'm only giving her that long 'cause she's a mate. Got that?'

'Yeah. I got it,' he said. 'And I'm so sorry.' He switched the phone off without saying goodbye (*accident, died*) and stared at the display, begging Elaine to get in touch. She didn't. What now? Anna? But the thought of her, the thought of the weeping and wailing and rending of garments was just too much for him to bear, too much weight.

One person goes to see her, ends up missing. Another I spoke to about her – who said he would go and talk to her – ends up (accident) dead. Is this a coincidence? Was it the doll? Did the doll get them? And oh my dear God, am I truly thinking this? Am I truly living *this? Please. If this is a dream, I want to wake up now. I want to wake up RIGHT NOW!*

He didn't. He just stayed there, outside the police station, one hand still around his Nokia, the other clasping a litter bin. *Who can I turn to? Who can help? Who knows about this sh...*

Then he had an idea.

Four

'No,' said Lillian Manning four hours later. Graham gaped at her, utterly astonished. He'd spent time and money tracking her down – first on her website, then via the electoral register, and he'd had to pay for that, money he could ill-afford now he was jobless – and he'd made his way all the way to Barnes to beg for her help, and now she was saying...

'No. Get out of here now, or I shall call the police and have you arrested.'

'Please,' he begged. He was almost crying. 'I don't know what else to do, I don't know who else to *turn to*...'

'Not my problem. Sorry.'

'But it *is*,' he went on. 'It was *you* who told her she had to appease the fucking thing...'

'Mind your language, please.'

He tried to step forward, to get in off the driveway. If he could just make her listen. 'This thing, this...'

'Don't you *dare* push your way in here,' she said, blocking his way, and then he saw it, in her eyes. She was terrified. For a second he thought she was scared of him – and he couldn't blame her, he probably looked a fright, all wide-eyed and babbling – but no, this was deeper. This was…this was…

'You *know*, don't you? *You know!* How long have you known, you *bitch?*'

'I'm warning you one final time, Mr Davis,' she said, but the tone she was no doubt searching for – indignation – wasn't there. Her voice was quavering, watery. 'If you don't get off my property I will call the police. And for your information, I have no idea what you're talking about. I visited your house and received the spirit of a lonely little girl, exactly what I told you. Now good day.' She reached out and pushed him. He could have fought back against it, but didn't. He was beaten, and he knew that. He knew one other thing as he saw the door close.

He knew she was lying.

Shoulders sagged, his face bleak, he took a pen from his coat and scrawled his mobile number on the back of a supermarket receipt. He dropped it through Lillian's letterbox the way a castaway throws a message in a bottle into the ocean.

He'd done all he could. He was on his own, stone alone, and clueless. Utterly clueless. *One missing, one dead, both been to see my wife. Do I go now? Do I go to my death?*

Five

Lillian closed the door – well, slammed it – and turned the deadlock. She peeked out from behind the blinds and saw the man eventually make his way down the path and leave. *Good. Nasty man. Nasty, rude man, coming here like that. Not that I could help him anyway, even if I still did that sort of thing. I was right about that house. Just a little girl. Nothing but a*

Trick.

She turned that thought over as she made her way upstairs. Yes, *trick*. Hadn't that been her thought after she'd returned home from that night? Hadn't she, in fact, reached out for the phone to call them, the nasty man (who'd been a cynic, let's not forget) and the nice wife? Tricks. Not *her* tricks, no; she'd been on that night, hadn't needed any. But tricks all right. Some tricks, by *somebody* or *something*.

Some *thing*.

The *thing* at the hospital, at the theatre? Could it be? No, there was no connection between them...none. But all the same, Lillian – a woman who trusted her instincts, who used her instincts to get by when the dead were quiet - thought there might be a connection, somewhere buried, somewhere buried in plain sight if she could but *see* it...

But who cares? Not me. I've had my warning. I know better. She made her way into the bedroom and pulled down a suitcase from the top of the wardrobe. *I nearly died, damn thing nearly killed me. You think I'm going to mess with* that *again? Even if it's not the same thing, the message was clear; stay out of things, you. And I won't poke my nose somewhere it can get bitten off.*

She pulled clothes – any random assortment she could find – and threw them in the case. Yes, best to get away for a while. No worries. Seaside. Abroad. Book something online - she'd been thinking about Antigua - get a bit of peace, a bit of perspective, no distractions...

'Going somewhere, Lil?' Asked a voice from behind her. Terrified, she took a year to turn and face it.

It was her dad, and he looked dismayed.

Six

'Daddy,' she said, and giggled. She was back to being a kid again. He was dressed exactly as he was the last time she'd seen him, standing outside the school, looking through the chainlink fence, telling her he had to go away for a while.

Well, it looked like he was back. 'Daddy,' she said again. Tears sprang up. He hadn't aged a jot. There he was, in front of her again, looking at her sadly. 'Oh, Daddy!'

'Somewhere nice?' He asked, looking at her suitcase. 'On your own? Well, never mind. I'm sure you'll meet someone.'

She wanted to run to him, hug him, bury her face in his security. Sometimes you didn't know how much you'd missed someone till you saw them again. But that look on his face…when had she seen that before? How long back? When she'd come back from playing and torn the knee of her new trousers? When she'd stood in dog dirt and tramped it across the carpet because she hadn't noticed? It was that sort of look, mild disapproval mixed with sadness and a touch of exasperation, *an oh, Lillian, what are we going to do with you*, look.

'Or are you running away?' he asked, voice sharp. Lillian jerked, her hand going to her mouth. 'Yes, that's it, isn't it? Running away. Someone asked you to help and you're running away.'

'Daddy,' she managed to say, 'you don't know what he wanted me to do. I can't…'

'There's no such thing as *can't*,' he said, voice unchanged, his eyes narrowed. 'You *can*. You just chose not to. And you know what? That's OK. Life's full of choices. It's the choices we make that define us. But consider this; your gift, this thing you can do, what is it for?'

'But…Daddy…'

'Don't "but" me, young lady. I know exactly what's going on, I know exactly what you're dealing with. Did you think I wouldn't? Why do you think I'm here? But answer me, what's your gift *for?*'

'To…' she swallowed, 'to help people.'

'And do you? Help people?'

'I don't know,' she said, looking now at the carpet. Yes, she was a child again all right. 'I try to. Sometimes though…I have to lie.' That last word came out as a choke, the way it always did when he got the truth out of her. *Yes, Daddy, I had the last bun. Yes Daddy, I said the Bad Word.*

'I know, and I'm not happy about that. But I know you do it with at least some good intentions. They get something out of it, and so do you, am I right?' She nodded, still unable to look straight at him. She saw his shoes instead. One of them was a little scuffed at the toe. Amazing, really. Even after death, after all those years, that shoe was still scuffed. *Can't get a shine in Heaven*, she thought. 'But forget that, just for now. You'll have to deal with it later, but for now we'll put it aside. You were given your gift to help people, to comfort them, and you mostly do that honestly. Am I right?' She nodded again. 'And who do you think *gave* you that gift? And do you think it comes for free?'

Once more she jerked, her hand to her mouth. She looked him square in the face, her dead father, speaking to her in her bedroom after a journey of God knew how far. She'd never considered this. It was just something she had, like her brown eyes. 'I…I don't know.'

'Come now, you think God just hands stuff out without asking something in return?' He almost laughed. 'There's *always* a price with God! He gives you something, some talent, and you live well enough from it. Better than most. Worse than some, granted, but you do fine. You don't *want*, do you? Got a full fridge, big house you can heat, nice car, holidays, all the stuff the living set their store by. So you didn't *once* consider that you may have to do something in return?'

'And...is this it? Is this,' her hands were shaking in terror, 'what I have to do?'

'It's what He wants you to do,' her dad said. 'He won't make you, not His style. He's a strictly soft sell kind've God these days, as we used to say when I was alive. He just nudges you a little, points at the choice, and says "Up to you now, kid." But I'll tell you something; He *never* forgets, and He stacks the deck. You turn your back on Him and He'll let you, He'll say "Yup, that's fine." But He'll get you back for it, somewhere along the line. Next time you lay with a willing man or woman – why, they may be a murderer! Next time you cross the road for a pint of milk – bam, here comes the drunk driver! God tells you that you have a choice, and He doesn't lie, but it's a bogus choice, Hobson's choice. You get what I mean by that, Lil?'

The tears dropped then, no stopping them, because of course she knew. The Bible was full of stories like that. The Old Testament was one long parade of people pissing God off or being tested for no very good reason other than He could do what the heck He wanted.

'So go on, make your choice. I've done all I can. All He's allowing me to do. Because this is important. You don't know how important yet, but you will, and soon. Things pivot on moments like these, crucial things.'

'But why me?' she sobbed. 'Why me? Why do *I* have to do it? Why can't someone *else?*'

Her dad shrugged. 'Don't know, can't tell you. Even His own son asked that one and got no answer. What makes you think He's going to tell me? All I know is that things are what they are. Scream against them, rail against them, won't make any difference. Make your choice,' he said, stern. 'And once made, stick by it.'

'Daddy,' she said, when she could speak, 'do you love me? Are you proud of me?'

He looked surprised. 'Oh, Lil. I love you more now than I did when I was alive, and I'm prouder of you than I could ever have imagined. And if you do the right thing here, I will burst with pride. Well, would,' he laughed, 'if pride wasn't such a big no-no where I come from.'

She stood for a very long time, thinking, feeling the weight of her father's eyes. *No choice at all, Hobson's choice. He stacks the deck. It's a bogus choice. But still a choice. I could keep packing, no one would stop me. I could forget all about the Nasty Man and the Nice Wife, I could...*

Could I? Could I blot them out, like they never existed, like this conversation never happened? Is that possible? Or would I see their faces in every glass I raised, in every man or woman who went down on me?

But I've been warned. That thing, that demon, knows me, pointed at me, marked me...

And God has sent your dad to tell you this is what you should do. *Not* must *do, but* should *do. And this is important. This is my moment. This is my time to actually, really help someone, help them like I've never helped anyone before. And could you ever say no to Dad?*

She shook her head. No. What little girl could? Dad was the final voice of authority, that's why he was here and no Voice from a burning bush. He knew she'd listen to her dad. She looked at him, loving him. 'OK Daddy. I'll do it,' she said, then shivered.

'Good girl,' he said, and smiled. 'I knew you wouldn't let me down.'

'But Daddy...can I have a hug?'

He held open his arms and she ran to him, buried her head in his chest, and cried terrified tears until he was gone.

Seven

Graham sat in his parents' front room, once more lost. Lost was his default setting these days. He had no home, no job, no direction, no clue.

'Drink that, son.'

He looked to the table and saw his dad had placed a mug before him. On reflex, he picked it up, sipped, and grimaced. 'Bloody hell, you put any coffee in this whisky?'

'Don't swear, your mother's in the kitchen,' Jim said, but he smiled. 'Decided it could do no harm.'

'Yeah, you got that right.' His own smile lasted barely a second, and they fell into silence for a while, broken only by the faint sounds of something being chopped in the kitchen.

'What you going to do?' Jim asked.

'Dad, what *can* I do? I don't know what's going on, I don't know what that thing *is*, I don't know what's happened to Elaine or to that copper, I don't know what's…'

'I didn't ask what you know, son. I asked what you're going to *do*.'

'But I can't do anything unless *I know what's going on!*' This was the loudest he'd ever spoken to his dad, and there was a hot burning in his cheeks that didn't have everything to do with the heavily laced coffee. But still, they kept their voices down. Out of respect for his mother.

'I'm with you on that,' Jim said, unperturbed, 'knowledge is power, they say these days. But kicking a door in and dragging your wife out of there is power too, son. And sometimes that's what's needed. Maybe now.'

Graham gaped at him. 'You think that'd work?'

Jim thought a bit before answering. 'We've tried leaving her alone, see what that did – and to get you away from that bloody thing, get you out of the line of fire; I'll say this again, you are my priority. As a parent you'll do *anything* to protect your own, and your own come before anyone else's. But…look, do you remember when you were a kid, burned your hand on that sparkler?'

Graham frowned, shook his head. 'No…well, maybe a little, but…'

'Well, you *were* wee,' Jim said, looking into the past. 'Four, maybe five at most. Anyroad, you were in the back with all the other kids, bonfire going, fireworks over, bundled and mittened six ways to Christmas, waving your sparkler about. Damaging your bloody retina, I daresay, but we knew no better then. So, the thing goes out, you look all puzzled, want to know where the fire's gone. That's how you put it, best as I recall. "Where fire go?" I tell you to put the thing in the bucket, it's over. You keep looking at it, all confused. "Where fire go?" I tell you a second time, louder, to *put the bloody thing down, put it in the bucket, it's still hot*. But you pull your mitten off, touch the stalk, and by God and all the saints did we know you were hurt! Surprised y've still *got* lungs! Your mother ran your hand under the cold tap for a full half hour and slapped butter on it – you sure you don't remember this?'

Graham did, and didn't. He *thought* he did – and butter had been his mum's magic cure for as long as he knew – but he wasn't sure if he *actually* remembered or just remembered being told. Who really remembered anything?

'The point is,' Jim went on, 'y'd not be told. You had to find it out for yourself, had to burn your hand to see how dangerous the bloody thing was. That's how we are, I suppose. Have to find out for ourselves. But you know what, son? There comes a point where you can't *let* people find out for themselves, where you have to stop them before they get hurt. Now this thing that's in your house…how sure are you, in your heart, that it did something bad to Elaine?'

'Certain,' he said without a beat. 'And to that copper, Lewis, as well.'

'And you love Hayley, right?'

'Yes.'

'Then the time has come, as the Walrus said, to stop telling her and to rip her away from the fire before she gets burned herself, am I right? And – now listen, because you won't want to hear this – but if she stops loving you for it, if she's that far gone, then that's the price you pay to keep her alive. Y'hear me, son?'

Yes, he heard. He heard well enough. It hurt, but yes, he heard. And after a second's deliberation, he decided it was a high price, an *enormously* high price, but a price worth paying. If he was right, then he already had two deaths on his conscience. He would not have a third. He would not put Hayley in any more danger. 'OK then.' He stood. 'I'll get going.'

Jim stood. '*We'll* get going, you mean.'

Graham grabbed Jim's arm, shocked. 'No. No way, Dad. You've no idea…'

'I'm your father, Graham,' he said in that implacably low voice. 'And I'll do anything to protect my own. You go nowhere without me. Not this time.'

Graham struggled, tried to find an argument, something that would put him off, delay him, and was coming up blank. *I can't, not him as well, I can't risk this, this is too much…*

Then his phone rang. He snatched it from the table, hoping he'd see Elaine's name on the screen. But instead was a number he didn't recognise. He hit the CONNECT button and said hello.

'Is this the gentleman who was at my house earlier,' a woman's voice he sort of recognised said in his ear. 'It's Lillian Manning. I've…' he heard her sob. 'I've changed my mind. I want to help you.'

Eight

'This is what I know,' said Lillian, two hours later. They were sitting in her living room, her, Graham and Jim, filling themselves up on tea and sandwiches. Nobody was really hungry, but it gave them something to do with their hands. 'And it's precious little, but it's all I've got.' She told them about the thing she'd seen in the theatre and again at the hospital, and the noise she'd heard in her home. 'Just above. Right there,' she said, pointing upwards. 'Some kind of warning, I think. This thing was trying to keep me away, to stop me...well, doing what I do. I know you don't believe in me,' she said, looking at Graham, who fidgeted a little. 'It's unsurprising. I encounter it a lot.' She sighed. 'And yes, sometimes I...augment a bit. I admit that.'

'Lie, you mean?' Jim asked. Graham looked at him sharply. The woman was going to help him, help Hayley, maybe put them back together again. The last thing he needed was his dad offending her and getting them thrown out.

Sure enough, she looked fit to explode for a second, then sort of subsided into the comfy chair. 'Yes, lie. Sometimes. It's not like turning on the TV, what I do. It wavers, comes in and out. Sometimes it's not there at all, and I need it to be. So I lie. But the rest of the time – *most* of the time – I don't have to. But believe this; *I don't care what you think*. I can do it, I can contact the dead. But this thing I saw, this...demon, for that's what I'm sure it is, isn't like anything else I've ever seen. It's not a person, it's never *been* a person. It's something darker, something evil.'

'But, you said it was...well, like a pig, didn't you?' asked Graham.

'That's what it seemed to be. I don't think that's what it *is*, really, I think it's the best way we can see it. Pigs have been associated with demons since the Bible. Jesus once encountered...'

As fascinating as a little Religious Education lesson would have been, Graham decided that wasn't why they were here. 'But there's *nothing* like that in our house, just this bastard *doll*. This little girl doll that wanders, that walks...*that's* the thing that's haunting us.'

'*This is not a haunting*,' Lillian said, sharply. 'Hauntings are ghosts. This is *not* a ghost, this is something psychical, a demon from Hell.'

'But when you came to our house, all you talked about was that little girl, about how we should make her happy, *nothing* about a demon!'

'Yes,' said Lillian, quietly. 'I think it tricked me. I think it hid, put on a face. Showed me what it wanted me to see. I'm sorry.'

'*Sorry,*' Graham screamed, standing. 'One dead, one missing – and I'm betting dead – *and you say sorry!*'

'*I didn't know,*' Lillian screamed back, also standing. 'Yes, it fooled me! I hope you're happy, it made me look *stupid!* How do you think *I* feel?'

Jim stood too, edged between them. 'I'm not sure this'll help,' he said, mildly.

He was right, but still Graham wanted to punch her. *Stupid*, stupid *woman! Because of her...because of* her...

But it wasn't because of her, was it? It was because of something else. OK so it fooled Lillian, but it had fooled Hayley also. Clever bastard *thing*.

'I'm sorry,' he said. She looked back at him and nodded. *Me too*, that nod said.

All three sat again, and after a pause Jim said, 'I think we need to find the connection between this...demon...and what's in your house, son. If there is one.'

'I think there *must* be,' said Lillian. 'I had...a visit from someone before, someone who made me see how serious this was, how I *had* to help you. He said there was one, he said we'd find it.'

'But they're different things,' Graham said. 'Totally. What you described, what I've seen...'

'Wait a minute, wait a minute,' Jim muttered. He turned something around in his head, then said to Lillian, 'You said that this thing put on a face, maybe, fooled you that way?'

She nodded. 'I think so.'

'Then that's it, isn't it? It put on the face of the doll as well.'

'Yeah, I suppose,' Graham said. 'But why bother? Why not just be itself?'

No one had any answer to that. Lillian dismissed it for a second. 'We're still in the dark. I mean, I think it's the same thing I saw as is in your house – no, I'm certain – but how did it *get* there? These things aren't ghosts, they don't travel easily. At least as far as I know, I'm a psychic medium, not a demonologist. Frankly, it's like consulting a plumber when you need an electrician.'

Great, thought Graham. *Gets better and better, doesn't it?* 'The only link I can see is you,' he said. 'You've been to our house, you saw it at the hospital, it came here to you as well…'

'Which hospital where you in?' Jim asked suddenly, a light forming in his eyes.

'St Jude's,' said Lillian. 'Just overnight. But when I saw that…what? What is it?'

'It was, wasn't it?' Jim asked Graham.

'Aye,' said Graham, unconsciously being his dad for a second. Then he turned to Lillian. 'That's where Hayley was. When they took the baby out of her. St Jude's.'

Nine

Hayley had found Connect 4 in the Red Cross shop down the street, and was delighting in teaching Angie, almost laughing at the concentration on her daughter's face as she worked out her plan of attack. Sometimes Hayley let her win, sometimes she didn't. That way she'd learn about the world, and also it would make her victories sweeter, the way ice cream tasted nicer when you only had it at weekends.

Angie was just about to drop a red counter into the slot – she always wanted to be red – when she stopped. 'This is the best, Mummy.'

'This game? Glad you like it. I had it when I was a little girl, your age. Used to play with…with…' She couldn't remember. Someone. Someone she'd been close to, but the name wouldn't come. Probably wasn't important. If it was, the name would come back to her sooner or later.

'Not the game. Well, yes the game, I love the game, I love the noises and the shapes it makes.'

'Patterns, sweetheart.'

'*Pat*-terns,' she repeated doubtfully. 'But Mummy….me and you. Isn't that the best?'

'Oh my love, yes. Yes it is.'

'I want to stay with you, Mummy, and play games for ever and ever.'

'And you will.'

'You promise, Mummy?'

'I promise.'

'You wouldn't let no-one hurt me, no-one take me away?'

'No!' She was furious at the thought. Furious…and a tiny bit scared, the way someone who has precious jewels feels. Scared at the thought that someone may steal them. '*Nobody* will ever hurt you, Poppet. You are my love, you are my daughter, and a Mummy would do *anything* to protect her child.'

'Anything, Mummy?'

'Absolutely *anything*. Nobody will split us up, nobody will hurt you. I swear, I would die before I let that happen.'

At that, Angie seemed to cheer up quite a bit, and dropped her red counter. She had three vertically. One of Elaine's yellows could block that easily…but no, let her have this one. She'd seemed so earnest and so scared just then. This little victory would cheer her up.

Ten

'So that's it, then,' Graham asked. 'Somehow this thing attached itself to Hayley in the hospital and came back with us. Set up house in the spare room, started moving the doll about. Is playing on her grief over *our* baby, making her see something that it isn't. Sound about right?' *Yeah, to anyone clinically insane.*

'Looks that way,' said Lillian. 'Maybe these things live in hospitals, feeding off the dead. That's the impression I got anyway – think of them as some kind of carrion bird, like a seagull or a vulture. But given a chance to get out, expand their feeding ground...well, wouldn't you?'

'We're certain it was Hayley's grief that did that?' asked Jim.

'No, not certain,' said Lillian. 'But it seems most likely, doesn't it? Strong emotions attract these things, and what's stronger than the grief of a mother for a child? So, yes. It probably hops onto her somehow, hops off when you get home, starts doing the damage. Splitting you up, rows – strong emotions, it loves that. And it's fooled your wife – hell, fooled *me* - into thinking it's a harmless little girl. It's playing on her maternal instincts, dragging those emotions out of her.'

'And running her like she's a robot,' said Graham. 'She's stick thin now, doesn't wash or change...'

'Yes. It may need to keep her close right now, keep drawing on her. And the stronger it gets, the weaker she grows. Also, the more hungry and tired she is, the less she's likely to notice the truth. Think of it being like the way they keep prisoners awake for days on end until they'll sign anything that's put in front of them. Now,' she went on, 'if it *is* a demon, and I'm sure of that, it'll want three things. The first it already has, despair. From my admittedly limited knowledge, they love that, makes them happy if we're at the state you are now, Graham. Secondly, food. Again, going on what I saw in the hospital, these things take something when we die. Don't know what, some energy maybe. So…I'm sorry, but I'm certain that your sister-in-law as well as that policeman are dead. That thing fed off them.'

It hurt to have that confirmed – well, almost confirmed. Didn't surprise, but it hurt. *Elaine. Damn this thing – Elaine.* He remembered her that day both families came round, when Hayley was back from the hospital, talking to him in the kitchen, telling him he had to have some time to grieve himself, looking out for him, loving him. Calling him 'brother.' *I let you down,* he thought. *I let you down and that bastard killed you.* Tears sprang. He wiped them away with the heel of his hand.

'What's the third thing?' Jim asked. Lillian hesitated. 'Come on,' said Jim. 'We need to know.'

'It needs to possess Hayley,' she said, slowly. 'It needs to put her on and go out and about in her body. To throw Hayley into the Void. I think it has something to do with expanding its feeding ground, like I said. In its own form, or hiding in the doll, it would get noticed. But as a young woman...well, it could go anywhere it wanted, couldn't it? Do anything it wanted. Who'd suspect her?'

Never going to happen, Graham thought. *I've given this fucking thing too much ground already. It ain't getting her as well.* 'OK then,' he said. 'How do we kill it?'

After a pause, Lillian said, 'We can't. Sorry.'

Eleven

'The *fuck* you say,' Graham exploded, standing again. What was the *point* of this woman? She'd said she wanted to help and was now telling them there was nothing they could do.

'You don't understand,' Lillian said, still sitting. 'You listen, but you don't hear. This thing we're up against is a *demon*, Graham. Not a ghost, not a lost, confused spirit. A *demon*. An Imp, one of Satan's minions – do I get through? We can't kill it, we don't have that power. Nothing on Earth has that power. The best we can do is to contact someone who'll cast it out for us, who has that strength. We don't. We'll die if we stand against it.'

Graham paced, ran his hands through his hair, barely restraining the urge to rip great clumps out by the roots. And then smash all her furniture. And then to smash her. *Fucking useless witch*.

'All right,' he heard his dad say. 'Then we'll go to…what, the church?'

'Yes,' said Lillian, but hesitantly. *Here we go, more bad news,* thought Graham. 'Your nearest Catholic one. But their procedure…even if they listen to you, they'll have to do an investigation, verify there's something truly evil there, then get permission from the Vatican.'

'Great,' said Jim. 'By which time this thing's in Hayley's body and walking around London like it's bloody ASDA. Isn't there *any* way we can speed it up?'

'The Catholic church is the world's oldest bureaucracy,' Lillian answered. 'And they're terrified of making idiots of themselves – hardly surprising given the number of scandals they've had recently. The last thing they want to do is admit all this still goes on. It does, but they won't say it publicly.'

Graham had hardly been listening. 'So what you're *actually* saying is we just leave my wife to die? Is that it? Because she will, won't she? She'll *die* if this thing possesses her, right? That's what "being flung into the Void" means, right? You're saying I just sit back and *let that happen?*'

'I'm saying,' said Lillian, 'that we don't have the resources to fight it.'

'You know something,' said Graham, quietly. He leaned over her. 'Fuck you. You said you were going to help. And what have you actually *done?* Come up with a load of horror stories and said "anyway, that's all folks." Well, *fuck you*. I'm going to go back there,' he said to Jim, 'and do what you said. I'll drag her out of that house. I'll knock her out if I have to. But I'll take her away.' Back to Lillian. '*That's* helping.'

'You'll die,' she said calmly.

'I don't care,' said Graham. 'I'll have died trying.'

That statement hung in the air, revolving, heavy. Jim broke the silence. 'Before we do anything – and I'm coming with you, son, don't even think about arguing – I want to run this past you, Miss Manning.' She looked at him. Graham could see her waiting to say *sorry, we're out of options* at the end of whatever he came out with. 'This thing, this demon...we reckon hitched itself onto Hayley somehow. Maybe using her grief as a kind of umbilical cord, am I right?' Lillian nodded. 'If she brought it,' he said thoughtfully...'could she send it back?'

Lillian looked slapped in the face. Graham could see it was something she obviously hadn't considered.

'If this thing's using her in some way, tapping her for energy, putting on a face to keep her happy...'

'Then if we made her see what it was *really* like...' Lillian joined in.

'Could she...I dunno, expel it, drive it out?' Jim concluded.

Lillian stood now, excited, turning it over. 'I think...yes, *maybe*. There's some kind of symbiotic link between them. If that was severed, it might be vulnerable. Maybe then even *I* could send it...well, home. I've got *some* power. It's limited, very limited, but if I called upon the others...but she'd have to *really* see it, be *revolted* by it. And...yes, it would have to be her, because she brought it, it's her responsibility.'

'We'd not be killing it though, would we,' asked Graham, caught up in the excitement now, caught up in the hope. 'Just sending it back to...where, the hospital? I mean, the thought of all of them...'

'That's their place,' said Lillian, shrugging. 'All things serve the will of the Lord, even demons; even Satan himself. They have their places, like spiders do and cockroaches and all the other things that revolt us. We don't know why they have their places and why God permits it, but He does. We've just got to accept that. It's when something sets itself *against* the will of God that these things happen, that people are placed in jeopardy. You know the rabbits in Australia story?' Graham didn't, but he saw Jim nod and decided to let it go. 'I think it's like that. Things are fine in their place, and should stay there. Overstep the bounds and something has to be done.'

'And it's going to be,' said Graham. 'Right now.'

He saw Lillian's resolve quiver a little, then she drew herself upright again. Graham, who would never like this woman, nevertheless found a small spring of admiration for her. She was clearly shitting herself brown, not to put too fine a point on it, but was still going ahead. That took *something*.

'All right then,' she said. 'Right now.'

Twelve

Hayley was on the toilet when she heard Angie start to cry – no, *scream*. Her heart sped up and she pulled her jeans up, not wiping, not washing her hands, she just hurled herself towards the nursery. Her poor little darling was in terror, by the sound of it, terror or awful pain, something she would not permit...

She flung open the door and rushed inside, her little angel screaming, face bright red, contorted in fear. Hayley picked her up, rocked her, tried to hush her, patted her back. 'It's all right, my love,' she crooned, 'Mummy's here, Mummy's here, hush now, everything's fine, Mummy's here.' Eventually, her daughter began to quiet, her racking screams dissolving into sporadic sobs. 'That's better, angel. That's better. Now what was it, eh? What was all that silly noise about?'

'Bad men coming, Mummy. Bad men and bad lady. They...' she hitched again. 'They want to *take me away*. I don't want to go, Mummy! *I don't want to go! I DON'T WANT TO GO!* I love you, Mummy! I want to stay! *I LOVE YOU MUMMY!*'

Hayley's eyes grew so dark they might have turned black. All the soothing dropped out of her voice. 'Nobody's taking you anywhere, my love,' she said. She clutched Angie tighter, feeling her slightly bristly chin, her cold, wet nose, loving her. 'Anyone tries to take you away and I will kill them. I will kill them. I will kill them.'

At that, Angie's cries turned to giggles of delight.

Chapter Eighteen

One

Jim called home during the drive, told his wife he and Graham were going round to see Hayley, back as soon as, no - don't hold tea, they'd get something on the way back. Then he finished the call with, 'Love you, Linda.'

I've never heard him say that, thought Graham. Never heard him tell Mum he loved her. He's a Scot; they don't do that in public. They've all sorts of exotic sayings and words that I keep trying not to use – 'I'm away to my bed,' for example, or calling the glass thing in the wall you open for ventilation 'the windy' – but they hardly express themselves where people can see or hear them. Except tonight.

If nothing else proved how serious and deadly this evening was, that did. *He's settling his estate*, he suddenly thought, and shivered all over. *He wants the last thing Mum hears is him telling her he loves her.* A fragment of a dream, half remembered, skittered through his brain. A long corridor, maybe in a hospital…had Jim been there? Jim and some others? He shook his head. It was a long time ago. Then, with an almost rueful grin, he realised it'd only been a month or so back. It just seemed longer. So much had happened. So much you just couldn't process.

Take this now, for instance. Were they really driving in his car back to his house in order to expel a demon? In 2015? In Crouch End, north London? Surely they'd have to be in a horse drawn carriage clattering around some park in Transylvania, wearing long coats and top hats, Lillian in a velvet evening gown of some description? He pulled up at the traffic lights and waited for the green light, and as he did he looked left and right. Houses. Some terraced, some semi, some with lights on, some dark. A man was walking his Staffordshire terrier. A woman was talking on her mobile, clutching a plastic bottle of milk. All of that normality. Deciding what to watch on telly, or whether they've enough money to go for a pint. None of them having a clue that parked up outside, waiting for the lights to change, three people are going to go face-to-face with an actual – get this! – demon.

'It staggers the mind, doesn't it,' said Lillian from the back, making him jump. He looked at her in the rear view and saw her smile a little. 'I know. I've had that look on my face before. I was a little girl when I saw my first ghost. In my room, I was. I used to look about me the way you just did. Look at the real world, yes?' Graham nodded. 'Takes time to process, but what you think of as the real world is only the bit we can see. Like icebergs.'

The lights changed, he drove on.

'You get used to it, eventually,' Lillian said. 'Well, you have to, or go mad. What's the point struggling against what you know to be true? It's like denying the existence of Luton.'

Graham, who had been to Luton once, didn't see that as a problem, really. But still, he got the point. *All around us, right now. The world we see, the world we don't. Overlapping, incorporeal, but just as real. And here we are, a retired building contractor, an unemployed draftsman and an occasionally fake psychic stepping into battle with one of the Devil's best mates. Yeah. Make a heck of a movie. I want John Cusack to play me, always liked him. Dad can be Sean Connery. And Lillian? That fella who used to drag up, does the chat show these days. That Scouse bloke.*

Incredibly, he laughed. Then he thought of the other Scouse fella, the one he once shared an office with, and wondered if he'd ever get round to sharing a pint with him. He stopped laughing.

Two

Hayley and Angie stood at the top of the stairs, waiting. 'They're coming, Mummy,' said Angie, and oh God Hayley hated that tremor in her voice, hated the people that caused it even more. She'd crucify anyone who laid a finger on her daughter. Crucify them and film them on her phone. And watch it every night. And laugh.

'Don't worry about a thing, babe,' she said. '*Nobody* takes you from me. *Nobody* splits us up.' She reached out her hand, and Angie took it. She had a strangely clumped hand, as if her fingers were very stubby, but Hayley didn't care. She was her daughter and she loved her. 'I'll protect you.'

'Thank you, Mummy,' said Angie. 'And I'll p'tect *you*.'

Bless her, Hayley thought. *As if she could. But that's how much she loves me. And nothing is stronger than the love a mother has for her child – and vice versa. Come on, if you're coming. Do your worst. It'll be nowhere near good enough. I promise you that. Nowhere near.*

Three

At last they pulled up outside his house and Graham all but leaped from the car and ran down the drive, pulling his keys from his coat pocket.

'Wait,' called Lillian. 'There's something we have to do first.'

'What, now?' asked Graham, almost dancing with impatience. 'We've got to get in there, Christ knows what's going on!'

She caught up with him, looked deep into his eyes. Jim came up last, his face set and grim. 'We have to be protected as best we can,' she said. 'This thing is old and powerful. It'll use every trick it can against us. It's strong, got me? And we are weak, so we need protection. God,' she said, 'I don't even know if I can do this. I'm hardly...well, I don't go to Church, but I need to...'

'Come on,' said Jim. 'Graham's right, time's a-wasting. What must you do?'

She looked at them both, then took their hands. 'I have to pray to God. If you two can, please do. Try to imagine yourself protected in His light, His *love*. If you can't do that, think of how you love each other, or Graham – how you love Hayley. Picture that as a nimbus around you, if you can.'

'What,' said Jim, coughing a little – Graham realised he was stifling a laugh, the way he'd stifled laughs years back, when they'd be watching TV as a family, Graham a small boy, and a dirty joke would be told, one Graham didn't get and Jim didn't fancy explaining. It brought back a feeling of nostalgia, warmth and safety. 'You mean like that old Ready-Brek advert?'

He expected Lillian to be offended, but instead she surprised him by laughing out loud. 'Yes, actually. *Exactly* like that.' The laugh died. 'Now please, concentrate. Think about God's love, if you can't manage that, someone you *do* love. Love is love the whole world over, I think.' *I hope* was the subtext. All three closed their eyes, and Graham saw – not God, he didn't know what God was – but Hayley as he'd first met her at that party, chatting to her friends, relaxed, laughing, beautiful, warm. He remembered how he felt – that *desire*. Not just a *physical* desire – though he wasn't going to deny that, he'd wanted to see her without her clothes on all right – but a higher, *purer* desire, a desire to know her, to talk with her, laugh with her, be beside her, comfort her, encourage her. Love at first sight? Maybe not, he had a feeling love was a complicated emotion, one that took time to develop. But desire? Yes, desire from the start. And love had followed quickly, and yes, love was complicated, but in the end you could boil it down to this; *love means sacrificing yourself for another person*. Not so grand a gesture as they were almost certainly embarking upon now, just the notion that their well-being was more important than your own, that you would do anything for them. God's love? No, that had no reference point for him. His love for his wife? Yes. He could visualise that all right, he could wear *that* out. It fit perfectly.

'God,' said Lillian, her voice catching. 'Please protect and save Your servants this night. Give us what strength You can. We are sinners and we admit that, but do not despise us for our sins. We are sorry for the times we offended You, truly sorry. Now we go to carry out Your will, we subsume ourselves to Your will. In Your name, Thy will be done.'

She broke the contact, drew in a shuddering breath, and said, 'That's the best I can do. OK then.'

Graham put his key in the lock and turned. He pushed the door open, and all three stepped inside.

Four

'Dear Jesus,' Jim breathed as he saw what was at the top of the stairs. Lillian crossed herself. Graham almost threw up. Standing next to Hayley, it stood, all disguises aside. A pig-thing, standing on its hind legs, vile drops of fluid dripping from its flexing snout, its hideous, impossibly wide mouth filled with rows of teeth so pointed and cruel they might as well have been called tusks. It stank. Its rank odour lined the back of their throats, the stink of animal sweat and thudding evil, the smell of sulphur. That stench almost hung over it like a cloud, and yet Hayley stood next to it, seemingly unaffected, holding one its hooves (*trotters*, Graham corrected wildly) like a mother walking her child to school. And that final, wonderfully terrifying absurdity – the fact it was wearing a white lace dress, the white lace dress he'd seen on that doll.

'Hello Graham,' she said, voice flat, uninflected, but the anger in her eyes was brutal.

'Hello love,' he replied, struggling not to stare at that awful thing. *A demon, a demon*, his mind kept repeating, *that's a fucking demon, an actual demon from hell*. He tried to blot that out, somehow knowing that thing wanted this confusion in his mind, wanted his thinking muddied up, but *oh dear God a demon, a fucking demon*.

'What you doing home at this time of night?' Hayley said. 'You should have rung and told me you were bringing company. I'd have cooked.' Then, to each of them in turn, 'Lillian. Jim. Mind telling me what you're doing here? Not that it isn't good to see you,' her eyes gave lie to that, all right, 'but it's late. I was thinking of going to bed.'

'We've come to help,' said Graham. This was his play, she was his wife. He had to see it through.

'I don't need help.'

'You do, babe,' he said, taking a very small step towards the stairs. He saw Hayley flinch, set her feet further apart. 'And we're here to give it. Because we love you. Because I love you.'

'You loved me so much you went away.'

'No babe. I was sent away. I was wrong to go, I should have stuck it out, but I didn't leave. I was pushed.'

'You walked out, you *coward*.' She spat that last word with such venom that he stopped, confused. She pressed on, 'I asked you to go along with me, I asked you to be on side, I asked you because you were my husband and you said you loved me but when it got tough you *packed a bag and ran out. That's* how much you loved me. Quitter! *Coward!*'

'No, that's…' *not what happened*, he wanted to say…but was it? Was it really? Why would she lie?

Beside her, that pig-thing squealed in delight, a terrible noise that broke his mind in two. He couldn't think straight, He'd tried to convince her, hadn't he? Make her see the danger they were in...no, the danger *he* was in, wasn't *that* the truth? That squealing, gibbering, slobbering thing hadn't attempted to hurt her, only *him*, and he'd walked, walked out, a quitter, a coward, a fucking useless...

'Hayley,' said Jim. 'I love you like you were my own, but sometimes girl, you do talk shite.'

The squealing stopped abruptly.

Five

Jim had seen his son wilting, doubting himself, and as he had that *thing* besides his daughter-in-law seemed to grow stronger, to take some energy from Graham's...despair? Yes, that was what this thing wanted, wasn't it, that woman had told them as much. The more Graham despaired the happier the bastard thing would be. *Despair and death, that's what it brings. But not to my son. I don't care about anyone else here, I'll throw them to the wolves, I'll throw myself to the wolves if it comes to that – I've had my time – but not to him.*

In the silence, he stepped forward, past the hunched figure of his son, to the bottom step of the stairs. He kept his eyes on Hayley. 'Y've not been a mother,' he said, quite astonished at how Scottish he sounded to his own ears – then, with some amusement, realised he sounded exactly like *his* dad, long in the ground. 'Not yet, anyroad, n'matter what y'may be thinking or seeing right now.' That came out as *richt nae*. 'But y've not. I've been a parent. Still am.' He mounted the first stair. 'And y'll do anything t'protect y'kids.'

'That's what I'm doing,' said Hayley. 'Stay there. I'm warning you, Jim. Stay there.'

'No y're not, that thing's no kid, that's been born of no man and woman,' he said, mounting the second stair. 'If y're kid has the bleach in his hand and looks like he's going t'drink it, what would y'do?'

That thing piped up again, squealing, tugging at Hayley's hand. There was something almost…yes, *appealing* about it, like the noise a terrified animal might make. It wasn't scared, or at least Jim didn't think it was, but it wanted her to *think* it was.

'It's all right, angel,' crooned Hayley. 'Nobody will hurt you.' To Jim; 'I mean it. Stay away.'

'Y'd take the bleach away, y'd slap the bloody kid's hand, y'd scream at it ne'er to do the thing again, and y'know what? For a second or two, the kid would hate you. Hate you because you're shouting at it.' Third step. Fourth. Six more and they'd be nose to nose. 'Hate you because y're stopping it doing what it wants t'do.' *Tae dea*, that came outs. 'But y're doing the right thing.' Fifth step, sixth, keeping his voice low, eyes on hers. 'Y'd no' let y're kid drink bleach, would you?' Seventh. Only three more *and dear Jesus, that stench! How could she stand it?* 'That's what we've got t'do now, hen. Y're about t'drink the bleach, and we've got t'take it off you. Because we love you.'

'Jim,' said Hayley, equally levelly. 'You're an arsehole.'

She stood aside, and the demon ran at him, awful hooves or trotters or whatever they were outstretched. It hit him with a force he didn't know existed, a strength that was impossible in something that size. He flew backward, chest burning where the thing had touched him. He seemed to be travelling an incredible distance before gravity overtook him and flung him to the bottom of the stairs. Pure agony flared as he felt his spine snap in two. For a second, he saw his wife, sat alone in their house, waiting for him.

Then he died.

Six

Graham screamed in grief and rage. His dad lay like a limp rag doll – like one of the rag dolls they'd bought for the baby who never was – at the bottom of the stairs. Blood had pooled from his mouth. His sightless eyes stared at the ceiling.

His dad was dead.

Graham crumpled beside the body, still screaming. He cradled his dad's head and sobbed, wailing inconsolably.

His dad was dead.

His dad was the bravest, wisest, kindest man he'd ever known, and he was dead. He lay there, dead, never to get up again, never to go to the Arsenal game with his son again, never to make anything again, never to smoke an illicit cigarette in his shed again, never to do anything again, because he was dead. *Cry on a Saturday, laugh on a Wednesday,* he'd once said, but there'd be no more crying or laughing for him, because he was dead, because that bastard *thing* had killed him, had killed his dad, and there it was, above him, squealing with laughter and joy and his wife, that bitch he'd married, the fucking *bitch* was laughing too, she was laughing, laughing at the fact they'd killed his dad…

Pure fury, hatred, rage flooded through him, made him cold. His screams turned from sorrow to anger. *'I'M GOING TO FUCKING KILL YOU FOR THAT,'* he screamed. *'I'M GOING TO KILL YOU BOTH!'*

He leaped forward, preparing to vault the stairs three at a time, when Lillian caught him by the coat collar and told him through her tears not to be such a fucking tool.

Seven

Lillian had stood with her back pressed against the front door, watching all that happened, and fighting an almost irresistible urge just to cut and run, to leave with her hair on end and her tail between her legs. They were screwed. She knew that as soon as she'd set eyes on that demon. Nothing on Earth could stand against that, not something that powerful. It was like looking at an infected, rotting tooth that had somehow put on a pig mask and grown to a ridiculous size. It was embedded in the world, rooted. It was cancer on porcine feet. It was death with a capering, gleeful, swinish face, and it would have them all, one by one. Then it would possess the woman – hell, it was almost halfway there already by the looks of things – and then it would wander off into the world, creating despair wherever it lit and feeding off the death it generated. This was the face every suicide saw when they got round to plugging in the car exhaust, egging them on, telling them this was fine, this was the way to solve all their problems for ever, go on, old mate, why not? This was the smell of millions of empty rooms where no sun had shone and love had long departed. It was the end, it was Omega, and it was...

Working on her.

She jerked back suddenly, banging her head on the door. As she did, she saw Graham's dad mount the stairs. So lost in her own desolation was she that she couldn't speak, couldn't shout out the warning in her heart...but she *was* thinking more clearly. Not by much. Not by nearly *enough*, but yes, clearly enough to know anyway that the oppression and anguish she felt was at least *partially* coming from that thing. *It doesn't want us to think we can beat it,* she thought. *And maybe we can't...but if we couldn't, why is it spending so much energy* telling *me we can't?*

She banged her head against the door again, hoping that would throw more things into focus. As she did, she saw the demon lunge at Jim, saw him flung backwards, heard the crack as he hit the landing and his spine severed, and once more the feeling of desolation ran through her. *Fight it? Fight* that? *We've no chance, it's too strong...*

And stronger *now it's killed. That's why it's pummelling me again. Why me, especially? Why...* Another bang of her head against the wood of the door, and she knew. *Oh God yes, because I'm the one here who doesn't have much to lose, I'm the one who can't be goaded. I don't love anyone here; I'm the one who can think clearly. That's why.*

She saw Graham about to run up the stairs and to his death and grabbed him by the collar. 'Don't be a fucking tool,' she snapped.

'I'll kill them,' he snarled, without looking back at her. She took hold of his lapels and glanced over her shoulder. The woman and the demon were smiling. Why shouldn't they? Hell of a good time they were having. Of course, definitions of good times were all a matter of perspective. 'I'll fucking kill them. My dad...'

'I know, I know,' she said. 'It's stronger now, because it killed him. If you go up there it'll rip you apart. Eat you up as well, I daresay.'

'Don't listen to the lezzer,' Hayley called down. 'She makes stuff up. She'd admitted it. What does *she* know? Come up and sort me out, hon. Come up and give me a right good seeing to.' She giggled. It hurt Lillian's ears. It was like a road drill. 'I'll even wear a school uniform for you. You wanna give me homework, sir? Wanna keep me after school? Ooh, sir, *not the ruler!*'

He nearly squirmed away from her, so desperately strong was he at that moment. *Fear, fear and anger give us strength we never knew.* She managed to hold him. Just. His coat frayed a little. 'Is that *her*?' she asked him, trying to keep his gaze on hers. 'Is *that* your wife? Is it? I only met her once and even *I* know that's not her! You want her back? You want her back, do you? Remember what we have to do!' Then it hit her. Not what *they* had to do. What *she* had to do.

Of course, it all became very clear, like Paul on the road to Damascus. Graham could help – a little – but only if she could break that grief, just for a little while. But this was down to her, this was the moment her father had spoken of, the chance to pay God back for her gift, her chance to make amends for all the times she'd abused it. *It falls to very few of us to make a difference on this kind of scale,* she thought, *to tip the balance of the world back to where the Almighty wishes it. Maybe this is the very reason I was given my power, for this one night. Everything else has led me to this one spot. I can do this.*

I can do this. Even if it kills me.

It almost certainly would, that was how God repaid his favours after all. Look at what he'd done to His only Son. But if it did, if it was her destiny to die in that hallway, surrounded by strangers, she would die with her conscience clear and her back straight. *Plenty of people die worse than that. Look at that poor bastard on the landing.*

'Graham,' she said, as firmly as she could. 'Listen to me. It's still doable. We can *win this*. We can *get her back*.' The squealing from the landing increased. The bastard thing was laughing at her. *Laugh away, Pinky,* she thought. 'Just don't listen to anything she says. She's not herself right now. But we can and *will* get her back. *You hear me?* Or do you want your dad to have died for nothing? You want that? Would that make you a good son?'

'Killed him...' he muttered, but yes, he was looking at her really looking at her now. That light in his eyes...was it hope?

'Yes, I know. I'm so sorry. But remember why we came. Think of Hayley, think of how much you love her – not *that* up there, but Hayley, the real Hayley, the one you married, the one you love. Not your dad. But *her*. Remember how much you love her. Can you? Can you do that?'

He boggled at her, lips trembling, but nodded.

'OK then. Keep doing that. And react to nothing.' Then she stood up, turned and faced the two on the landing, and said, 'So. Here we go, then.'

Eight

Hayley stared down at them all, strong, taking comfort from and giving strength to her daughter. How pathetic they were! Useless wastes of space! Didn't they *know* a mother's love was impossible to break? How could they be so *stupid!* And Jim...brought it on himself, sticking his nose in, interfering. That's what happened to nosey bastards who'd split families up. They wound up dead. Tough shit.

So, she'd seen off Graham – he was useless now, just lying there in a heap, staring up at her – she'd seen off Jim, and now there was only the dyke. No contest. What did *she* know about being a parent? What did *she* know about *anything*, the lying dyke bitch?

'So. Here we go, then,' she said.

'Just get out of here,' Hayley said, 'while you're still upright.'

'Mummy, Mummy,' said Angie. 'Why won't they go away? Mummy, *please* make them go away.'

'I will, angel, don't worry. They'll be gone soon.'

'Who're you talking to, Hayley?' the dyke asked.

'My daughter. The one you're going to take from me. They one you'll *never* take from me. Look at him,' she said, pointing at Jim. 'Look at what happened to him.'

'I don't *have* to look at him. I know what you did. You killed him.'

Hayley laughed. 'Collateral damage!'

'Oh, not you physically, you didn't lay a finger on him, but you *allowed* it to happen, didn't you? You didn't stop that thing from killing your father-in-law.'

'Don't call my daughter a *thing,* bitch!' Hayley yelled. She picked Angie up and hugged her tight. The poor little girl was terrified, wriggling in her arms.

'What daughter?' the fake psychic said. 'Hayley, you don't have a daughter. Your daughter died – no, even *that's* not right. Your daughter *never even lived.* You've *never had children*, never fostered, never adopted. *You have no daughter.*'

Hayley looked at Angie and shook her head. 'What a silly, silly woman, eh?' Angie smiled at her and once more the sun filled Hayley's heart. In the midst of all this, she'd made her daughter smile. *This* was what she was made for, *this* was why she was on the planet. 'What's this in my arms, or are you blind as well as a lying dyke? What's *this?*'

'Hayley,' the woman asked. 'Who told you I was bi?'

Nine

That got through, Lillian saw Hayley pause, grow doubtful. It wasn't a killing shot, far from it, but it *got through*. 'Come on,' she said, trying to press home whatever scant advantage she may have gained, 'who told you? I never did. Why would I? Graham couldn't, he didn't know. So who told you? Where did you get that from?'

'You...you just look like one,' Hayley said, floundering a little, trying to regain some ground. 'You look like a big lezzer dyke.'

'Really? Do I? And if I did, what does it matter? Who cares?'

'*I care*,' Hayley screamed at her, and oh this thing was strong, its hold tough. She could feel it wresting back total control. 'I care because you'll abuse my child! I know what you're like, your lot, dirty, all of you, grooming little children for your perverse...'

'Hayley,' Lillian interrupted. 'Should you be talking like that in front of the child?'

Again, another good shot – this one went even deeper. She saw the demon squirm in Hayley's arms, almost as if it wanted to leap down and go on a killing spree. Ah, but it had done its work just a little *too* well. Hayley almost smothered it. 'How *dare* you tell me...'

Lillian kept talking, she had to, had to keep control of this. 'And all that stuff about dressing up for Graham? Is *that* what you want your daughter to hear? Not that you have a daughter...'

'I *have*, you stupid...'

'*I'm* not stupid, *I'm* not screaming my head off, I'm not swearing or behaving inappropriately. *You* are. Is that good parenting skill? Maybe you deserve to have the baby taken from you. Not that I can.'

'Damn fucking *right* you can't!'

'Please,' said Lillian, reasonably. 'The language! What *will* people say! People will say,' she pressed on, talking quickly, confidently, hoping nobody would notice just how terrified she was, 'that you're an unfit mother. All that swearing, all that shouting. All that *death*. I mean, look at us, look at how nice we are, how calm, how reasonable – why Graham's dad has just died. Just minutes ago, and look at him, standing there thinking about how much he loves you.' She saw Hayley glance away, troubled, and that demon pig-thing wriggled even harder. But the harder it fought, the harder Hayley held it. How soon before the thing lost it completely and turned on her? 'He still loves you, after that thing killed his father,' she pressed on. 'How *good* is he? How good a *man* is he? That must be *real* love, Hayley. Real love he has for i. You drove him out, you stood by and let his father die, and *he still loves you*. That's more than human, I'd say. That's a *saint*, don't you reckon?'

'He...they...' Hayley stuttered. 'They came to take my...'

'*You have no child*,' Lillian said again, strong but not shouting. 'That thing you hold is not your child, it never walked the Earth as a person, your child never took a breath. Look at it, Hayley, really *look at it*. Not at Graham, not at me, look at the thing you're holding. *Look now!*'

Hayley did. Her eyes bulged, her mouth dropped. And she screamed in terror.

Ten

She was holding something that looked like a pig, but wasn't a pig. It was a grotesque sham of life, a writhing, squirming, wretched thing, something that stank, something that oozed liquid from its snout and its mouth, something covered in gross hairs…

Her slightly bristly chin…her cold, wet nose…

…something that snuffled and choked and squealed in rage…

…her gobbling, wet laughter…

…something with hooves for hands and feet…

…her oddly clumped feet…

Hayley screamed again, and dropped it. It scampered up, casting itself this way and that way, like a dog trying to track a scent, then it fixed itself on the people below, and it bellowed a terrible cry of frustration, and Hayley looked down and actually *saw*…

'JIM,' she shrieked in sorrow. '*AW MY GOD, JIIIIM!!!*'

From below her, she heard Lillian scream, '*Now Hayley, now! Send the bastard back – tell it you don't love it, tell it you don't want it, JUST SEND IT BACK!*'

Eleven

In that moment, Lillian thought *we've done it.* Then slightly more vaingloriously, *I've done it.* All Hayley had to do now was banish the Godforsaken thing, and they could all move on. If moving on were still possible. 'Go on,' she shrieked. 'Tell it to go!'

Hayley opened her mouth, maybe to scream, maybe to say something...then stopped.

Oh fucking shit, thought Lillian. *We're in deep trouble now.*

Twelve

Hayley's bewilderment was total. Nothing was making sense, nothing at all. She was so deeply repulsed by the thing in front of her – the thing she'd held, she'd kissed – that she couldn't process anything. She could feel her brain cells jumping ship and by God did she want to join them.

Not just them, she wanted to join Graham, to run down the stairs and comfort him, rock him...just *hold* him. How *long* had it been since she'd had him in her arms? It seemed like forever.

Then she heard Lillian shout something about sending this alien horror away, telling it to go, and it seemed so insane (but what wasn't right then?) that she opened her mouth to tell it just to fuck right off, when it stared right back at her, quiet and still, and those hideous eyes started to *grow*, to transfix her, to *show her something*, to make a picture...

Her sister is climbing the stairs. These stairs. She's a little apprehensive, she's calling Hayley's name, she reaches the top, and when she does that monster runs from the nur...the spare room and hits her full tilt, and her sister falls, screaming, the way Jim fell, exactly the way Jim fell, and there's a horrible crunch, and Elaine, Hayley's younger sister who would like to pretend sometimes that she was a bit scatty just so nobody would know how clever she was, lay dead in her hallway. And then the thing that had fooled her so well and for so long ran down the stairs to the body – that's all Elaine was now, a body – raised its awful tusks, and started eating.

Hayley howled in dismay, and sank to her knees. 'Oh my dear sweet God I'm so sorry I'm so sorry I'm so sorry.' She gibbered over and over. Jim's death. Elaine's death. Both planted firmly at her door, both her fault, both her responsibility. *I'm damned,* she thought. *Damned.*

The pig-thing squealed in triumph.

Thirteen

It's got her, thought Lillian, *got her somehow.* She tried calling Hayley's name, but the woman didn't even blink. *I'm out of options, out of ideas, I do not know what to do next.*

Fortunately, someone else did.

Fourteen

'Babe,' said Graham through his tears. 'Hey. Babe. Hayley. You with me?'

They were close now. Very close to the end of it, one way or the other. Lillian had somehow managed to break the spell, or illusion, or whatever the hell it was, but the thing was still strong, still linked to her in some way – and then when he heard Hayley call her sister's name he knew. That *despair* again.

Should hang out at White Hart Lane, you'd see all the despair you ever need. 'Hayley,' he called again. 'I love you hon. You want to know how much? Shit, I don't care if I *never* see you as a schoolgirl. That's how much. I just want you back. *You.*' She looked to him, tears down her face as well...but she almost smiled. Almost, but almost was enough in this game. *Love, that's what it's about.* 'Whatever the rest of the shit is, we can *get through*. We *will* get through.' That demon was turning to him, itching to run and get him...to kill him...

(*So why doesn't it?*)

...but it stood there, quivering all over in rage. Its fetid stench grew to a point Graham could almost *see* it.

'Go on, Hayles. Don't listen to it, ignore the bastard. Whatever it's doing to you, showing you or whispering to you, *ignore* it. We'll deal. Just tell it to fuck off. That's all it takes.' *We hope.*

'Gray,' she said, voice watery. 'I missed you.'

'So you should. Now go on.'

She nodded, gathered whatever strength she had left, and faced the demon. 'Get out,' she said flatly. 'Get out, I don't love you. Get out. *Get out of my home!*'

Now, thought Graham. *Now.*

But the bastard thing just *stood* there. It didn't go anywhere. Then it ran for her.

Fifteen

Graham ran too. There was no way he could make it before that thing grabbed her, but he ran. He'd be too late, but he ran. When he got there, she'd be dead, but he ran anyway, he ran not caring about his own fate, his own life. He ran because he loved his wife. He ran because he'd lost one person he loved that day and would do anything he could to avoid losing another. He wouldn't make it, it was impossible, they'd lost, but that didn't stop him running, like Arsenal, two nil down in a Champion's League semi-final with eighty-eight minutes on the clock. Just because you were down, just because you were out, you kept trying. Lillian's plan hadn't worked, they were all doomed (*doomed*, the word clanged through his head as his knees pumped and his thighs flexed, as he pulled in air and pushed it out, *doomed, doomed*), this thing would win, life wasn't a movie and sometimes the bad guys triumphed, but he still ran.

Of course, he was too late. The thing grabbed Hayley, hoisted her upwards, chuffing and screeching in delight, and Hayley was screaming, screaming in pain, and Graham could see the smoke rising from where this thing held her. *Burning her, the bastard's burning her*...but she was still alive. In pain, but alive.

He ran, didn't slow, dropped his left shoulder and hit the thing square on its back. It uttered a *squawk*, lost its grip on Hayley and hit the wall. Graham saw his wife sag a little, but she stood. Barely, but she stood.

And...what next? *Wait for it to jump at me, push me down, break my back? Yeah well, guess what? I'm ready. I'll take you with me. Maybe I can break your back.*

But it didn't. It stared at him with a terrible malevolence, its stench growing heavier if possible, almost choking...but it didn't move for him. *Why?*

'Hayles,' he gasped. 'Get away from it. *Stay* away from it.'

He looked away for a second, saw her nod, then stared the bastard thing down. *Mexican standoff, isn't that what they call this?* Then he thought, *fuck it, I* hate *Westerns*. He leapt at the thing, grabbed it, felt his hands blister and burn, but held on, despite its struggles, its noise, its smell. He held it so Hayley would be OK, he held it with no idea what he would do next. He screamed in pain and fear, but he *held on*.

As he did, he felt terror and revulsion so complete, so exquisite that it should have engulfed him. Holding in his hands a being that had no soul, that existed on a plane no man was ever meant to *glimpse*, let alone *interact* with, he should have been so overwhelmed that his heart should have just popped like a Juicy Fruit bubble.

But he didn't. This terror was…familiar. He'd felt it before. *Twice* before. 'Oh dear God,' he whispered, as he realised why the thing hadn't attacked him, as he *remembered*.

Making his way down the hospital corridor, finding the Klix machine, putting in his coins and feeling…what he's feeling now.

Picking up the stuff in the room, taking it to the attic. Last thing left is that doll. That awful, horrible doll. Picking it up…and that same feeling. The goosebumps, the heart tripping, the hairs on the back of his neck upright, the bugging eyes…

Once when it hopped on my back, once when it ran out. Into the doll. I brought it here. Me. I am the bringer. I am responsible. I'm *the one it hitched a ride on. Not Hayley,* me. *And if I brought it…*

In pain from his hands, in pain in his heart, terrified beyond human belief, he nevertheless started to laugh. As he did, the thing writhed even harder, frantic…scared. *Don't be scared, little piggy. I can't kill you. But I can…*

'GET OUT OF HERE YOU FUCKING TWAT,' he screamed. *'GO BACK TO WHERE YOU BELONG, YOU UGLY MOTHERFUCKER! FUUUUUUUUUUUUCK OOOOOOOOFFFF!'*

The screaming, the noise, the pain built to an unendurable crescendo. Plaster fell from the ceiling. The walls shook. The glass in the windows rattled. Bizarrely, Graham heard the toilet flush. A bellow of rage sprang from its inhuman throat, fine, hot spittle splashed Graham's face.

Then it was gone, and all he held was a doll. A little taller than most, with plastic limbs and a china face. It had curly false hair and painted on freckles, a button nose and an expectant *I want to play games I love you smile*. It wore a long white lace nightdress.

It was just a doll though. Plastic, china, cloth. He stared at it for a moment, waiting for it to come to life and throttle him, but it didn't. It was only a doll, and dolls just don't do that sort of thing. Not on their own, anyway. Not without help.

He dropped it, staggered a bit, raised his hands and looked at the blisters – didn't look so good, but he thought they'd heal. Then he heard a voice say, 'Gray? You OK hon?'

He looked at his wife. She looked at him. Then they held each other and cried.

Sixteen

In the hallway, ten minutes later.

They formed a circle – Hayley, Graham and Lillian – holding on as they looked at Jim's face. After a second, Graham broke contact and closed his father's eyes. He wanted to say something but couldn't.

Hayley did. 'I'm so sorry,' she sobbed. 'Ah, hon…Jim…Elaine…ah God, I'm so sorry.'

'It wasn't your fault,' said Graham. 'It was me.' He looked to Lillian. 'I didn't know, not until the end, but…' he took a shuddering breath. 'I felt it, at the hospital. Went to get a coffee while Hayley slept. Had this…I don't know, bad feeling, I suppose.' *Yeah, that sums it up, well done.* 'And when I was putting the stuff away, I picked up the doll and…there it was again. I brought it here,' he continued, turning to Hayley. 'You're blameless, babe. All of this was my fault.'

'Sorry, but no,' said Lillian. 'Neither of you can take the blame. There's no blame to be taken. You got in the way of something, that's all. This was just an accident.' She actually laughed. A bitter laugh, but a laugh. 'An act of God. Fuck Him sideways for it, but that's all it was. No blame anywhere here. You can't even blame the demon, it was just doing what it was made to do. And who made it? God, the sick bastard. Oh, don't look so shocked. Everyone who loves God hates Him a little bit too.'

They sat in silence for a while – how long they would never know – until Hayley said, 'What do we do now?'

'Call the police,' said Lillian. 'If one of your neighbours hasn't done it already. We have to…' she swallowed with a clicking noise, 'see to your dad, Graham.'

'What do we say?' Graham asked, tears welling again.

Another pause. 'Fucked if I know,' said Lillian.

Chapter Nineteen

One

In the end, they settled for the truth – or at least, *some* of the truth. Yes, there'd been a separation in the marriage; yes there'd been some tension. That night they'd all attempted to sort it out. There was some argument, the way there often is. At one stage Jim had gone upstairs to use the bathroom. They'd heard a crash, when they came to see, well…

'And you,' the constable had said, looking at Lillian. 'Why were you here?'

'Friend of the family,' she said.

There was some suspicion, some things that didn't quite jibe, some suggestions that Jim might have been thrown, rather than just fallen – but nothing that would really stick. There were no signs of a struggle, for instance, and it *could* have been just a fall. There was an Inquest, and the coroner ended up recording an open verdict.

Linda, Graham's mother, grieved hard. One day, in August, she sat Graham down and asked him exactly what had happened. He told her. She was silent for a long time. Eventually Graham said, 'Do you believe me?'

'I don't know,' she answered after a seemingly eternal pause. 'I don't think you're lying, but…' she trailed off again, had a cry, then said, 'if what you say is true, then he died being very brave, didn't he?'

'Yes Mum. He did.'

'Well then. There's that.' She cried again, and so did Graham.

Elaine, of course, was never found – there was nothing of her to find. Anna, Hayley's mum, never recovered from that. *More fallout from all that shit,* Hayley would think. They looked after her as best they could, they did what they could, but the guilt they carried around with them was sometimes so hard and so heavy that they felt they would collapse under it.

Easy for Lillian to say it was an act of God, Hayley would think, *but for those of us who survived, the days are so hard.*

Lillian gave up her old life – no more appearing on stages, sometimes telling the truth and sometimes lying, no more private readings – and enrolled in the Church as a minister. She had seen the great evil that walked the world, had been a tool of the great good that opposed it, and was determined that *something* positive would come out of it all. She was still visited by the dead, but when they asked her to pass on a message or two, she politely declined. The only thing she would say from then on was that there was hope. Whenever anyone asked her about the future, about what lay beyond this world, she would answer with that word. 'There is hope,' she'd say.

She never saw her father again – not while she was alive, anyway. But she knew she would someday, and that sure and certain hope was good enough for her.

Two

Hayley and Graham kept hold of the house – just. Jodie had replaced Hayley at the beautician's – she just couldn't wait any longer, sorry, she had a business to run, after all – and Hayley bore her no ill will. Well, not *much* ill will anyway. She found another salon in Tottenham, though, and worked like a Trojan, putting in all the hours she could, moonlighting when the opportunity presented itself.

For Graham it was harder. The blisters on his hands took a month to heal, and Maitland solidly refused to give him a reference, and without one it was tough to get through any employer's door. One day in May though, he took a phone call on his mobile. 'All right mate, up the Blues, Arsenal are shite!'

'Danny?'

'None other, big as life and twice as beautiful. Listen. I read in the paper about your dad. Sorry, mate.'

'Thanks, man.' Tears – tears that were never far away – sprang into his eyes. Hayley muted the TV and held him.

'An' you an' the missus, how're you?'

'We're OK mate.' He held her tighter. 'We're OK again.'

'Bastard, I was hopin' I could gerra bitta that, she' a fine piece o'tail.'

'Yeah. You got that right.'

'So anyways, you workin'?'

'No so much, no.'

'Wanna?'

Something in his chest loosened. 'Christ, yes. What d'you know?'

'Nesmith's in Neasden are hirin'. They need a dog's bollocks draftsman. Now, I *may* just be nailin' the boss's PA. An' I *may* just have a file of your work sittin' on me Mac right now, which I *might* just be able to send over to y'. I know Neasden's a trek, but I reckon you could work from home a couple o'days a week. So, waddya say?'

'I say big thanks, but Maitland won't give me a ref…'

'What,' Danny interrupted, 'no reference, say you? I 'appen to 'ave one right 'ere, mate, all ready to go, full of lies about how good you are. And, weirdly, it's Maitland's name. And, when Nesmith's email him back for confirmation, why, they'll use the email address at the top. The one I've just created. And lo and befuckinhold, I'll say "yes, all spot on, Gawd bless y', Guv'nor!"'

'And if they ring?'

Danny laughed. 'Then you're *fucked*, pal! So…do I hit SEND or what?'

'You hit SEND,' said Graham. 'And I owe you.'

'Too fuckin' right you do, mate.'

Graham sent the file off to Nesmith's, and three days later was asked to attend an interview. A week later, he took a phone call offering him a job. The day after he signed the contract he took Danny out and the two of them got standing up, falling down drunk.

Three

In September, Hayley missed her period. She bought a test that afternoon, did it, and saw it had turned blue. She showed it to Graham. He held her and they cried together.

They told no one, not wanting to tempt fate. But they also did *not* stock the spare room with toys or cots or dolls. This time they knew better, they knew better than to plan.

But the months went on, and Hayley's stomach grew, and the more it grew, so did their hope.

Four

It was a girl. They named her Elaine. She was born in St Jude's hospital, Crouch End, North London. As she took her first breath and gave her first cry, Hayley thought, *somewhere in this place there are demons feeding off people's deaths. But here there is life, and so there may also be things that guard that life, that treasure it. Things other than us. Things which are good.*

But then they put the baby in her arms and she cried. Hayley and Graham joined in. *No plans,* Hayley thought. *But you're going to be Prime Minister one day.*

THE END
January 2014 – January 2015

Printed in Great Britain
by Amazon